RECKLESS WITCH

Illumina Academy Reverse Harem Book One

TARAH SCOTT

Scarsdale Publishing

Acknowledgments

To the greatest editor around, Kim Comeau. You've taught me everything I know.

Now if I can just get you to teach me everything *you* know.

Many thanks to my friend Liv Chatham.

Glossary

- *Margidda*—All magical beings
- *The Illumina*—World government that rules over all Margidda
- *Abaddon*—Magical underworld where magic is practiced illegally
- *Zidruhin*—Religious order that follows Damien, demi-god of The Shadows
- *Elohim*—Ancient god of the angels
- *Elyon*—The Most High
- *Anunnaki*—Followers of the old god *Elyon,* God of creation, God of the angels

Clans

- Silwood: Sirens and Fae
- Longthorpe: Warlocks/Witches
- Middlewich: Mages and potions
- Penncarrow: Wolves/Shifters/Vampires

ONE

Leilah

I was four when The Shadows came. Perhaps the vague nightmares and the images I can't quite identify stem from those days. I don't really know.

I don't want to know.

World governments attributed the near annihilation of Margidda as a pandemic virus that science cured. But those of us who survived face constant reminders of the apocalypse: a flash of fear that arises from the illegal use of magic, the unexplained disappearance of one precious remaining member of our kind, and our need to hug natural shadows in an effort to cloak ourselves from The Shadows. According to my grandmother, the apocalypse left behind a compulsion to hide our true selves from humans.

For me, it's first nature to hide what I am from the mundane world. Margiddians were once numerous. Now, we number fewer than three million worldwide, which makes each life valuable. Still, despite the fear of discovery and the threat of annihilation, we find a way to live.

It's ten past midnight at The Witching Hour Cabaret Club. From my table at the rear, I watch three long-legged drag queens strut down a twenty-foot runway. Leave it to vampire queens to own glittering, sequined evening gowns that any woman would kill to own. The lead queen tosses loose blonde hair over her ebony shoulder and the crowd cheers as she sashays back to the stage, the other two close behind.

A man in the audience shouts, "You free after the show, baby?"

All three queens spin toward the crowd and throw kisses as they back toward the rear curtain. I sip my vodka. How would the man who wants to hook up with the queens react if he knew the three beauties had lived a collective millennia? The blonde, Desiree, owner of The Witching Hour, is over six hundred years old. There are older vampires, though many ancients perished in The Shadow War. A few were murdered by Margiddians who fed on The Shadows in an attempt to grab power during the war—as well as after the fall of Margidda. According to Grams, those criminals were almost as hard to extinguish as The Shadows had been to drive away. At least, we were able to kill the criminals. The Shadows never die.

My heart clenches as her words haunt my memory. *"Sweet pea, when we began to reveal ourselves, the world called it the dawning of the Age of Aquarius. Then The Shadows came."*

This last Shadow War was even worse than the war in fifth century BCE Athens, which killed nearly three hundred thousand people. Modern historians attributed the deaths to everything from smallpox to typhus to the bubonic plague. They classified the *plague* that swept through Egypt, Libya and Greece as the most lethal in all of Classical Greece. This most recent war, however, claimed twenty times those numbers. It'll be millennia before Margidda recovers the eighty percent loss of our population.

A shiver slides down my spine when I remember the evil that I seemed to inhale at the deserted academy Grams took me to in Massachusetts. If what I experienced were remnants of

The Shadows, how much worse had it been for the victims when The Shadows spread their infection of fear and hatred?

What would life be like if The Shadows hadn't destroyed the possibility of our acceptance by humans? I wouldn't have to hide my magic from the Illumina.

I gulp half my drink. As a result of the war, the Illumina now rules our magic with an iron fist. What right have our leaders to forbid Margidda from practicing magic without their permission? Guilt stabs. It's the one subject Grams and I argued about with heat. She informed me I would one day attend The Academy, just as she did. Admission to The Academy is by invitation only, but Grams had an uncanny way of knowing things. I told her I wouldn't attend that prison. Was that why she'd kicked me out at fifteen?

"Stop it, Leilah," I mutter.

Seven years is long enough to have tortured myself over that question.

She's gone. You'll never have the answer.

Maybe I made a mistake in returning to New York. So far, I've only succeeded in dredging up old resentments I've worked hard to put behind me. Why should I care that the only family I've ever known is dead? Is taking possession of the only real home I've ever had worth facing the memories that fill every corner of that house? In the two weeks I've been here, why haven't I visited her grave...or tried to call her from the dead?

Loud applause jars me from my thoughts and I realize the queens have left the stage. Dammit. My customer is late. I scan the club but see no sign of him. The door opens and I tense when, instead of the large, muscled shifter I'm expecting, tall, dark and handsome steps inside. I blink. That isn't just any tall, dark and handsome. That's war hero and Illumina Academy student recruiter Commander Ethan Bordeau. I've only seen Ethan from afar, and that was before I left New York seven years ago. Ethan Bordeau and Illumina Cadette Commander

Raith Vanderkoff are two of the oldest beings to have survived The Shadows. Grams said that Ethan's strategy and Raith's sheer strength saved The Academy forty miles north of the City, maybe even saved what remains of Margidda.

Since when do the high and mighty slum with peasants?

Ethan's eyes slide over the crowd until—

I go perfectly still. No way he's looking at me. He's got to be looking at someone near me. I glance left, where a man and woman hold hands across a table. To the right, two blondes have their eyes glued on Ethan. I grimace. Their breasts, practically spilling out of their tiny dresses, look as fake as their hair color. So, the dragon is on the prowl for bleach and silicon.

He starts forward. I hunch over my drink and allow my long, dark hair to cascade round my face. If there was a way out without passing him, I would take it. He's not a Watchman, but he's too damn close to the law for my taste. Hell, if he gets in the way of tonight's deal, I'll kick his ass and take whatever's in his wallet.

A shadow falls over my table. Through the veil of my hair, I glimpse jean clad legs that go on forever. I lift my drink. When Ethan slides into the chair opposite me, I freeze, the glass barely touching my lips. I snap my head up and lock gazes with the bluest eyes I've ever seen. Dragon eyes are almost as compelling as a siren's.

I STARE FOR THREE HEARTBEATS. "YOU'RE SITTING AT the wrong table." I tilt my head toward the blondes. "You'll get a twofer there."

He lifts a hand to signal the waitress who, I realize, must have followed him. "Glenfiddich, neat," he says without taking his eyes off me. "Would you like another drink?"

I only stare. He flashes a smile at the waitress and she hurries off. His attention returns to me.

I command my pounding heart to slow. "I'm not in the mood for a hook-up." Damn, if he were anyone else, I would hook up, down and any way he wanted me. I'm dying to run my fingers through that dark hair.

Something flickers in his eyes. Amusement? I blink. Can't be. Dragons aren't known for their sense of humor.

"Maybe some other time," he says in a deep voice that could melt sin on a frigid winter's day. "I'm here on business."

"Business?" I blurt before catching myself. He—the Illumina—can't possibly know about my *business*.

"You have the honor of being chosen to attend Illumina Academy New York," he says.

I stare. Of all the things in all the worlds—hell!—in any dream I might have dreamt, that is the last thing I could have imagined him saying.

"What?" I stupidly reply.

The waitress arrives with his drink and sets the glass on the table in front of him. He looks up at her and murmurs, "Thanks."

Her eyes widen and I half expect her to melt into a quivering puddle of estrogen right there at his feet.

"I'll let you know if we need anything more," he says.

She hesitates, then leaves.

His looks back at me. "You are to report to Illumina Academy in the morning. Like all students, you'll dorm at the school. Your classes have already been assigned."

Well, fuck a duck.

"Not interested," I say.

His eyes narrow almost imperceptibly. Most likely, he's never been refused by a recruit. When Illumina Academy informs you of your acceptance, you don't refuse. You jump for joy. It's like winning the lottery. Newly chosen students are beyond thrilled. But my grudge against the Illumina is huge. Their laws are the reason I practice magic illegally. Why I can't sleep in my bed in the house that is now mine. Well, Grams started the whole mess when she exiled me, but they finished the job by seizing her home a month ago, right after she died.

As one of the only three academies left standing in the States, the prestigious school wields unholy power, which gives commanders like Ethan and Raith god-like power. Raith, in particular, is known for his unyielding ruthlessness. He's intensely private and spends most of his time behind the walls of the massive fortress-school.

On the brightly lit stage beyond Ethan's broad shoulders, a woman dressed in a slinky, short nightie belts out, *"Hush. Don't tell Mama. Hush. Don't tell Mama."* While the orchestra crescendos, she lets her slinky robe fall to the floor. The crowd cheers and whistles.

"Don't be a fool," Ethan says so only I can hear.

"Does the name Crowe ring a bell?" I struggle to keep the hostility out of my voice.

I'm careful about wishing people ill. I'm not saying I never have, just that I'm cautious about doing so. Those sorts of *wishes* have a way of biting you in the ass when you least expect it—kind of like the three too-good-to be-true wishes those trickster jinns grant. But I too easily envision Ethan's gorgeous body smeared across asphalt after being struck by a double decker bus. Of course, it would be simpler to drop just the right tincture into his drink and watch him melt into a pile of dragon goo. That, however, will get me into deeper trouble with the law than I already am. In this post-Shadow War era, I walk a fine line as a street witch. Which means I'm not going to tell Ethan to fuck off, like I want to.

His eyes remain locked with mine. Most women would melt under those icy blues, but my talent for sniffing out secrets causes a stir in my solar plexus that tells me he has a whopper. A being as old as him must have many secrets. Sadly, I don't always figure out the secret. But when I do…

He's still staring as if trying to read my soul and I have the unexpected desire to press my cheek to his chest and listen to the rhythmic beating of his heart. No human heart beats within that chest. He's pure dragon. Any witch who forgets that is likely to find herself bowing to his will as easily as that waitress. Small wonder he's The Academy's most renowned recruiter.

"Miriam Crowe," he murmurs.

Grams' name coming from those full lips ignites a new wave of anger. I grasp the glass tumbler sitting in front of me in order to keep an eye on my hands. They've been known to smash noses without my permission.

"You've got balls," I hiss. "The Illumina seizes my grandmother's home and drags her good name through the mud—a name I share—and now they decide to mess with *my* life?"

Ethan takes a large swallow of his drink then says, "She broke the law."

That's the news on the grapevine, but I don't believe that rumor for a minute. Hell, witches of her stature practically *wrote* the laws all witches live by.

An image of Grams' brown eyes, snapping with anger, flashes across my mind as she shoves me through her shop door and says, *"Leave and don't come back. You're dead to me."*

I thought she was being overly dramatic. I didn't know the exile would last years…that I'd never see her again.

Why? *Why?*

I shove aside an avalanche of pain and focus on the dragon shifter across the table. "Broke the law?" I repeat. "My grandmother helped the Illumina enforce the damn law," I scoff in an effort to head off tears. "It's damned easy for the Illumina to act as judge, jury and executioner against a dead woman. No investigation—no trial necessary."

He hesitates.

There it is. That secret. What the—

My grip tightens around my drink as his eyes shift past me. In the corner of my eye, a tall blonde sashays past our table. I tamp down my anger and do my best not to envision him getting hit by that bus. The Illumina has ripped away my past and intends to steal my future, and I'm supposed to wait while their messenger boy watches some tall, thin lovely walk past.

He gives a tiny nod in the woman's direction and I realize he knows her. Ethan reaches for his drink and the sleeve of his expensive dark suit jacket drifts up to expose the edge of a silver-laced tattoo. Most dragons love showing off their clan markings. The symbols are considered prestigious, and human women have an almost obsessive need to rub against bronze muscle bearing silver markings they don't understand. Maybe it's the magic that draws them.

I lift my gaze to his face and glimpse his darkening pupils in the instant before his eyes returns to me. Magic? Hell, it's the pure maleness that radiates off dragons that ensnares women.

He sets down his drink. "What makes you think there wasn't an investigation?"

Well, well, Ethan Bordeau might get distracted, but he gets back on track in a trice.

"Fucking evidence," I retort. "The precise lack thereof."

"The Illumina doesn't publicize its business."

I snort. "Sure they do. Miriam Crowe, consorting with Shadows? Not a chance." I'd heard the vicious rumors clear over in Chicago. "And don't try giving me the bullshit that she committed suicide." He opens his mouth to reply, but I cut him off. "What right does the Illumina have to prevent me from living in my grandmother's home? That's my home now."

I don't mention that I still can't find the damn house. He doesn't need to know that Grams' defense spells against me are still effective, even after death. When she kicked me out, she made the entire structure invisible—to my eyes only. I can wander around the vicinity all day and never see or touch the damn place. But come hell or high water, I'll find the house. It's mine now. My chance to have a real home again, neighbors who will notice if I go missing, even a reputable business.

Ethan arches a brow. "All your needs will be met at The Academy. Your grandmother's house no longer matters."

The part of me that longs for the security he's offering jumps to life. Little does he know that's the part that's going to get me possession of Grams' house.

"It's an honor to be accepted into the hallowed halls of Illumina Academy," Ethan says.

I snort. "Man, have you got the wrong Crowe. I dropped out of high school and took my sweet time getting my equivalency. I'm definitely not 'advanced' educational material." A flash of shame washes over me at just how far from Academy material I am. I sell fake IDs—too often, to people who shouldn't be walking this planet. Hardly the kind of student to set foot in one of the most illustrious magical institutions in the world.

"You've been identified as a High Potential," he says.

I blink. "You are out of your ever-loving mind."

He tilts his head. As I stare into the cerulean depths of his gaze, a strange tremor simmers in my belly. He's sinfully ripped, even for a dragon, but there's more to his allure than that god-like body. I uncross my legs, suddenly aware of how warm the packed club has become. My short leather skirt sticks to my legs. Thank God, I'd opted for a black bra and fishnet top.

Ethan waits, silently watching me.

"Trot on back home," I say. "I'm not about to set foot in that place."

"Don't do this," he warns softly. "It won't end well."

My fingers twitch.

His gaze flicks to my hands. He gives a slow shake of his head. "Don't do anything stupid."

"You're worried I'll kick your ass."

He lifts his glass and sips his whisky. Then, his hand shoots out so fast I feel my flesh burn before the silver rune on the back of my hand registers in my brain.

"What the—"

The strange rune scores my skin, twinkling in the bar's dim light. It feels like a spider crawling under my skin. I grit my teeth.

"The sigil will grant you access to the school," Ethan states, then adds in a soft voice, "Just as it will ensure you arrive."

Dragon magic.

I glare. "You better fucking hope you're wrong, because if I am forced to show up, I'm coming for you."

Ethan rises, slowly walks around the table, and stops behind me. I remain motionless as he leans close. The hair on my nape prickles as his warm breath heats my skin. My traitorous heart responds on a level that unsettles me.

"You know how dangerous it is to practice magic on the streets," he whispers. "You're exposing more than yourself to danger."

I twist in the chair and meet his gaze. I'm aware only of the raw maleness that makes my skin sizzle. His gaze drops to my mouth and I'm startled by the need to find out what his lips feel like on my body.

Heart pounding, I bolt to my feet and grab my jacket off the back of my chair as I head for the door. I have to get as far away from him as possible. My legs feel strangely heavy, as if I'm slogging through quicksand.

Damn you, Ethan Bordeau.

Already, his sigil is bending me to its will. I can break the damn spell. I have to find Jax. He'll know how.

I shove my arms into my coat sleeves and force my way through the standing-room-only crowd. The Witching Hour Cabaret Club is one of the most popular clubs in the City, not only because the cabaret acts are the best or because the club is owned by the vampire queen Desiree, but because Margiddians blend nicely with the alternative lifestyles of the customers. I sense two vampires and several shifters. They're Desiree's biggest fans.

Halfway to the exit, I glimpse shadows near the main door. I slow, caught in the strange rhythm that pulses in sync with the music. My heart pounds harder. Dark magic? Fear slides down my spine. I hadn't sensed a black witch earlier. How did I miss her?

Someone jostles me and my gaze sharpens as if I'd been staring out of focus. The man who bumped me mumbles something and pushes past me. I quicken pace toward the front door. I may engage in a dubious profession, but I don't dabble in black arts. Everyone knows black magic is like candy to The Shadows.

I reach the door, burst into the cold December air, and stumble two steps right while dragging in deep gasps. Strong fingers grasp my arm. I pivot, leg raised high for a roundhouse kick. I register Ethan's face as he clamps a hand around my ankle. I leap upwards and yank my leg free while whipping around to kick with my other foot. My skirt rides up nearly to my crotch.

Ethan ducks with the speed unique to his kind then bands an arm around my waist before my feet touch concrete. He yanks me against an impossibly hard body and drags me toward the alley. Instinct summons my magic, but the sigil on my hand burns. I blink in surprise.

"Don't fight me, Leilah."

His order, spoken low in my ear, only infuriates me all the more. Rage has been a near-constant companion since the day Grams ripped me from all I'd known. I'd been fifteen. *Fifteen.* Tears well from some dark corner of my fifteen-year-old self.

Once in the alley, Ethan releases me. I spin and face him.

"I'm not your enemy," he says.

I can't speak. If I do, I might embarrass myself and cry. Then I *would* have to kill him. I can't have him telling anyone Leilah Crowe cried. The door to the club creaks open and music blasts in the instant before the door slams shut.

"I want to know what's going on," I say.

Ethan releases a breath. "Zadkeil is leading the investigation—"

"You've got to be kidding," I cut in. "For Christ's sake, *demons* are more reliable than angels. Zadkeil can't be trusted."

In my experience, few angels can be trusted. Maybe none. Talk about self-righteous beings who think they're right all the time… They make Ethan look like an amateur.

"Would you feel better if I told you we did, in fact, get corroboration of her guilt from a demon?" he asks.

I stare in shock. "Angels and demons don't take part in earthly matters."

"In fact, they sometimes do."

I start to reply, but he says, "You'll get answers when we have them."

We? Who the hell is *we*? Raith Vanderkoff runs The Academy. Ethan is, essentially, his second in command. Does Raith have something to do with the investigation into Grams' death? As Cadette Commander of Illumina Academy New York, Raith has a buttload of power, but he's not a council member. What could he or Ethan have to do with an investigation into my grandmother's death—and why the fuck are angels involving themselves in a witch's death? Witches and angels aren't on the best of terms given the old testament, *'thou shall not suffer a witch to live'* deal. Sure, their leader later denied having anything to do with that clusterfuck. After all, it's not his fault his followers misunderstood. Right?

I consider casting a truth spell on Ethan and the sigil on my hand heats. What the fuck? I pin the dragon with a glare. "Your little sigil is more than a compulsion spell to enforce attendance."

"You know it's against the law to practice magic without proper training," he says.

"And the permission of the Illumina," I snarl.

"You're too young to remember The Shadows." Sorrow clouds his eyes. "Be glad for that."

I'm startled by the sense that his secret is closer to the surface than it normally is, and realize I'm extending my magic when his damn sigil heats my hand again. I yank back my magic. It's best Ethan doesn't know how hard I'm willing to work to break through his dragon magic. I'll save that for just the right moment. Like when I get the fucking thing removed from my hand. Then he and Raith will get a nice surprise.

While dragon magic isn't as encompassing as that of a natural witch, with dragon magic at his disposal, Raith is a powerhouse. Dragons are natural enemies of vamps—everyone is a natural enemy of vampires, when you get right down to it —but I guess Ethan isn't afflicted with a sense of loyalty to his clan. He's obviously Illumina first, and that means he's Raith Vanderkoff's man, dragon, and anything else Raith wants him to be, including—and most importantly, today—what they call a recruiter and what I call a henchman.

A man turns into the alley, stops short, looks from Ethan to me, then backs away and heads up the street.

I return my attention to Ethan. He's given me more information about Grams than I've discovered in the two weeks I've been here.

"Maybe you'll find the answers you seek at The Academy," Ethan says.

I narrow my eyes. "You'll never convince me that my grandmother, a High Witch of the Light, was consorting with Shadows." Grams was a lot of things, but this... I shake my head. "No way. I would have known."

Yet even as I make the claim, I see Grams in the cellar pouring over an ancient scroll in the dead of night. Alone, that isn't suspicious. Witches are known for reading ancient scrolls. However, another time, when I sneaked up behind her and shouted 'boo,' she'd whirled and thrown a flame spell that singed my hair as it flew past and hit the wall. Normally, Grams was unshakable. Something had scared her for her to react with such violence.

I once saw her standing in the dark, arms outstretched, eyes closed. Shadows danced about her feet. Perhaps most damning of all had been our last encounter. I'd awakened to find her standing over me in the dark, chanting. The next day, she tossed me onto the street and cast a spell on the potion shop to prevent me from finding it again. I grimace and cut off the thoughts. Dammit. Fifteen minutes with Ethan and he's already summoned more memories than I'd thought about in years.

"These are underhanded, false accusations to justify the Illumina's actions," I snap. So much for the school mantra of *Light, Honor and Duty*.

A corner of Ethan's mouth lifts. "You can't honestly think your grandmother's shop is worth anything to the Illumina?"

His comment is insulting. Grams had specialized in one-of-a-kind Shuhadaku potions that allowed users to harness elemental magic. They'd been the best on the East Coast. Plenty of people would kill to get their hands on the formulas.

"Her recipes are invaluable," I say.

"The Illumina doesn't need her magic," Ethan states. "The dark arts leave an undeniable imprint. Once the Illumina finishes its investigation..." He shrugs. "The house will be disposed of."

Disposed of? My heart beats faster. Over my dead body. I step closer, grab the lapel of his expensive shirt and yank his head down so I can look him in the eye as I tell him they had better not touch my home. *My home.* But this close, his eyes capture mine. Despite being the granddaughter of the whitest witch who ever lived, I'm comfortable with natural shadows. I see in the dark as almost as easily as a cat, so I don't miss the silver dragon energy swirling in those irises an inch from mine. Something deep inside me hums, as if I'd just stuck my finger in an electrical socket.

His brows shoot up in surprise. His secret rushes to the surface. I reach for the answer. The sigil on my hand burns. I grunt and take a faltering step back. What the hell? I haven't summoned any magic. Then I understand.

Dragon energy.

I shoot him a dagger-filled glare, then spin on my heel and leave him standing in the cold alley.

TWO

Ethan

I stand frozen in the alley. She has finally returned. My heart thunders in my ears. *Forty years*. The blink of an eye. An agonizing eternity. Leilah Crowe, Illumina's newest High Potential. I break from my shock. *Illumina's newest High Potential*. I race from the alley, halt, and glimpse her dark hair as she ducks into a taxi. The cab takes off and I stare until she's long out of sight.

An hour later, I'm out of the city and nearly at The Academy. Icy flakes strike the windshield with a relentless staccato that grates on my nerves. After all these centuries, I should be immune to the mingling of euphoria and fear I experience every time Ciarah returns. The Illumina Academy's stone wall comes into view up ahead on the left and my hands still shake as I turn into the drive, pass under the archway and enter the school grounds.

I heave a breath and will my heart to slow, but my thoughts continue to race. I'd entered The Witching Hour Cabaret Club to recruit a student and felt an attraction to Leilah the moment I laid eyes on her. But who wouldn't? Hazel, kohl-lined cat eyes. Tall, with long raven hair that fell down her back, and long legs.

I swallow. I'd sat across from her in the club without a clue as to her true identity. Hell, I'd touched her, dropped a sigil on her skin. In the past, physical contact had always been enough to stir the recognition. Why not this time? Only when she collared me in the alley did my dragon energy leap to meet hers.

I slow, pull into the parking garage attached to the instructors' living quarters, park the Aston Martin in my designated spot, then turn off the car. I close my eyes and drag in a long breath as I let my hands drop from the steering wheel onto my thighs.

Ciarah is back. This time, as Leilah.

Can we do this again? Can *I* do this again?

Over the years, I've known many beautiful women and even loved a few. But not the way I love Ciarah. I've known her by many names. But to me—to us—she will always be Ciarah, the slave girl we met millennia ago, the one who keeps appearing in our lives again and again. Even after centuries, we still haven't discovered the reason why.

Each time, the pain of losing her hurts more than the last.

I need a long vacation. The Orient. It's been too long since I've visited Japan. A couple months surrounded by soft spoken geishas would soothe the fire raging in my gut. At least, for a little while. No, that's a lie. The pain of knowing she's here and being so far away from her would kill me.

I consider staying in my off-campus apartment, but the idea is a fantasy. Rest isn't on the docket for tonight. Probably not for the next ten years; fifteen, if I'm lucky. Not until we lose her again. Besides, I have to let Raith know I found her. He would toss me into a deep grave if he learned I'd found Ciarah and hadn't told him. That's one trait vampires and dragons share; neither is forgiving.

I step from the car into the frigid garage. The dragon in me recoils. I long for a whiskey, a raging fire, and an opportunity to recall every second of the fifteen minutes I'd spent with Ciarah. Instead, despite her return, we have work. I start toward the door leading into the building.

Fear that practice of the dark arts empowered Damien, demigod and Lord of The Shadows, to wage the latest Shadow war, has kept tensions high these last twenty years. Damn the Illumina's fear. It's almost as if the mindless wisps of dark energy that are The Shadows still infects our leaders.

The discovery that Miriam Crowe died while dabbling with Shadow magic rocked the Illumina to its core. Her estranged granddaughter being identified as a High Potential set off another shockwave, one nearly as powerful as the first.

And now?

Now, I have to tell Raith that Leilah Crowe, granddaughter to Miriam Crowe, an Illumina High Potential, is also Ciarah.

I enter the main foyer, a carved white marble monolith. I nod to Jace and Michael, who stand guard on opposite sides of the room. The only indication they notice me is the lightspeed flick of their eyes in my direction.

The school's coat of arms, wings spread over the Illumina Academy name, hangs on the arch above the stairs that lead to Raith's office. I take the steps two at a time. His door stands open. The room is dim, lit by an antique brass lamp positioned on the edge of his desk. He looks up from paperwork arranged before him, then leans back in his chair.

Blade isn't present. Not that I expected him to be. He deals with Ciarah's absence by burying his cock deep into the soft folds of his latest flavor of the month. Or week, if I want to be more accurate. I can't remember the last time Blade kept a woman for longer than a week—aside from Josephine, but she doesn't count. She's as big a playgirl as Blade is a playboy and she makes no demands on him.

Raith tracks my progress across the room. If not for the special bond created when we battled The Shadows—and the fact I've known him for millennia—I wouldn't have the slightest idea what he's thinking. But the darkening of his pupils reveals the fact that he knows me as well as I know him.

"I'm all right," I assure as I drop into the chair across from his desk.

"You need a vacation."

I grunt. "A vacation from you," I say, although I have seen him little these last two weeks.

He gives a slow nod.

Without Ciarah in our lives, too much time spent together can be dangerous. Maybe Caleb and Matthias had the right idea by disappearing. In all this time, we've yet to discover just why her presence balances our life forces. Hell, despite complete access to the Illumina archives, we still haven't figured out what keeps bringing her back to us—or why our bond grows stronger each time.

Raith still watches me. His lips are compressed lines and I wonder when he's last fed. He can survive as long as a year without feeding on human blood, but he doesn't do well. It's been decades since he's kept a stable of humans, as most vampires do. It's been forty years since he's fed off Ciarah, and I know that's the hardest. Maybe that, at least, will change soon.

"What happened?" he asks.

I lock gazes with him. "She refused."

Surprise flashes across his face.

Part of me finds the situation amusing. In all my decades recruiting, I've never had a student look disappointed, let alone resist. Leilah has courage.

"I slapped a sigil on her," I say. "She'll show tomorrow."

Raith frowns. "Just who does this little witch think she is?"

"Ciarah," I say in a hoarse whisper.

He goes rigid. "No," he responds with vehemence, but I know it's because he wants to convince himself I'm wrong. "No," he repeats, this time, in a whisper.

I give a single nod.

"If I had… Leilah?" he says. "*Crowe?*" He sucks in a long breath. "If I'd had the slightest idea… I should have sent Zadkeil back to Olympia. Fuck. Leilah Crowe can't be Ciarah. You have to be wrong."

He knows dragon energy is never wrong.

"She's angry we took possession of her grandmother's home," I say.

He shoots me a narrow-eyed scowl. "You shouldn't have marked her with your sigil. Why didn't you let her walk away?"

"You know as well as I do that Olympia would have found her," I say. "She's a High Potential."

"Fuck," he curses again.

I nod. "She's strong. Even stronger than last time."

He slams his fist on the desk. "Where the hell are Caleb and Matthias?"

I don't say what I'm thinking.

"If they were dead, we'd know," he says, although we have no idea whether that's true.

We five have never died, so we have no idea what happens if one of us dies. Even if we attempt to call Caleb or Matthias from the dead and get no answer, we wouldn't know whether their silence meant they were alive, they reside in Shadow Hell, or they'd died in the Shadow War and their—lost—spirits are unable to reincarnate.

In truth, with the Hell Gates closed, no one is certain if souls bound for Hell can enter. Aside from another Shadow war, the thing we most fear is that those we love, those mired in bitterness and fear and most vulnerable to The Shadows, might be trapped in Shadow Hell with the evil deceased who can't enter Hell.

I hope Raith's right and we would sense if something happened to Matthias and Caleb. I wish I could say I'm more worried about Matthias than Caleb but that's not so. Despite Matthias's grotesque gargoyle features, when he shifts, he's the closest thing to an angel that walks the earthly plane. One of The Most High's grand jokes.

As the quintessential guardian, there's simply nothing that will induce Matthias to desert Ciarah once he learns she's alive. He's just made that way. Just as Caleb is made to pick at every wound until it festers. Since her last death, we haven't heard from Caleb. During the intervening years, I've often wondered if, this time, he'd died of a broken heart. Not that I would blame him. I'm not sure I could survive if Ciarah had died in *my* arms.

Raith slowly shakes his head. "A street witch, specializing in black market potions. I should have known," his tone is grimmer than usual. He taps the topmost folder of a stack on his desk. "Leilah Crowe. Twenty-two. Young to be breaking the law with such abandon."

"You're just getting old," I say.

He flicks me a 'fuck you' look, but his pique doesn't halt the memory that rises.

"Remember Venice?" I ask.

His expression remains stormy. "Even in the eighteenth century she made a habit of breaking the law."

"There wasn't a chance in hell she would agree to marry that fat old merchant—in any life," I say with a laugh.

My amusement dies when I recall the man she *did* marry in the early eighteenth century. Gregory Warwick. Despite the three hundred years that have passed, my gut twists. It took all my willpower, and the strength of the others, to keep me from killing him. He'd been good to her, but how does a man watch the woman he's loved for millennia marry another man?

Raith releases a heavy sigh that puts me on guard. Vampires

are almost unshakable and Raith is a rock amongst his kind. But there's a weariness in that sigh I've never heard before.

"She shouldn't attend The Academy," he says.

Shouldn't attend The Academy? "We have no say in the matter," I reply carefully.

He hesitates, and I realize that he wants to argue. "She'll have one helluva welcome."

I force my fire to cool. "What do you mean?"

Raith meets my gaze. "We never did learn who leaked the news that Miriam Crowe killed herself while practicing Shadow magic."

"Now most, if not all, the students know about Miriam and they will not be kind to her granddaughter," I finish his thought.

He leans his head against the back of his chair and closes his eyes. "Tomorrow, then." There's a strange note in his voice I don't recognize. "Tomorrow...it all begins."

Before I can ask for an explanation, he vaults to his feet and crosses to the sideboard positioned to the left of the bookshelves behind his desk.

"You want a drink?" he asks.

My earlier desire for whiskey has vanished. "No thanks."

He half fills a crystal tumbler with bourbon then drinks it in two gulps, and I know he's remembering what I'm remembering: the last time all five of us were together, the day Ciarah died in Caleb's arms.

"Olympia's on her way from Greenland," Raith says suddenly. "Be here at noon."

Too much is happening at once. Olympia, Grand Witch of the North and Superintendent of all Illumina Academies, is coming to set up the virtual Shadow world we will use for our War Games. I don't trust those who manipulate, and Olympia's done nothing but manipulate from the moment I met her at that tavern on the Rhine in 1862.

"Has she said anything about filling the Headmaster position here?" I ask.

Since we lost George Brown last year to retirement, Raith has taken on extra duties I know are wearing on him. We fought alongside the tall black man during the Shadow War, and Raith had a great deal for respect for him, which is largely why Raith didn't mind that George was his superior. I'd bet Raith isn't looking forward to answering to someone new.

"She said we would discuss candidates on this visit." Raith returns to his desk, picks up his cell phone, and thumbs the lock. As the screen lights, he hits the number two: speed dial for Blade. The first ring sounds. A second, third and fourth follow before voicemail switches on and Blade's cultured English voice announces, "Sorry I've missed you, but no one answers phone calls anymore. Text me instead." After the beep sounds, Raith grates, "Blade, get over here. We found Ciarah." He jabs the End Call button on the screen. I notice he doesn't text.

It's cruel for Raith to break the news to Blade like that, but Raith can be cruel—just as Blade can be an asshole.

THREE

Blade

I IGNORE THE WHIP OF WIND THAT LASHES STRANDS of hair loosened from its tie into my face and stuff my hands into the pockets of my tailored black slacks. I lean against the brick of the building in the alley across the street from The Witching Hour Cabaret Club. As if on cue, Leilah bursts from the club with Ethan close behind. I wince when he seizes her arm, then laugh when Ethan barely blocks her roundhouse kick and grabs her ankle. If he'd been a little slower, she would have caught him in the nose. Everyone hates a solid nose hit, but dragons more than most, something about the septum cartilage in their noses when they shift. As Ethan grabs her waist and drags her into the opposite alley, I know I've kept Ciarah to myself longer than I had a right to.

How did he find her? Even as the question forms, I know the answer. With the power oozing from her, it's surprising it's taken this long. *Quid erit, erit.* There's no turning back now. In truth, The Academy needs Leilah. Though Ethan and Raith will, no doubt, disagree with my assessment once they learn she's Ciarah. I had wondered how long it would take before she was identified as a High Potential. She is too powerful for the famed Illumina Stone not to name her.

I wonder if Leilah Crowe being named a High Potential is why Olympia, the Grand Witch of the North, is dragging her creaking bones from Greenland to visit tomorrow. She has a controversial plan to have our students fight the most real mock Shadow battle we've ever staged. But I'm not fooled. She's equally interested in discovering why a High White Witch like Miriam Crowe turned to Shadow magic.

Leilah seizes Ethan's collar and shoves him against the wall and I shake my head. Trust a dragon to poke the wrong witch. Now, there will be hell to pay. My humor fades as I acknowledge I've created a little hell of my own. When Ethan and Raith learn I already know that Leilah is Ciarah, they'll be furious. I don't plan to confess, but I've lived long enough to know such secrets never stay secret. If I'm lucky, they won't find out for a century or two. My one saving grace is that I haven't taken advantage of the situation and fucked her. *Yet.*

Leilah emerges from the alley. I drink in her every curve. She's a heavenly body to shame all others. She's clearly furious with Ethan, and Ciarah and fury make for the best sex.

My cock twitches. Leilah stalks to the curb and flags a passing cab. The cabbie veers across two lanes and halts two feet from her. Ethan emerges from the alley as she enters the cab.

I discern another approaching cab and silently command the driver my way.

Ethan is watching like a forlorn puppy as her cab merges into traffic. I'll be damned, he has the hots for Leilah. No, I realize with a start. It isn't Leilah he's lusting after. It's Ciarah.

He takes a couple steps toward the curb. Dammit, he's going to follow her. Instead, he spins and stride's down the sidewalk. I step from the shadows and slip inside my taxi the instant it halts at the curb. With my mental command to follow Leilah's cab, the driver takes off.

Now that Ethan knows about Ciarah, he'll run straight to Raith.

City lights blur past the window. There's no more keeping Leilah to myself, even though I never really had her to begin with. I focus on her cab, which is slowing and stopping in front of Studio 59. *Perfect.* She's gone from cabaret and leather to jazz and cigars. The girl always did know how to get around.

Leilah exits the cab, then my driver pulls into the spot vacated by her cab. I tip the driver an extra fifty, slide from the cab and squint as I enter the club. The lighting is low, and a tall, leggy brunette is playing a baby grand located in an alcove at the corner window facing the street. Cigar smoke hangs heavy in the air and I breathe deeply of the aroma. Cigar clubs are among my favorite in the city.

Leilah is heading toward the stairs leading to the second level. It's not quite midnight, but the place is almost full. The crowd is a little older, and much more mainstream than the patrons at The Witching Hour Cabaret Club. Still, I know the club will stay busy until its two a.m. closing.

I sidestep a group of men, step up to the bar, and order a Grey Goose on the rocks. Leilah reaches the top of the stairs and leaves my range of vision. The bartender sets the drink in front of me. I leave a twenty on the bar then casually climb the stairs.

She's seated at a corner booth, a drink in front of her, her raven hair concealing half her face. I'm betting she's drinking tequila. She's a whiskey girl at heart, but when she wants to forget something, she drinks tequila, and often a lot of it. I near her and she looks up. The sorrow in her eyes kills me. I stop as if just noticing her, then smile.

I change direction. "Something wrong, love?"

The moisture welling in her eyes tells me she's on the verge of tears. What the bloody hell did Ethan say to her?

Leilah shakes her head. "Just a long day."

"Want company?"

"You'll do better to find one of your lollipops."

I chuckle. Her way with words remains consistent throughout her incarnations.

"I'm not in a licking mood tonight," I lie. I'm always in a licking mood.

I slide into the booth to her right and immediately sense the heat of magic. Ethan's work. He must have marked her with a sigil. So, the little hellion refused to accept her admittance into The Academy. That's what I most love about Ciarah. Her unpredictability. Being forced to appear against her will must be killing her. Ciarah hates being controlled.

"What do you think of The Illumina Academy?" she surprises me with her bluntness.

"It's a prestigious institution," I keep my voice neutral. "Those who train there are the best of their kind."

Leilah hrmph. "Well, not anymore." She lifts her hand.

Ethan's silver lace tattoo glitters on the back of her hand. I give a low whistle. "Are you a recruit?"

She scowls. "A prisoner."

I pretend to inspect her sigil and work hard to ignore the rose scent she must have bathed in. I sense magic roiling deep inside her, just as angry as she is. I'm tempted to stretch my arm along the back of the booth, but I'm not keen on getting stabbed or punched in the stomach. I know she carries a small blade hidden somewhere in the skin-tight skirt. Instead, I lean a causal elbow on the table.

She takes a sip of her drink and crosses her legs. My vantage point allows me to see her skirt ride up so high on her thigh that I'm sure I glimpse red lace. A hiss escapes my lips before I can stop myself.

"Something wrong?" she asks but doesn't look up.

I'm grateful for that small mercy, before I realize the reason she isn't looking is because she understands my reaction. My chest tightens. What man has already taught her to be so attuned to a man's reactions?

I don't reply. I can't reply.

She lifts her head and looks me in the eye, but I can't read a damn thing she's thinking. Despite knowing her all these centuries, she remains an enigma. But aren't women just that? Unsolvable mysteries?

Her gaze sharpens and I startle. Bloody hell, she caught me staring. I may not know *exactly* what she's thinking, but I recognize that look. It's the universal female look for *I'm figuring you out*. She's smart—which means I have to step up my game, and quickly. Any other woman, I could outwit by using my Fae talents of seduction. With Ciarah, that's like throwing gasoline on fire.

"I don't care for organizations that become too powerful." She startles me with the sudden change in direction. She lifts her glass, then pauses, the glass an inch from her lips. "The Academy shouldn't have the right to upend lives whenever they choose. Or take what doesn't belong to them." She slams her drink down. Tequila slops onto the table. "They're abusing their power."

I can't tell her the truth about her grandmother. I'm just relieved she was nowhere near the damn house while Miriam was playing god and consorting with the bloody Shadows. The woman deserved her fate. I should feel guilty about withholding the truth, but guilt has never been my favorite pastime. Plus, I figure Leilah will understand when she finally learns the truth. I pray so, anyway.

"The Academy must protect Margidda," I say.

"So they claim."

I sense a powerful shifter headed our way. I won't mind

getting Leilah off the streets, away from these kinds of characters.

The wolf halts and towers over the table as Leilah looks up. "There you are." At six foot five, he's a solid wall of chiseled muscle. Even in human form, he can't hide his power; plus, he's got some Middlewich in him somewhere.

He ignores me. "Got the goods?"

Leilah looks at me and says, "Business."

She shifts in her seat and pulls a small vial from a front pocket hidden in her skin-tight skirt. The glimpse of her tanned skin sends a message to my cock that will demand satisfaction before the night is through. I grab my drink and slide off the booth with an easy smile that promises I'll be back, but her attention is focused on the shifter.

A lovely redhead in a black miniskirt sashays past as I lean against a nearby booth. Her four-inch silver stripper heels catch my eye. I imagine Ciarah in my bed wearing those shoes and nothing else. The fantasy is going to remain just that.

I glance back at Leilah and her customer in time to see him disappear down the stairs leading to the men's room. I sip my drink, my eyes on Leilah as she turns slightly aside and stuffs the bills into her bodice. She throws back the remainder of her drink. I take a another sip of my drink, push off the booth, then halt when a pale, anemic man of about twenty-one emerges from the stairs leading to the men's room. I stare as he walks past, astonished that I can barely detect Leilah's shifter lurking inside. How did she accomplish such a feat? Leilah rises and starts toward the stairs behind me. I step into her path. She halts and narrows her eyes.

"Impressive," I say.

She studies me. She doesn't trust me, but the gleam in her eyes tells me she's confident of getting herself out of any trouble I might start. "Thanks."

She abruptly seizes my collar. I realize her intent and allow her to yank my mouth down onto hers. Her lips. God, how I've missed that moist satin skin against mine. Our tongues stroke, but not nearly long enough, before she ends the kiss by sliding the tip of her tongue under the seam of my upper lip. Funny how she remembers the action through every incarnation. I grab a fistful of her hair. Soft as corn silk, as it's always been. She grunts, then pulls back.

"My place?" I growl.

Fuck Ethan and Raith. They wouldn't say no after that kiss, either.

"You wish," she snorts, then walks away.

I force my breathing to slow and order my cock into submission while my eyes caress her curves, her buttocks. We've shared so many 'first' kisses, but this one surprises me the most. I've always been the one to initiate. I'd have much preferred a different ending to the night, but this rejection is better for both of us.

She's going to be angry once she discovers I'm the one investigating her grandmother...the one who pronounced Mariam guilty of evoking Shadow magic.

FOUR

Leilah

I HEAD BACK INTO THE COLD BEFORE THE HEAT OF Blade's mouth against mine cools. The nighttime temperature has dropped several degrees in the short time I've been in the club and the cold wind burns my skin. Why *hadn't* I accepted his invitation? I shiver, but not because of the cold. I have a weakness for Fae, and Blade Tyrion is a prime specimen, all loose-limbed grace and elegance, his every muscle coiled with easy power. Tonight isn't the first time I've wondered what it would be like to pull his long blond hair from its tie and tangle my fingers in the softness while he drives his cock so deep that he touches my soul. He would have made me forget about Grams, her house…and now, the fucking Academy. Maybe I would even be able to vanquish the memory of Ethan's body against mine in those seconds before I broke free of his hold.

I halt abruptly. I shouldn't want the man who is forcing me over a threshold I swore never to cross. What do he and Raith have to do with the Illumina's decree against my grandmother? How did she *really* die? Not for an instant do I believe the police report of suicide. Grams wasn't capable of killing herself.

Was she?

My heart twists. Grams was sixty-five when I last saw her—middle-aged in these modern times—seventy-two when she died—barely across the threshold of elderly. I expected her to live at least another twenty years. I told myself I would eventually return and demand to know why she'd kicked out a kid whose worst problem had been figuring out how to not get caught sneaking home after curfew. Hell, I hadn't even reached the really tough teenage years when she exiled me. What did I do that made her hate me so?

I go cold. She hadn't wanted me. Neither had my parents, who left me on Gram's doorstep and then disappeared.

I stalk across the sidewalk and hail an approaching cab. The cab stops at the curb as I arrive. I slide inside and give the driver Jax's address in Yonkers. It's late. I'm tired. But I have no intention of trotting over to The Academy first thing in the morning just because Ethan Bordeau branded me like livestock.

As the cab pulls away from the curb, I squint at the sigil. It's delicate yet strong. Real dragon magic. Jax should be able to handle a little dragon magic. I met Jax in Chicago three years ago. He's the only contact I have here in New York.

Half an hour later, I knock on the dingy wooden door of Jax's apartment. His mother is a harpy and his father a demon, making him a devious mix, if there ever was one. Right now, deviousness is exactly what I need. A TV abruptly blares in the apartment next door and some guy yells something I can't make out. On the fourth knock, the door opens beneath my upraised knuckles and Jax beckons me inside with a hurried wave of his hand.

"I'm not being followed," I say as I enter his tiny apartment.

I know he'll crane his thin neck and look in the hall anyway. He does. Then closes the door, faces me, and leans against the wood. He's tall and wiry and his round eyeglasses give him even more of an owlish look than he inherited from his mother.

"What's that on your hand?" he asks, zeroing in on the sigil before I can speak.

"Ran into a bit of trouble." I brandish the mark.

He squints at my hand for less than two seconds. "Yeah, that's not coming off."

"You didn't even really *look*," I carp.

Jax shuffles into the dingy realm of his living room, an area littered with video game paraphernalia and empty pizza boxes.

"Don't have to look," he grunts. "That's high-grade persuasion, right there. You're going to do exactly what that spell wants." He pauses, then faces me as he folds his arms across his thin chest. "That's a real Illumina spell. Can't fake those, you know."

I scowl. "I thought you could hack anything."

He dashes any remaining hope with a final, "You're not getting out of that."

The air leaves my lungs with an audible hiss.

"Looks like an Academy summons." A quirk of his lip announces he's impressed.

"Well, they might force me to show up, but I won't stay," I say.

"This is the Illumina you're talking about, Leilah." There's genuine awe in his voice, and precious few things evoke that kind of reaction from Jax.

"I'm not playing their game. Not after what they did to Grams. They can't just drag her name through the mud and expect me to heel when they wave a fucking carrot."

Jax shakes his head. "That can't happen. Acceptances come from the school itself."

Again, I wonder if my name actually appeared on the Stone. The same shiver that zipped down my back when Ethan informed me that I was to attend The Academy returns. Who writes the names on the Stone? How powerful was the mage who created the Stone to have knowledge centuries into the future? The Zidruhin preach that the identity of the Stone's creator is a dark mystery we aren't supposed to question or understand, but what do priests know?

I scowl. Stone or no Stone, the Illumina won't win—won't control me—not after they ruined Grams' reputation and stole my home.

"I'm with Grams," I say. "And that means I'm against—"

"Stop being a baby," Jax cuts in as he pushes his glasses up the bridge of his nose. "The Illumina sealed the house and initiated court proceedings. You're not getting the house."

"It's mine," I blurt.

Jax's intense gaze spears me. "You can't go home again." Embarrassment warms my cheeks, but he saves me from a stupid denial by adding, "You want the truth about your grandmother's death?" He motions with his chin at my hand. "This is your chance."

He's right, which I hate.

"That'll be fifty." Jax holds out his hand.

I can't really spare the money, but Jax isn't much better off than I am. I reach into my bra and withdraw the cash I got from the shifter, count out two fifties, and slap them into Jax's waiting palm. "Thanks," I say as I head for the door.

"Be careful," he calls. "That dragon protection is good stuff, but you never know."

I halt at the far end of the living room and turn. "Dragon protection?"

He rolls his eyes. "The sigil binds your magic, right?"

Jax really is too smart for his own good. "Yeah," I say slowly.

"Without protection, you would be left at the mercy of some demon or asshole Margiddian who wants to take advantage of you. Dragon protection is serious shit. Still..." He shrugs.

"There's a protection spell in the sigil?" Why hadn't I

sensed that? "Thanks." I say, then hurry from his building and step into the cold for the last time this night.

I keep my head down, but keep an eye on my surroundings. My place is a quick jog five blocks down and two over from Jax's place. Just far enough to enter an even worse part of town. What would it be like to stroll home instead of walking fast while pretending to appear nonchalant? I picture Stony and I eating breakfast in Gram's sizeable kitchen. I'd always wanted to learn how to really cook. That kitchen is the perfect place to learn. My fingers itch to leaf through Grams' potion books. She wrote everything down. I could easily take over the potionary business and be a true and respectable witch. God, what would that even look like?

Ten minutes later, I climb my building's rickety stairs to the second floor. The wards I put in place almost hum like a live wire at my approach. My keys jingle loudly in the darkness as I unlock my apartment door. I open the door a few inches and wait until Stony's snout appears in the crack.

"All clear?" I whisper.

She snuffles and turns back into the apartment.

Stony, a white micro pig with one black ear, is on the small side as micro pigs go, maybe forty pounds. She's not one for English. She's an equal-rights familiar who expects me to inter- pret her range of grunts, squeaks, and squeals as often as she has to deal with my words. When she was a piglet, we were fairly well balanced—an equal fifty-fifty—although, with the passage of time, communication is downright ridiculous. The last time she spoke English was nearly a month ago, and only because she wanted Chinese takeout. We've been together only three years, but I trust Stony with my life. Having to deal with grunts and squeaks in lieu of words is a small price to pay for safety and loyalty.

I flip on the light and survey my studio apartment. Furni- ture consists of a futon, a plastic lawn chair I found in a dumpster and a tiny, plastic table I got at a yard sale. The table is wonky. As I toss my keys down, even that sleight weight makes it wobble.

I spin left, drop onto the futon, and fall back. Something sharp digs into my thigh. I shift my leg and lift a fork. On the floor to the left is an empty carton of Chinese fried rice I'd left in the fridge. I give Stony a glare. She doesn't care. She's already comfortably sprawled under the window, snoring.

"Clean up after yourself," I mutter.

She snores louder.

I stare at the sigil glittering on the back of my hand. If Jax is right, I can twist this to my advantage.

I roll onto my stomach. "Stony, wake up."

She flicks an ear.

"You'll have to get up early," I warn.

She's going with me. I don't want her locked in the apartment in case I can't get back. More than one rumor claims The Academy is a one-way trip.

Stony lifts her head. I read her look. She doesn't do 'early.'

"Got an appointment at the Illumina Academy in the morning," I say. "Summons, rather."

This time, she grunts, "Illumina?" in her cute piggy snort.

Stony's not a fan of The Academy, but for entirely different reasons than mine. Several months ago, we passed a couple of Academy students sitting outside a Starbucks. One of them called her a 'porker' and said she'd make a tasty side of bacon. He hadn't known what thin ice he'd treaded.

I squirm onto my back and stare at the ceiling. Exhaustion washes over me. I'd been stressed before Ethan introduced himself and made things worse.

"Trouble follows me like shadows," I groan.

It's a phrase Grams used to say, but not one most witches would make a habit of using. Grams thought that fearing a word like 'shadows' was just plain silly. She'd garnered criticism for that stance. Still, how could anyone think she would stray to the dark side? She was nothing *but* light. She'd surrounded her shop with crystals to encourage the light to remain long after nightfall. We positioned herbs throughout the house to encourage harmony and peace—and, generally, we had peace.

Memory jumps to a fuzzy view of Grams leaning over me, chanting powerful words, her face drawn with fear. A prickle creeps up my spine. Behind her, candles flicker in the nooks and crannies of a cave wall. When was I ever underground with Grams? As a jumble of images follow, I sit up abruptly, unwilling to remember more. Tonight, I've had enough of the past.

It's tomorrow that worries me, now.

FIVE

Ethan

I STAND AT THE WINDOW IN RAITH'S OFFICE AND watch the sun's early rays dapple the gray Mercedes that glides up the school's drive. Olympia, the Grand Witch, Head of the Illumina Council that controls all Illumina Academies and ensures the Hell Gates remain sealed, has come to set up the first virtual world created since virtual worlds were outlawed during the Shadow War.

I release a breath. I'm not looking forward to our war games this year. A virtual Shadow world is a space that swallows light. Without light, love cannot grow. Hate and fear are sure to slither like brackish water in this created void. That reminds me too much of the myriad of nights Raith, Blade, and I prowled the streets of New York stopping crimes the NYPD had no idea were taking place while we searched for the source of The Shadows. Little had we known they were waiting in our dreams.

The virtual Shadow world is a huge undertaking, even for the Grand Witch. But I wonder if there's more to her visit, even more than her concern over Miriam having killed herself while practicing Shadow magic: she's unearthed news of Damien.

My fire warms. We kill Damien, The Shadows cease to exist. At least, that's the theory. I've lived long enough to heed caution when dealing with demigods. The last time someone other than a god tried to kill a demigod, Yissa, son of Erra, the god of plague, sent the Black Death in retribution for the attempt on his life. I doubt Damien will go as quietly.

The Mercedes stops in front of the building. If we do manage to kill Damien, that will lead to the next big crisis: do we open the Hell Gates? Olympia has kept the gates closed, despite efforts by demons and religious zealots to break the spell. Even some among the Zidruhin want the gates opened. One would think that the followers of the ancient god of angels—the god responsible for hell's creation—would accept that if their god wanted the gates open, he would open them himself. Interestingly enough, *Elohim* has remained silent on the matter.

I grimace as Olympia's driver opens her car door and she steps out. Even *Elohim* might think twice about tangling with the Grand Witch of the North. She has no intention of relinquishing her power.

Five minutes later, Raith's assistant, shows Olympia into Raith's study. I nod thanks to Madeline and she closes the door on her way out of the room.

Despite her great age, Olympia's skin is virtually wrinkle-free and, while the sparkle in her eyes lends a light-hearted, youthful appearance, she's anything but a dust-sprinkling fairy.

The Grand Witch settles into the Spanish leather chair in front of Raith's desk. Head held high, she surveys the room as if she's seated on a throne and holding court. But then, I suppose she is.

"Ethan." Her smoky voice is deep for a woman.

Even though we both protect Margidda, Olympia's a schemer, yet her voice fascinates, slides under your skin. Somewhere in her veins, Fae blood must flow.

"Grand Witch." I angle my head, then sit to her left, and we wait.

Two minutes later, Raith enters followed by Blade. So, the Fae got Raith's message last night. I send him a look that says we'll talk about Ciarah after this meeting. Blade gives a barely perceptible nod and, ever the charmer, approaches Olympia. His smile melts her like butter. She extends a hand. He grasps her fingers and brushes his lips across her knuckles.

"Blade." A coquettish gleam lights her eyes.

"An honor, Mistress Olympia," Blade murmurs.

She watches him saunter to the window as Raith settles behind his desk. Raith and Blade are polar opposites. Blade enchants women. Raith...well, Raith demands loyalty.

"I've found him," Olympia says without preamble.

My heart picks up speed. Am I right? Has she found Damien?

"The perfect man to fill the position as Headmaster of Illumina Academy New York," she says. "Mage Edd Domini, Master Extraordinaire of potions, brews and concoctions."

"Never heard of him," Raith says.

I haven't heard of him, either, which is odd. Still, there must be something extraordinary about the man if Olympia chose him.

"Impeccable credentials," she says. "He is Italian. You will love him."

"I'll consider him," Raith replies.

"Ah, but he's already hired, my dear," she says. "He's waiting in the library."

Raith arches a brow.

She waves dismissively in my direction. "You'll see him settled."

"I thought we were going to discuss candidates," Raith says coolly, but I note hesitation in his eyes.

Leave it to Raith to be blunt.

The subtle compression of Olympia's lips reveals her irritation. "There is nothing to discuss. As you know, Leilah Crowe being named a High Potential has caused a disturbance in the houses. House Maywen is demanding we deny her entrance into The Academy."

I tense.

"Perhaps they're right," Raith says.

"Are we going to allow the Houses to dictate who attends The Academy?" Blade asks.

Olympia grimaces. "No. But that doesn't mean I can ignore their concerns."

Blade laughs. "Forgive me, Grand Witch, but I've known you to ignore concerns far more serious than this."

Her eyes glow. "More serious than a White Witch—a White Witch powerful enough to have replaced me—who has crossed over to The Shadows?"

Blade half smiles. "Miriam Crowe hasn't been drafted into The Academy."

The glow vanishes and Olympia's eyes darken. "No, she hasn't. But I want to inspect Miriam's shop."

"We are still investigating," Raith says. "As is Zadkeil."

She bestows an indulgent smile. "We cannot count on Zedkeil to share every detail. I knew Miriam. I may be better qualified to detect the source of The Shadows she used. Meanwhile, you and Ethan can welcome Domini and see him settled in."

I smile, but only because it's expected.

"Blade, you will take me to Miriam's home," she says.

We're on edge with Leilah's impending arrival. I'm betting Blade is in no mood to deal with Olympia's machinations. Yet, with her power and position, we cannot refuse.

"Will two this afternoon suffice?" Blade asks.

Her mouth thins and I can tell she's preparing to insist they leave right away, but her assistant arrives, a slim male with a self-important swagger. He whispers in her ear and Olympia stands abruptly.

"If you'll excuse me, Gentlemen?" Without another word, she leaves.

I look at Raith and Blade. "What was that all about?"

Blade glances at the door. "Can't be good," he says.

I hate it when he's right.

SIX

Leilah

WITH THE WAY THE DRAGON'S DAMNED SIGIL BURNS my skin, I know there's no turning back. It's nine in the morning as I crack the twelfth egg and drop it into the frying pan. Despite feeling like I'm marching to my death, I'm determined to make Stony's breakfast as I do every morning. Even though she's a micro-pig, Stony eats enough for a full-sized hog. Her grocery bill is four times the cost of mine.

"Time to chow down," I announce.

Stony's grunt announces her bad mood, and not only because she's awake before noon. She watched me cook and knows I've used the last of our eggs, so her breakfast is at least a dozen eggs short.

"Suck it up, Buttercup," I say. There's apology amidst my sarcasm.

She stares at me through her beady black eyes and heaves a sigh. Apology accepted. She likes her eggs runny, so, after a minute of stirring, I switch off the stove, grab the pan's handle and squat beside her dish. I scrape the eggs into her bowl. As I slide the spatula under the last egg, she knocks my hand. I can't miss the caring concern in her eyes. She's indicating that the last egg is mine. My eyes mist. Her ears flick back as she attacks her breakfast with gusto.

I sit at the table to eat my share. "We make a pair," I comment sourly. Stony snorts between bites and I scowl. "Oh yeah, we should be thrilled the prestigious Illumina Academy wants us. Let's hop up and down for joy. Remember why we're doing this," I say. "You're going to love Grams' house. The kitchen is huge."

At that, she looks up, her eyes alight with interest. I hide a grin. I knew that would capture her interest.

After I eat, I scrawl a quick note to the landlord and fold the paper around most of the cash I received from the shifter last night. It'll cover next month's rent. By then, I'll be done with The Academy.

I reach for the small metal lockbox under the table and flip open the lid. I have only one fake identity potion left. I pick up the last bottle and grab my wand from the counter, then cross to where Stony is circling like a dog atop her bedding.

The wand is one of the few things I managed to stuff into my backpack the day Grams threw me out. I seldom use it; wands are more the purview of wizards. But Grams taught me that a good witch needs a basic understanding of different types of magic. I heft the wand and hope it allows me to bypass Ethan's damn sigil so I can change Stony into a mouse.

I stop beside Stony and pull the stopper from the vial. "Sorry to disappoint, but I was serious. You're coming with me."

I tip the bottle, the liquid touches her hide, and she squeals. The potion is as safe as Baby Shampoo, but Stony prefers drama. Technically, I don't need additional magic for the potion to work, but this is my last vial. Besides, Stony's obstinate. She'll try to outwit me by choosing a new identity of 'micro-pig,' thus leaving me exactly where we started. Right now, I can't take that chance.

A poof announces the potion is ready to take form, so I point the wand at Stony and murmur, "Mouse."

She squeals and flattens her ears. I don't miss the defiant gleam in her beady little eyes.

"*Mus*," I say louder. I rarely use old Latin, but once in a while, old trumps new.

Magic shimmers over Stony as the sigil on my arm flares. I grit my teeth against the increasing heat. I want to shout at Stony to quit fighting me but if my concentration breaks, she wins. I push my will into the wand. The sigil grows more painful. My shoulder muscles burn with the effort of pushing back at Stony—which distracts a little from the burn of the damn sigil. She resists for a full three minutes and I try not to think about how much hotter the sigil might get. At last, sparks engulf her. My muscles relax. I toss the wand onto the futon and rub my right shoulder as I hold my breath, as much in anticipation of the outcome as out of relief that damn sigil is cooling.

I chose a mouse as something I could easily hide in my pocket. There's an audible poof and I see I only get half my wish. I groan. Stony has definitely gone for 'pig.' On her bed sits a pissed, grumpy guinea pig. She's chunky and definitely won't fit in any pocket.

"What the hell, Stony?" I growl.

She lifts her lip and bares her two elongated teeth.

So, neither of us is happy.

I scowl as I grab my backpack, packed with a few clothes and my cell phone. I stuff my wand in an inside pocket, then grab Stony by the scruff of her neck. She squeaks when I dump her inside the biggest pouch.

"Be quiet," I hiss over the grate of the closing zipper.

She gives a final peeved grunt, then settles down as I slip the strap over my shoulder. I scoop up a hair tie from the kitchen counter and pull my hair back into a ponytail as I give the place one last look. The sigil on my hand begins to warm, this time in warning that it's time to go.

"Damn you, Ethan," I say. I grab my cell phone charger, head for the door, and add for good measure, "Damn you, too, Raith."

Ninety minutes later, I'm waiting on the train platform. I've discovered that as long as I'm on track for the school, the sigil on my hand doesn't heat up. Stray more than a foot and it zaps me back on track like a cattle prod. By the time I arrive at The Academy, I suspect my hair will be standing on end like a frazzled dandelion seed puff.

The train arrives and I cradle my backpack in an effort to keep Stony safe as I shove my way through the crowd toward the train's open doors. The third time I'm elbowed in the gut, I succumb to temptation and send Ethan a double dose of ill intent.

"Next time, Ethan, you and your sigil can kiss my ass," I curse under my breath.

I board. We're packed in like sardines, and the man sitting to my right is watching the news on his phone. The volume is low, but I hear the voice of a local newscaster say, *"What's the weather today, John? Are we headed for our first snow of the winter?"*

The weatherman forecasts a clear day and dry weather for the coming week.

"Thank you, John," the newswoman says when he's finished. *"In other local news—"*

The phone's owner switches to a game as the train descends into a tunnel. The interior dims and I glance out the grimy window into darkness and shadows. Both should make a Light witch uneasy, yet I've always found darkness and shadows strangely comforting. I stare at the darkness, looking for shapes and patterns, as if I'm taking one of those ink blot personality tests. When a hand suddenly forms and beckons, I blink and my concentration breaks. Uneasy, I glance around to see if anyone else noticed.

The train curves to the right and the sigil on my hand warms. My ire returns. *Damn you, Ethan. I can't control the direction the train takes.*

The rest of the ride further succeeds in frazzling my temper and, by the time I emerge from the station at Pound Ridge, I'm in the worst mood I've been in since I learned of Grams' death.

I hail a cab and, fifteen minutes later, I spot a stone keep above the trees in the distance. A few more minutes and massive gate comes into view up ahead. Stone pillars support an intricate, wrought-iron gate. Each black spire is tipped with a spear. There'll be no escaping over that thing without impaling myself. I wonder if that's the intent. The place exudes a high-class prison vibe. Embedded in each pillar is a gold emblazoned Illumina Academy coat-of-arms. The gold looks real.

The cab pulls over at the gate. "You one of those rich genius kids?" he asks.

"Rich?" I snort. "Not hardly. Genius? We'll see." I pay him, grab my backpack and get out.

I stare at the gate. My heart begins to pound. I'm about to enter the Illumina realm of control. Determination overcomes misgivings and I stride toward the gate. I see no guards and no way of getting inside. Scarcely do I begin to wonder how I'm going to enter when the gates begin a slow inward swing, gliding smoothly without a sound. I enter the widening gap and sense the wards that guard the gate. Past the gate, I slow as I start down the tree-lined drive that winds out of sight through the trees. It's strange, I can almost sense the school. Even stranger, I feel like I'm suddenly home. The thought smacks of betrayal—mine—and I scowl.

I shoulder the backpack and mutter, "Here we go, Stony. There's no turning back now."

Of course, she doesn't answer. Knowing her, she's asleep. I take half a dozen more steps, then stumble under the sudden weight on my back and drop to my knees as Stony's spell breaks. The backpack rips under the strain. With grunts and squeals from both of us, I struggle to free myself from the straps as she kicks me in the ribs in her efforts to scramble away. Then, she's free, back in pig form, and wearing the backpack like a life jacket around her neck. She's pleased as punch to find herself restored. I'm not.

"So much for hiding." Dammit, the wards probably deactivated the spell. No unregulated use of magic on Academy grounds. Fabulous.

"You're a witch," a voice says.

I whirl to find myself staring at a middle-aged man with an unusually pointed nose wearing a green John Deere baseball cap, wool-liked jean jacket and jeans. The gates click closed behind me and a sense of panic bubbles up.

"Welcome to Illumina Academy New York," the man says. "I'm Daws Flitwick, Groundskeeper." He points up the drive that winds through the trees out of sight. "Just keep going. Follow the 'New Student' signs."

As he finishes, a click sounds behind me and I turn to see the gates swing open again and a dark-haired young woman of around my age enters. Leather pants are visible below the knee length black pea coat, buttoned to her chin.

"Fran Shelton," she says, her lively brown eyes crinkling at the edges in a smile.

"Leilah," I reply. "Leilah Crowe."

Before she can respond, the groundskeeper urges, "You'd better hurry. They're starting and it's not good to be late." He nods his chin at the road and then cocks a brow at Stony. "Not sure about the pig."

"She's fine." I step in front of Stony to cut off his view.

He doesn't seem interested in a confrontation and, with a nod, enters the trees. Relieved, I begin herding Stony down the drive.

Fran falls into step beside me. "You're a witch, huh," she observes.

"Yep," I answer, even though I know she's not asking. My mind is on Stony. Will they kick her out? After a few more steps, I pause and crouch beside her. "Maybe you should chill in those trees for a bit while I check this place out." I point across the drive to a nice stand of birch and willows. The ground looks soft there, mud-like. Just Stony's style.

Her beady eyes light with interest. After all, rooting in the woods is a far sight more interesting than being cooped up in our shabby one-room apartment. Knowing Stony, she'll head straight to a warm place beneath a tree and plop down for an all-day nap.

"She's cute," Fran says as Stony trots off, snout held high.

"Yeah." When she is in pig form, anyway. "You go on ahead. I'll just wait till she's settled." I smile politely but Fran's brown eyes sparkle with amusement. She knows I just told her to bugger off.

"Catch you later." She waves, then heads down the drive.

I wait until Stony vanishes into the trees before I resume my walk toward the school.

Halfway around the first bend, a castle-like structure comes into view. Towers rise at each corner, each crowned with a steeply conical, black-slate roof. Brick buildings behind the castle extend beyond the sides of the main building. Behind the main building, at what must be the center of the compound, the keep I saw on our approach rises at least a hundred feet into the air. I feel like I've stepped back in time.

Ivy clings to the walls, threatening to cover the many arched windows where small stone gargoyles perch above each window. Warmth ripples through me at the memory of Grams' stories of how well gargoyles guard their assignments. My mood breaks at the wonder of how many schools had gargoyles when The Shadows came. I guess gargoyles' powers aren't all-encompassing.

I reach a cobblestone walkway that leads to the grand entrance, complete with a portcullis gate, and can almost feel the prestige that radiates from every brick. I half expect knights in full armor, riding white destriers, to charge and am not disappointed. Half a dozen men in body armor come into view beyond the *New Student* sign up ahead.

Watchmen on Academy grounds?

I veer right onto a path that parallels the castle and hurry past the Watchmen, who walk in twos, clearly on alert. The path leads to half a dozen small stone buildings that form a circle with the tower rising beyond them. Here and there, students stroll in groups of two or three. Finally, the last sign directs me between two large buildings. I emerge from the shadow of the buildings and stop short. Twenty feet ahead is the tower.

A sign over the door reads *New Student Orientation*. A strange tremor ripples through my stomach as I start forward. As I approach the tower, the door swings open and I enter a dimly lit chamber. Flickering beeswax candles are the only source of light. The floor and walls are stone, and large wooden beams span the ceiling. This time, I feel as if I've truly stepped back in time.

Before a stage, red-cushioned benches are arranged in rows, seating about two dozen students wnts. The red-haired woman standing on the stage before a blue velvet stage curtain facing the audience. Every head angles my way.

"Sorry," I mumble, and drop onto the nearest bench, just behind Fran.

"Punc-tu-al-i-ty." The woman on the stage enunciates each

syllable as icy disdain rolls off her in waves. "Punctuality is *key*. Without punctuality, you will *not* succeed here at Illumina Academy. Rules are to be *obeyed…*"

She keeps going on, but she's staring straight at me through her gold, horn-rimmed glasses. What the hell? Does she know me?

"Students, before we move forward with the ceremony, I must warn you against repeating to anyone outside these walls what goes on here. You are High Potentials, our strongest line of defense against any enemy. We cannot allow these enemies to learn our secrets." She slides her gaze across the audience and I swear her attention snags on me. "Now, we have a very special guest with us today. It is my distinct honor to introduce the Grand Witch of the North herself."

I stare in awe as a woman emerges onto the stage from the left. She moves with fluid grace, the silver cloak flowing around her like liquid metal. She looks like the legend she is: tall, long silver hair piled atop her head, and magnificent.

Grams had worshipped the Grand Witch with the frenzy of a zealot—a hero worship that changed three months before she tossed me out on my ass. By then, Grams had withdrawn from everything, starting with Olympia and ending with me. My troubles started the day I came home from school to find Grams swearing and tossing out every magazine, paper, and book that contained a picture of the Grand Witch. When I'd asked why, she'd zapped a bolt of lightning at me. I'd been too busy diving out of its way to ask any more questions.

"Welcome, all," the Grand Witch says in a smoky voice, and lifts both hands. "I am honored to welcome each one of you. Thank you, Miss Mack." She bestows a gracious nod upon the woman with the horn-rimmed glasses, then faces us once again. "The four clans welcome you. Silwood, Longhorpe, Middlewich, and Pencarrow. Welcome to our New York students, and a special welcome to students from Colorado,

Texas, and North Dakota." A few claps and whistles go up. The Grand Witch smiles indulgently, then continues, "Joining me today, I have Illumina Academy New York's new Headmaster, Mage Edd Domini, and Academy recruiter, Commander Ethan Bordeau." She turns to the side and claps.

Ethan emerges from the right of the stage and every female in the room straightens. It's genetic, I suppose. He's wearing black pants and a crisp, white shirt that can't hide the lean muscles rippling beneath the cotton. I bet every girl in the room is mentally undressing him.

Ethan's eyes latch onto mine and I'm tempted to point to his damn sigil with my middle finger. A corner of Ethan's mouth quirks. To hell with it. I give his sigil the finger, but he's already turning away. The new headmaster follows Ethan onto the stage and startling green eyes lock onto me.

I freeze. I have the strange sensation as if I know him. Have I met him before? Where? He's tall, well-built, with stylish chestnut hair and a sinfully chiseled mouth that ends in a dimple on each cheek. He's not the kind of man you forget any more than Ethan is. Headmaster Domini nods at me and I realize I'm not only staring, but my middle finger is still on display.

I quickly hide my hand and mouth, "Sorry."

He turns away, leaving me unsure if he understood.

I wince. *Great job, Leilah. Less than ten minutes and you've made an enemy of the guy who runs the school.*

I hunch down on the bench as the Grand Witch waves at the velvet curtain behind her. The curtain pulls back with an audible whoosh to reveal a jagged block of obsidian about eight feet high and five feet wide.

My breath catches. This can't be the famed Stone. I don't know what I'd been expecting, but it hadn't been a block of black stone that exuded magic like a live wire. I could fall into that river of magic and never come out. The Stone looks cold, but I instinctively know it warms to the right magic. I smile to myself. How interesting that the Illumina Academy of Light has within its gates a black stone, the embodiment of shadow?

As Ethan and Domini position themselves on each side of the Stone, Olympia calls a student by name to join them on the stage. When the student arrives, she speaks with the girl, but from where I sit, I can't discern the words. After a short exchange, the student places her hands on the Stone, then Headmaster Domini escorts the student to the stairs that descend the stage as the Grand Witch calls out another name and the same scene plays out again.

A sense of discomfort tightens my belly. I wait my turn, and notice my ass feels hot, as if I'm sitting on a seat warmer. I shift my weight to cool off as my gaze strays to the shadows dancing in the room. It's odd that the Illumina's New Student orientation is taking place in a candlelit room. The shadows capture my attention and, once again, I find myself mesmerized with the many shapes; fanciful beasts, geometric patterns, and even clawed hands. It's not until I discern the wavering form of a large, black spider on the ceiling over the Grand Witch's head that I tense. Searching for shapes in the darkness isn't exactly a pastime that's condoned. I should know better.

SEVEN

Leilah

"LEILAH CROWE," THE GRAND WITCH'S THROATY voice startles me to attention.

There's something in the way she says my last name. There's a secret there. Normally, I find secrets interesting. Now, however, I'm not sure I want to know anyone's secrets. I rise and hurry to the stage, too aware of Ethan's piercing gaze.

When I reach her on the stage, she smiles. "Leilah." Her expression is as sympathetic as the smoky overtones of her voice. "I'm so sorry for your loss, my dear. I knew your grandmother well."

I blink, shocked. I hadn't expected anyone to mention Grams, let alone the Grand Witch. She knew Grams? Grams never mentioned that. I shouldn't be surprised, but I am. The Grand Witch grasps my hand. Her fingers are warm, strong, and she radiates a kindness that robs me of my desire to demand answers concerning the Illumina's seizure of Grams' house.

"Thank you," I say as I shake her hand.

A tear slips down her cheek and I tense when her eyes search my face. "You have your grandmother's eyes." She smiles and I detect a hint of dry humor as she glances at the sigil on my hand and adds, "And, clearly, her passion."

I jerk my gaze onto Ethan. Even as relaxed as he appears, he dominates the stage. An electric current zips from the hairs on the back of my neck to the base of my spine. It takes me a second to yank my mind back to the conversation. What were we talking about? Right, the damn sigil that has marked me as a troublemaker.

How do I reply? "Grams was special," I say.

"Indeed, she was." So many secrets swirl in her voice, but in a Grand Witch, that's got to be expected.

I suddenly want to demand answers. If anyone knows what really happened to Grams and why the Illumina took possession of her home—my home—the Grand Witch does. Hope surges. Of all people, a Grand Witch is sure to understand the connection between two witches...granddaughter and grandmother. She will understand that Grams' home is mine. Maybe the Illumina seized the house not thinking I would return?

"Justice shall prevail," she says.

My heart speeds up. Has she discerned my thoughts? Does she really understand? Will she release the house to me?

Her expression brightens. "But today is about you, child, is it not? Touch the Stone and let us see what The Academy has to say of you."

I frown, confused for a moment, then realize what she's said. "The Academy actually speaks?"

"The keep is the heart of The Academy," Headmaster Domini says with a slight Italian accent. His deep voice sounds exactly like it should for a man with deep and sexy looks. He's overwhelmingly male—and so very familiar. "This is where the Stone lives."

I'm dimly aware of Ethan's scrutiny as I ask the headmaster, "Have we met?"

His eyes light with amusement. "I don't see how, Miss Crowe. Unless you've visited Italy?"

His voice rumbles through me, sinfully delicious, but I'm sure he's lying. Still, I feel drawn to him in a way I can't explain, like a moth to a flame...a flame hellbent on burning the moth to a crisp. The strength of my response makes me uneasy and I step back.

"The Stone. Touch it," Ethan urges.

I turn toward the dragon and find myself drawn toward him, as well. Fuck, what's wrong with me? I'm like a cat in heat. He's all strength and hard muscle and every cell in my body forgets the headmaster in favor of the dragon energy sweeping over me. That's the thing about dragons. They're bigger than life. They leave no room for anyone else. The edges of the silver tattoos visible beyond his shirt cuff call to my fingers like a siren. Then I remember his sigil has jolted me one damn time too many and I'm back to being pissed.

"Today sometime?" Ethan arches a brow.

The Grand Witch smiles. "Touch the Stone and your name and clan will appear as proof of your acceptance."

I turn my attention to the black slab. "I thought my name had already appeared on the Stone." I slant a narrow-eyed glance at Ethan. "Isn't that why I was *invited*?"

"Correct," the Grand Witch replies. "But we must be sure of your identity. We cannot risk anyone impersonating a student." Her gaze shifts to the Stone and a soft emotion fills her eyes. "The Stone is imbued with magic as ancient as the Shadow attack in Greek fifteen hundred years ago."

So, there's a chance—a big chance—I'll get booted out on my ass. What are the chances I could get any answers before they kick me out? I hesitate, then brush my palm over the cool surface of the Stone. The sigil burns. I withdraw my hand. As expected, nothing. A vision flares of Ethan grasping my arm and escorting me off the stage to the front gate.

The three of them study the Stone, brows drawn. My heart takes a dive. I don't want to be here, but I had counted on getting answers before I leave. Damn the Illumina—

Letters of luminescent white fire flicker on that shiny black surface. I take an involuntary step back. A series of names appear, names I don't recognize. *Ciarah, Brin. Emma. Nova.*

Ethan draws a sharp breath. He *knows* he's made a mistake. I'm not the High Potential he claimed. My mind races. Shit, shit, shit. Now, I've got to…

New letters form the name *Leilah Crowe*. My breath catches. I stare at the name in disbelief. It's really true? I'm a High Potential? I'd known from a young girl that I was a powerful witch. Grams made sure I understood the responsibilities that accompanied my abilities. But a High Potential? The name scrolls upwards to make room for the clan name *Longthorpe*. I open my mouth to speak, then freeze as another clan name appears: *Penncarrow*. I frown. Ethan and Headmaster Domini frown, too.

"What is this?" the Grand Witch demands, but before anyone can answer, the names Middlewich and Silwood appear on the Stone. "This is…" her voice trails away.

As the silence drags, my heart speeds up. It takes a lot to stump an Illumina Grand Witch. It takes a lot to catch *me* off guard.

"Something's off with your precious Stone," I mutter.

"No," Ethan murmurs, but he's looking at the Grand Witch. "She's connected to all four clans."

"This is impossible. Who are the other names?" The Grand Witch looks at me. "Do you know these people?"

I shake my head. "Never heard of them."

She studies me for a long moment and I feel the subtle probe of magic. A truth spell, no doubt.

She abruptly swings her gaze onto the headmaster. "Domini? Isn't this impossible?"

He's still staring at the Stone. "Apparently not."

"The Illumina Stone does not err," Ethan says.

I'm not convinced, not with the succession of names I'd seen, but I'm not about to rock the boat. I have no desire for Ethan to slap another sigil on me. The current of power radiating at the base of my spine makes me shift in growing discomfort and I wonder if the magic in his sigil is running amok.

"But, of course, Miriam Crowe's granddaughter would prove the most unusual student," the Grand Witch says with a laugh that doesn't quite sound genuine.

"As each clan has claimed you, you'll have rights to access each tower," Ethan informs me.

He stares down at me through half lowered eyelids with a strange look that starts a tingling in my stomach. I force my gaze from his eyes and wince at how downright hot my ass is getting.

As the Grand Witch calls the next student, Headmaster Domini motions me to him. I walk to him and, as he escorts me to the stairs, he says, "Student Crowe, take your rightful place within these hallowed halls." We reach the stairs and Domini drops a hand on my shoulder. My awareness skitters atop my arms. "Welcome, Leilah. Go through that door." He nods toward the door the other students exited through.

I descend the stairs. Unable to stop myself, I look over my shoulder. He's watching me, eyes intense. Damn, the man is fine. I turn to face forward and catch sight of Ethan staring, brow cocked. I continue toward the door. I'll deal with him later, and demand he remove his sigil now that I'm officially enrolled.

I force myself through the door and into the next room. A variety of low, curving couches are clustered around potted trees in the large room. Crystals hang from a high ceiling.

There's lots of light, and the whole place makes me feel like I'm standing in a hotel lobby.

Before I can take another step, a zap radiates from the base of my spine to my buttocks with a sizzle; the exact same discomfort I've experienced all morning. Am I having some kind of allergic reaction to the damn sigil?

I hurry past my fellow students in search of a bathroom and enter a hallway that stretches out longer than the square keep should allow. Fucking Academy magic. I walk past closed doors. My sigil stirs as if it's getting ready to zap me back on track.

"You can just kiss my a—" I stop, mid-curse.

As understanding sinks in, my ass takes the full force of my backfired spell. I'd cursed Ethan on the train. Something about his *fucking power kissing my ass.*

"This is not a kiss," I growl as pain radiates deep inside my butt muscles. I'll blister at this rate.

When will I ever fucking learn? Wishing others ill has never failed to bite me in the… No, I don't dare think that blasted word. The way the curse is building, I'm headed for real trouble unless I can break the spell fast. I concentrate. After a minute, I recall mint is used to sooth rogue magic.

The sigil begins to heat. "I'm here at the fucking Academy," I shout at it.

With an extra urgency to my step, I begin trying doors but they're locked. At last, an unlocked door. A classroom and—thank God—it's empty. My backside is burning now and it's all I can do to keep from ripping off my jeans and running through the halls in my thong. The classroom is filled with desks, but not a single herb. I hurry from the room and glimpse an exit sign in the hallway. I'm intent upon cornering the first student I encounter in order to demand directions to the infirmary before my clothes ignite.

I pass an open doorway and I'm flooded with relief. The shelves are lined with jars of herbs. A potion classroom. I kick the door shut and shove my jeans down my hips. I kick them aside as I stumble to the shelves and scan the labeled jars. St. John's Wort. Mustard Seed. Ashwagandha. Hell, where is the mint? Tears sting as I bend down, still searching. Then, I see a jar labeled mint.

"Halla-fucking-lu-yah," I sing, and grab the jar.

In my haste, I fumble the lid. It falls to the floor and rolls away. I grab a handful of mint and rub it on my ass. The heat begins to cool. I slap some on the damn sigil, as well, then rub more on my ass.

I freeze when the door creaks open behind me.

EIGHT

Ethan

FIRE WARMS MY CHEST AS I TRACK LEILAH THROUGH the hallway. She has no business being here in the Restricted Zone. We haven't finished cleaning residue from the magic spill last week when Professor Cornwall's students lost control.

Strange, how the Stone picked up all Leilah's past identities in the four clans. I didn't miss her name, Ciarah, being the first. Leilah hadn't understood, of course. Neither had Olympia and her new pet, Headmaster Domini. No one knows of the relationship we've shared with Ciarah in her many incarnations. Blade, Clan Silwood. Raith, Clan Longthorpe. Myself and Caleb, Clan Penncarrow. As for Middlewich? Matthias, as Gargoyle, claimed kinship to that clan. She's part of all of us. Somehow, the Stone knew.

I close my eyes, breathe deeply, and locate her scent coming from the Advanced Potions Class. Leilah's a loose cannon, but her sheer raw power is impressive. I'm irritated, but can't deny the pride I feel that she's managed to bulldoze her way through the wards set in the Restricted Zone. How the hell did she power through that level of pain?

I open the door, half expecting to find her passed out on the floor. Instead, she's at the shelves, bent over, and I'm presented with the finest view of her perfect ass. It's hard to count that barely-there, wisp of a lace thong as a legitimate article of clothing.

I growl and my dragon blood roars. "What are you doing?" I start toward her. "This area is restricted."

She whirls, eyes wide in embarrassment. Still, she doesn't attempt to hide, but stands straight as I stop before her. Dragon fire answers the defiance in her eyes. I tower over her, needing to yank that thong aside and taste her. I smell her desire. She's responding to me on that soul level we've always shared. She's as much a beast as I am.

"This is your fault." Leilah thrusts a handful of mint beneath my nose. "You and your damn sigil."

I sense the magic running riot over her skin. It's concentrated on that firm ass of hers. "That's none of my doing," I say. That spell is hers and hers alone.

"Your sigil has caused me nothing but problems."

Her heartbeat quickens. There are only a few buttons separating our beasts. My tattoos rise, some already shifting into armor. I'm dangerously close to taking that first step to slake our mutual desire and, once I step on that road, we won't stop. We never have. As for Raith and Blade...well, I've done my duty. I've informed them. They know she's back. The rest is going to happen, just as it always has.

I lean an inch closer and whisper, "I put a mark on your hand, not your ass." Yet. I can and will put a second one on her ass.

"Take this sigil off. *Now*," she demands. "I'm done."

Raith won't say a word if I make love to her, but he will be furious if I remove the sigil. He's right. She can't be allowed to run around the school with that much power at her disposal, not when her temper runs so hot. There's another reason I won't remove the sigil, one that makes my dragon growl. The satisfaction I feel at seeing my mark on her flesh, the next best thing to a mating mark.

"Now," Leilah repeats.

"No. You need a little…" I lean closer to breathe the one word I know will infuriate her animalistic side the most, "taming."

The power that surges through her doesn't disappoint. It's all I can do to keep from flipping her around to bury my cock deep inside that tight channel of hers, the one I smell growing wetter by the second.

"Taming?" her voice is dangerous.

"I'll compromise." There's no way she can miss the lust in my voice. "I'll remove the curse you're trying to break. What was it?"

She hesitates.

"Or not." I crook a smile.

"Fine," her voice turns waspish. Ciarah never did like to lose. She lifts her chin. "I simply said, *You and your power could kiss my ass.*"

I'll kiss her ass and *more*. I would start with running my hands over her smooth backside and not stop until I'm inside her, where I belong.

"Turn around. I'll remove your curse."

She hesitates. The way her lashes dip signals she knows where this is going. She turns. God, she's gorgeous. There's no outer sign of her discomfort but I feel the strength of her spell even without touching that smooth skin. With such power running in her veins, her magic finds it hard to leave her. I wonder if she knows that's why her spells backfire. Blade will have to teach her proper focus.

I drop my gaze to the thong that disappears between her ass cheeks, caressing the parts of her that I will soon caress. My fingers twitch, wanting to slide that soft scrap of lace aside to pillow my hardened cock there. Flesh on flesh. It's been so long. She's better than gold. I inhale the scent of her hair, vanilla, then place my hands on her hips. Her magic flows up over my arms, teasing my tattoos.

That's all the invitation I need.

NINE

Leilah

THIS ISN'T HOW I IMAGINED MY FIRST DAY AT THE Academy. The famed Ethan Bordeau fucking me in a classroom. I knew dragons were sexual, but I had no idea just how sexual. Animalistic. Raw. I arch my back and push against him. His cock is rock hard—and huge. He grasps my hips and I draw a sharp breath when the fingers gently squeeze. I need him.

His hands slide over my skin and leave blessed coolness in their wake. A new heat builds that sends a different electrical current straight to my core. I close my eyes and will his fingers lower. He slips a finger under the lace of my thong and I draw a sharp breath at the warmth of his touch.

The classroom door creaks open.

A shocked female gasp is followed by, "Commander *Bordeau!*"

I whirl as Ethan steps back. I want to melt through the floor. Miss Mack gapes, her horn-rimmed glasses balanced precariously on the tip of her nose. Fury swirls in her expression. She's angry—with *me.*

Fuck. She has the hots for Ethan.

"Miss Mack." Ethan graces her with a casual nod.

He doesn't explain, and I don't look at him as I take two steps and scoop my jeans from the floor. Miss Mack watches me, eyes narrowed and clearly thinking the worst...but the worst is exactly what Ethan and I had in mind. Why couldn't she have come fifteen minutes later? No, half an hour. This dragon had been in no hurry. God have mercy.

"You shouldn't be here, *Student* Crowe," Miss Mack snaps.

"I was just leaving," I lie.

"You should be with the other students, touring your clan dorm."

"On it," I say, then pause. "Which clan is that?" I had ranked in all of them.

Miss Mack's expression fills with contempt. "The clan on the Stone, of course." Her tone clearly states just how stupid she judges me to be.

I turn to Ethan. He's leaning a shoulder against the shelves, arms crossed over his broad chest. Heat floods my core. What had I wanted to ask him? I blink. *The clans.*

A corner of his mouth twitches in amusement. "You will be assigned a clan," he says.

Is he making fun of me?

"You should go, Ms. Crowe," Miss Mack snaps.

Ethan flicks a cool gaze her way. Poor woman. She's obviously out of her league. She's not his type. He's raw, animalistic...*my* type. His eyes return to me. My breath catches. His dragon energy promises we're not finished. He straightens, walks past me without a word, and passes through the door. I follow before Miss Mack corners me.

By the time I reach the lobby-like waiting room, I glimpse a line of students outside the open left-hand door. I hurry outside to join them, curiosity over which clan I'm saddled with momentarily displacing memories of Ethan's thick cock pressed against my ass.

A tall, good looking guy steps up and waves his arm. "If I

call your name, please stand over here." He motions to his right.

He begins to call off names of students. My name is called last and I join the group of waiting students.

"Welcome, students of Clan Penncarrow," he says. "My name is Thomas and I'm your student advisor as well as the male student body RA." He pauses to survey each face before his eyes rest on me. His brow furrows.

Fabulous. The name Crowe precedes me. I scowl. What exactly have I gotten myself into?

Thomas turns away, arms raised, and starts down one of the paths running between buildings. I trail the other students. I hope Stony is having fun. Likely, she's snoozing, warm and cozy. Can't say I'm having much fun. Well, the classroom was kind of...exciting. My mouth dries when I remember Ethan's warm hand so close to my—

"Welcome," a silvery voice interrupts my thoughts.

I startle to see the group's stopped before the two-door entrance to a four-story brick, Tudor-style building that's one of the circle of buildings. Ivy covers the weathered red bricks. The speaker is a slender blonde, her body as delicately exquisite as her voice. She looks so fragile that I wonder why a good gust of wind doesn't blow her away.

"My name is Ariel." She pauses to bestow a lofty smile at Thomas.

Meow. There's clearly a power play going on between them. I watch for his reaction, but he remains stone-faced.

Ariel looks back at us with a smirk that conveys, *You are my subjects.* "This is a coed dorm, students. Boys on the third floor. Girls on the Fourth. I'm the Room Assistant for the Fourth Floor. So, girls, if you encounter any problems, Room 401 will solve them."

I notice the subtle shift of responsibility. Room 401 will solve problems, huh? Not her? I absorb her expensive clothing.

Yeah, she isn't the type to work. No doubt, she delegates to a gaggle of students who make sure things get done.

James lifts an arm and barks, "Men, this way. Follow."

The guys fall into line behind him. The ages of the students strike me as strange. The youngest can't be more than thirteen while, accounting for the paunch of that belly, the oldest seems closer to thirty. This clearly isn't a normal school. But then, I knew that.

From the front of the group, Fran makes eye contact with me and waves. I wave back and trail after the girls who surge through the door. Their ages are closer to mine, maybe a shade younger, although Ariel seems to be in her early twenties. I pass her and catch a whiff of...*Cartier Oud and Santal Parfum?* Yeah, she's rich. That perfume costs more than I charge for a fake ID, and I only know that because I'd once met a customer at Bergdorf Goodman.

We climb the stairs to the fourth floor. There's a grunge vibe here. Chalkboards are decorated with colorful graffiti and mysterious symbols cover the walls. The ceiling is painted dark gray and fairy LED lights are strung the length of the carpeted hallway.

A young tattooed woman stands in front of Room 401 with a clipboard. "Room assignments. Line up, quick," she says.

I hang back and eye the girls around me. They exude an impression of belonging, a real sense of clan blood and loyalty. Grams had described the many clan battles that had taken place before the war, each group vying for control in Margidda. Power struggles stopped the day The Shadows arrived.

"Room four ten," the tattooed girl says the instant I step up. "Leilah Crowe."

That she already knows me is disconcerting; more so is the wary look I glimpse in her blue eyes.

"Thanks," I mutter.

I turn and lock eyes with a dark-haired girl who can't be more than fifteen. She's staring as if she knows me.

"Do I know you?" I ask. I'm sure I don't, but what does a person say to someone who blatantly stares?

Her eyes darken with distaste before she whirls and hurries away. I sigh. It's anyone's guess as to why the kid doesn't like me. Because my name showed up on the Stone under all four clans, or because I'm Miriam Crowe's granddaughter? These last seven years, I've been a loner, not an outcast. I guess there's a first time for everything.

I find room four ten. My room is a far sight better than my futon mattress with garbage-variety lawn furniture. This place is something you'd upload on Pinterest. Dark, geometric patterned carpets cover the floor. The twin bed has plump, canvas throw pillows. One wall is a chalkboard covered floor to ceiling with symbols and welcome messages from other students. I wonder if the students knew they were welcoming a Crowe. The desk is an artful twist of gray steel. I slide my gaze past the closet where a dozen hangers are filled with clothes, to a rack where knives hang beside— Are those real swords?

I reach the wall in three steps and pull the short sword and its leather scabbard from the wall mounting. With care, I draw the blade. Celtic writing runs down the center of each side of the blade. Roman Celtic, I bet. The blade is hefty and—I carefully test the edge with a thumb—sharp as a razor. What the hell? On a shelf above the knives lay a bow and a quiver of arrows. These aren't cheap target-practice arrows. These steel bolts are meant to kill. I swallow.

At a knock on the door, I shove the sword back into its wall sheath. "Come in."

"Just visiting," Fran's cheerful voice sounds through the crack. She pushes the door open and steps inside, her nose wrinkling in a smile beneath those sparkly eyes of hers. "I saw you after orientation, but you disappeared. I was afraid something had happened."

Well...something *had*. I shift my gaze back to the sword as I recall Ethan's hard cock against my backside. Somehow, I don't think that's what Fran meant.

"Nice sword," Fran says as she follows my line of sight. "I didn't get one."

I lift a brow. "They're not standard issue?"

"The Commanders assess each students' strengths to find the best weapons match." She grins as she plops down on my bed. "I got a chakram when I arrived last year." When I just stare at her, she adds, "Think of it as a razor disc."

I shrug. "I'm still confused. What's with the weaponry?"

"In preparation for the return of The Shadows."

Fear coils in my stomach. Physical weapons are powerless against The Shadows. The weapons are defense against those of our kind who become so infected with The Shadows' darkness that they turn on one another like rabid dogs. Some people still talk about Elijah Walker, a vampire crime boss in New York, who fed on The Shadows and, for nearly a year, ruled the criminal underworld with an iron fist, unlike any crime boss New York had ever seen.

The infection spread by The Shadows empowers those who practice the dark arts. Elijah employed a witch by the name of Jessica Bailey who trapped Shadows and used them to spread fear and hatred to their advantage. People like Elijah and Jessica were as bad as The Shadows. They were killed by Watchmen, the Special Forces of Margidda. I shudder and wonder if Elijah and Jessica become Shadow hybrids.

I cross to my desk where a black, ringed binder called *New Student Information* sits. I open the binder and see a syllabus on page one. Reaping Preparedness is my first class tomorrow morning.

I look at Fran. "What's Reaping Preparedness?'

"The first class all new students get. It's the bare bones of what to expect should the Reaping take us."

The Reaping—an ancient, twisted version of the Olympics that separates those capable of fighting from those who aren't. Whoever set that spell—no, *curse*—into motion was one twisted sorcerer. Many speculate over who created the powerful magic that snatches Illumina students every twenty years or so and drops them into an alternate reality that tests their metal against The Shadows. Just another reason not to be here. I shake off the thought. I'm here to find out what happened to Grams.

"The last Reaping was five years ago," I say. "I don't plan on being here another fifteen years. Do you?"

Fran laughs and grabs a canvas pillow to prop beneath her head. "You never know when it might hit." Her eyes cloud. "Last year, I met someone who was taken in the last Reaping. They were…not quite well."

I'd heard similar rumors of people who returned from the Reaping as different people. Whatever mage set the Reaping in motion all those centuries ago had to have been one sick puppy.

I return my attention to the syllabus. *Defense Magic. Battle Magic. Potions. Mage History. War Games.* I look at the date, which is nine days from now.

"War Games?" I murmur.

"They're a big deal," Fran says. "Alumni come from all over to participate. Some who fought in The Shadow War come. It's loads of fun. The Academy does something different every year. That way, past students can't give current students a heads up."

I look at her. "How do you know so much about all this stuff?"

"This is my third semester."

"Oh, I thought you were a freshman. Sorry."

She shrugs. "No biggie."

"There were quite a few freshmen," I say. "I guess there are a lot of High Potentials."

"Not really," Fran says. "The Stone is the only one here in the States, so any students named in the country have to come here to be confirmed."

I grunt. "I didn't know that."

I liked Fran. Maybe she is a good person to have as a friend, as friends go. I scan the rest of the classes. The list goes on. My schedule is on the last page. I blink. Each class lasts several hours with little time for lunch. Wow, this is like real work.

"They're light on details." I turn.

Fran isn't there. I glance at the open door, then return my attention to the syllabus. Reaping Preparedness. Hopefully, it'll be challenging enough to distract me from the memory of Ethan Bordeau. Damn dragons.

TEN

Leilah

THE FOLLOWING MORNING, AFTER A FORTY-FIVE-minute search for Stony on Academy grounds, I give up and trudge across campus to the dining hall. She's, no doubt, punishing me for trying to turn her into a mouse—though, she's likely turned into a mouse and is sneaking crumbs in the dining hall. I'm stupid to worry, but in our three years together, we haven't spent a single night apart. Oh God, I'm acting like a tween who's missing Mommy at her first sleepover. I'm glad Stony isn't here to witness my humiliation. She would never let me forget that I missed her so much.

I reach the dining hall and my stomach growls at the dozen wonderful smells that assail my senses. I survey the food line where they're serving everything from any style eggs to fruit and yogurt or bagels. At least I'll save a bundle on food while I'm here. Typically, I eat a light breakfast, but my stomach gives another growl, so I choose eggs—no bacon, that is an offence Stony would not forgive—coffee, blueberries and yogurt. The bagels smell so damn good, I can't resist taking an anything bagel.

I grab two cinnamon bagels for Stony and stuff them in my

coat pocket, then turn from the counter and scan the room. Eighty or ninety people have come for breakfast and it's clear that several cliques have already formed. The prettier than average, teenage to twenty-something girls hold court at a corner table, and a dozen geeks are trying to hide in another corner on the far side of the room. The older students are gathered in pairs or small groups and talk quietly. I'd bet the different clans gravitate toward each other. It's always been that way.

I carry my tray toward an empty seat a few tables down. Two young men at a table nearest me glance my way. One leans close and whispers to the other. Several students stare as I pass. If I didn't know better, I would say my hair is sticking up or my fly is down. I near the table and the two students seated to my left slide closer together, so the vacancy becomes a sliver of space I'd have trouble sliding an arm into.

I halt and survey the other girls seated at the table, but they murmur amongst themselves as if I'm not there. Oookay. I turn and scan the room. There's another vacancy at the end of a table two tables to the right. I head that way. I reach the spot and set down my tray. The girl sitting closest to me slides away.

I sit and look at the girl sitting kitty corner from me. "Hey," I say.

She smiles. The young man next to her nudges her and whispers in her ear. Her eyes widen. She and the young man pick up their trays and leave. An unexpected stab of hurt catches me off guard. What do I care if I don't fit into their cliques? It's not like any of them know me. My thoughts skid to a halt. Or is it? Well, fuck. Between the Stone naming me as a member of all four clans and me being the daughter of Miriam Crowe, I never really stood a chance. So much for feeling at home. Fuck them. This isn't my home. Grams' place is my home, and Stony is my family. I don't need any of these people.

"Don't let them get to you," a guy says as he passes.

I look up to see broad shoulders as he keeps going. My

chest tightens. Okay, so everyone here isn't an asshole. I peel back the cover on the yogurt and eat my breakfast.

After breakfast, I find my Reaping Preparedness classroom and stop just inside the room. The sudden sense of featherlight weight that swirls around the sigil on my hand draws my attention to the dragon mark. I flex my fingers and release a breath. Apparently, some sort of energy inside the room deactivates dragon magic. I'm surprised at the relief that ripples through me. I hadn't realized how much the absence of my magic bothered me.

I scan the octagon-shaped classroom. Directly ahead is a framed chalkboard on a scrolled woodwork stand. Beakers, Bunsen burners, and jars filled with herbs and the like fill tables along the far wall. A collection of black, spiral notebooks on a metal shelf near the door completes the mad scientist vibe.

At least fifty old-fashioned school desks fill the center of the large room and the students sitting in them range in age from teens to the thirty-year-old I saw in orientation. Awareness tingles in my gut and I sense that the teenage boy sitting in the desk to my left has a secret he fears will ruin him. At that age, a secret like that could be something as simple as his family not having as much money or influence as other students.

Then again, I bet he's born of the Longthorpe clan, like me. Being connected to the Longthorpes has the potential to make the kid a pariah., considering witches were blamed for dabbling in the dark arts and empowering The Shadows in the first place. Not warlocks so much, mind you. After all, women get blamed for everything.

Fran sits in the middle, flirting with a group of guys. I wave and she waves back, but doesn't skip a beat batting her eyelashes at the boy to her right. I spot the same young girl I caught staring at me yesterday. Her attention is on her desk, but I'm not fooled. She's seen me. At least, this time, she's keeping to herself.

Thomas, the RA I saw yesterday, sits at a desk in deep conversation with another student. Where to sit... The thirteen-year-old kid is slouched in his seat in the far corner of the room. His body language says he wants to be as anonymous as I do. A pang of sympathy stabs. Poor kid, it's got to be tough being a High Potential at that age. So much for regular school, weekend movies and committing general teenage mayhem. Maybe his parents will be smart enough to allow him to be a kid during summers.

I grimace. I haven't been in a classroom since...well, since I was fifteen. Even when I got my GED, I didn't set foot inside a classroom to study for the test. I would love to tell myself that means I'm a genius. Truth is, the equivalency test is a joke.

I start toward the empty desk to the right of thirteen-year-old kid and ignore the glances as I pass other students. The cliques I left behind in high school are clearly alive and well here at Illumina Academy.

I slide into the desk next to the thirteen-year-old and brows go up. Interesting. He glances at me from the corner of his eye, then ducks his head. My guess is he's of the Silwood clan, sirens and Fae. A siren, most likely. His eyes give him away. Sirens have eyes the color of the sea, crystal blue or an emerald green that makes you feel as if you can fall into their souls. I wonder what it is about him that makes the other students give a damn that I've sat near him.

A door in the wood-paneled wall next to the chalkboard opens and a woman enters. One glance at those gold-rimmed, horned glasses and my heart sinks. *Miss Mack.* She's dressed in a tight green dress and her red hair hangs in perfect ringlets that give her a medusa look. She appears much older than what I'm guessing are her thirty or so years.

Miss Mack makes eye contact with me and I can't help but

feel she's read my mind. I scrunch down in my seat to hide behind the tall boy in front of me as her heels click across the tile floor. The scrape of chalk on the chalkboard makes me wince and I lean sideways to see she's writing *Light vs. Dark* on the chalkboard. She finishes the last letter with a flourish and drops the chalk onto the tray with a chink.

She faces us. "Can anyone tell me what the Reaping is?"

"It's when we're taken," one girl says.

"Taken?" Miss Mack repeats.

"Taken to fight The Shadows," a boy says.

"The illusion of Shadows," Miss Mack corrects. "We never know when a Reaping will occur, which is why *Reaping Preparedness* is your first class. It's our hope that we have time to train you before a Reaping takes you, but, inevitably, some will be taken before they've had much training."

She takes three paces and stops in front of the desk of the delicate, fairylike blonde dorm RA. In a t-shirt and gray sweats, I look like a maid next to Ariel's blue mini skirt with a tight matching tank top. Her makeup is perfection. I ended my morning toiletries by brushing my hair into a ponytail.

"The one thing you must remember is that The Shadows cannot be beaten with magic—not regular magic, at any rate," Miss Mack says.

"Regular magic?" a young boy asks.

"Spells, curses, elemental magic," she says. "Earth magic, herbs, meditation and the like can help protect you, but cannot defeat The Shadows." Miss Mack slowly walks along the front desks. "You see, The Shadows feed off magic."

"We all know that," a young boy cuts in. "What we don't know is why." I recognize fear in his voice.

"That is correct," she replies, and I'm surprised at the compassion in her voice. "We aren't certain when our ancestors *first* encountered The Shadows. All we know is they appeared sometime before the Hell Gates were sealed. We don't know exactly when our ancestors created the Reaping, but we suspect it happened sometime after the Great Shadow War of the fifth century."

"Didn't do us much good in the last war," says a guy who looks a little older than me.

"Are you sure?" Miss Mack asks. "How do you know what we learned in the Reaping isn't what saved us?"

"Saved us?" the guy snorts. "We got our asses kicked."

She tilts her head. "But we are still here." Miss Mack runs her gaze across the class. "The one thing we know for sure is that one of our ancestors discovered The Shadows' one and only weapon is the sowing of fear and hatred."

"That sounds stupid," a guy in the back says.

Miss Mack takes a few steps left and stops in front of another desk. "You think so? Let's say that"—she glances around the room and her gaze halts on me—"Leilah Crowe tells Commander Vanderkoff that you intend to spread a rumor that he tried to kill you because you want his job."

Every head swivels toward me as if I'm guilty of Miss Mack's hypothetical accusation.

"Raith would never believe such a ridiculous lie," I blurt.

Something flickers in her eyes and I realize she's peeved that I called Raith by his first name. What the fuck, are we in junior high?

"He might," she says, "*if* The Shadows have infected him. Feed fear, and doubt multiplies, leading to psychosis, which can result in violence."

"How do we stop them?" a dark-haired girl asks.

"Stopping The Shadows is both simple and difficult," Miss Mack says. "The greatest weapons used to defeat The Shadows are trust, love and harmony."

Murmurs of "What?" and "You've got to be kidding," and "That's stupid," ripple through the room.

Miss Mack walks along the front desks. "Yes, at first glance, the idea that love and trust can defeat The Shadows is preposterous. But consider that, with trust present, fear and doubt have little foothold. Trust accompanies some positive emotional attachment—real trust, that is."

"Sounds easy," another student says. "So why were The Shadows able to infect so many people?"

"Is it easy not to get angry when you learn that someone has told lies about you?" she asks.

More glances come my way and it occurs to me that Miss Mack is exacting revenge for my fooling around with Ethan. Yeah, she's got a thing for him.

"It's far easier to become angry when we perceive we have been wronged than it is to remain calm and try to ascertain if we really have been wronged, especially if you are already angry, bitter or just very sad."

"So, you're saying The Shadows fuc— mess with our heads?" asks the young boy I peg as a wolf. "They use our emotions against us."

Miss Mack pushes her eyeglasses up the bridge of her nose. "Right, Billy. They play upon our vulnerability. If a husband lost a wife to illness and blames the doctors or maybe just fate, The Shadows can amplify that sorrow and anger. An enemy that can sow dissent can walk away and let their enemy destroy themselves. What's tricky, is that they first center you, give you a sense of peace, of purpose. Then that sense of purpose is funneled into your greatest fears and sorrows. The most important thing—the one thing that can save your lives and your sanity—is to remember that you need one another. You must resist the urge to distrust. Stay in the light." She points at the chalkboard. "Light versus dark. What does that mean?"

"Light vanquishes dark," Ariel answers with a smug note in her voice.

"Good, Ariel. And?" Miss Mack prompts as she slides her gaze across us.

I slump farther down in my seat.

"What about you, Leilah?" she asks. There's a hint of harshness in her voice.

I hesitate. I'd never bought into the idea that all light is fluffy and good, while all darkness is unequivocally bad. Grams hadn't either. *Nature isn't all rosy and light. There's a dark, destructive side that's necessary to the force of regeneration*, she used to say.

"Leilah?" Miss Mack's tone ratchets up a notch.

"There's no light without darkness," I say. "And no darkness without light."

Several students gasp and heads swivel my way.

My cheeks warm. *Shit.* Wrong answer.

"Spoken like a Crowe," Miss Mack observes in frozen tones.

I blink. The students' snubs I get, but the teachers'?

Students turn in their seats and stare at me. After three heartbeats, all but Ariel swivel around and begin minding their own business. She watches me with a cold calculation that makes the street witch in me stand at alert.

Miss Mack returns to the chalkboard and writes a spell in Mandarin. Many of Grams' potion books contained Mandarin spells. I know a thousand or so, though not this one.

"Light *vanquishes* darkness. It was with light, L-I-G-H-T"— Miss Mack jabs the chalk against the board with each letter —"and *only* light, that the Commanders used to banish The Shadows." She faces the class. "From birth, we're taught meditation and creative visualization with color. Who here knows what the different colors mean?"

"White is for protection," Ariel says with haughty righteousness. "Green removes toxic emotions."

Several other students call out different colors and their uses.

Miss Mack nods. "Excellent. "Now, what about armor?"

I try not to roll my eyes. Any witch worth her salt understands metaphysical armor. Without it, we leave ourselves open to all kinds of attacks on the spirit and magical plane—something we're taught from childhood, as well. Though, I'm ashamed to admit, I don't rebuild mine as often as I should. With Stony around, I've gotten lazy about adding protection.

"My armor is like a medieval knight's," a guy in the back says.

"Excellent," Miss Mack says. "What about herbs? As per law, I'm sure everyone here has sachets hung about their homes that contain herbs like chamomile, calendula, basil, angelica…" Her gaze sweeps the classroom.

"My mother adds allspice and grass," says one student.

"Yarrow," another says.

"Verbena," another adds.

Miss Mack nods. "Good, very good. Protection against negativity, along with the cleansing of toxins is our first defense against Shadow infection."

"Isn't that a spell?" Billy points at the board.

"It is," Miss Mack says.

"But The Shadows feed on magic," another student says.

"That's right, which is why we are very careful about how we practice magic. You High Potential students are here at The Academy because of your power but, as everyone knows, all citizens of Margidda are required to attend school in order to learn how to practice light magic—and light magic only."

Translation: that's the excuse the Illumina uses to control Margidda.

Miss Mack returns to the board and taps the spell. "This spell is unique because it is performed within a lucid dream."

I come to attention. A spell within a lucid dream? That would mean—

"That means you are casting the spell while maintaining an altered state of mind," she says, finishing my thought.

Or an alternate reality.

"That's like an alternate reality," a guy says.

"There are some who believe dreams are an alternate reality," Miss Mack says.

"But lucid dreaming is knowing you're dreaming and taking charge and even creating in that dream," the guy says. "That's different than regular dreaming. You're creating that dream world."

Miss Mack nods. "That is what we have found to be the case."

"So it's a virtual world," the young shifter says.

"Virtual worlds are created in the waking world," Miss Mack replies. "They are not created solely with the mind, as in a lucid dream."

"So I can go to, say, Hawaii and check out the chicks in bikinis," another male student says.

Laughter ripples through the room.

"With lucid dreaming, you can create a version of Hawaii in your mind," Miss Mack says. "But you are not actually visiting Hawaii."

"So close," the guy says, a more laughter.

"The Shadows can't feed off magic cast within a dream?" Ariel asks, and I'm surprised at the genuine interest in her voice.

"There is a fragile balance," Miss Mack replies. "But, yes. Only a small amount of magic works within a lucid dream—and I do mean lucid dreaming. You must be in total control of the dream. And—this is paramount—the person casting the spell must be at complete harmony within themselves." She laughs. "Something not easily accomplished in everyday life, much less when facing a foe as insidious as The Shadows."

She runs a finger alongside half of the symbols. "This is the section that guides one into the meditative state. Once focused in the meditation, you purposefully step into the lucid dream."

My mind races as I scan the instructions. *Calm body and breath. Remember something you are grateful for. Affirm: I will focus my attention…I can do it. I will do it. I am doing it. Once in the meditative state, no distractions.* From there, you tell yourself to dream, that you own the dream…and the dream begins.

Then comes the spell…

"The second half is the incantation that is spoken while in the lucid dream." Miss Mack points to the symbols that begin the spell.

I'd never thought about casting a spell during a dream. Why would that be necessary? The spell is complex. Even with all my illegal street witch experience, I know I can't succeed. Is the focus and concentration that the meditation achieves before the dream begins what is needed to cast such a complicated spell?

"Let's have a student demonstration, shall we?" Miss Mack asks. She adjusts her eyeglasses on her nose and scans the room, but I already know who she's going to pick. "Leilah?"

I rise and start toward her, but she says, "No, Leilah. Sit back down at your desk. You will enter a dream state. We don't want you falling and hurting yourself."

Thomas sends me a smirk that says that's exactly what he'd like to see.

I return to my seat.

"Typically, a person lies prone while working this magic," Miss Mack says.

A shiver of dread slides down my back. Fight The Shadows while lying down? That's scary as hell. I fix my attention on the blackboard.

"If you will, Leilah," Miss Mack orders.

She retreats to one of the lab tables, leans against it and folds her arms. I try my best to ignore her and the few scattered snickers. Slipping into an altered state of mind is as natural to me as breathing. Grams used to say that I must have spent many lifetimes learning how to achieve altered states. I relax my body as I study the spell's five symbols. The first four are easy enough: fire, light, peace, earth. I know how to draw my power into the shapes and breath them to life. After all, they were the first things Grams taught me, even before ABCs. But it's the last symbol I don't understand. It's not one I've seen more than once or twice, I think. I'm only half sure it means mirror. It's definitely not a shape I've ever breathed life into.

"Sometime today, Ms. Crowe?" Miss Mack prods.

More snickers.

I commit the spell to memory.

Earth. Check

Fire. Check.

Light. Check.

Peace. Check.

I close my eyes and am instantly surrounded by trees, blue skies as far as the eye can see, and tall, gently swaying meadow grass. I shift my attention skyward and close my eyes as the sun warms my face. This is one of my favorite places. I've come here since childhood. I release a breath, then pull the first Mandarin symbol up in memory.

Earth.

Solid. Grounding. My feet connect with the soil beneath me.

Fire.

Energy flares inside me, nearly breaking my concentration. I breathe deeply and ignore the commotion that accompanies the symbol. I can't break the rhythm. To break rhythm while casting a spell is to open a door to chaos. All kinds of bad things happen when a witch halts before finishing a spell. I focus on the next symbol.

Light.

Purity, but also power. I wince as brilliant light penetrates my closed eyelids and try to block the roar in my ears. Quickly, I call up the next symbol.

Peace.

The roar in my ears dulls and breathing grows less strained.

Inside me, the force kicks into a higher gear, like someone just switched the volume to high. Now, for the final symbol.

Mirror.

The memory resists.

Concentrate, Leilah.

Mirror.

For a split second, I'm cocooned in an orb of light. Perfect. That's what I want in the dream.

The light surrounding me abruptly shatters with an ear-splitting crash. Light folds in on itself, sending bolts of energy back at me. I scream. The lightning jolts are a thousand tiny needles piercing my body.

This isn't supposed to happen. This can't happen.

A deep voice booms over the chaos. Pain doesn't allow for distraction or concentration. He said something in Fae, I think.

The lightning vanishes, but the needle pricks still stab. I blink back tears and find myself curled in a ball on the floor, hair covering my face. Someone gently, carefully, pulls me to my feet.

"Rather irresponsible to cast that spell without full understanding of the magic. Wouldn't you agree, Miss Mack?"

I recognize that British accent. I snap my head up. Familiar deep blue eyes meet mine.

"Commander Tyrion," Miss Mack breathes. "An unexpected pleasure, sir."

I yank free of his grip.

"The pain will dissipate soon," Blade says.

I stare. Did she say 'Commander'? Blade Tyrion? The Fae commander who rallied others during that last stand to save Margidda?

The smolder in his eyes isn't sensual, as it had been last night. He's angry, but not at me.

"I didn't think she could cast the spell, sir," Miss Mack hurriedly explains. "It's such an advanced spell. It's like asking her to solve the Hodge conjecture. Who thought she'd get that *far? I…*"

Blade smiles at me. "The last symbol is a mirror, Ms. Crowe." Elegance drips off his every syllable. "Not a literal mirror. It is, instead, the difference. You cannot have light without darkness. Nor can darkness exist without light. The challenge is to understand the difference. That is the symbol's meaning. Difference."

I'm so caught in the alure of his eyes that I struggle to hear what he's saying. He hasn't once looked away from me, but I don't feel awkward. His expression is almost tender. Strange, he hadn't seemed the tender type in the club. Sexy, likely very inventive in the bedroom. But tender? I feel as if I can fall into those eyes because, beneath the sensuality and polish, he's there to catch me.

Those gorgeous eyes crinkle at the edges. "Shall I escort you to the infirmary, Ms. Crowe?"

I drop my gaze, a little unsettled that, in the span of a few seconds, I've so easily fallen under his spell. I'd never had that reaction to a Fae before. Why this one?

"I'm fine." I turn toward Miss Mack.

She's wide-eyed and obviously mortified that Blade caught her torturing a student. She blinks rapidly and says, "Well done, Ms. Crowe. How brave of you to volunteer to attempt that spell. Please, take your seat."

Obviously, Miss Mack wants to sweep the incident under the rug. I'm half tempted to call out her bullshit, but with the anger I sense bubbling in Blade, she's already in trouble. I decide to vacate the limelight and sit down. My legs are a little weak, but I manage to smoothly lower myself into my seat. Ariel shoots me a dagger-filled look, but I don't care. Living on the streets, I've come across a lot tougher characters than her who don't like me.

"Commander Tyrion," Miss Mack's coo is a little unsteady.

Her guilt rings like a bell. "This is such an honor. What brings you to our class? It's not often we see you here."

"I'm observing," he replies curtly. "We shall speak later. Until then, Miss Mack, continue."

Miss Mack pales and grips the edge of the lab table. All eyes follow Blade as he walks to the back of the classroom. He leans a shoulder against the wall and looks like a damn movie star. His eyes lock onto mine and all I can think is that I haven't noticed the crease in his cheek before.

"Shall we move on?" Miss Mack's high heels click across the room to her desk. When no one responds, she claps her hands. "*Students!*"

I turn in my seat along with the rest of the students—all except Fran. Her big brown eyes stare at me. Her faint smile never wavers. I glimpse Blade. He hasn't moved and his eyes are hooded. I slide down in my seat and face the front. My cheeks heat with the memory of how I'd grabbed his collar and kissed him at the club. I now regret not having gone home with him. If he ever again says 'my place' within earshot, I'm going.

"*Voila.*" Miss Mack says.

The gasps in the room jerk my attention back to her. She's holding aloft a crystal shard, but it's the dark streaks running through it that make my heart skip a beat.

"Shadows," Miss Mack murmurs.

My heart begins to pound. On the black market, those are worth a king's ransom. Shadow magic is supposed to be among the most powerful magic in existence. A tremor ripples through my stomach. Grams was certainly powerful enough to harness Shadow magic. Was that why the Illumina pinned the crime on her? There certainly weren't many witches capable of harnessing that much power. Framing Grams still didn't make sense.

"Isn't that *dangerous*?" Ariel's voice is at least two octaves higher.

"These are husks," Miss Mack stresses. She twists the crystal back and forth. "Think of them like deactivated viruses."

Deactivated? All sound from the classroom fades as I stare at the crystal. Even Blade vanishes until there's just me and the trapped Shadow husks. The dark ribbons inside the crystal don't appear dead. The more I stare at them, the more I imagine them breathing, pulsing. Do I hear soft whispers emanating from the crystal? The sound reminds me of black velvet. So beautiful...

"*Ms. Crowe?*" Miss Mack's strident tone shatters the spell.

I shiver and clear my throat. "Yes?" I croak.

"Do you have something to say?"

I frown in confusion, then realize I'm standing, fists clenched at my side. I quickly drop back into my seat. The students around me shift nervously. Hell, I don't blame them. What the hell just happened?

Miss Mack stares at me a good three seconds before resuming her lecture. "As you saw, control is key. As hard as this type of magic is to learn and control, it's infinitely more difficult with live Shadows present. Does anyone have any idea what went wrong when Leilah attempted the spell while in a dream state?"

"She was probably calling on The Shadows," Ariel mutters.

A murmur sweeps the room. My heart races. They really think I'm like Grams. I start. She isn't guilty of a damn thing—other than trying to help the Illumina—and neither am I.

"If Ms. Crowe had called on Shadows, those husks would have risen from the dead like Lazarus," Blade's voice cuts through the light murmur.

Everyone turns toward him.

"What went wrong was an overload." He pushes away from the wall and walks to the front of the class. When he faces us, I'm certain the eyes of every female in the room are glued to him. "This is a prime example of why you're here. Untrained, your abilities have the power to destroy you."

"Only if The Shadows return," a guy of about twenty says.

Blade nods slowly. "Who here wants to chance The Shadows aren't going to return?"

The room goes quiet. Even I don't have a pithy retort. The power I felt moments ago is a fraction of what I sensed in the meadow and I ended up on the floor in the fetal position. Looking at Blade, however, I easily imagine the discipline—the power—the courage, it must have taken to face The Shadows. He would be nothing short of a god with sweat on his brow, his sinewy muscles straining as he controlled that magic within a world of complete harmony. A world he controlled.

He crosses his arms and my mouth goes dry when his biceps bulge. My inner core tightens. Fuck, what is it with me of late? First Ethan and now Blade? If I'm honest with myself, I'm brewing an attraction for them both.

Miss Mack glances at Blade, then focuses her attention on the class. "If you find yourself taken in the Reaping, the first thing you must remember is not to succumb to distrust and depression. Do not allow yourself to give into any fears, bitterness or anger that you harbor deep inside. Control begins here, in this world."

One girl to my left shakes her head. "I can barely do that now. How am I supposed to do that if The Shadows infect me?"

Miss Mack opens her mouth to answer, but Blade says, "Find someone and ask for help." The compassion in his eyes tug at my heart. I'm right. This man is so much more than a sexy playboy.

"Easier said than done," the girl mutters.

"You're right," Blade replies. "It's hard."

The girl looks at him and, instead of the dreamy lust so clear in on the faces of other female students, gratitude appears in her eyes.

He smiles gently. "One day at a time," he says. "That's how we get through. That's how we beat The Shadows."

"One of your strongest defenses against fear is meditation," Miss Mack says. "Deep mediation. Go to the place that brings you the most peace."

Blade flashes a dazzling smile that sets my heart racing—probably the reaction of every other woman in the room. "On that note, I'll take my leave." Groans go up amongst the girls—and a couple of the guys, I notice. "Never fear," Blade says. "You'll see me in different classes." He faces Miss Mack. "We'll speak later, Miss Mack."

She blanches and I can't help but savor a rush of satisfaction even though I know her reprimand will only worsen matters between her and I.

Blade leaves and we spend the next two hours on deep meditation and simple earth magic without incident and without Miss Mack calling on me. Class lets out, and I'm on the path, headed to my next class, when Fran catches up with me.

"Hey, Leilah," she says. Her brown eyes sparkle, but there's tension at the corners of her mouth that warns me she's troubled.

"Hey." I keep walking. I catch sight of two men, Watchmen, descending the half dozen steps from the Administration building. "What's with the Watchmen?" I ask.

"Since the Shadow War, they patrol the grounds," she replies without her usual warmth.

I glance at her. She's obviously got something on her mind.

We walk in silence for a minute before I say, "Spit it out, Fran."

She surprises me with a blunt, "What's going on between you and Commander Tyrion?"

I'm startled by the question, but keep a neutral expression and say, "I'm not after any favors."

"The commanders have no say in who graduates. Do you want him?"

"Want him? What—"

She grabs my arm and pulls me to a stop. "He's mine."

"Not sure he's the kind you can own," I counter.

She shrugs. "I'll have him in my bed within the week."

The proclamation incites an unwanted stab of jealousy. God, I feel like I'm back in high school.

ELEVEN

Leilah

EARLY AFTERNOON, I PASS A GROUP OF THREE GIRLS on the walkway, then scrutinize the trees on the southeast corner of the campus where I last saw Stony. Maybe I should skip the sparring class and search for her. I really had expected her to find my dorm room last night. I think of Grams' house, my house, my and Stony's chance at something solid. She never complains—not about where we live or not having much money or hiding from the Watchmen—but she wants a home as much as I do. Stony knows we're here to claim what's mine. I hesitate. Skipping first-day classes won't endear me to The Academy.

So, you don't really care what happened to Grams, then? my inner voice asks.

"Hush," I mutter, and refocus on the building that marks my next class. I have to clear Grams' name in order to get the Illumina to release the house. Finding out what really happened is part of the deal.

Five minutes later, I reach the field on the north side of The Academy compound. The sun is shining and there's a crisp bite in the air that will keep me from working up a sweat. Still, I could use another cup of coffee.

I join the students who mill about until a thirty-year-old man announces, "Today, there's no magic on the field. Hand to hand combat only. Line up and stretch first."

I follow orders. At least, I'll be able to keep in shape while I'm here, and a good sparring match will help me work off the residual sexual tension remaining after my *encounter* with Ethan the day before yesterday and all the subsequent classmate snubs. In bed alone last night, I'd taken matters into my own hands—it was that or insomnia—but my hands aren't as warm and strong as his. I shiver at a flash memory of his green eyes locked with mine and I wonder for the hundredth time what his mouth would feel like on mine.

As I stretch my arms over my head, my attention snags on three unfamiliar men strolling near a distant building. If their black body armor didn't give them away, their walk would. Watchmen.

"Good morning, class," the teacher says. I tear my attention from the Watchmen as the teacher halts near the students opposite me and says, "Pair up with the closest person to you."

The closest person to me, the girl who'd openly stared at me the other day, meets my gaze, then whirls. Too late. The other two students nearest her have already paired up. The look the two girls send her way carries open spite. So, no one wants to pair up with me, and they think it's funny she's stuck with me. I don't have to ask how I've garnered their disdain. This is just a continuation of breakfast in the dining hall. Though I do wonder what she's done to garner their disfavor.

"Chelsea, you're with Leilah," the instructor announces, then begins walking the line. "No magic, this time, Ariel. I won't warn you again."

Chelsea faces me and my body hums with anticipation. She circles me like an animal. In the fifteen years I lived with

Grams, I learned more about magic than most people might in a lifetime. Add my street survival to that knowledge and skill and I'm a formidable opponent, with or without magic.

I dodge Chelsea's sluggish punch, then whirl and lightly kick her in the ass. She spins to face me, eyes blazing.

"You should spar with someone more on your level," I say.

Her eyes darken. "I don't need to change partners, *witch*."

I startle at her venom. Her hatred feels way more personal than the *like grandmother like granddaughter* attitude I've received.

"Do I know you?" I ask.

Chelsea lunges, legs kicking in an awkward semblance of martial arts moves I've never seen. I block with my arms and retreat. She puts her weight behind her kicks and my arms take a beating.

"Do you really want to do this?" I demand when she lands, breathing hard. "You're going to force me to hurt you."

She surges toward me, fists up, legs kicking. I seize her right ankle and she teeters, barely managing to stay on her feet.

"All I have to do is yank and you'll go down on your ass," I warn.

Chelsea yanks her foot free and starts kicking, again. She adds a punch, which I block, then I grab her left leg and yank. She drops onto her butt like lead. To her credit, she rolls away from me and shoves to her feet.

I grin. "That's not bad."

She backs up several paces, but before I can advance, a tall, dark-haired man I can only describe as a Greek god steps between us. He's dressed in a tank top that showcases sculptured muscles hard as marble, and tight sparring pants that leave nothing to the imagination.

Vampire.

He's an instructor of some sort, or I'm Bugs Bunny. God have mercy. Are all the instructors at The Academy gods?

I register the tension in his body and turn sideways an

instant before he leaps. He's all grace and power. I swing my leg up in a roundhouse kick, but my foot slices through air. I start at the sting of a slap to my arm and swing around to find the vampire standing three feet away. Of course, he's not even breathing hard.

"If you can use your powers, I can use mine," I snap.

"Powers won't always help you," he retorts.

With this damn sigil on me, I can't prove him wrong. An idea strikes. The sigil is dragon magic. Fire and I are very good friends. Maybe I can teach Mr. Greek God Asshole a small— very small—lesson.

I snap the energy inside me into a dense ball of energy, thrust out the hand with the sigil and mentally shout *Fire!* Heat races down my arm, hits the sigil like a brick wall and a fire hot as a branding iron mashes against my flesh. The pain intensifies the force of my will and a small ball of fire appears in front of my palm.

His mouth falls open. "What the fuck—"

The fireball explodes like a smoke bomb.

Not very elegant, I know, but sometimes, there's just no time for frills. I drop to a squat, hook my right foot around his ankle, and yank with all my might. A satisfied *whoof* sounds, but I don't wait to see the fruits of my labor. I roll away and leap to my feet only to feel another slap, this one to my ass.

I whirl to face him. "What the hell kind of lesson is this?" I demand.

"The kind that teaches you how to survive."

"You want me to survive? Then have the dragon remove his muzzle." I thrust my hand forward to show the damn sigil and reddened flesh. I ignore the sigil's growing heat.

"You'll hurt yourself," the vampire replies coldly.

I open my mouth to tell him to fuck himself, but he leaps upward. I jump into the air to meet his assault, left leg drawn up beneath me, right leg shooting out for a vicious kick.

My foot makes contact with something hard—which could be any part of his body, including his very thick skull. Arms of steel band around me and we hit the ground with a thud, me on top.

I drag in a harsh breath and yank my arm up, intent upon ramming my elbow into his ribs, but he rolls on top of me. My breath catches when our eyes meet. The man is so damn beautiful it's almost a crime. I could fall into those dark eyes and never return. I squirm beneath him and, to my shame, the hard planes of his body pressed against mine send an unexpected wave of desire through me.

What the hell?

"No using your damn vampire charms on me," I snap.

I center my thoughts in my core and send my power up through my chest to shove him off me. The sigil burns my hand. I push through the pain and force my energy.

"Off, mother fucker," I wheeze.

His crushing weight eases, and evil glee bubbles up with the thought of how I'll kick his ass, even if the damn sigil burns a hole through my hand. His weight abruptly crushes me, again. Cries go up from other students and my mind registers the high-pitched battle cry of a…pig.

Stony's squeal causes the vampire to look up. His brows plunge in confusion as she barrels over him and they topple to the ground in a flaying mix of legs and hooves. Stony lands on top of him and bites his arm. He growls and seizes her head.

"No!" I shout, and shove to my feet.

Stony shifts and rises to full height. In her natural form, she resembles something like a Wookie, only with claws and teeth that would make a saber-toothed tiger jealous.

The vampire leaps to his feet and demands, "Whose familiar is this?"

I step between them and whisper, "Down, girl."

To my relief, Stony shifts back into her pig form but leans against my legs.

The vampire pins me with his dark glare. "Yours, I see, Ms. Crowe. No familiars are allowed at Illumina Academy."

"Fine," I snap. "Stony and I will leave." I start to turn.

The vampire lifts a staying hand. "You stay."

I snort. "I don't take well to commands."

Behind me, someone sucks in a shocked breath and I realize a deadly silence has fallen. So. People don't talk to Mr. Obnoxious this way?

His eyes glitter. He's angry. *Really* angry. He's coiled tight, muscles bulging beneath that damn tight shirt, and suddenly, all I can think about is just how gorgeous he is, even furious. No, *because* he is furious. There's fire running through him that's contagious, a force I want to unleash, touch, and experience.

He jerks his head, the motion causing a strand of dark hair to fall over his forehead. He's beyond sexy. "Back in line," he commands.

His obnoxiousness shatters whatever spell I'm under. "I'm out of here." I get three steps and he's in front of me, blocking my retreat. I narrow my eyes. "So, Illumina Academy keeps prisoners?"

"When they don't have the sense to know when to stay," he replies. I start to tell him to go to hell and he says, "It's this, or we strip you of your magic."

My heart pounds. What he's threatening is monstrously wrong, but it's the law and he can enforce it. I glare. "This is about you being pissed that Stony tackled you and was about to kick your ass."

The vampire steps so close I swear I can feel his heat. His eyes lock onto mine. "Order her to leave."

The need to blast him with my magic is so strong, the sigil heats again. Fucking dragon fire.

"Do not further test my good graces," he says.

A man pushes through the crowd. Ethan. He glances from the vampire to me, then to Stony. His gaze snaps onto the sigil. "Put magic from your mind, Leilah."

I keep my eyes locked on the vampire.

"Enough, Raith," Ethan says.

Raith? The name is a punch to my gut.

"Raith Vanderkoff." I step so close I can see myself reflected in his perfect dark eyes. "I should have known. Trying to prove that you're better than the newest High Potential? Is this how you get your kicks? Or are you just trying to finish off the last Crowe for good?"

Those eyes turn colder. "You're here to learn, Ms. Crowe. I'm here to teach."

Stony growls. If you've never heard a pig growl, it's because they don't.

"Get that familiar off the grounds, immediately." Without another word, he turns and walks away.

Ethan watches him for several heartbeats, then faces me. "Raith is right. No familiars allowed."

I try to slow my pounding heart. "She has nowhere to go."

"You must have a friend."

"A friend who will care for a forty-pound pig?" I say. Past his shoulder, I notice Miss Mack, almost hidden behind the audience of students. A tiny curve of her mouth causes me to return my attention to Ethan. "You're telling me that no other witch has their familiar here?"

He shakes his head. "Who can we call?"

I'm at a loss. I can't leave her. I found her a squealing piglet on the road, little more than hide and bones. She might die without me.

"I'm leaving." They can *try* to rip my power from me. I sure as hell won't make it easy for them.

Shock flashes across Ethan's face. "Don't be a fool."

I shake my head. "I won't leave her."

He steps closer and whispers, "You realize the moment your powers are stripped, you will no longer *have* a familiar?"

I blink.

"Don't do this," he warns.

Stony bumps my leg. My throat closes with emotion. Stony begins to shimmer. In the blink of an eye, she morphs into a hawk.

"Stony," I gasp, but she's not listening—not that she ever does. She unfurls gold-tipped wings and lifts off the ground. I reach for her, but she evades my grasp "No!" I stumble after her.

She swoops toward me but stays out of arm's reach, voices a hawk scream, then lifts higher. I choke back a sob and stare until she's out of sight.

Then I whirl on Ethan. "When is this sigil coming off?"

He hesitates, then says, "When you graduate."

Or when I kill Raith Vanderkoff.

TWELVE

Ethan
______

I reach Raith's office to find him sitting behind his desk, cell phone pressed to his ear as if he hasn't just practically challenged Ciarah to a death match.

I don't wait for him to get off the phone. "What the hell was that all about?"

"We look forward to seeing you, Carter," he says into the phone. "Someone just came in." A pause. "Yeah, it's Ethan. I'll talk to you later." Raith disconnects the call and places the phone on his desk. "That was Carter. He'll be here for the War Games next week."

"Forget Carter," I snap.

"She's out of control," he replies before I can say more. His tone is colder than ice. A warning if ever I've heard one.

I stare. "What are you talking about?"

Raith isn't one to give in easily. So, of course, he waits a long moment before saying, "You know it's true. Her last few lifetimes, she's become more and more volatile. Now she's a street witch. She's going to get herself killed, or worse, and take down others with her."

"You've lost your mind," I say.

He shakes his head. "It's undeniable."

"If you push her like this, she'll let us strip her powers."

His face remains an unreadable mask. "That's the preferable solution."

"What?" I can scarcely believe my ears. "She's wielded magic her entire existence. She—"

"Look what it's gotten her," he cuts in. "In the fifteenth century, she was burned as a witch in Great Britain and again in Salem. Remember?"

I remember. We hadn't reached her in time to stop the English burning. When witch mania reached the New World, all five of us knew Ciarah would show up. She did.

"Remember, Persia?" I ask. "She was revered as an oracle."

"It seems she hasn't learned a thing since then."

The anger behind his glare startles me. Something is dreadfully wrong.

I recall my sigil on her hand. The magic had burned her. I should have seen to the wound. I'll have Lacy look at it.

"She used her magic on you," I say. "She's never been this powerful. Name another student who's ever conjured magic while wearing my sigil."

He shrugs. "That only proves my point. She's dangerous."

"I'm not buying it," I shoot back. Then I understand. I sink down into the chair to my left and say in a gentler voice, "Stripping her of her power won't protect her."

His eyes darken and I see part of the old, vicious vampire lurking close to the surface.

"The last thing we want is for her to be vulnerable, especially if The Shadows return," I say.

"If?" His lips curl in derision. "There's no 'if.' Damien won't rest until he's found his Demon Bride. You never did like facing the hard truths."

It's my turn to scowl. "Not true. I'm just not a fatalist like you."

"Realist," he corrects. "She's going to get herself killed. She needs a lifetime or two without magic."

"Are you forgetting those early years?" I ask.

"I haven't forgotten a thing," he snaps. "Despite the struggle, she was better off before her magic came into fruition."

"Struggle?" I repeat. "She was a mess. Half the time she hid from her powers, the other half, she feared she was going mad." I release a breath. "She's a witch. Magic is who she is."

"Bullshit." The ice mask returns. "Did you get the damn howling night pig off the grounds?"

"I didn't have to. It shifted into a hawk and flew away. You didn't have to be so cruel."

"It's cruel to let her go on as she is." He scowls. "The howling night pig shifted into hawk form and flew away? It'll be back. They're stubborn as hell."

"Loyal," I say. "Leilah is fortunate to have such a familiar. I didn't think there were any left. I wonder if Leilah knows what the creature is. If you're right, and The Shadows return, Leilah will be fortunate to have the creature protecting her."

Raith grunts. "Keep an eye out for it." He stands, signaling the end of our conversation. "When it returns, I'll need to kill it."

"Kill it?" I blurt. "Why?"

Raith flashes a cool smile. "I don't think it likes me."

THIRTEEN

Leilah

IN THE SHOWER THE FOLLOWING MORNING, I examine the remnants of the burns on my hand. Yesterday afternoon, Ethan ordered me to go to the infirmary and have the burn looked at. Lacy, the healer, is quite good. Only the barest of scabs is visible. By this afternoon, I'll be as good as new.

I skip breakfast. I'm in no mood to face the stares and whispers of the other students. I slow my walk along the campus walkway and look left—south—in the direction of the apartment I shared with Stony. Might she have returned there? At least there are plenty of holes in that dump for her mouse form to squeeze through and get inside. I return my attention to the pavement and pick up the pace. I'm stupid to worry about her. She's not helpless, not by a longshot. She can turn into pretty much any animal and eat almost anything. Hell, by now, she's probably lying on a plush carpet in some old lady's home in the guise of a cat—a well fed cat. Still, I can't help worrying.

So far, all I've gotten from The Academy is trouble, and separation from Stony. I had thought I could get close to Raith Vanderkoff and learn something about Grams' death, but yesterday assured me that particular idea is about as idiotic as they get. He clearly doesn't like me. Why should he? Aside from Blade and *maybe* Ethan, no one else wants me here.

Truth is, I have no one to blame but myself for getting nowhere in finding out what really happened to Grams. I wasted my first two weeks in New York grappling with the past, then got drafted into The Academy. I've got to make a plan, a real plan that will force the Illumina's hand.

I finally locate my 102 Conjuring classroom in Redwood Hall. I sigh in relief. As with Miss Mack's class, when I step into the room, the sigil on my hand feels feather light. In the last few days, I've grown accustomed to the damn thing, but I can't deny I'm glad to be rid of it, even for a couple hours.

Unlike Miss Mack's classroom, this room is filled with desks and shelves of books. Spell books, I imagine. I notice the same thirteen-year-old kid I'd seen in Miss Mack's class. He sits at the back of the room. I pick a desk near his. Other students filter in and find seats, and a short balding man wearing a wizard's robe strides into the room. I want to laugh, but he radiates an endearing quality that kind of makes me like him.

He lays an old satchel on the desk at the front of the class, then faces the blackboard. He picks up chalk and says, "I am Mr. Cornwall," as he writes his name on the board. He next writes, *Is all magic equal?* Then he faces the class and says, "Witch or Wizard?" He scans the room.

"Middlewich is better," a guy calls out.

The Middlewich clan has been at odds with the Longthorpes from the beginning of time. As mages and wizards are masters of potions, the Middlewich clan brags that their magic is better than that of the Longthorpes. I have yet to see any evidence they're right.

"Is that why you're wearing a wizard's robe?" a girl asks.

"Are you finally going to show the Longthorpes that Middlewiches rule?"

"On the contrary," he says. "I intend to demonstrate the synergy."

The students groan. He turns and, again, writes on the blackboard. It's a simple conjuring spell, something I could accomplished when I was ten. Written in Latin, of course. Most believe the old language has more power than other languages. Grams taught me that power comes from the witch.

The door opens and Fran enters.

"Thank you for joining us, Ms. Shelton," he says.

She smiles at him from under her lashes. "Sorry, Mr. Cornwall." She slides into an empty seat in the second row and leans forward as if anticipating the fall of pearls from his mouth.

Mr. Cornwall scans the room. "Who wants to try this quick spell?"

A girl of about eighteen raises her hand.

He nods at her.

"*Ignem spirans draconem,*" she says.

A shimmer appears face level to the teacher's left, then evaporates in a puff of smoke.

He lifts a brow. "Any idea what went wrong?"

The girl slumps in her chair. No one replies.

"Anyone else wish to try?" he asks.

A guy stands, tall, with dark hair, probably of the Penncarrow clan. He has the cocky attitude common among young wolf shifters. I hide a smile. This fine male specimen is sure that brute strength will call forth magic. All creatures in Margidda have some sort of magical powers, but witches—and yes, those of Middlewich clan—are the embodiment of magic. Still, this young wolf should be able to conjure a small fire-breathing dragon.

"*Ignem spirans draconem,*" he booms.

To his credit, a small fire-breathing dragon appears near the window to our left.

WHOOPS AND APPLAUSE GO UP. I GLANCE AROUND the room. These are High Potentials and they're impressed with the conjure of a small fire-breathing dragon?

The dragon screams and breathes fire—then disappears in a bigger puff of smoke than did the girl's dragon. The shifter drops back into his seat.

"What happened?" a girl asks.

Mr. Cornwall lightly punches his stomach. "You must pull the magic from your center, then push it out with your will. That applies to Longthorpe, Middlewich, and anyone else who uses spells of any kind."

"Everyone knows that," another girl says.

I'm betting this girl hails from the Middlewich clan. She would know how to call forth a dragon.

"*Ignem spirans draconem*," she says in a clear voice.

A dragon twice the size of the others appears to the teacher's right. The dragon bellows fire. Mr. Cornwall moves faster than I would have thought possible for a man of his size and dives for the floor just in time to miss being turned into toast. The girl tosses me—*me*—a satisfied look.

Fiddlesticks.

"Fire breathing dragon," I mutter.

A dragon twice the size of hers appears. Both dragons scream. The smaller one swoops right in an obvious attempt to get behind my dragon. My dragon whirls. His huge wings brush the heads of the front-row students. They duck as his wicked tail sweeps books from a front row desk. Screams go up as the dragons breathe fire on one another. Mr. Cornwall leaps to his feet and shouts something in a language I don't understand. Both dragons evaporate.

He faces the students. "Thank you, Ms. Hanson and Ms. Crowe, for demonstrating today's lesson."

Ms. Hanson shoots me a dagger-filled look and says, "I understand the lesson perfectly well. I just didn't feel the need to show off. But what can you expect from a Crowe? She probably threw in a little black magic for good measure."

Fury rams through me. "My grandmother didn't consort with Shadows," I snap.

"Everyone knows she died using Shadow magic," Ms. Hanson says with cruel satisfaction.

I leap from my seat and shout, "Muzzle."

Something that looks like string cheese stretches across the girl's face. Laughs and cries of 'Oh my God!' and 'Look at that," along with laughter, fills the room. The girl screams. Well, she screams as best a person can when their mouth is covered by magical sting cheese with the strength of duct tape. Duct tape is some strong shit, evidenced by the girl's futile yanks on the muzzle.

"Ms. Crowe," Mr. Cornwall's voice rings out above the din.

The students quiet, all except the girl who's muzzled. She continues her muffled screams and continues her attempts to tear the muzzle off her mouth.

The teacher motions with his chin toward her. "Do you mind, Ms. Crowe?"

I do mind, but say, "Muzzle remove," and the muzzle disappears midscream.

The girl's ear-piercing scream causes me to wince.

Muzzle girl whirls on me. "You bitch. Do you know who I am?" She starts toward me.

"Tut, tut," I say in a low voice. "The next muzzle won't be so pleasant."

She halts, eyes wide. Then fury returns in full force and she spins toward the teacher. "Mr. Cornwall, I demand satisfaction."

"Satisfaction?" I repeat. "What, like a duel?"

"Be careful," someone whispers, and I realize it's the thirteen-year-old kid.

I look at him. He's giving me a pleading look and shaking his head almost imperceptibly. What's wrong with the kid?

"I don't want to have to talk to my father about this," the girl snaps.

"Have a seat, Jennifer," Mr. Cornwall says. "This is a magic class. Magic will sometimes run amuck."

The girl's eyes narrow. "Either report her or I will. Olympia will not be pleased to learn her favorite niece was attacked by another student."

"Attacked." I snort. "You want to see attacked—"

"That's enough," Mr. Cornwall cuts in. "Ms. Hanson, take your seat. You, too, Ms. Crowe."

There is no mistaking the steel in his voice. Wow, the short bald guy has balls. I like that.

"Please sit, Ms. Crowe."

I drop back into my seat. Jennifer looks from him to me, then sits back in her seat. The glare she throws my way says her grudge against me has gotten very personal. So this is what it's like to be popular?

FOURTEEN

Leilah

THAT AFTERNOON, I START DOWN THE MAZE OF garden paths that leads to the dining hall when Thomas emerges from the tall hedges to my right and blocks my way. He's bigger than me, but lean from strenuous exercise, not because he's a fighter.

"You recognized them, didn't you?" he accuses.

"Them?" I repeat.

His face darkens as the delicate Ariel from Reaping Preparedness class steps out from behind the hedgerow. "She ought to recognize them," Ariel says. Hatred radiates from her. "You know where they got those Shadows Miss Mack showed in class, don't you?"

"We all know," Thomas says before I can ask what they're talking about. "They came from Crowe Potionary."

His words hit me like a punch in the gut.

Ariel steps closer to Thomas. In the afternoon light, she reminds me of a shrew more than a delicate fairy. "You were talking to them, weren't you?" she hisses. "I heard you. You called them beautiful."

I want to reply, but all I can think about is the accusation. The Shadows from Grams' Potionary?

"She was probably chanting black magic." Thomas rakes his eyes down my body. "What else can you expect from a Crowe?" He looms over me. "You're dangerous."

Anger whips through me. "That's right." I clench my fists. "And you'd better fucking remember that the next time you spread lies about my grandmother."

Ariel's eyes flick to my clenched fists and she pulls Thomas back a step. "You've been warned, Crowe. We don't allow black magic here."

"*Leave,*" Thomas says. "If you want to survive."

Survive? I keep my gaze locked on them as they step around me and head down the path. The instant they vanish from view, the hedges to my left shake.

"Be careful," someone whispers, and I recognize the voice of the thirteen-year-old kid from Defensive Magic class. He pushes through the bushes. The knees of his pants are stained with mud. I squint at the dirt smudges on his cheek, then glance in the direction Thomas and Ariel went.

I look back at the kid. *Oh, no they didn't.*

"Did they do that to you?"

He doesn't reply.

I will beat that fucking asshole and his sidekick Ariel. "You're the one who needs to be careful, kid," I manage in a low voice.

He nods and scurries away.

I head to the dining hall and eat, but can't shake the feeling I'm being watched. I shove my tray aside and head back to my dorm. The feeling of being followed persists and I'm convinced I'm a victim of some kind of spell. I break into a run. It's with some sense of relief that I finally reach my room and lock the door. I back up to the bed. I wish I could set wards, but I can't, not with the damn sigil embedded in my flesh. The best I can do is shroud my room and myself in white light. The back of my legs bump into the edge of the bed and I drop onto the mattress.

I burrow beneath the blanket, wishing Stony were here. I need to find her. Maybe I can convince her to assume the shape of a proper mouse and return to The Academy with me. Why did she leave?

She's not Grams. *She isn't.* And she's not my parents. She flew close before she left. My throat constricts. Had that been goodbye? I bury my head in my pillow. Maybe I'm wrong. Maybe she can survive without me. But I can't survive without her. I try to picture myself alone in Grams' big house, but can't.

By the time the moon rises high in the sky, I'm done tossing on the bed. I can't live with the stress of wondering why Stony left.

As I shrug into a black hoodie, the Penncarrow Hall clock chimes in the common room below, announcing the 11:00 p.m. curfew. Curfews and I have never been on speaking terms. Probably one of the reasons why Grams kicked me out. I don't follow orders well. Why start now?

I slip from my room and hurry down the dorm hallway as quiet as a cat, a trick I learned when I was thirteen. Grams wasn't easily fooled. Aside from the spells she cast to keep me inside, she had damned superhuman hearing.

I reach the main doorway, which is, of course, locked with a key and a damned good spell that's likely to fry the sigil if I attempt to break through. I would have preferred to leave by the front door because that exit offers a shorter route to the wall I plan to scale, but I'll have to settle for the girls' bathroom, which has a small window. I turn and hurry back the way I came, then duck into the bathroom at the far end of the hallway. The window has an old-fashioned crank. It probably hasn't been opened in a decade, but I don't sense any magic surrounding it. A painted shut window is doable.

I wind the handle and quickly break the paint seal. A dozen more winds, and I have the window open wide enough to squirm my skinny ass through. I'm one of those lucky women who has a high metabolism. The downside is, I'm hungry two hours after a meal.

I drop three feet and land on the moist ground in a crouch. One of the perks to studying martial arts is learning how to land on your feet from just about any position. The bathroom, being on the ground floor, saves me from trying something foolish like rappelling down the side of the building using tied sheets.

I creep along the building to the rear. The stone wall is a hundred feet beyond the trees, but I must cross the school grounds without getting caught by the patrolling Watchmen. I consider trying to reach the perimeter wall in one shot.

About thirty feet away stands an old willow that'll provide cover while I observe the patrols. I scan the darkened grounds. No Watchman; although, one can never be sure they *aren't* there. I dart across the path and hightail it across the grass to the tree. I reach the tree and wait. I consider making a run for the stand of trees. I'm fast, I can outrun any Watchman. Yeah, and I can sing like Beyoncé. I climb the tree and find a comfortable branch.

The night is warm for early January, just the way I like it, so I lean against the trunk and wait. No more than ten minutes pass before two large figures materialize on the pathway ten feet away. They're quiet. If I hadn't been looking for them, they might have been able to sneak up on me. I breathe in controlled breaths as they approach.

Moonlight illuminates two very large men in black body armor. I wonder whether this is what Raith, Ethan and Blade wore when they fought The Shadows. No, that can't be how they dressed. They defeated The Shadows in their dream worlds. But they might have worn armor like that to fight the crime bosses who used The Shadows to acquire their power. I grew up in the aftermath of the apocalypse, yet the reality has never hit me as hard as it does in this moment. Irrational, I know. But The Academy wouldn't employ men in full body armor to patrol school grounds just for the hell of it.

For some strange reason, needing Watchmen on school grounds makes me angry and sad at the same time and I fight an unreasonable need to cry. I bite down on the inside of my cheek and hold my breath as the Watchmen pass below me. After they vanish into the darkness, I slowly release the breath.

God, I need Stony.

Minutes tick by as I contemplate the strange actions of my familiar. Bright moonlight provides more than enough light to observe the Watchmen patrols for the next hour. They patrol every twenty minutes. All I have to do is wait for the next patrol, then I can reach the wall and scale it.

The crunch of bootfalls snaps me to attention. Not a single one of the patrols made this kind of noise. I squint down through boughs and leaves and a shiver ripples through me. I'd recognize those wide shoulders and that fluid, powerful gait anywhere.

Ethan.

Part of me—the newly discovered nymphomaniac part—wants to drop from the tree and pick up where we left off that first day. Memory of his hard cock pressed against my ass sends butterflies skittering across the insides of my stomach. I lift my leg over the branch and silently drop down to the branch below me.

"Ethan, wait!" a female calls.

I stiffen. Fuck, it can't be...

Ethan slows. He's nearly under the willow when the woman catches up with him and a shaft of moonlight reveals, as expected, Miss Mack. She wears a slinky, slip-like dress that screams 'desperate.' Am I witnessing a lover's quarrel? Was that why Miss Mack had been shocked to discover Ethan's cock pressed against my nearly naked ass? I'm startled by the mixture of jealousy and hurt that swirl in my stomach.

"Miss Mack."

The formality in his tone is like cool water on the burn of my jealousy. I grin. No one talks to a lover with such distant reserve.

"Commander," Miss Mack sounds suddenly breathy, and it's not the breathiness that results from sprinting. "Ethan."

He stands backbone straight and waits. If I were a betting woman, I'd bet he knows what's coming. With all that dragon energy, he's got to be accustomed to women throwing themselves at his feet. He's probably got a Webster's Dictionary-sized manual of come-on ploys used during attempts to seduce him.

"I can't help but notice how you've been looking at me lately." Miss Mack steps closer.

"Pardon?"

Ouch. Even though I'm thrilled with his response, part of me cringes on Miss Mack's behalf. I can't stand the woman, but it's got to be rough to hear that.

"Ethan." Her voice trembles. Apparently, she's decided it's all or nothing, because she drops a spaghetti strap as she steps even closer.

Ethan sidesteps her. "Miss Mack, I'm flattered, but I'm simply not available. Now, if you'll excuse me?" He turns and hurries away.

She gasps, but I hardly hear her over the thudding of my own heart. He's not...*available?* Who is the woman? And why did he almost have sex with me my first day here?

Miss Mack unexpectedly looks up through the leaves. I freeze. Oh God, did I make a noise? She continues to stare up into the tree. There's no doubt she knows I'm here. I tense in readiness for her to call me out, but she doesn't. Then I realize that to acknowledge me would only magnify her humiliation. She stands another long moment, then spins and hurries away.

I wait until she's out of sight, then drop from the tree. My feet touch the ground. I freeze for a long moment and listen. Silence. I turn toward the wall. A hand clamps down on my shoulder. I grin. Unavailable, huh? This time, we won't be interrupted.

"What are you doing here, Ms. Crowe?" demands a familiar, deep male voice.

My heart plummets.

Raith.

FIFTEEN

Ethan

I PICK UP THE PACE AROUND THE CURVE IN THE walkway. I knew Miss Mack had a thing for me, but I'd hoped she had the good grace to take my subtle rebuffs to heart. I suspect that finding me with Leilah lit a fire under her determination to throw herself at me. My cock pulses with the memory of Leilah's body pressed against mine.

A blur whizzes past me. I whirl. I've known Raith long enough to recognize him even when he's traveling at vampiric speed—something he doesn't do except in emergencies. I break into a run and follow. But when I find him at the willow tree, I'm astonished to discover him towering over Leilah as if he intends to eat her.

"What is it?" I demand.

Raith's eyes glitter in the moonlight and I'm struck by the thought that he needs to feed.

"Ms. Crowe has apparently decided to get herself expelled," he says.

Leilah gasps and, even in the dark, my dragon eyes discern the rise and fall of her breasts through the thick fabric of her hoodie. God, it's pure torture being so near her and not being able to touch her. A realization strikes. It's been forty years since Raith has fed on Ciarah. Being this close to her has got to be as hard on him as it is on me. In one very big way, even worse. Vampires languish if they don't feed often enough, and there's something about our connection with Ciarah that incites tenfold Raith's need to feed from her. Maybe his aggression is a manifestation of that need. Hell, we haven't seen Caleb since Ciarah died in his arms, and Matthias disappeared twenty-five years ago when he went in search of Caleb. Maybe they just couldn't take any more of the roller coaster ride.

For the first time in eons, I consider what their absences might mean for me. In the beginning, almost too long ago to remember, we all wanted her for ourselves. Hell, how could we possibly have conceived the need that bound the six of us together? Now, however, if Caleb and Matthias have decided they can't deal with the huge emotional swings in their lives—having Raith, Blade and I share her—maybe that leaves more of her for me.

Leilah lifts her chin and faces Raith. Pride and sadness war to fill the eternal hole in my heart. She is magnificent. I could love her forever—have loved her for eons. My heart beats faster. Our short time with Ciarah is always fraught with trouble and chaos...and the sweetest love that ever existed.

"She's broken curfew." Raith's voice is a low growl I recognize all too well. He may be angry, but he wants her. Hell, the challenge that radiates from her body has my cock hard as a rock.

"That's punishable, but not an expellable offense," I say. I grasp Leilah's arm and pull her away from the tree, away from Raith. "Return to the dorm. We'll settle this in the morning." Once I get to the bottom of what's eating Raith.

"No," Raith countermands.

He steps toward Leilah. She retreats until her back presses the tree trunk. Raith braces his hands against the trunk, one on each side of her. He looks like he's about to attack—or fuck her. If I'm honest, I'm torn. Once he admits how much he wants her, life will get easier for all of us. Until then, I can't allow him to hurt her.

"She's not going anywhere until I find out what she's doing here," he says. "It's past midnight."

I start to step toward them, then stop when Leilah angles her face within an inch of Raith's and says, "You're the one who forced me here by having the dragon put this damn sigil on me."

"We all make mistakes," Raith murmurs.

"Even though your precious Stone named me a member of all four clans?"

"What's the ruckus?" Blade's cultured voice reaches us before I detect him.

I keep my eyes locked on Raith as Blade stops beside me. "Leilah's out after curfew," I inform him softly.

The Fae chuckles and claps softly. "*Bravo, bella mia. Bravo.*"

Raith growls and my fire rushes to the surface.

SIXTEEN

Leilah

From the corner of my eye, I see the dragon's tattoos glow silver at the edges of his cuffs. My heart pounds. I lock my knees to control a tremor and keep my gaze on Raith's face. His eyes bore clear through my soul. God help me, the sheer magnetism of the man is overwhelming.

"Ms. Crowe," his voice is low and devoid of compassion. I'm pretty sure he's honeying a trap to lure me to my death. "You still have yet to answer," he says. "Why are you out in the dead of night?"

"You have no right to ask me."

"I have the right to ask any question I please," he hisses.

"Raith," Blade begins, but I cut him off.

"If you're tossing me out, what does it matter?"

Sure, I'm being unreasonable, but he's so fucking close I can feel the heat from his body, which makes me want to irritate the hell out of him. The frustration radiating off him says I've hit the mark. Raith says nothing for three heartbeats, then straightens. I tense.

He emits a low laugh I know is at my expense, then he

turns. "Make sure she's at Domini's office first thing in the morning. He'll deal with her."

I stare, heart pounding, as Raith walks away. I'm not sure if it's the threat of expulsion—why the fuck should I care?—or his proximity that has me shaken. The guy has been nothing but a jerk from the moment we met.

"What the fuck is his problem?" I start at the realization that I've spoken out loud.

"You won't be expelled," Ethan's gentle voice knocks me off balance as much as Raith's aggression did.

Ethan lifts a hand and my heart races with the anticipation of his touch. He hesitates, then drops his hand back to his side. He towers over me, the epitome of protection. Add his dragon heat and my head spins. What woman can resist him? His volcanic fire warms the soul instead of burning the skin.

He sighs. "Raith can be—"

"An asshole?" I finish for him.

"Do not sow the wind, lest you reap a storm," Blade murmurs.

I frown. "What does that mean?"

I have no defense against his easy laugh. He says something low in what has to be Fae, then adds, "I will leave you in the care of your guardian, Leilah. But if you need me, just whisper my name."

I sense the magic an instant before a tiny ripple washes over me. Blade turns and begins walking away. His name rushes to my lips and I barely silence my voice as need sets my heart to pounding again. A mixture of fear and...is that joy?...fills me. I watch until Blade disappears into the darkness. What the hell kind of magic is this? Fae magic? I have no experience with fae magic.

I start as Ethan steps closer.

"I'll walk you to your room." He waves toward the dormitories.

My cheeks warm and I'm glad for the darkness. God, these three men have completely thrown me off my game. I've got to get a handle on my emotions.

We walk in silence to the dorm, then up the stairs to my room. Ethan opens the door and I step inside before he catches my wrist. The warmth of his fingers sends a shiver through me and I yank my eyes up to his face. Memory flashes of his darkening eyes the day he found me in my thong. I'm suddenly sure he's remembering that moment, too, and I'm tempted to pull him into my room. But I remember him telling Miss Mack that he's spoken for and I yank free.

"Have a care, Leilah." He steps back as I swing the door shut. The last words I hear are, "The school grounds are dangerous at night."

SEVENTEEN

Leilah

AN HOUR LATER, I LAY AWAKE IN BED. I HAD WANTED badly for Ethan to stay with me...make love to me, but confusion had—still—muddles my brain. Memory jumps from Blade to Ethan and, damn it, to Raith. Blade's easy charm, Ethan's gallant but off-limits protectiveness, and Raith's...whatever. He's done nothing but specialize in being a jerk. So, why can't I get him out of my head?

Vague images hover like *déjà vu* in the back of my brain. Stark beauty, a desert, maybe. I hate *déjà vu*. Grams always said *déjà vu* meant we were on track, but the elusive sense of familiarity leaves me off balance. I snort. I guess it's not strange that thoughts of Raith should confuse me. But then, all three men confuse me. My feelings for them confuse me. If Stony were here, she would know what to do. How can I feel so strongly about all of them—even if my feelings for Raith aren't that charitable.

I wonder...

An alarm blares and I jolt.

Sunlight streams through the window and my pulse skips a

beat when I don't recognize the gray curtains hanging at the single window.

"Stony," I rasp, and push up onto an elbow before I remember.

Fuck. I drop back onto the bed. I'm at The Academy. I must have dozed off. The alarm still blares. I slap the top of the old-fashioned alarm radio and blow out a breath. I consider staying in bed, then remember I'm supposed to see Headmaster Domini this morning. I can't have Raith thinking I'm afraid to see the headmaster.

With a groan, I roll out of bed. A hot shower does little to revive me and I'm still yawning when I stumble into the dining hall and grab an apple for breakfast. I eat it on the way to the Headmaster's office and barely finish it before I reach his receptionist's desk. No one is manning the desk. I toss the core into her trash can and take the four steps to his open office door.

The place is utilitarian, without even a plant to soften the starkness. Just a clean desk with a pen holder and an old-fashioned lamp placed on opposite corners. A black leather office chair sits behind the desk and three armchairs for guests face it. Except for a few framed portraits gracing the walls, that's pretty much it.

On the far left wall, two French doors lay open to a balcony. Who leaves doors open in winter? Headmaster Domini steps into view on the balcony, his back to me. He's wearing a crisp white shirt with dark slacks. The man must be freezing. Why— He turns slightly and I see the tip of a cigarette glow. A smoker. That's why he's outside.

He turns and his eyes lock onto me. A tiny smile curves his lips. He takes a final puff of his cigarette, then exhales smoke as he crushes the butt in a crystal ashtray on a small table to his left.

"Ms. Crowe, is it not?" he says in a slight Italian accent.

The sexy smile hovering about his lips sets off a spark of

attraction, so I'm not prepared for the wash of despair that follows.

I realize I'm gawking and clear my throat. "Commander Vanderkoff ordered me here, sir," I say. I wince inwardly. God, did I just call Raith by his title and address the Headmaster as 'sir'? Grams would be thrilled.

"Ordered you here, did he?" Domini murmurs.

"He didn't tell you?"

"He didn't." The headmaster brushes past me into his office and I can't shake the odd impression that he's pulling away from me as I watch him walk to his desk, sit, then relax against the back of his chair.

"Perhaps the question is why the commander ordered you here, Ms. Crowe."

"I…broke curfew."

"Why?"

I'd considered a host of excuses on the way over, but had finally settled for a half truth. "It's my familiar. I'm worried about her. I didn't know she couldn't come, so I brought her onto school grounds. Long story short, she flew off and I'm worried." Most likely, Stony has established a royal lifestyle as a mouse in a Chinese Restaurant, but until I have proof, I am going to search for her.

"Admirable." Headmaster Domini smiles.

I want to melt into a puddle of soppy goo.

"Your feelings are quite natural, Ms. Crowe."

My heart jumps before I realize he's not talking about my attraction toward him.

He removes a laptop from a desk drawer and opens the lid. "We should always see those we are responsible for safe. Familiars are cherished creatures and an important key to a witch's power."

His incredible green eyes latch onto mine and I sense a

secret. It's a whopper—no, it's the king of all secrets. I clear my throat.

"I'll shoot an email to Administration to send someone round to perform a wellness check at your home," he says. "The policy that forbids familiars is one of the restrictions I want to change here. I believe all familiars have rights to be here and I'm working with the Grand Witch to change Academy policy."

I blink. I no longer sense his secret and I'm struck by the kindness in his eyes. My lack of sleep must be affecting my abilities. Or maybe it's the damn sigil.

"Thanks," I reply and find myself relaxing.

"Just respect the curfew, eh?" He lifts a brow.

I smile. Maybe Domini will be able to offset Raith's coldness and make the other students as comfortable as he has me. The thought tightens my stomach. Fiddlesticks, is that jealousy? I groan inwardly. Yeah, I'm off balance. Shit. If only I could take a nap before class, but I can't risk pissing off Miss Mack more than I already have.

"Rest easy, Ms. Crowe." Domini chuckles. "If there's anything you need, feel free to drop by. I'll have Admin contact you if there's any news."

"Thank you," I say, and leave.

So, no punishment. I mentally cheer.

I imagine that since I've been caught and reprimanded for breaking curfew, no one will suspect I would try again. Especially not as soon at tonight.

EIGHTEEN

Leilah

IT'S PURE DISCIPLINE THAT ROLLS ME OUT OF BED when the 11:00 p.m. alarm blares. I yawn and stumble to the closet, but can't find my standard-issue gym hoodie. After a search through my room leaves me empty handed, I give up and shrug into the school jacket. It's a bit formal for a stealth mission to break out of school, but at least it's black and I don't have time to waste.

Sorry, Headmaster Domini, I project. I can't wait until you change school policy. I have to find Stony—and make one stop along the way.

This time, no one will catch me.

I scoop up my cell phone from the desk, then head to the bathroom even though I fully expect to find the bathroom window bristling with wards. To my shock, it isn't. I stare at the painted glass. It's got to be a trap. Is it possible Ethan never investigated how I'd escaped yesterday? The possibility makes me even more suspicious. I've got about twenty minutes before the Watchmen reach this side of the grounds.

I don't look a gift horse in the mouth. For the second time in as many nights, I slither through the window, land on my feet in a crouch, and listen. When the music of crickets and night frogs continues without interruption, I edge along the building to the corner. A hundred feet beyond the scattered trees, I discern the hazy silhouette of the perimeter wall through a break in the trees. The wards that surround the school are intended to keep The Shadows—and any other nasty beasties—from entering, although no one really knows how well the wards will work until The Shadows return. The wards are some pretty damned powerful magic, which is why there are no spells to prevent students from leaving.

I glance left, then right, and discern no shadows moving within the darkness. I reach the trees and the crickets and night frogs fall silent. To my left, something rustles. I drop to the ground and grimace at the moisture that seeps through the knees of my pants.

Carefully, I shift and search in the direction of the noise. Nothing moves. Damn, four days at The Academy and I'm already losing my edge. I push onto my feet then hurry forward in a crouch until I reach the next tree, press my back against the bark and listen. Silence.

I creep from tree to tree and, five minutes later, reach the wall. I crane my neck and look up at the top. Only about eight feet. I leap, grab the top, and pull myself up in one fluid motion. When I drop down onto the other side, I sprint toward the road. I walk two miles before getting a signal on my phone, so I can call an Uber.

Half an hour later, the Uber drops me on the street where I grew up. The house/potion shop is located ten miles southeast of The Academy in beautiful Westchester County. Streetlights are few and far between on the county's residential streets. I don't mind. Unlike most kids, I don't fear the dark. Sure, night-time may be the province of the boogie man, but the boogie man isn't the badass most people think he is. There's so much beauty in the night.

I glance at the sky. Clouds obscure the January moon, yet it's warmer than it was five days ago when Ethan Bordeau walked into *The Witching Hour* and changed my life. I breathe deeply of the crisp night air. The familiar scents evoke a surge of emotion that catches me off guard.

Why, Grams? Fifteen wasn't old enough to be pushed out of the nest, even a witch's nest.

I should turn around. There's nothing but pain for me if I keep walking this direction; the pain of never finding Grams' shop no matter how hard I try.

The knowledge that she hated me so much that she felt the need to hide her home still hurts as much as it did the first time I tried to return home and couldn't. Yet, I can't make my feet veer away from the familiar road.

The red glow of a cigarette flares to my left, near a large tree a mere ten feet away. I freeze.

"Looking for something?" A man's rich baritone reaches me.

Something deep inside me stirs. That voice seems familiar. Before I can respond, an overweight, orange tabby darts out of the shadows from the opposite direction. The cat skitters to a halt five feet away and arches. With his many fat rolls, he can't quite make the high arch and ends up looking supremely uncomfortable, like he's a victim of a vet sticking a ther-mometer up his rear.

"You're dangerous," the cat hisses.

I blink in surprise. I'd never had an affinity for cats, but more than that, witches can only understand their own famil-iars, although I can understand the odd pig on occasion.

"I see you for what you are," the tabby growls, reminding me of a bitter, old woman harping about the younger genera-tion. "You shouldn't be here."

"You must know Grams," I reply acidly.

"Go," the cat hisses.

I fold my arms over my chest. "I'm not inclined to take orders from a cat. Who do you belong to?"

He exposes more teeth, but he only appears more awkward. "You're dangerous," he repeats.

"Right." I lurch forward and flap my hands.

The cat jumps back, trips, and rolls in the street before regaining his feet—or, at least, I assume he has feet under all that chub—and bounds off into the night. I grin, even as his words haunt me a little. A forgotten memory of Grams hovering over me whispering 'You're dangerous' surges from the depths of my mind. Unexpected shame washes over me. Wasn't that what Thomas had said, as well? Of course, he was right. I was dangerous—to him. But to Grams? Was that why she betrayed me?

A chuckle comes from the direction of the cigarette.

Again, the depths of my soul stir. I whirl. The cigarette is gone. So is the man—I think. "Who are you?" I wait expectantly through silence. My temper flares. "Enough already."

Even though I know I won't find the house, I start walking. I don't have any potions, and the damn sigil will limit the types of magic I can use in my search for the house.

I'd grown up in this neighborhood. It's crazy that I can't find my childhood home using landmarks. I experience the same sense of the neighborhood being frozen in time I did the previous two times I've been here. Mrs. Campbell's corner grocer is still there. So is Sam's Barber Shop and the Tip-Top Tresses hair salon. I recognize the ancient oak up ahead. I always see the tree. It's as if Grams left that memory just to taunt me. I could climb onto one of the limbs from my bedroom window. Until Grams pruned the tree, that is, which didn't stop me for long. By age thirteen, I'd studied martial arts for six years. It was a simple matter to leap from my window onto the limb.

I cross the street, my spirits flagging, and half wonder if I shouldn't just head to my apartment to look for Stony. Maybe Stony can root out the house. I'm surprised I hadn't thought of that before.

A flicker teases the corner of my eye. I stop and look. My heart stands still. Amidst a tiny shimmer I glimpse...is that gabled window part of Gram's house? A car horn blares. I jump back onto the sidewalk.

"Get out of the road," a sedan's driver shouts as he speeds past.

I stare after the car. I hadn't realized I'd stepped from the curb.

I return my attention to the shimmer and start running toward the house. I draw closer and my heart pounds. The house isn't a mirage. Two stories, an attic, and a sharply pointed roof come into focus. Wooden shingles. A house straight from a storybook. A painted sign reading *Crowe's Potionary* and looking as fresh as ever hangs from a post in the yard. Potionary wasn't a word until the original Crowe potion master coined the term centuries ago. Since then, the rest of the Crowes kept the tradition alive.

I run up the walk, clear the four steps onto the porch, and stop in front of the door. The repel of the ward stings an instant before the damn sigil on my hand heats. Anger bubbles over. Shadows swirl in a vortex around me. My head spins in rhythm with the shadows and power surges. The wards splinter. Tiny lights flash as my fingers close around the doorknob, the door opens, and I step across the threshold. I start at the pain on my hand and glance down. The sigil glows like a glow stick in the dark. That's going to hurt like a bitch when the adrenaline fades from my system.

I reach for the light switch to the left of the door before I realize the action. Even after seven years, old habits die hard. The overhead light flares to life. I fix my gaze on the left hand table, which stands in the exact place it occupied the day I left.

I hold my breath. Everything is exactly as it had been when I last saw the inside of the house.

Above the table hangs a picture of Grams' grandparents. Portraits of even more distant ancestors follow the stairs to the second floor landing. My gaze shifts to the right-hand wall and my heart cracks a little when I recognize photos of me hanging among more valuable portraits. Why did she leave my pictures hanging?

Her essence lingers like a physical presence. I laugh bitterly. If any part of her is present, it will be furious that I've returned. So, why can I now see the place?

I head across the foyer toward the living room, visible through the arched doorway to my right. As I pass through the archway, the motion-sensor floor lamp in the near-left corner turns on. I blink, surprised the thing still works.

I stop short at sight of a man dressed in jeans, a t-shirt and a leather jacket sitting in the wing backed chair on the far side of the room. Raven hair grazes his shoulders and long legs attached to a six foot-three-inch frame are crossed at the ankles. He's gorgeous. Lately, the world seems overrun by gorgeous men.

"Who the hell are you?" I demand.

"Forgive the intrusion," his velvety voice is colored by a slight accent I can't quite place. "I didn't have your phone number and the neighbors were looking through their curtains after I'd waited at your door for half an hour." The accent could be Eastern European, though it really is faint.

"Most people leave after they realize no one is home," I say.

A corner of his mouth turns up. "I am not most people."

Chances are, the guy isn't evil. Unless, of course, he figured out a way to get past Grams' warding spell. Damn, maybe Grams' concealment spell faded, along with her wards. No. The ache where the sigil marks me reminds me how acutely I felt her wards. I eye him. He doesn't seem to know that Grams died and the potionary is no longer open for business.

"I don't do business after five," I say.

"Shall I return tomorrow before five?" he asks.

I shake my head and start to reply when the rapid click of small hooves on wooden floors approaches from the foyer. I know that sound. The man's eyes shift past me and I cry out in delight as Stony trots into the room, snout high as she sniffs the air.

The man's eyes shift to me, brows lifted. "A pig as a familiar?

"You don't want to see her true shape, so I suggest you leave without causing any trouble," I say, and suddenly wonder why Stony hadn't sensed his presence in the house. Had she just arrived? I hadn't heard the click of her hooves on the front porch.

Stony continues to the man, then sniffs his pants leg. His brows lift, but when she turns and waddles away, he relaxes. "She likes me," he says. "That should count for something."

"Stony's easier going than I am." That's a complete lie, but she isn't going wonky, so I relax a bit.

A breeze wafts the curtain to the left of the fireplace. I keep my eyes on the man. Grams never left windows open. Did someone leave it open during the investigation or is that how the man got in?

"Enough chitchat," I say. "It's been a hard day and it's late."

He rubs the arm of the chair. "Does the hard day have anything to do with your shop being closed?"

So, he *does* know.

Somewhere in the house, a door slams.

Dammit.

"Who the hell are you?" Before he can answer, I add, "If you brought friends, I'll—"

Stony squeals and rams the back of my legs. I fall to the

floor. Something green and iridescent grazes the sleeve of my jacket. The man dives for the floor. The green goo burns a hole through the chair back and continues out the other side. *Not the armoire.* Yes, it continues through Grams' armoire. I push to my knees. I have no idea what the hell that was, so have no idea how to stop it. How far will the goo go before losing momentum?

The man jumps to his feet. "There will be more."

Stony growls.

"You said she liked you," I snap.

"She isn't growling at me."

A shudder shakes the house. The man weaves toward me. I scramble to my feet and take a step toward the foyer, but Stony bumps my legs, again. The man reaches my side as a green, eight-foot-tall demon ducks through the archway. Green demon. Green goo. Of course.

The man yanks me into a bear hug and dives for the back of the couch. The demon bellows. Stony squeals. The man and I hit the carpet. He releases me and we both peer over the back of the couch. Stony has shifted to her full seven-foot height.

She charges the demon. The creature emits an ear-splitting scream. How the hell did a demon of this magnitude get past Grams' warding spell? I didn't think it was possible for any amount of real evil to enter this house. The demon flings another green goo ball at us. We dive left, me landing on top of the stranger.

He grabs my shoulders. "Maybe another time, eh, sweet?" He sets me aside and leaps to his feet.

Fuck this. I jump to my feet and see Stony swipe at the demon. Her claws slice down the creature's left side and she ducks when the thing dives for her. Thankfully, this green thing must be some kind of lower demon—slow and very stupid. But deadly. The creature begins to whirl toward Stony, but not before Stony sinks her fangs into its rump.

Green goo splatters Stony's face, but she holds on for dear life. The demon throws its head back and claws the air above its back. My heart nearly stops when one long talon sweeps perilously close to Stony's side. I throw my hands out to my sides and pool all my focus. The sigil burns like a bitch, but balls of thick, swirling black energy rise from my palms.

"Jump, Stony," I shout.

I throw first the right, then the left shadow ball. Stony drops to the floor, bites the demon's leg, then rolls into the foyer before the demon's talons swipe the empty spot on the floor. The demon whirls toward us and the first ball hits its stomach, the second, its chest. It manages two steps, then explodes in a rainfall of green goo.

NINETEEN

Blade

I ENTER RAITH'S OFFICE. IT'S ALMOST MIDNIGHT BUT, as usual, he's still working. With Ciarah back, none of us are getting much rest.

He looks up from his desk and frowns. "Ciarah?"

I nod. "She's gone."

"Gone? What do you mean, *gone*?"

"Bertha found her bed empty."

"So soon?" he whispers.

I release a breath at the stark fear in his eyes. Raith's reaction, and his display during Leilah's first day here, reveals the passionate heart that beats beneath that cold exterior.

"She's not *gone* gone," I say. "My guess is she's headed to her grandmother's."

Raith blinks. Confusion flickers across his face, then is replaced by anger. "You're sure?"

"I found an open window in the girls' bathroom where she sneaked out."

His mouth thins. "This is grounds for expulsion."

I chuckle. "There's not a chance of that and you know it. Besides, that's what she wants."

"I will take her over my knee," he mutters.

"You might want to recall where that got you when we caught up with her down in Virginia."

Emotion flickers in his eyes. Yes, he remembers.

He grabs his phone, dials, presses it to his ear, and says, "Ethan, get over here," then hangs up.

One might say Raith is autocratic, but all vampires are. While Raith isn't the average vampire, it is in his nature to expect obedience. Still, his species traits are enhanced when Ciarah is involved. Ethan knows that. We all know it. In truth, we're all different when she's involved.

I'm not looking forward to the dragon's fire once Ciarah's energy fills us, as it inevitably will. Already, his green eyes swirl with a little more fire than they have these last forty years. At least, I don't have to worry about a sulking wolf and a vicious gargoyle. The thought doesn't comfort as much as I would like. Life is easier without these four men in my life, but they are as much a part of me as is Ciarah.

Minutes later, Ethan enters. He takes one look at us and says, "Where is she?"

Raith shoves to his feet. "Her apartment."

"Her grandmother's," I say.

Raith shakes his head. "She can't find the potionary. Miriam's spell makes the house invisible to her. She's looking for that damn howling night pig."

"The little fool doesn't think we know she can't find her grandmother's home," Ethan mutters. "She can't get in." He blows out a breath before Raith or I can reply. "Or, maybe she can. She pushed through the pain of my sigil and used magic on you, Raith."

Ethan's dragon magic isn't weak. Pride swells in me. I wonder just how far she can push through Ethan's magic before the sigil stops her. Knowing Leilah, we'll soon find out.

· · ·

Forty minutes later, we pull up to Miriam Crowe's home and potionary.

"The lights are on," Ethan says.

"Told you we should have skipped her apartment and come here first," I say.

A crash sounds. Ethan and I are out of the car and up the front porch steps in an instant. With his blasted vampire speed, Raith is already through the door and standing in the foyer when we rush inside. At the base of the stairs stands the pig. Through the arched doorway to the right, Leilah stands amidst a half-destroyed room. She stares at us as if seeing a ghost.

I watch her closely. With all three of us in the same room, she's sure to have some reaction. Ciarah has yet to remember us from any of her multiple lives, but she always has a reaction. Her reaction to Raith was to attempt to kick his arse. Same with Ethan. But then, Ethan did mark her with a sigil that compelled her arrival at The Academy.

The pig trots past us to Leilah, turns to face us and drops its butt onto the floor beside her foot.

"What the fuck happened?" Raith demands.

The pig snorts what is clearly intended as a warning, but for once, I'm in agreement with Raith. Never mind the hole in the armoire or the overturned furniture. It's the green goop that catches my attention.

"A Thol'guk," I murmur.

Ethan gives an almost imperceptible nod.

"What are you doing here?" Leilah demands, but I discern an unsteadiness in her voice. "Out," she orders. "All of you. You, too," she adds, and glances over her shoulder. Her brow furrows. "What the hell? Where—" She faces forward again. "Where did he go?"

Through the long sleeves of Ethan's white shirt, his dragon tattoos glow. So it begins.

"The Thol'guk?" Ethan demands.

Uncertainty flickers in her eyes and I realize she wasn't referring to the green demon.

Ethan takes a step toward her. "Who else besides the Thol'guk was here?"

The glow beneath his shirt now covers his arms and dragon armor is nearly bursting the fabric of his shirt.

"How did you get past the wards?" Leilah counters.

"Wards only keep out evil," I say.

Her eyes narrow. "Too bad it doesn't keep out assholes."

I laugh. "If that were the case, darling, you wouldn't be here any more than we are."

Her eyes narrow. "What are you three doing here? Since when do Academy instructors take part in investigations outside The Academy?"

"We're not here to investigate Miriam Crowe's crimes," Raith says. "We're here to collect you."

She lifts her chin. "Try. Grams keeps a stash of silver stakes here."

Even with the sigil glowing on her hand, magic radiates off her. By God, she's magnificent. I half wonder if I can devise a way to send them home and have my way with her. But that's a fantasy. We do have to share her, but it's too early. Plus, I've got to figure out what's different about her this time. Well, that last might be able to wait. I'm not one for denying myself any longer than I must.

"Easy, Leilah," Ethan warns. "You have only pushed the limits of the sigil a little. Push too hard and you *will* injure yourself."

She thrusts forward the hand with the sigil. "Then take it off."

He hesitates.

"No," Raith says.

Leilah throws him a thin-lipped scowl. "I wasn't talking to you."

"Ethan isn't in charge."

She laughs harshly. "Neither are you."

"Ethan doesn't have the authority to remove the sigil," Raith says. "Your name is written on the Stone. We've been through this. You know the law. Anyone's name who appears on the Stone must attend The Academy."

"I thought you wanted me expelled," she shoots back.

The pig snorts and Leilah laughs, clearly in agreement with whatever the animal said. I shake my head. Witches and their familiars.

"Stony says she'll take care of the three of you while I go upstairs to bed," Leilah says. "As Miriam's only living relative, this house belongs to me."

"Talk to the Illumina once the investigation is over," Ethan says. "For now, you're coming back with us."

Her eyes spark and the pig snorts loudly.

"Don't force us to kill the howling night pig," Raith says.

I wince. Raith isn't known for his tact.

Leilah frowns. "Howling night pig?" She looks down at the pig. "I thought— Stony, you never told me that's what you are." She drops to her knees. "You're alone. Just like me."

The pig snorts and nuzzles its nose against her cheek.

"Don't worry," Leilah says. She stands and faces us. "I'll come, but this place is mine. Stony gets to stay here. I want food sent to her every day."

Raith opens his mouth to answer—or refuse, is my guess— but I say, "I think that can be arranged."

Raith snaps his gaze onto me.

"I'll see to the feeding of the familiar myself," I say.

Leilah looks at the animal. "If you miss even one meal, tell me." The pig snorts. "Yeah," Leilah replies. "Grams warned me about men."

I don't have to ask what it is about men Miriam warned her

about. *Men are idiots,* is a universally accepted fact among women of all ages and species.

Leilah looks back at us. "I want to look around."

I'm not surprised when Raith shakes his head. "No."

It's a bad move. Leilah will return. But he's right. We still haven't found the source of The Shadows Miriam Crowe contacted. Not to mention the Thol'guk and whoever the bloody hell else had been in the house with her. For now, Leilah is safer far away from this house.

"What happened here?" Ethan asks. "How did the Thol'guk get past your grandmother's wards?"

"The green demon?" Leilah shakes her head. "I...I don't know."

"Who was the other person with you?" Ethan asks.

Something flickers in her eyes. Leilah was never a great liar. At least, she was never good at lying to us. I'm relieved to see that hasn't changed.

"I don't know. Some guy dressed in leather was sitting in that chair." She points to the wing-back chair lying on the floor to the left of the couch. "You showed up and"–she shrugs—"he left."

I exchange a look with Raith. Just what we need, a mystery man. Not to mention, a damn Thol'guk. Was the demon after her or had it followed the mystery man? Or did the creature have something to do with Miriam's death? If she really was dabbling in the black arts, then her wards could have been defective.

Raith motions with his head toward the door. "Let's go."

Leilah shoots him a dagger-filled glare, then drops to one knee and hugs the pig. "I'll make sure you get lots of Chinese food," she says.

The pig snorts.

"Of course, all vegetarian. I'll see you soon." She rises then walks past us.

I follow her. Ethan is close behind. I descend the few steps from the porch then halt. I should have known. Leilah is getting into the driver's seat. A blur passes me and, in the next instant, Raith stands in the street on the driver's side and stops Leilah from pulling the door shut.

"Get out," he says.

I bite back a laugh when she says, "You're not afraid, are you?"

"I'm afraid for my car," Raith replies.

Leilah revs the engine. The car purrs like the well-tuned animal it is. "Get in," she says, and reaches for the gearshift.

To my surprise, Raith doesn't use his vampiric speed to pull her out of the car or to reach the passenger door. Instead, he slowly walks around the hood to the passenger's side. He opens the door and stands aside as Ethan and I slide into the back, then he slides into the front seat. Once he's arranged his long legs and pulls his door closed, Leilah shifts the car into gear, slowly. That is unexpected. I exchange a puzzled look with Ethan. Then, she jams her foot down on the accelerator and all is right in the world.

As the tires squeal and the car shoots forward, I know a moment of fear. Raith, Ethan and I cannot die. Not in a car accident, at any rate. Leilah can. I wish I could say that with the three of us here she couldn't die, but that's a lie. Raith has tried twice to turn her, but in some cosmic joke that holds the six of us in thrall, our powers are useless when death comes for her.

The headlights cut through the dark as she shoots through a stop sign at the end of the street and takes the corner way too fast.

"You'll only succeed in killing yourself," Raith says in a conversational tone, but I detect an edge to his voice.

"My name appeared on your Stone," she replies.

Raith gives a mirthless laugh. "That doesn't guarantee your safety."

"So I've heard." She doesn't slow for the next curve.

"What if you kill someone else?" Raith asks.

Her head jerks in his direction. She mutters something unintelligible under her breath, but I glimpse the corner of Raith's mouth lift. Not amusement. Heaven forbid. Satisfaction, I'm guessing, for she slows. Headlights appear up ahead, and I wonder if she'd sensed the oncoming car.

"Stony will need food tonight," she says.

"Vegetarian Chinese," Ethan says.

She nods.

Before I can respond, he pulls his phone from his pocket and taps the screen. "Lo mien should do the trick."

"And egg rolls," she says.

He taps the screen another moment, then says, "Done."

Leilah glances in the rearview mirror. I'm certain her gaze lingers on Ethan a heartbeat longer than necessary before she returns her attention to the road. Right now, she despises us all —me less than Raith, of course, or so I fantasize. Either way, her anger won't stop her from wanting us. It never does. In all our lifetimes together, she has never remembered us. I've never once had the courage to ask her what she thinks of the fact that she loves us all simultaneously.

Deep down, I think there's a part of her that does remember. She's questioned our strange love far less the last few lifetimes. I pray that brings her some peace—or, at least, causes her less confusion.

"What do you want from me?" she asks.

The abrupt question stumps us all.

"You're an Academy student," Raith is the first to reply.

She snorts. "Try again."

"There's nothing to try," Ethan says.

"Even I know Academy instructors don't chase after a

student—*en masse,*" she retorts.

She isn't wrong.

"I'm not sure how you know that," Raith says. "You've never before been a student."

She glances at Raith. "How many students does Illumina Academy Cadette Commander Raith Vanderkoff let drive his McLaren?"

I chuckle. "Most wouldn't try."

Two heartbeats of silence pass before she says, "So, which of you is going to see me to my room?"

Tension, thick enough to cut, suddenly fills the space.

"Ohh, so it's all three of you?" she purrs.

I envision her straddling my hips as she rides my cock into a mind-numbing orgasm. The silence tells me Ethan and Raith are envisioning similar fantasies. Each time Leilah reappears, our hunger for her grows wilder. Centuries of discipline keep us in check, but I wonder when—and it is inevitable—one of us will snap and take her at all costs.

"You're going to bed alone," Raith says.

I wager the strain in his voice matches the strain of his cock against his jeans.

Ethan shifts in his seat and I know he's feeling the sexual tension, as well.

Leilah doesn't come back with a witty reply. The silly girl is wondering how seriously we're taking her flippant invitation.

More seriously than she can imagine.

I wonder what she might do if I slipped into her room once she lay warm and cozy in her bed. I release a breath. It wouldn't be the first time I sneaked into Ciarah's bed. Raith and Ethan have done the same, as has Caleb. Matthias is the only one who hasn't. To my knowledge, at any rate. But I can believe Matthias has not taken that liberty.

My chest constricts. Now that Ciarah is back, I wonder if her return is enough to draw Caleb and Matthias back to us.

TWENTY

Leilah

MY HEAD IS SPINNING. I'VE KNOWN SOME GORGEOUS men, but these three are causing my heart to beat an erratic rhythm. Maybe I'm simply surrounded by too much testosterone. The sexual tension in the car is so thick I'm tingling. I've been starved far too long. I could probably blame Ethan for leaving me unsatisfied the other day. Or Raith for pushing me against that damn tree last night. Or maybe even Blade. I know he mentally undresses me. Once we get back to the dorm, I've got to take care of business—again. Hell, forget that. I need to find a guy at the Academy and fuck him—hard.

I cast a covert glance at Raith. Would he...? I've heard conflicting stories about how cruel vampires can be, all the way to how they can drive a woman mad with desire. My gut tells me Raith is the *drive a girl mad with passion* variety with a twist of cruelty. There's a lot of speculation about his origin and when he was turned. Whatever the case, the guy has been around forever. He's an asshole, and he's been true to form tonight, but God, why do I want to stroke his cheek and assure him everything will be all right—and then fuck him senseless?

Saints have mercy! I have lost my mind. No way I'm getting

involved with a vampire who treats me like a minion. Blade, at least, treats me as the woman I am—or he would, if I let him.

I slow for a curve and catch a glimpse of Ethan in the mirror. The dragon energy in his sigil alone threatens to burn through my soul. The way his armor began to form earlier…. God, I've never seen a dragon in armor. What would that shell feel like beneath my fingers as he drove his cock into me from behind? I've never seen a dragon's wings unfurl, but I've heard they're magnificent. To have him stand before me, wings widespread, cock erect, I just might fall to my knees and—

I'm suddenly aware of the deathly silence in the car and how fast I'm driving. I wince, but don't slow down. I resist an urge to glance at Raith and keep my eyes on the road. I'm damn glad telepathy isn't a gift of vampires and dragons. Fae sometimes claim it, but I've never sensed that gift in Blade. Still, the silence unnerves me.

Hell, none of this matters. Raith will likely expel me. I'm surprised by the jump of my pulse at the thought. Does he really believe Grams was a dark witch? Does he believe I will turn to Shadow magic? Do Blade and Ethan agree? I recall Ethan's body pressed close to mine that first day. There's no denying what would have happened had Miss Mack not interrupted us. Does he fuck dark witches? Oddly, a quick fuck wasn't how that encounter felt. That puzzles me, just as his manner in the alley that first night does. His reaction hadn't been the typical male lechery that results from contact with a woman's body. He'd been caught off guard. I can't place the emotion, but I swear, I noticed some tenderness and maybe longing.

As for Blade, he's a natural flirt, but I've already witnessed the kind heart beneath that façade. He immediately offered to take care of Stony. Relief that Stony's safe floods my soul and I curse inwardly at the sting of tears. I will not cry in front of these men. I concentrate on Stony and how happy she'd been to see me.

Wait. *Stony was in Grams house*. How—my mind whirls—how did she find the house?

The truth hits like a Mack truck and I want to scream at how stupid I am. Grams didn't cast a spell to make the house invisible. She cast a spell on *me*, so I couldn't see it. I'm a complete idiot not to have figured that out long ago and, worse, not to have gotten Stony to find the house for me when we arrived in New York. Was Stony finding the house what broke Grams' spell on me?

Another thought strikes. Why did Stony decide to find the house now? Has she known all along where the house is? Oh, that pig and I are going to have a long talk the next time I see her. For the moment, she's safe in Gram's house. Stony didn't know Grams. My heart squeezes. Grams would have liked her.

We're halfway to The Academy, but I feel Grams' presence as if she's in the car with us. I shove the sadness aside. The feeling is nothing more than the fifteen-year-old me wanting to believe she didn't throw me away. I have to get over this shit. She didn't want me. End of story.

That, however, doesn't mean the house isn't mine. Now that I found it, I can search for information on any lawyer she might have employed. I have no idea if Grams kept a will, but this is the first step to finding out.

Headlights come into view up ahead. I pass the oncoming car in a blur. I glance at Raith. He's staring ahead, mouth thin. Sure, I'm driving recklessly, but there's something therapeutic about speed. Who says you can't run from your problems? The MacLaren temporarily loans me a freedom I long for, even if the car is just a teaser of dreams I may never find.

A stop sign comes into view ahead and I apply the brakes. Raith throws out a hand to brace himself on the dash. Two cars approach, both with their high beams on. I flash my high beams, but the two cars ignore me and speed past. Assholes. I stop at the stop sign, then proceed a little slower. Grams' lawyer isn't the only person I need information from.

"What really happened with my grandmother?" I hope to surprise one of them into an answer.

No one replies.

"Don't play coy," I say.

"Miriam died while practicing Shadow magic," Raith says.

I hate that overconfident voice. Worse, I hate how it glides over my flesh like velvet, leaving a trail of gooseflesh, even when he says things I despise.

"Sounds cut and dried," I say.

"It is," he replies.

"Why allow Zadkeil to be a part of an Illumina investigation?"

"It's not the first time the Illumina has worked with angels," Ethan says.

I grunt. "Then the Illumina hasn't learned its lesson. Angels can't be trusted."

"They have a vested interest in keeping the Hell Gates sealed," Ethan says.

Hell Gates?

"None of this is your concern," Raith says.

I hit the brakes and veer off onto the shoulder, then shove the car into park and face him. "She was my grandmother."

"Your duty—"

"My *duty?* Don't you fucking lecture me about duty," I snap.

Raith's brows shoot up.

"My duty is to my family. Everything else is secondary." It's bullshit. I have no family—blood family, that is. But I'm not letting them in on that juicy secret.

No one answers.

"Grams was no black witch. She would never summon Shadows."

Ariel's words blare in memory, *"You know where they got those Shadows Miss Mack showed in class, don't you?"*

"We all know," Thomas had said. *"They came from Crowe Potionary."*

"You can't say she summoned Shadows," I say with a jab of my finger in Raith's chest, but their silence tells me they can and do.

I put the car in drive and pull off the shoulder. "Is it true that the Shadow husks Miss Mack showed us are from Grams' house?"

"Yes," Blade says without hesitation.

The words are laced with kindness and I detect no deceit. Oh God, I might embarrass myself and cry. "Who told you that?" I whisper.

"Leilah…" he begins.

"No," I cut in. "Answer the question."

A moment of silence passes, then he says, "The Illumina watched her for a year."

"A year?" I blurt. My heart pounds.

"The Watchmen detected dark magic," he said. "It wasn't consistent. They weren't a hundred percent certain. Then came an explosion in the basement. They immediately detected dark magic and…Shadows. They investigated and found a hole in the floor."

"Her body?" I whisper.

I discern the shake of his head in the mirror.

"Who the hell is buried in that grave at Westwood?"

"No one," Raith says.

I grip the wheel tighter and force myself not to slam my foot down on the accelerator. "So, you don't really know what happened."

Another heartbeat of silence passes and I know I'm wrong —again.

"The three of us dealt with The Shadows in Miriam's house," Raith says.

Liar! my mind screams. Grams stood for everything the opposite of darkness. My mind races. I have a thousand questions.

How can you tell such terrible lies?

Why would you tell such terrible lies?

Angels teaming up with the Illumina? Are you crazy?

Shadow husks in her—my—home?

You don't know my grandmother.

Fucking Shadows. If they didn't exist, Margidda wouldn't have been nearly annihilated, magic wouldn't be regulated, and we wouldn't be in this fucking situation.

We drive in silence for a long moment, then I say to Raith, "You defeated The Shadows in the final battle."

He doesn't reply. I look at Ethan in the rearview mirror. "You were there, too. The two of you together." Before he can answer, a thought strikes, and I add, "You too, Blade. Miss Mack called you Commander, but I didn't know you were there. Why?"

"Because my part was more...covert," he replies.

"What did you do?"

Ethan's gaze snaps onto Blade, and Blade says, "It's best you don't know."

"How did The Shadow war begin?" I ask.

"People began to disappear," Ethan says. "When they returned, they were...different. But not all who changed left. We don't know where those that left went to." He pauses. "None of them are alive to tell us."

A chill slides down my spine. "Miss Mack says you beat The Shadows with trust and love projected through a lucid dream."

The same embarrassment that washed over me in class does so now. Love and trust? From birth, we're taught meditation and earth magic as protection against The Shadows. I hadn't thought of it before, but I now wonder why we weren't taught exactly how The Commanders beat The Shadows. Shouldn't that knowledge be standard teaching, as well?

"How can you defeat pure evil with trust and love? I mean, that part about meditating to center yourself. Sure, we're taught that from childhood—we're taught almost everything Miss Mack shared in Reaping Preparedness from the time we're babies. But killing while inside a dream? That's science fiction."

A look passes between Blade and Ethan.

My third chakra tightens in my solar plexus. Raith has a secret. I glance at him. He's not telling me everything that happened when they defeated the Shadows. But that's not his only secret—not his big secret—I realize.

I slow for a stop sign, glance both ways, then accelerate through the intersection. "I know there's more to the story than the drivel Miss Mack taught us in class."

"That *drivel* may save your life one day," Raith says.

I cast him a sideways glare as I maneuver another curve. "How did you drive them away?"

"We put a stop to all magic," Raith says.

"Buffalo chips," I mutter.

A weird silence descends.

"Buffalo chips?" Blade repeats.

I wince. I've probably just lost any ground I *might* have made in convincing them I'm a no-nonsense badass.

"There's no fucking way you eradicated all magic," I say. "That's simply impossible. Hell, the crime bosses' use of black magic would have fed The Shadows' hunger."

Raith turns his steely gaze onto me. "You know nothing."

"I know that, at four, my magic had a life of its own." Which is likely why Grams sent me away from the age of two to four. She didn't want me near the big city where The Shadows ran rampant. Many in the bigger cities sent their young away.

Raith stares through the windshield. "That flow of magic fed The Shadows."

I blink. "Are you saying *I'm* responsible for The Shadows' attack?"

"He's saying that even innocent magic fuels The Shadows," Ethan says.

I shake my head. "Uh uh. He said that I contributed to The Shadows' reign of death. I assume, then, that you stifled your own magic. How very clever of you to have saved Margidda without magic." The Academy's turrets come into view above distant trees. "Magic is practiced every day. What's stopping The Shadows from returning?" I ask.

"Enough," Raith growls. "You're too young and inexperienced to have an opinion on how to deal with The Shadows."

"Isn't that why I'm here?"

"You're here to learn what we teach you."

"Blade and Ethan don't agree with you."

"Raith is right," Blade says, and I'm disconcerted by a wave of betrayal.

"I assume when you spoke with Headmaster Domini, he didn't explain that breaking curfew means you aren't allowed to leave school grounds without permission," Raith says.

"This isn't high school and I'm not a prisoner," I snap.

"Then why did you sneak out?" his tone remains steady.

"To avoid a conflict like this. What the hell is really going on?" I demand. Everyone knows that once a High Potential is drafted into The Academy, their lives aren't their own, but I had never given that much thought. "Are we prisoners?"

"You are aware that everyone in Margidda has to attend magic school. High Potentials attend an Academy. It's the law."

"Sure," I say. "But—"

"But nothing," he cuts in. "You think anyone can be trained without rules? You think people learn discipline when discipline isn't imposed or enforced? Do you think untrained High Potentials are ready for a Shadow attack?"

"There are over two thousand years between Shadow Wars. I think—"

"You don't think," he cut in.

"Fuck you," I mutter, then clamp my mouth shut.

Thankfully, we reach The Academy, and I'll soon be freed from the prison of this car. The gates swing open as they did that first day. Two minutes later, I park behind Penncarrow Hall, cut the engine and bolt from the McLaren. I reach my room, probably before the last man has time to leave the car and slam his door.

Again, I spend a sleepless night. Images of Grams' house keep replaying in my head. What happened that I can now see it? Who was the man inside her house? Was the demon part of his act or was it after him? Few are strong enough to conjure a demon.

How did Stony find Grams' house? That pig—

"Howler night pig," I murmur.

I should have argued harder and stayed at the house.

I groan and flip from my left to my right side. Why did *The Three*—as I've come to call them—drag me back to school? The biggest question of all: what do *The Three* know about Grams' death that they're not telling me?

It isn't possible that Shadow husks were found in her house.

Just like it wasn't possible for a demon to enter that house?

TWENTY-ONE

Ethan

I didn't sleep well after getting Leilah back to The Academy.

I haven't slept well since she reentered our lives. I won't sleep well until she's lying in bed beside me, or, at least, beside Raith or Blade.

Thunderous clouds blanket the early afternoon sky. I leave Raith's office, stuff my hands into the pockets of my hoodie and dash along the walkway toward the east sparring gym. I want to get back to Miriam Crowe's house and nose around. That Thol'guk didn't arrive there by accident. No one lives in the house, and no one could have known Leilah was going there. Yet, she's the most likely target. Which means someone is watching her. Raith and Blade agree, and we would all like to know who that someone is.

I arrive at the sparring gym ten minutes later to find a dozen students paired up, sparring, while another six take turns with the Teacher's Assistant. The clash of steel and the thud of hardwood bo staffs fill the air. Martial arts is the only subject I teach and, I must admit, I love seeing the students grow in patience and skill.

I pull off my hoodie, toss it onto the floor near the wall, then motion the TA off the mat. Billy Mills, a young shifter with great promise, takes the mat. He's talented and, once he matures, he'll go far. Like many males his age, his biggest vulnerability is the belief that he's indestructible.

In the corner of my eye, I glimpse Leilah enter the far door. Billy rushes me. I nimbly step aside and whirl to face him. What's Leilah doing here? She wasn't assigned this class. Billy spins. I recognize embarrassment in his eyes.

"Remember," I tell him, "emotions have no place in battle."

He circles me, embarrassment still swirling in his eyes.

"Come on, Billy," Preston Phillips calls, "show Teach what you're made of."

I don't reply. The students know better than to heckle or encourage their fellow classmates during sparring. I'll deal with Preston when his turn comes. This is hand to hand combat, but I'm tempted to pull one of the bo staffs from the wall and give Preston's butt a memorable whack.

Leilah leans against the wall, eyes glued to me, and I wonder whether Blade or Raith made the change in her classes. Billy rushes me and, though he knows better, I suspect he's going to shift into wolf form. If the boy wants to play with the big dogs, I will oblige. I summon fire. My palms heat and—

A lance spear is yanked from its wall mounting, controlled by an invisible hand. Even before the point turns toward its intended victim, I know.

"Leilah!" I shout.

My armor warms my flesh and my shirt rends. The silver tattoos across my body morph into hardened silver. Students shout. Billy spins toward Leilah.

Leilah throws up her right hand, palm out, and shouts, "Deflect!"

My sigil on her hand glows. The spear merely wobbles. Billy shifts as fire bursts from my palms. I race toward her, heart hammering. Billy passes me, his wolf form faster than my human form. Leilah lunges left.

"*Deflecto,*" someone shouts.

The spear veers right, then whips back on course toward Leilah. I throw a fireball into the spear's path. The wood sails through a flame hot enough to melt steel. My heart thunders. Billy leaps and snaps at the spear, but his powerful jaws close around air.

I speed past as he lands in a crouch and throw another, then another fireball, to no effect. An eopy materializes in the spear's path. The giant ape bellows as it swipes at the spear. The point passes through its hand, then through its massive chest and the creature falls.

Leilah starts to turn as if to run, but my youngest student leaps between her and the spear and throws up both hands. Leilah shoves him aside as she spins, throwing a lightning fast roundhouse kick at the oncoming spear. I throw another ball of flame and want to cry out in relief when her foot makes contact with the spear. The wood splits in two with a crack. The point shoots through the blaze and buries itself in the right side of Leilah's abdomen.

She gasps and looks down at the broken spear protruding from her body. Blood spreads in a dark stain across the hem of her t-shirt. She crumbles and I catch her before she hits the floor, dropping to my knees.

"Back," I shout, as students rush us.

My vision blurs. Fate can't be so cruel as to take Ciarah away so soon. I haven't had a chance to stroke her face, taste her lips, show her how much I love her.

There is never enough time to show her how much I love her.

Her eyelids flutter. She murmurs, "It isn't your fault."

I shake my head. Anger rips through me. I won't let her die. *Not this time.* I surge to my feet and race toward the door.

"Someone open the door," I shout.

Billy speeds past me in human form, naked. He reaches the door seconds before me, pushes through and holds the door open as I burst into the rain. Wings burst from my shoulder blades and, in three running steps, I leave the ground, Ciarah a feather in my arms.

"Don't you *dare* die," I hiss.

In less than a minute, I reach the instructors' offices and land at a run. My wings retract as I hit the front door with a shoulder. I take the stairs three at a time and burst into Raith's office, breathing heavily. He's not at his desk.

He doesn't have classes at this hour. Where is he?

"What the hell?"

I whirl.

Raith's standing in the doorway that connects to his private chambers.

"Someone attacked Ciarah," I pant.

Her head lolls against my chest.

God, don't die.

I rush to the leather couch and lay her on the cushions. Raith reaches my side.

"She needs your blood," I say.

He stares at her.

"Raith," I growl.

"Maybe it's better this way," he whispers.

"What?" I shout. "What the hell are you talking about?"

"Life with Ciarah never ends well."

"Life without her is hell." I seize his collar. "Save her or I'll put a stake through your frozen heart."

His eyes meet mine. "Too late. Ciarah cut out my heart forty years ago."

I drive him so hard against the bookshelf that several books hit the carpet. "Give her your blood or I'll bury you so deep no one will find you for a millennium."

Leilah moans. Raith's head snaps in her direction and his pupils dilate. His gaze fixes on the wound...on her blood. I pull him over to the couch and shove him onto his knees.

"Don't you think this is as hard on her as it is on us?" he asks.

Fear twists through me as I grab the broken spear and yank it from her body. She convulses. I throw the spear to the carpet. As blood gushes, I rip her t-shirt and expose the wound. Raith draws a sharp breath. He starts to rise, but I shove his face into the blood. He throws his head back and I stumble two paces before catching myself. Raith shakes his head as if he's been drugged.

Good.

I grab his head and force his face into the blood. Ciarah draws a stuttered breath. I hold Raith's mouth in the pooling blood. He relaxes in my hold and grasps her waist. When he begins sucking the blood, I drop to my knees, breathing hard.

Blade bursts into the room. I shake my head in warning, and say, "Hand me the letter opener on the desk."

Blade rushes to the desk. An instant later, he slaps the handle of the letter opener into my open palm. By now, Raith is sucking hard. Just as I thought, it's been too long since he's fed.

I grab his right hand and cut the vein in his wrist. He grunts but doesn't stop drinking. I press his bleeding wrist against Ciarah's mouth. After a second, she thrashes her head aside and loses contact with Raith's wrist.

"Blade," I call.

Blade grabs her head and holds it still as I force the bleeding wrist against her blood-smeared lips. She grimaces, but closes her mouth around the wound. I shift my attention to Raith. He has sunk his fangs into her abdomen. The wound no longer gushes blood. I release Ciarah and straighten.

Now we wait to see if Raith saves her...or kills her.

TWENTY-TWO

Raith

THERE IS A FINE LINE BETWEEN HEAVEN AND HELL... love and hate. Heaven and hell are often one and the same, as love and hate are two sides of the same coin. Too often, love leads to hate.

Then we lose control.

The sweet, thick blood that slides down my throat sets my lust on fire and feeds the fury that lives so close to the surface. This moment is the sweetest of hells I can imagine.

Ciarah has never died by our hands. What will happen if I drain her? Take all her life force? Will that end the torture? Perhaps that would give her the strength to stop seeking us —me—out.

She tastes so good, as good as I remember. Perhaps even better. I feel her life force stirring. There is only her and I, and our blood.

Yes.

Only us.

She draws harder on my wrist. Anyone else, I would fear changing them into a creature without a heart, but Ciarah can't be changed.

I suck harder.

She sucks harder.

Lust streaks through me. My cock hardens. I smell her desire, taste her need. Memory rises of her on the floor on all fours, my grip tight on her hair as I take her from behind while my fangs are buried in her neck.

"More," she pants.

I draw harder—drive harder into her channel.

"Yes," she whispers in a hoarse voice. "I need more."

I need more.

She always needs more.

Maybe it will be her who drains me.

TWENTY-THREE

Leilah

WHAT IS THE MAGIC LIQUID SLIDING DOWN MY throat? Nothing ever tasted so sweet. The pain that permeates every fiber of my body is ebbing, but the ache in my heart hovers close to the surface. Still, with each beat of my heart, I care less and less about anything except the sweet nectar.

Strong fingers squeeze my waist. Cool air washes over my skin and gooseflesh raises on my arms. There's something familiar in the fingers that tighten on my flesh. I breathe deeply and swallow more of the magic fluid. What is that scent? Male —yes. But, also something else… Sandalwood?

The mouth pressing my flesh is full and warm, conveying a need that pulls forth an answering desire that staggers. I drink greedily. I can't get enough. More. I need so much that I want to drown in this need. Nothing else matters. I want—*need*—to drink more. Need to be touched by those long fingers. Need to feel that mouth on all of me. Everywhere.

That mouth…so familiar.

I stare into a canyon.

Overhead, a hawk screams. A cool evening breeze wafts across my warm flesh. Those familiar hands span my waist from behind, then slide around as strong arms pull me against a muscular body. That mouth so close to my neck. I shiver. Need rises. Not just to have his arms around me, or to have him inside me, but to warm his cold heart. I'm not certain he's ever felt the joy of warmth.

His need, hard and demanding, presses into my ass. I sigh and he growls low in response. The hawk cries again. The scream pierces my ears. I wince. The cry grows louder. Fear clenches my belly. I've never felt fear while with him. The cry grows louder. The sound isn't a bird's cry, but a scream. A woman's scream.

My scream.

I bolt upright, heart pounding. The room wavers, then snaps into focus. Ethan and Blade stand over me. What the hell? Except for the collar of Ethan's shirt, he's shirtless and blood stains his jeans. I'm half laying on a leather couch. Raith kneels on the floor beside the couch. I gasp at sight of my ripped shirt drenched in blood. I jerk my gaze to Raith. The front of his white shirt is stained with blood. The tips of his fangs indent his full bottom lip. I've never allowed a vampire to feed on me. I've never considered the possibility. The idea that Raith took that liberty without my permission is paramount to rape.

"How dare you?" I say in a hoarse voice.

I kick him hard with the heel of my foot and he tumbles onto his ass.

He looks at Ethan. "No good deed goes unpunished."

"Good deed?" I repeat. "You have one hell of an ego."

"Leilah," Ethan cuts in, "he saved your life."

"What—"

Memory slams into me. The spear. My belly. My mind registers the bloody, broken spear lying on the carpet a few feet away. Heart pounding, I look down at my belly where the wound should have been. I run my fingers over the spot where the spear pierced my stomach. Smooth as a baby's bottom.

I lift my gaze to Raith. "I didn't know that a vampire feeding could heal."

"It can't." He shoves to his feet.

I look in confusion to Ethan and Blade.

"Raith healed the puncture by feeding on you," Blade says. "But it was you drinking his blood that healed the internal injuries."

I stare. Did I hear right?

"I drank his blood?" I whisper.

"You're welcome."

I wince at the sarcasm in Raith's voice and, in the instant before he turns away, I glimpse the thin line of his mouth. He crosses to the large mahogany desk located near the left wall and sits in the chair behind the desk.

"How much did I drink?" I try to control my racing pulse.

"Not enough to be turned," Blade says.

I'm not feeling anything strange. In fact, for someone who's just been skewered by a spear, I'm feeling pretty damn good. I'm almost...relaxed, and I feel oddly safe—despite my racing heart.

I shift my gaze to Raith. "Thank you."

His eyes don't shift from Ethan. "What happened?"

I'm not one to embarrass easily, but my cheeks heat at the obvious rebuff. He's angry with me. Because I kicked him?

Blade takes two steps and sits on the couch beside me, heedless of the blood that slicks the leather. "You sure you're all right?" he asks.

His smooth British accent usually makes everything he says sound sinful. This time, however, it's the concern in his voice that causes the insides of my miraculously healed stomach to gel. He actually sounds like he cares—a lot. My cheeks warm, again, not with embarrassment, but due to the intensity of his gaze.

I scoot backward toward the couch arm so that I can pull my legs up and swing my feet onto the floor. I stand. To my surprise, my legs are steady. I feel as if I could run a marathon.

"I seem no worse for wear," I say.

"Is someone going to tell me what happened?" Raith demands.

I want to tell him to go to hell, but Ethan says, "Someone used magic to pull a spear from the wall and…"

My stomach somersaults at the roiling cloud of emotions in the dragon's eyes. Fuzzy images jumble in my brain and I recall strong arms around me and the shwoosh of powerful wings taking flight.

"You brought me here," I say. He'd unfurled his wings and I'd missed the whole thing. God, that must have been a majestic sight.

A corner of his mouth lifts in a tiny smile. "The hospital was too far away."

And they don't have any vampires on staff, I mentally add, but say, "I need to thank you, too."

My gaze catches on the spear. I take three steps to where it lies and pick it up. The sigil on my hand warms.

Blade comes to his feet. "Put it down, Leilah."

Before I can reply, Raith is at my side and knocks the spear from my hand. The shaft hits a shelf with a loud crack and splinters.

"Do you know even the most basic rules of magic?" he demands in a voice so cold, I shiver.

I frown. "What are you talking about?"

"You could have triggered any magic remaining in the wood."

I'm startled at the hurt that stabs. Then anger boils over. "Why the fuck did you save me when you clearly hate me?"

"He doesn't hate you," Ethan says.

Raith snorts. "This isn't about you, Ms. Crowe."

He starts to turn away. I grab his arm and swing him around to face me. "The hell it isn't. You don't know me, but you've decided you don't like me. Maybe you really believe Grams was a dark witch, and the apple doesn't fall far from the tree. I can live with that."

Blade surges to his feet. "Leilah—"

I cut him off with a harsh laugh, my gaze still locked on Raith. "It's not like it's the first time someone hates me. But I'll respect you a lot more if you're honest about your feelings."

Raith's eyes darken and awareness reminds me that this vampire has a big secret.

"I know you all too well, Ms. Crowe," he says, and I feel as if he's punched me in the stomach.

He really believes I'm…bad. I'm struck with the memory of calling up a dark ball of energy at Grams' house to fight the green demon. The energy was eerily similar to the Shadow husks. Obsidian wisps of energy tangled with themselves. Raith pulls free and I fall back a pace.

"Blade, get the spear out of here and have it analyzed," he orders.

Blade takes three steps and reaches my side. "After I've seen Leilah safely back to her dormitory."

Raith's mouth thins, but he gives a curt nod. "She's to stay in her dorm for the remainder of the day." He turns and heads for the door.

I draw a sharp breath.

"Raith," Ethan begins.

I fist my hands at my sides. "I will not be a prisoner—"

Raith whirls, those vampire eyes swirling with emotion so hot that the room tilts around me. "You will do exactly as I say, Ms. Crowe, or I will have you sealed in your room. *Indefinitely.*"

An unexpected image flashes of me locked in the room—with him. Lust wars with fury. The sigil on my hand heats.

His gaze flicks to the sigil then back to my face. "If one sigil can't keep you in check, I'll have Ethan put one on the other hand."

I take a step toward the vampire and Blade steps in front of me.

"He's right," Blade says. "We need time to find out who tried to kill you."

I blink. *Someone tried to kill me.*

Raith turns and strides toward the door. I stare, torn between wanting to throw some kind of spell—any kind of spell—at him, and confusion. Of course, anger wins out, and I say loud enough for him to hear, "I can't leave before I apologize to Mr. Stick-Up-His-Ass for getting his couch bloody."

Raith stiffens, hand on the doorknob of the open door. In the next instant, he steps through the doorway and the door clicks shut with a finality that startles me.

TWENTY-FOUR

Ethan

Five minutes later, I nod at Rebecca, Raith's assistant who's seated at her desk outside his private chambers, then enter his room without knocking. "What the hell was that?" I demand.

Raith looks up from the document lying before him on his desk.

I've known Raith far too long to get angry over his typically cold and calculating manner. But his *laissez-faire* attitude after Leilah's near death—and his willingness to let her die—kindle my fire almost as violently as did the attempt on her life.

"Don't think I won't make good on my threat," I say.

"Leilah is alive," he says, unperturbed.

"No thanks to you," I snap.

His brows rise. "It was my blood that saved her."

I stare for half a dozen heartbeats, as much out of the need to gain control over my temper as shock. "Would you have really let her die?"

With a deep sigh, he leans back in his chair. "Think about the last forty years," he says.

"You mean the years we spent mourning her, then fighting a war, then trying to protect Margidda from The Shadows?" I say.

He nods. "We've been focused, calm, content, even."

"Content?" I snort. "We haven't seen Caleb and Matthias in decades. Lie to yourself all you want, but I see the strain in you."

Anger flashes in his eyes. "Nothing compared to the strain of having them in our lives."

I stare, this time in complete shock. Only days ago, I was contemplating how I might have Ciarah more to myself if Caleb and Matthias weren't here. Can I really be angry with Raith for being honest about how much easier our lives are without them? Is it possible that the issue is more than just not wanting the others in his life?

"You don't love her anymore," I whisper.

Something flickers in his eyes.

"You can't even successfully lie to yourself," I say.

"Love and hate are two sides of the same coin," he replies.

"What the hell has gotten into you?" I begin, then his words slam into memory.

Ciarah cut out my heart forty years ago.

Why hadn't I seen it before?

Forty years have passed, and I still don't know exactly what happened the day Ciarah put a knife through Raith's heart.

Ciarah's grandmother owned a popular bakery in Chicago's Latino district. That got Ciarah noticed by John Cordero. Her grandparents immigrated to the US from Greece, and their only daughter married a young Cuban bookkeeper who helped run the bakery. With jet black hair that brushed her waist, olive skin worthy of the gods, and emerald eyes, Ciarah was as much of a beauty as she is now.

But that beauty proved her undoing. Try as we might, we couldn't convince her to stay away from John. Even if he'd intended to marry her, she would have been miserable inside of a year. Men like John know only how to conquer. But, like most women, she foolishly thought she could control the mob boss. As a result, Raith nearly died by her hand, and she *had* died, shot by John. Then died in Caleb's arms.

Raith had been too weak to save her. I often wondered if Caleb never forgave him for that. No one was surprised when Caleb disappeared. A wolf licks its wounds in private. What surprised us was that he never returned. Just before The Shadow attack, Matthias went looking for Caleb and also disappeared.

"You haven't forgiven her for her relationship with Cordero," I say.

"Her *relationship* with Cordero?" Raith repeats in a deadly cold voice. "She put a stake through my heart and left me there for Cordero to find."

"She didn't—"

"She did," he snarled.

"We have known Ciarah for millennia," I say. "She has never truly done anything to hurt us."

"You're the one lying to yourself," he says. "People change."

I give a slow nod. "Yes, they do." I start to turn, then stop and add, "If any harm comes to her as a result of your actions— or inaction—I'll make what she did to you seem like love play." Without another word, I stride from the room.

TWENTY-FIVE

Leilah

Heads turn as Blade and I walk across campus. He has given me his shirt, which hangs down far enough to cover most of the blood stains on my pants, and his jacket. Of course, Blade is left in a tank top. The temperature can't be above thirty-five but, being kin to nature, fae aren't easily touched by the elements. He has stuffed his hands in his jeans' pockets but, otherwise, gives no outward indication he feels the cold.

Female passersby—and a couple males, I notice—openly stare at Blade. And why not? The damned tank top lays bare his muscled arms and emphasizes a taut torso that I could probably bounce a quarter off. Oddly, bouncing quarters isn't what I want to do. I want to wrap my arms around him, press an ear to his hard chest and count the beats of his heart. Does he agree with Raith? Does he believe I'm no good? I can still hear the quiet click of the door when Raith left. Why did they bring me here? That obsidian energy ball I called forth to fight the green demon. Obsidian. I'd never called forth energy that dark.

"Leilah."

I start and snap my eyes up to Blade's. He lifts a brow and

my heart jumps. God, did he read my mind? "What happened back there?" I blurt, then inwardly wince. *Great cover, Leilah.*

"Raith saved your life," he replies.

"I'm not in the habit of drinking blood. How did he get me to do it?"

Blade gives me a sideways glance. "There's no shame in liking it."

I flush. "That's not what I asked."

"Vampire blood is…good stuff," he says.

I stare. "You drank his blood?" I wasn't sure whether to be disgusted or fascinated.

"Drinking from female vampires is just as pleasurable," he says.

Three twenty-something girls pass, their eyes glued to Blade's chest. His eyes remain fixed on the path ahead and I find I'm a little surprised. He clearly finds me attractive. Why not them? No way he can have any real feelings for me. A wave of self-consciousness washes over me and I suddenly feel like that starry-eyed seventeen-year-old girl who fell in love with the local bad boy she'd met on the streets. That love affair had been doomed from the start. Never mind Alec was ten years older than me, and that my commitment issues set the relationship on a path to crash and burn. Which it did in spectacular style when I bound him with magic to our bed and left him there.

"Who might want to kill you?" Blade asks.

I grimace. "What, no sweet talk before you ask a girl who hates her enough to kill her?"

His mouth twitches in amusement. "We could have dinner and discuss the matter. I promise to ply you with lots of wine and tell you how beautiful you are before we get down to business."

Something in the way he says *get down to business* sends a shiver down my arms. "I'm serious," I manage in a level voice.

"Hmm," he intones.

"What about that girl—what's her name—Hanson. Jennifer Hanson," I ask.

"Jennifer?" His amusement vanishes. "She wouldn't have the courage to make an attempt on someone's life."

"People can surprise you," I say.

"Indeed, they can."

I can't prove it, but I know he's not talking about Jennifer.

"Look, I've gotten flak from the students who believe the lies about Grams and think I'm like her. I'm not, you know."

"I know," he says in a gentle voice.

"I mean, Grams isn't like that, and neither am I."

"Will you settle for me believing you're not a black witch?" he asks. "At least for the moment?"

Before I reply, he slows, his attention on something to my left. I look and spot a girl, about fourteen or fifteen, with head bowed, seated on a bench half-hidden by sculpted bushes. Blade cups my elbow and veers toward the girl. We near her and she looks up, eyes moist and red rimmed. Has she been bullied like the thirteen-year-old? Blade's hold on my elbow tightens slightly and he brings us to a stop, then steps past me to the girl. She swipes at her eyes, clearly embarrassed, and jumps to her feet.

She starts to hurry past him, but he grasps her arm. "What's wrong, Alisha?"

Wow, he knows her name. Does he know all the students by name?

She keeps her head low. "Nothing, sir."

He gives a gentle laugh. "I'm not one of the paid instructors here. You can call me Blade. Now tell me, what's wrong?"

"Nothing," she insists, and I understand exactly what's wrong.

"It's hard being way from home, isn't it?" I say.

She looks up in surprise. "I'm not a baby."

I shake my head. "Of course not. Missing your family doesn't make you a baby. I miss mine."

Her brows furrow. "But you're old."

Blade dips his head, but I glimpse the smile on his mouth.

"That's my point," I tell her. "Age has nothing to do with missing your family. I miss mine a lot."

"Does your mom know how to cook oatmeal the way you like it, too?"

Bittersweet sorrow squeezes my heart at the memory of Grams' soft, home baked cinnamon rolls, sure to appear on particularly gloomy days.

I smile at the girl. "I never knew my mom. Want to know who my family is?"

Alisha nods.

"My familiar. She's a pig."

Her mouth falls open. "A pig? Really? That is so cool."

I laugh. "It is. And it's me who cooks for her. She has a weakness for Chinese food."

"She's got good taste."

I lean in and whisper conspiratorially, "But Stony eats only veggie Chinese food, and I'm not allowed to eat anything with pork."

"Of course not," Alisha says with gravity. "That would be like cannibalism."

"Exactly." I release a sigh. "I miss her a lot."

Alisha touches my shoulder. "It's okay. She loves you and you'll be together soon."

I'm touched by her kindness and will away the tears that press the backs of my eyes. "When I see her, maybe I can introduce you," I say.

"I would love that." She looks up at Blade, shyness clear in her expression. "I have to get to class."

"Of course. I suggest you see Ms. Rose later on today. She is a very good person to talk to when you're feeling a little blue."

Alisha nods and gives me a tiny wave as she starts away. I sense subtle magic drift in her direction and whip my head back toward Blade.

His eyes shift to me and the tenderness in his expression knocks me off my feet. The emotion is directed at me, not the kid. But why? Because, unlike Raith, he doesn't believe I'm—

"Come on." He cups my elbow and heads toward the walkway.

"You did something," I say.

"Something?"

I snort. "You can't kid a kidder. You cast a spell on her."

"Doing something isn't the same thing as casting a spell on someone."

My dorm comes into view and I recall I'm about to be put under house arrest. "I haven't had anything to eat today," I say, then grasp his arm and add, "Stony is getting her daily order of Chinese food?"

He smiles. "Indeed, she is. I have a friend who owns a fabulous restaurant half an hour from the house. I sent him a key. He delivers twice a day and has instructions to puts the food on paper plates on the kitchen floor."

I raise my brows. "He doesn't think that's odd?"

"I suspect he thinks it's very odd," Blade says with a laugh. "But, as I said, he's a good friend. Now, what would you like to eat?"

"Burger, fries, and a beer."

His eyes light up. "I can oblige."

"Really?" I say, then realize my surprise is evident in my voice. I'm some smooth operator.

"One of the best burger joints around delivers," he says.

I narrow my eyes. "And here I thought we were going for that dinner."

His eyes darken and my breath catches. "Everything in its

time, love." The British have a way of making everything sound sexy, but sin drips off his low-spoken words.

I can't halt the lowering of my gaze to his chest. The man's chest is as sinful as his voice. And those damn arms... God have mercy. I return my attention to his face to find him staring. Well, damn. He knows exactly what I'm thinking.

I shake my head. "Seems I forgot who I'm talking to."

His brows lift in surprise. "Who might that be?"

"The lollipop man."

He blinks, then begins to laugh—hard. We reach the dormitory and he pulls the door open for me. I glance left, toward the trees that hide the wall, and consider making a run for it.

His eyes sparkle. "I'll give you a head start."

I blink. "What?"

"What do you say to a twenty-foot lead?"

"Then, what, you'll catch me?"

He steps a hair closer, but it feels as if he's practically pressed against my body. Or is that wishful thinking?

"I will, indeed, catch you," he murmurs.

Something jumps to life in me. I feel as if I'm the prey and the hunter at the same time, and the thrill that goes through me is palpable. I'm tempted to try just to see what he'll do.

"If I reach the wall, will you let me go?"

I read the challenge in his eyes.

"You won't reach the wall."

Damn, my feet itch to try him out.

"I'm pretty fast," I say.

"I should hope so," he drawls. "Otherwise, it wouldn't be any fun."

Fun. He makes even that word sound dirty.

His gaze drops and I realize he's looking at my blood-stained jeans.

His mouth hardens. "Let's get you inside." He motions with a nod.

I sigh and precede him through the doorway. He falls into step alongside me as we cross the expansive foyer and head up the stairs. We ascend in silence until we reach my room.

When he opens the door and steps aside, I say, "I have no intention of staying locked inside this room."

His expression softens. "I know."

He cups my elbow and urges me into the room. I pull his coat off as I whirl to face him, then thrust the coat toward him. His mouth twitches in amusement, as he takes the coat. I try to ignore the flex of muscle as he shrugs into the leather.

He grasps the door handle and says, as he's pulling the door shut, "I'll have the burger and fries sent up once they arrive." I take a step toward him as the door clicks shut in my face.

An instant later, I feel the spell that turns my room into a prison.

TWENTY-SIX

Blade

FURY BOILS MY BLOOD AS I STRIDE THE WALKWAY that parallels Penncarrow Hall. When I discover who tried to kill Leilah, I will bury him to his neck and set the wood demons on him. My phone buzzes. I pull it from my jacket pocket. Josephine's name flashes on the screen. Damn, I haven't spoken with Jo since Leilah arrived and I have no time now. I decline the call and drop the phone into my pocket as I round the corner of Penncarrow Hall. I nearly run headlong into Chelsea Nightlow. We both stop short and I seize her arms to keep her from falling. Her head snaps up, eyes wide.

"Sorry, Chelsea," I say.

Her brow furrows. "Are you all right?"

Chelsea is only fifteen, a slip of a girl with strong mage powers, and even stronger empathic abilities.

I release her. "I'm fine."

"You've got a lot on your plate," she whispers.

I close my thoughts and smile. "Such is the way of life."

She studies me, clearly intent in reading my mind—something that is not allowed.

Although she's a High Potential, her affiliation with House

Nightlow concerns me. They aren't members of the religious guild, but they are strong supporters and are deeply religious. In her youth, Lady Nightlow avoided an Academy draft by attending religious school. At fifteen, she spoke passionately in favor of the Hell Gates remaining locked and was offered a position among Margidda's leaders.

I'd seen her speech and had half expected her to come to fisticuffs with Jess Santillana, who'd argued for opening the gates so the souls of loved ones who had paid their karmic debts could ascended from Hell. Lady Nightlow countered that anyone who tried to open the Hell Gates must be found guilty of treason. A crime on par with consorting with Shadows.

I'm not certain her daughter inherited Lady Nightlow's passion, a passion that sometimes crossed over into fanaticism. I have seen no fanaticism in Chelsea, but then, I have never seen Chelsea in a situation where fanaticism might be evoked. I hope I never do.

Raith emerges from between Penncarrow and Middlewich Halls. Chelsea casts a quick glance his way, then continues down the walkway.

Raith reaches my side and demands, "Why are you still here?"

"After what just happened in your office, I'm not leaving The Academy anytime soon," I shoot back.

"Don't make the same mistake we always do and allow Ciarah to rule our lives," he says.

"What the devil are you talking about? Someone nearly killed her."

"Exactly," he says. "You need to figure out the magic used on that spear."

"Of course. By the way, I looked into the Thol'guk that showed up at Miriam Crowe's house the other night. Someone called it from the underworld."

Raith scowls. "Of course, someone called it from the underworld."

"Don't be an ass," I say. "The magic was fresh. Someone sent the creature to kill Leilah."

"You can't be sure of that."

"I said, don't be an ass. The attempt on her life today is the second attempt. How the bloody hell did her attacker get past Ethan's protection spell in that sigil—never mind his fire?"

Raith's eyes flash. "Whoever it is, is using some powerful dark magic. I want to know how that's possible on Academy grounds." His gaze shifts past me and his mouth thins.

"Gentlemen," Olympia says behind me.

Bollocks.

A silent promise to continue our conversation later passes between Raith and I before I turn toward the Grand Witch. She stops beside us and her assistant, Franklin, halts behind her. Her silver gown shimmers as she extends a ring bedecked hand toward me.

With a viper like Olympia, it's wise to keep her sated. "You grace us with your presence," I imbue my words with the seduction I know she loves. It's a damn good thing I ran into Raith before meeting Olympia. She would have read my anger in an instant.

She gives a soft laugh. "Please say you've changed your mind. You must teach at The Academy. After you fulfill your obligations to me, of course."

Right willingly will I fulfill my obligation to her. Then, never again will I yoke myself beneath the Grand Witch of the North. However, my smile doesn't reveal my thoughts as I caress her hand with my thumb.

"As you know, teaching is not my forte." I lift my lips in a hint of the smile that melts her every time.

Amusement lights her eyes. "You cannot resist me forever,

child," she says in a voice both cold and beautiful. "I will have you."

I know she is referring to more than my obedience, but I say nothing as she faces Raith.

"I'm running late," he says and, before she can respond, he turns and strides down the walkway.

The Grand Witch watches him for several seconds, then faces me.

"Surly fellow," I comment dryly.

"Indeed." She loops her arm through mine and leads me through the maze of paths running behind Penncarrow Hall. Her assistant follows a few discreet steps behind. "I've never understood your friendship."

This isn't the first time Olympia has tried to learn more about the connections among Raith, Ethan and me. I can't imagine her reaction if she knew Raith was one of the First. Raith hadn't been made a vampire. He'd been born a vampire.

"I don't always understand our friendship, either," I murmur.

"We haven't discussed your progress with my request," she says.

"The Zidruhin are tight-knit," I say. "They choose their high priests from those whose families have been members of the order for centuries."

"We have had spies within their ranks for centuries," she counters.

I tilt my head. "But none of our people have been invited into the inner sanctum."

"Our ancestors would have been wise to have infiltrated their ranks when The Shadows attacked in the fifth century. How can the Greek gods continue to aid Damien after he cost them that war? Spiteful creatures," she snarls. "After nine thousand years, they still hate the Atlantean pantheon and continue to sacrifice their own people for revenge."

"I don't think the Greek gods consider dead Margiddians to be part of their people," I say.

She snorts. "Of course, they don't. But many Greeks died, as well. Had we paid attention to the Zidruhin then, we would control them now, and Damien would likely be dead."

I think she's oversimplifying the situation, but keep that thought to myself.

"Rumors of Damien have reached Greenland. Samayaza paid me a visit."

I look sharply at her before I can catch myself. "The fallen angel has surfaced?"

She gives a single nod. "Strange, yes?"

I don't like this one bit. "Yes," I admit. "What did he say?"

"That Damien believes he has located his demon bride and is no longer hiding."

Samayaza, the fallen angel—one of the direct Sons of God—in hiding for nearly five hundred years. I curse silently. This news could have waited until we had Ciarah settled and safe.

"What does he care if Damien has found his bride?" I ask. "The world could fall for all he cares."

She casts me a sideways glance. "I love it when you pretend to be naïve. It is so at odds with your true self."

"Damien may find his bride, but that doesn't mean he can open the Hell Gates," I reply.

"Nothing is forever," she says. "Someday, someone will break the spell and open the gates. Even Samayaza does not want that."

The opening of the Hell Gates is something none of us are prepared for.

"We must know Damien's plans," she says.

"Our men are watching the Zidruhin." A light breeze ruffles my hair as I match her sedate pace down the path.

"The strange doings at Miriam Crowe's home are harbingers of things to come."

I know she refers to Miriam's connection to The Shadows and her subsequent death. Out of deference to me, however, she will not name them in my presence. Fae hurt more deeply than most when magic scars the earth. Occasionally, the Grand Witch is almost human.

"I came across a demon in her home last night," I say.

"A demon?" she demands.

Franklin sucks in a sharp breath.

"In Miriam's home?" she whispers.

I nod. "He has been disposed of." *I think.* "Unfortunately, before I could learn his intent."

"Highly unusual," her assistant murmurs.

"Indeed." Olympia halts and turns. "Franklin, see that the demon is investigated. We must find out who conjured it."

Bloody hell, Franklin will find Stony. "Leave that to me," I say.

"There is no need for you to waste your time on such a mundane task."

"I wouldn't call Miriam Crowe practicing Shadow magic mundane."

She studies me and I keep my expression neutral. Olympia is not Grand Witch for nothing. Her ability to read a situation without resorting to magic is highly developed.

At last, she nods. "Franklin, leave the matter to Blade.

"As you wish," Franklin replies.

We resume our walk.

"I expect this new task not to interfere with our search for Damien," she says.

The investigation into the appearance of the Thol'guk at Miriam's home won't interfere, but the investigation into who tried to kill Leilah will.

"Of course not." I offer my most winning smile.

She narrows her eyes. "Do not be deceived into believing I am always moved by a pretty face."

"On the contrary, I suspect that is never the case," I say, and mean it. The Grand Witch of the North might like male company but, in the end, nothing interferes with her goals.

She faces forward again, her expression grim. "It is my fault we do not have the answers we need. I should have been watching the Zidruhin these last fifty years."

I'm struck by her return to the subject of the Zidruhin. Olympia will protect her position, and she's given to dramatics, but only to a point. Might she be right in worrying about the rumors that Damien has located his bride? Or might she have a hidden agenda behind these new machinations?

"Nothing from Zedkeil on Miriam Crowe's death?" she asks.

I wince inwardly. Since Ciarah's arrival, I had let slip most of my duties, with keeping an eye on Zedkeil being at the top of that list. The angel might have agreed to work with us to discover how far Miriam Crowe got in her dark magic and how she managed to kill herself, but angels aren't known for keeping their end of a bargain. Which made me suspicious of his offer of help.

With the Morning Star trapped in Hell, he has been unable to make mayhem. Yet demons are gaining unaccountable power, particularly since the recent Shadow War. Hence, I suspect, the reason the angels are looking closely at anything that might empower evil. A high white witch suddenly practicing Shadow magic qualifies.

"I haven't spoken with him in a week," I lie. It's been closer to two weeks. "I'll contact him."

"See that you do—immediately," Olympia replies. "Then report to me right away. I hope his examination of Miriam's house is more revealing than my own."

"You've been to the house?" I ask.

"The first night I arrived." She looks up at me. "You did not honestly think I would wait upon your convenience to escort me?"

I dip my head in a slight bow. "Of course not. Forgive me for not escorting you. You found nothing, then?"

"Not the tiniest trace of remains. As for Shadows, thankfully, the husks you captured seem to be all that is left of what she used. "

It's a relief that her investigation confirms ours.

"I also assume you have heard nothing from Abaddon?" she asks.

"The usual," I say. "Those in the underworld might practice magic illegally, but even they have a code that doesn't tolerate dark magic."

"By 'the usual,' I assume you mean things like Leilah Crowe selling false identifications?"

I keep a neutral expression. "Yes."

"I want Leilah Crowe watched."

I look sharply at her. "We cannot condemn Leilah for her grandmother's wrongdoings."

Olympia lifts her chin. "We are not condemning her. But neither are we naïve. When was the last time you heard of a High White Witch turning to The Shadows?"

I can't tell her the truth, for that would give Olympia more power in my life than is wise, but I've heard of such a thing once, in Mesopotamia. Even now, after all these millennia, I dare not speak the witch's name. The Grand Witch wouldn't know her. No one who hasn't lived as long as Raith, Ethan, Caleb, Matthias and I would know her. But the ancient witch was as powerful a witch as any I have ever known. She was caught dabbling with Shadows and was burned to death. Thankfully, I wasn't present, but I understand that her screams and the curses she spat at her killers were heard centuries after she died.

"It doesn't matter," I say. "We do not visit the sins of the parents upon the children. We are not the god of the angels."

"Four names preceded Leilah's, and the wall named her as part of all four clans," Olympia says. "This, after her grandmother died while consorting with Shadows."

So much for Olympia's humanity. Four of Leila's names from previous incarnations—especially one as old as Ciarah—shocked me. In all the thousands of years that Ciarah has passed in and out of our lives, we have kept secret our connection to her and, until fairly recently, our connection to one another. We wondered what the consequences might be if the wrong person discovered that beings as ancient as we five were bound to one woman. The Grand Witch of the North is a perfect example of the *wrong person*.

"Have you consulted an oracle?" I ask.

She shakes her head. "I have yet to decide who I might trust."

That is not a good sign. "I sense no evil in Leilah Crowe."

"Neither do I. But then, I was completely unaware Miriam was practicing Shadow magic."

"The Stone would never name a High Potential who practiced dark arts," I say.

"There is only one thing in life that is unchangeable, Blade." Olympia tilts her head and makes eye contact with me. "Nothing stays the same forever."

We reach the southern edge of the garden and the scrape of a boot on the rocky path announces a newcomer. Olympia and I turn to find the new Headmaster, Domini, approaching. There's something about that man that bothers me. His eyes lock onto mine and I realize he knows about the attempt on Leilah's life.

He stops in front of us. "I just learned of the attempt on Ms. Crowe's life. I was on my way to her dormitory."

Franklin gasps in unison with Olympia's, "A murder attempt?" Her eyes snap onto my face.

"Ms. Crowe is fine," I say.

"Why didn't you tell me?" the Grand Witch demands, but before I can answer, she demands, "What happened?"

"She was in Ethan's martial arts class when a spear was yanked from the wall and thrown at her," Domini says.

"Who is the culprit?"

I shake my head. "We don't know. Magic was used. We have yet to discover who cast the spell."

Her mouth thins into a hard line. "In all the Illumina Academies' years of existence, this has never happened in *any* school."

"I know," I say.

"I have our Watchmen investigating the crime scene," Domini says. "I will want to speak with Ms. Crowe, as will the Watchmen Commander."

"Ethan and I are conducting an investigation, as well," I say.

Olympia frowns. "Blade—"

"I must insist," I say before she can tell me no. "You can well imagine how Ethan feels with one of his students attacked in his own classroom. As you said, Grand Witch, this has never before happened. Our students have always been completely safe at The Academy. This attempt on Ms. Crowe's life must be met with swift, hard justice."

Olympia purses her lips. "I expect you both to report to me upon finding any information."

"Of course," Domini says, and I'm surprised to read genuine worry in his eyes. Maybe the guy is all right, after all.

She begins walking and Domini and I fall in on each side of her, with her assistant close behind.

"Domini, we must implement a spell that protects our students." Her attention shifts to me. "Blade, I find this attack too coincidental given her grandmother was consorting with Shadows before she died."

"I do, as well," I say."

"Look into the matter at Miriam's home immediately. I have yet to receive information from Raith concerning the Watchmen's investigation into Miriam's death. Franklin?"

Her slim assistant steps forward. He's a strange man, his face so hard to read it might as well have been carved in marble. "Yes, Grand Witch?"

"Retrieve the Crowe investigation report from Raith. I've asked him twice, and I'll wait no longer."

"Yes, Grand Witch," the young man replies.

When he doesn't move, Olympia's already low voice deepens, "Now."

He spins smartly on his heel and heads down the path.

Olympia faces Domini. "I am sorry that you are walking into this... There are no words."

His smile contains the same deadly charm as my own. "No need to apologize. No one could have foreseen this."

Her eyes darken. So, the Grand Witch of the North finds the headmaster attractive. He's a good century younger than she... or, at least, I think so. Perhaps that's what bothers me. He's a bit too perfect. Too accomplished. Too appealing...and he's not even Fae.

Olympia gives a small smile and I seize the opportunity to say, "If you will excuse me, I am going to have a look at the sparring room."

Her eyes snap onto me and she's all business. "Any news at all, Blade..."

"Of course." I hurry away.

When I step from the garden into the center of the campus, my phone buzzes with an incoming text. I pull my phone from my pocket and read, *See me. Now.*

I growl.

Raith.

TWENTY-SEVEN

Leilah

I'M UP AT DAWN, ALREADY CLAUSTROPHOBIC AFTER spending less that twenty-four hours locked in my room. At least, Stony is safe—and she didn't really leave me, after all. I miss her comforting snore, but I'm relieved she's at Grams' house. I can imagine all the fun she'll have, lazing about and eating Chinese food all day. She's probably going to hope I never return from school. At least, with Stony in the shop, demons will think twice about entering the house.

I pace my room. I'm not used to being this sedentary. I pause and glance at the desk where my useless phone sits. If I could get a signal, I could, at least, distract myself with something on Netflix. I growl and pace again. The Academy doesn't have to bother with a jammer. There's just no signal out here. Nothing to distract me from wondering who tried to kill me and why. Almost more unsettling is wondering exactly what happened in Raith's office yesterday.

I still can't fathom the idea of drinking Raith's blood...or him drinking mine. Sharing blood with a vampire is highly personal. They might drink from willing—or unwilling—

donors, but they seldom share their own blood with anyone except those they care for.

I snort. There is just no fucking way Mr. Greek God Asshole cares for me. Ethan took me to Raith because I would have died, otherwise. Still, I haven't been able to shake the feeling that a lot more happened when I was dying than *The Three* have confessed. I'm ashamed to admit that I haven't been able to get them off my mind—Raith, in particular.

Last night, I didn't sleep as well as I usually do. Vague images of a dark-haired man too much like him plagued me. The murky image is replaced with Raith's dark hair curling around the nape of his neck. Fuck, what am I doing? There's only one explanation for the attraction—yeah, it's an attraction, as much as I hate to admit it: vampire tricks. Vampires are naturals at manipulating pheromones. And it doesn't hurt that he looks like a god. But personality and good character overrule looks. Period. *Right?*

I shake my head. Forget Raith. Concentrate on figuring out who wants me dead. I've never been one to run away from conflict, but nearly dying has me spooked. As far as the students are concerned, I'm the granddaughter of a black witch who died practicing Shadow magic. Yeah, that hurts. It hurts like a bitch. But I can't blame them for hating and fearing me. They can't know they're wrong. If they were right, I should be shunned. But killed? I stop. If the Grand Witch believes Grams is guilty of the crime, she must not love that Grams' granddaughter has been named a High Potential.

"Goddammit, Grams. What the hell were you doing?"

And where is your body?

An intense sorrow stabs. I can't even visit her remains. If I didn't know better, I would almost think that Grams is still punishing me.

Can a spirit be called from the dead when there is no body on the earthly plane? Were there any pieces of flesh, bone...

blood? I wish I'd asked for details. Even if I could, do I want to call her from the dead? Magic dances along the hairs of my arms. The sigil heats and the magic evaporates with a zap.

"Ow," I cry, and rub my arms. "Damn you, Ethan."

I cross to the window and stare out at the burgeoning light stretching across the sky.

The Illumina is claiming that Grams died while using Shadow magic. I detected no lies when *The Three* told me she'd died while practicing dark magic, so they must believe that's the truth. That, or I'm wrong.

Or she's guilty, my inner voice says.

No fucking way.

My spidey sense isn't right a hundred percent of the time. I have to be wrong this time. But wrong about all three men? They *believe* what they told me. Including that the Shadow husks in Miss Mack's class were gathered from Grams' house.

Impossible.

Grams hated evil. She lived her whole life in the light and helped others learn white magic. Yet, *I* am perfectly at home in the dark…in the shadows. I make deals with unsavory characters who operate in the shadows. Despite my efforts, I recall a particular drug lord in Chicago who wanted a disguise that would fool the police when they came looking for him at his girlfriend's place. He'd paid me enough money to keep Stony and me in our tiny apartment for six months.

Eddy Hanks hadn't been the worst drug dealer in Chicago, not by a long shot, but he had a mean streak that would give a badger pause. He did give me pause, but I can't blame fear of him for my decision. Eddy is human, but his girlfriend is Fae. When the Fae go bad, they're akin to demons. I'd tried telling myself she was the reason I took his money, but it's a lie. I was simply weary of being two months behind in rent and fending off my landlord's sexual advances and his threats of eviction.

The money got us out of that dump. Yep, I stiffed the

bastard of a tenement owner and got Stony and I into a one-room basement apartment with a tiny fridge and a hotplate. We stayed inside the apartment that first week—no criminals, no fake IDs or disguises—and ate Chinese food, a little Mexican, and binge watched half a dozen Netflix series. When I finally took a stroll in my old neighborhood, I learned Eddy was looking for me. He liked my disguise and wanted half a dozen more for the boys in his crew. Bottom line, he wanted to make me his newest bitch.

I can't repress a grim smile. I'm good at making fake IDs and disguises; the best, really, and Eddy knew it. What he didn't know was that when pushed, I can give a badger pause, too. I regret not being there to see the look on his face when the cops busted down his door after getting an anonymous tip that the drug dealer was back at his girlfriend's place. But, although I might give a badger pause, there wasn't a chance in hell I was going to be anywhere that Fae bitch could sense me when the cops hauled her boyfriend away.

I lean my forehead against the cold widow pane. I wish I could say I turned Eddy in because he was a world class asshole, but I did it to save my and Stony's bacon. What's worse, Eddy isn't the only person outside of the law I've helped. Maybe Raith is right. Maybe I am no good. Maybe Grams wasn't any good, either. She did kick her fifteen-year-old granddaughter out onto the street.

I straighten. Did she kick me out so that she could practice Shadow magic?

A loud knock on my door brings me bolt upright in bed. It takes several heartbeats before I remember that I'd crawled back into bed just as sunlight began to reach across the sky. Sunlight now streams in through the window. The knock persists.

"All right, all right," I mutter, and jump from bed.

I cross to the door and sense the absence of magic as I open the door. I blink at the sight of a man the size of a troll, dressed in body armor, standing at my door. *Watchman.*

He informs me that he's my escort for the day while I attend classes.

I blink. "What time is it?"

"Nine," he replies.

I have a 9:30 class, but had assumed Raith would keep me incarcerated indefinitely. Hell, I'm not going to argue with good fortune.

I tell the Watchman to hold on, then close the door, quickly change my sweats for jeans and a t-shirt, grab my jacket, and rush out the door before word can arrive that Raith wants to keep me locked up. I ignore the Watchman as he falls in beside me in the hallway.

I grab a quick bagel and coffee—also ignoring the stares the Watchman elicits—then head to History class. *History.* I can't believe it. I really am in high school. I walk a little faster. The damn Watchman keeps pace alongside me without breaking a sweat.

We reach the classroom and I give the Watchman a cool look as he turns and leans against the wall outside the door, arms crossed over his broad chest. I enter the room and head for the back of the class. Stares follow my walk to the far corner desk. Apparently, everyone has heard about my near death. Popularity isn't as grand as I thought it would be.

I drop into my seat as Thomas and his sidekick, the shrew fairy Ariel, enter. Their gazes lock onto me. One look at their dark expressions and I tense. Thomas brushes past Ariel and reaches me first.

"Proud of yourself?" he hisses under his breath. Before I can ask what he's talking about, he adds, "You got Miss Mack suspended."

I blink. "She's gone?"

"There's only one way you could have succeeded in getting her out of The Academy," Ariel spits as she joins Thomas.

The other students in the room are now openly staring.

I keep my gaze glued on Ariel. "The fact Miss Mack experimented on her students had nothing to do with her getting tossed out?"

Ariel's eyes narrow.

"Look," I force a calm tone, "I didn't say anything about Miss Mack." I'm betting Blade did, though, and the knowledge elicits a strange wave of affection.

I catch sight of Fran as she enters and heads my way.

"We don't allow black magic here," Ariel says.

Black magic? That's their gambit? I should have known it wasn't my near death that has everyone whispering. I never really stood a chance of being accepted here.

Thank you, Grams. I direct the thought outward before catching myself and stifle a gasp as Thomas steps closer.

"You don't belong here. *Leave*," he hisses.

I will my suddenly thundering heart to slow, and throw up my mental armor with the command that no one, not even a loved one—especially a loved one--can penetrate the thick, turtle shell-like steel I envision as a second skin. I lift my arm and the weight of the armor is as familiar as an old friend just returned home as I drape it over my chairback. Then, slowly, I lift my eyes to Thomas. His pupils dilate and he falls back a pace before catching himself.

Fran reaches us and gives Thomas and little Ariel a dagger-filled look. "Scram," she orders.

Thomas's head snaps in her direction. He glances at me, face red, then says to her, "You'd better be careful who you associate with, Fran." He spins away and Ariel casts me a last venomous look before following him to desks near the door.

As Fran slips into the desk beside me, her expression

softens and she says, "I heard what happened in the sparring gym. Are you okay?"

"Right as rain."

"They say Ethan actually flew off with you in his arms."

"I heard that, too," I say. Not that I remember anything beyond the thwap, thwap, thwap of wings. I still regret that.

"Any idea who tried to…" Fran's voice trails off.

"Could be just about anyone."

She shivers. "That's really terrible. I'm so glad you're all right. I've never heard of anyone trying to murder someone at *any* Academy."

I hadn't, either. Fran natters on about her classes and I'm surprised by the desire to return to the solitude of my room. I glance at Thomas and Ariel. The fear in Thomas's eyes a moment ago tells me he glimpsed my armor. *Good.* Are he and Ariel capable of murder? Maybe. Do they have the ability to use magic that can't be stopped by dragon fire?

I haven't forgotten the shock and fear on Ethan's face when the spear sailed unharmed through his fire. Need yanks at my heart. I start. Uh oh. That warm, fuzzy feeling means—

I shake off the thought. I do *not* have genuine feelings for that damned dragon.

A tall, good-looking blond enters the room.

Fran glances at the guy and smiles. "I have to go. We'll talk later, okay?"

"Sure," I say.

She jumps up and hurries toward the newcomer. Halfway there, two other girls descend on him like vultures. I'm not worried about Fran, though. She'll get what she wants.

"Thomas and Ariel are after you," a voice behind me says.

I turn and watch the thirteen-year-old kid crawl out of a gap between a bookcase and the window to the left. My face softens in sympathy. This kid keeps popping up at the oddest times.

"They don't like you," he whispers. "You're a Crowe. They

say you're calling The Shadows. That you tried to wake them—you know, the husks in the classroom." Clearly warming to the subject, he slides into the seat to my left and continues, "They say you pulled The Shadows out of the crystal and ran Miss Mack out of her room in the dead of night and possessed her."

"That's some story," I mutter. The only thing that possesses that woman is desperation for a man she can't have.

The kid's thin shoulders droop. "They say a lot about me, too."

I'm curious about that, but he clams up like he's said too much, so I simply ask, "Is Miss Mack really gone?"

"Dunno."

I study him for a few seconds, then say, "Thanks for the info, but maybe you should find a seat far away from me." No point in making his apparently miserable existence any worse.

He surprises me by flashing a genuine grin. "Maybe they'll leave me alone if I'm in the company of a badass."

"Street witch," I correct.

"Even better," he says.

Creaking wood draws everyone's attention to the front of the classroom, and I tense as one of the panels in the wall opens and Headmaster Domini enters. He's wearing the Academy's formal hooded Professor robe with long, sweeping sleeves. The Academy crest embroidered on the sky blue silk stands out. The silken threads glisten as they catch the light. A few rows in front of me, Fran straightens and flips her hair. I roll my eyes. The girl really needs a hobby.

"Good morning," Domini greets us with a smile that dimples his cheek. "I'll be covering for Miss Mack today."

Several pairs of eyes flick in my direction. So, Thomas and Ariel have been busy worker bees, pinning Miss Mack's departure solidly on me. I haven't forgotten the strange occurrence when Miss Mack showed us the Shadow husks. I had thought them beautiful. No one should find Shadows beautiful. Did Grams find them beautiful? Is that how they entice a person into letting them in? Had The Shadows infected Grams? That's not possible. The Commanders drove The Shadows away. Yet, I saw the Shadow husks myself. They are beautiful.

I suddenly want to cry so badly I consider leaving. Leilah Crowe running from a room. Yeah, that would get everyone talking. They'll talk a helluva lot more if I burst into tears in class. What the fuck is wrong with me?

Returning to New York was a mistake. Letting Ethan Bordeau mark me with his sigil was an even bigger mistake. Caring about Grams' house and thinking I could have a real home and legitimacy is the mother of all big mistakes. Who am I kidding?

I hold my breath and order my body to simmer down as Domini walks to the massive mahogany desk in the front of the room.

He leans a hip against the front edge. "How many of you have heard the tale of the Demon Bride?"

"She's the Shadow Mage," a girl says.

"The most powerful mage to have existed," Ariel interjects. "So powerful and perfect that when the demigod Damien met her, he knew he had to have her."

Domini arches a brow. "He didn't just meet her, he created her."

"Created her?" A girl at the front sniffs in disdain. "A man clearly wrote *that* account."

"Perhaps." Domini shrugs. "Damien had many apprentices, but the Shadow Mage was the only one who could control his Shadows."

"And a woman clearly wrote *that*," says the blond-haired guy that Fran went after.

Muffled snickers circle the room.

"Regardless of who wrote the accounts, there is truth in

them." Domini folds his arms across his chest, his black robe pulling against his bulging biceps.

Again, Fran flips her hair.

"His equal, though?" the blond-haired guy challenges. "He's a demigod. She was mortal."

"True," Domini agrees. "But humans should not be underestimated. Was it not the sorceresses Senorn and Eledin who sealed the Hell Gates? A spell that, to this day, the demigod himself cannot break."

The room goes silent, every eye fastened to Domini, including mine. He pushes off the desk. "Perhaps, to truly understand the Shadow Mage, we must first understand Damien, the demigod of Shadows. We know that Hades left Hell and fathered Damien with a wealthy shipmaster's daughter, Aella. When Aella's father learned that his unwed daughter was pregnant, the shipmaster threw her out onto the streets. She lived a life of misery and never revealed to Damien the identity of his father."

I shift in my seat. We all know the story, but it still hits close to home for me. Getting tossed into the street hurts.

"After his mother's death, Damien met a sorcerer by the name of Falco"—Domini's eyes gleam—"who discovered Damien's powers. For years, Damien apprenticed with the sorcerer. Eventually, his father, Hades, revealed himself to Damien and granted him entrance into Hell. But it wasn't until Damien found an Atlantean sorceress of great power and strength that he knew he had met his destiny."

"Elexea," Ariel said.

Domini smiled. "Exactly. She learned to control The Shadows and became known as the Shadow Mage. Like Damien, she, too, grew up on the streets of Atlantis and, in her, Damien believed he'd found his Demon Bride."

A shiver slides down my back. I know these stories. We all know them. Damien, who created The Shadows, is responsible for the genocide of our kind. I hate him as much as everyone else does. Still, my heart goes out to the woman who felt so alone that she fell in love with the wrong man.

"What was that, Miss Crowe?" the headmaster's baritone shatters my thoughts.

I tense. I hadn't said anything...had I? As every head turns my way, I blurt, "Who really knows what happened?"

"Trust a Crowe to claim the Shadow Mage isn't evil," someone murmurs.

"That's not what I said." *Was it?*

Domini raises a hand, commanding our attention. "A true scholar retains an open mind." He glances around the room. "Who knows what happened next?"

"Archon realized the Shadow Mage was becoming too strong," the blond guy says. "He warned the Atlanteans about her."

"The kings sent an assassin to kill her." Domini winks. "We know the true fate of Atlantis, don't we?"

"Could anyone really be powerful enough to destroy an entire nation?" Fran asks.

Domini's brows raise. "The possibility boggles the brain, doesn't it?"

The hint of accent in his voice snags my attention. The sense of familiarity I experienced the first time I met him returns, but stronger.

"Too bad she didn't take Damien down with her when she sank Atlantis," a guy in the back says.

"Demigods are not easily killed," Domini says with gravity.

"If he didn't die when Atlantis was destroyed, what hope do we have of killing him?" Fran asks.

"Are you saying we should give up?" Domini asks.

Cries of "Of course not" and "Hell no" and "Fuck The Shadows," go up.

"There's your answer," Domini says. "So, why rehash a

history that we're taught from the cradle?"

"That's what I'd like to know," a guy mutters.

Domini chuckles. "It's wise to know one's enemy, right?" He walks slowly past the front desks, his robe billowing slightly. "Why does Damien want to find the Shadow Mage and make her his bride?"

"He's in love with her," Ariel says.

"Perhaps," Domini says.

"She died when Atlantis was destroyed," Thomas says.

"That is what Archon tells us," Domini says. "But let us remember that, at the time Atlantis fell, Atlanteans were no longer magicians of light. They had become power hungry, which is why Damien and the Shadow Mage flourished. The Atlanteans didn't try to kill her because they wanted to stop an evil being. They sent an assassin because they feared her."

"They didn't fear Damien?" a girl asks.

Domini lifts a brow. "Interesting, isn't it, that we have no legends from the Atlantean pantheon about them trying to destroy Damien. I suspect they feared his father, Hades, would bring war upon them if they tried to kill Damien."

"I guess that's one reason to keep the Hell Gates closed," Thomas says.

"Yes." Domini nods. "We must never allow the Hell Gates to reopen."

"It is possible to keep them closed forever?" a girl asks.

"We had better hope so," Domini says. "If Hades is ever freed, he will exact retribution on Margidda for locking him inside all these millennia. And the gods help us if he and Damien join forces with The Shadows."

I abruptly remember why Domini seems even more familiar today. The other night, when I found Grams' place, the man smoking the cigarette. I recall Headmaster Domini's office, the other day, he'd been out on the balcony smoking a cigarette. I stare. What was Headmaster Domini doing near Grams' house?

TWENTY-EIGHT

Leilah

THREE HOURS LATER, I LEAVE MY SECOND CLASS OF the day, Reaping Preparedness, the Watchman at my side. "Remember, don't get angry," Mr. Denney had said. Trust. Meditate. Sing fucking Kumbaya, if you have to. Okay, so I added the last part, but that's about what Reaping Preparedness amounts to. Oh, and, whatever you do, *don't use magic.*

Bottom line, make sure no one dies.

It takes a helluva lot more than mediation and sweet songs to keep from killing another person.

We break from the path between dorms and I slow at sight of the Grand Witch standing outside Penncarrow Hall. A skinny man hovers beside her like a vulture, her assistant, I bet. He watches my every step as I approach, and my heart is pounding when we reach them.

The Grand Witch smiles and says in her deep alto, "My dear Leilah."

The Watchman angles his head in acknowledgement to her, then steps aside as I say, "Good morning, Grand Witch." I give a slight bow, first to her, then to her over-attentive assistant.

He smiles.

"How are your studies, my dear?" she asks.

"Fine."

"Are you being treated well, child?"

"Sure," I hedge.

Her expression turns serious. "I have learned of the attempt on your life."

It hadn't occurred to me that might be why she's here.

"Are you well?"

I'm startled by the embarrassment that washes over me. I had a couple of friends in Chicago, where I'd lived for the last five years, but they seldom asked if I was all right—and never had someone of the Grand Witch's status noticed me.

"I'm fine," I say.

Two girls approach and she motions me to walk with her. Her assistant and the Watchman follow at a respectful distance.

We stroll to the large oak twenty feet from the door and she faces me. "Can you tell me what happened?"

I give her the basic rundown, which isn't much, and by the time I finish describing how even Ethan's dragon fire hadn't stopped the spear, her expression is grim.

"Only very powerful magic is unaffected by dragon fire," she says. "I don't like this, at all." She studies me for a long moment. "Have you any idea who might want to kill you?"

I want to tell her to talk to Thomas and Ariel. They're spoiled and troublesome, but murderers? If I'm honest, I'm far angrier at the possibility that they're bullying the thirteen-year-old kid.

I shrug. "Not everyone loves me, but I don't know anyone who might dislike me enough to kill me." Uncertainty niggles, and I say, "Maybe someone has tried and convicted me of practicing black magic because the Illumina convicted my grandmother of the crime. Rumors are floating around about how I practice black magic."

She gives a slow nod. "Yes, you believe our judgement against your grandmother is unjust."

It's not a question.

"You're damn right, I do. My grandmother was a very powerful *white* witch. She didn't practice black magic and she sure as hell didn't play with Shadows."

Her expression softens. "People often change. Miriam... well, she wasn't the same woman you knew all those years ago."

"You talk as if I've been gone eons. Seven years isn't that long."

"It can be an eternity, child."

The kindness in her voice makes me wish I could drop the issue. I hesitate, then ask, "Exactly how did my grandmother change so much?"

A soft light enters her eyes. "Miriam was once amongst the most law-abiding citizens in Margidda. Yet, she kept Shadows, used Shadow magic. She became secretive, reclusive."

I can't argue with that last.

"The evidence is irrefutable," she goes on. "Sadly, I saw her little these last few years. Had I made an effort to spend more time with her, perhaps I would have noticed how far she'd strayed from the light."

Strayed from the light? Oh God, don't tell me the Grand Witch of the North is a religious zealot? Whatever happened to separation of church and state? Oh, yeah, that's the American government, not the Illumina. Is this why everyone in Margidda has to be vetted through the Illumina before they can practice magic? Our leaders are getting religious?

"Are you certain you don't know the people who were named on the Stone with you?" she asks.

"No," I blurt. She's caught me off guard.

"What about your grandmother? Are they friends of hers?"

I frown. "I don't recall anyone by those names." I want to

say that it's strange that the names appeared on the Stone before mine and stranger still that I've been associated with all four clans, but it's clear she's as much in the dark about those names as I am. It's also clear she's troubled by the appearance of the names. Does she think I had something to do with the names or maybe that I'm lying? Does she, too, think I'm a dark witch?

"If you recall anything, you will let me know?" she asks.

I nod and hope my confusion doesn't show.

She waves toward the Watchman. "Stay close to your protector. I would never forgive myself if anything happened to you."

Frustration supplants my confusion.

She lifts a brow. "I have displeased you."

She read my mind. *Stupid, stupid, stupid.* Of course, she'd read my mind. She's the Grand Witch.

She laughs softly. "I am old, my dear, but not so old that I have forgotten the look of frustration from a young person who feels an older person of authority has dismissed her."

I search her gaze. "Grams and I had our differences, but she was no black witch."

"That is a hard case to make. She died while casting spells using Shadow power." Before I can reply, her eyes slide past me and I turn to see her assistant waving at her. Her gaze returns to me and she smiles. "I must go. We will talk more. Until then, you are to do as Raith commands."

I stiffen.

She laughs again. "I know. He can be a complete prig."

I blink.

Her eyes twinkle. "But he is very nice to look at. Still, it's a shame his parents taught him how to speak."

A laugh bursts from my lips. I clap a hand over my mouth. Warmth spreads across my cheeks.

"He is very good at what he does," she says. "Do as he asks, at least until we find the person who tried to kill you." She sighs. "If I do not attend to Franklin, he will have a stroke. I will see you again soon." She brushes past me and she and her assistant walk away.

I turn toward my dorm, then reconsider and veer right. I want to have a talk with Raith. The Watchman steps in my path.

I stop short and frown up at him. "What are you doing?"

He nods toward Penncarrow Hall. "You're supposed to go to your room."

I narrow my eyes. "Says who?"

"Raith."

A group of girls pass us and stare as they ascend the half dozen steps to the door. No way do I want gossip getting around that a Watchman tackled me and dragged me back to my dorm room.

I'm going to find a way out of my room and hunt down Raith. And not to talk.

TWENTY-NINE

Leilah

I LAY ON MY BED AND STARE AT THE CEILING OF MY room. A little less than a week at The Academy and I've managed to get myself imprisoned in my room—with no tree outside the window. Grams would love that.

I glance at the Excalibur sword on its rack in the closet. At least, I was able to work off a little energy this afternoon during the war games training. Ethan allowed me to spar only with him and at some distance from the other students. I should have been embarrassed by being singled out but, at this point, what difference does it make? It's clear he drew the short straw and has to protect me from flying weapons, teenage and twenty-something angst, and the occasional psychopathic Academy student who's got a hard-on for killing Crowes. On the upside, Ethan is a superb warrior, and sparring with him was the most fun I've had at The Academy. I would never tell him, but I know he went easy on me. If I'm lucky, maybe he'll continue sparring with me and I'll actually learn something in my time here.

His protection should be enough, dammit. So why am I recalling him telling Miss Mack he isn't available, and hating the mystery woman who holds his affection? His attitude during sparring had been as intense as usual, but without a hint of the dragon fire I touched that first day.

"His change of heart is not," I say with vehemence intended to drown the fear twisting like a snake inside my belly, "because he agrees with Raith that I'm a bad seed."

I sit upright. Maybe he told Miss Mack he's unavailable in order to save her feelings? Oh God, that would only mean his change of attitude toward me isn't because he has someone else. I lay back down and release a breath. Fuck, I'm acting like a lovesick teenager. If Stony were here, she would make so much fun of me.

I don't need Ethan Bordeau, Blade Tyrion or Raith Vanderkoff. The wargames are three days away. I have to admit, I'm looking forward to the games. We're supposed to train hard these next two days in preparation. Which only means more time with Ethan. An odd sense of *déjà vu* washes over me and a watery picture springs to mind filled with images that press against my consciousness like an insistent itch just out of reach. I tell myself not to reach for the picture, but it's impossible not to and the picture vanishes. The itch intensifies.

I jump from the bed, cross to the window, and gaze across the southern part of the campus. In the distance, I can just make out the bridge connecting Westchester and Rockland counties.

Think about something else, anything else other than this place.

My home. The home I won't let anyone take from me.

Who besides *The Three* and the Grand Witch know what's going on with Grams' investigation? I learned of Grams' death through the grapevine. The death of a powerful witch is big news, especially when people believe she committed suicide— and consorted with Shadows. A thought occurs. *The Three* told me there was no body, yet there has to be an ME's report to confirm suicide. Without a body, the Illumina had to call in some serious favors in high places to get the ME to sign off on a fake death certificate.

The police... I had put off contacting the police about Grams' death. Guilt stabs. Did a part of me believe that Grams might have committed suicide? I shove the thought aside. Damn. The Illumina—and *The Three*—have gotten inside my head.

I need to visit the police ASAP and get a copy of the ME's report, if there is one. Disquiet tightens my stomach. Margiddians are taught early on not to involve people without magical abilities in our business. Death, however, isn't easy to hide from the mundane world. We all know that. While the general population isn't aware of what we are, some individuals high up the food chain do know of our existence.

Grams kept me ignorant of specific connections and warned me to keep quiet about what I am. Just who up the food chain knows of Margidda? Police Chief, mayor, governor...president? How many details concerning Grams' death had the Illumina shared with those in the know? Maybe if I shake that tree, someone of interest will fall out. Once I prove Grams isn't guilty of treason, the Illumina won't be able to stop me from taking possession of the house. I'll be able to put her to rest, and squash this fucking self-doubt that's eating its way through my brain.

Pursuing that line of action is a moot point. My keepers have locked me up good and tight. There will be no crawling out my window or the window in the girl's restroom. Even if I wanted to rappel from my window to the ground, the magic surrounding my room would knock me on my ass—as it did the two times I've tried.

What kind of fucked up school is this? I've heard rumors about students who entered and never left. Were they murdered? The words of the song *Hotel California* come to mind: *'You can check in, but you can never leave.'*

A shiver snakes down my back. Is Blade right? Is Jennifer Hanson too gutless to attempt murder? She belongs to the mean-girl club, and those chicks can be pretty ruthless. Not long before Grams kicked me out, I heard of a group of white cheerleaders who beat a black girl so badly they put her in the hospital, all because the boys from the football team were flirting with her. Thankfully, the girls were arrested. At least, there's a smidgen of justice in the world.

The door handle jiggles. I whirl. I have no pending class. Does Raith intend to free me, or… The knob slowly turns. The latch disengages and the door swings open a few inches. I glance at the swords, too far away for me to reach before the door opens. Fingers curve around the edge of the door, which opens farther. Eyes peek around the door and I recognize the thirteen-year-old kid.

I blow out a loud breath. "What the hell are you doing here, kid?"

He shrugs.

"You don't know what you're doing here?"

He shakes his head.

"You'll get in trouble for being here."

He nods.

I scowl. "Get out of here."

He hesitates, then starts to back away.

A thought hits me. "Hey, how did you get past Blade's spell?"

"Easy," he replies.

"Easy, how?"

"I redirected the spell to the empty room next door."

I blink. "You're joking."

He shakes his head.

"Is Blade's magic that easy to get around?" I murmur. *Or am I just that inept?*

"No way," the kid says. "Blade's magic is pretty invincible."

"Not so invincible. A thirteen-year-old kid circumvented the spell," I say.

"I'm twelve."

I snort. "A tween. That's even worse."

He shakes his head. "I'm using Blade's magic against him."

"What do you mean?"

"The spell I used to redirect *his* spell is magic I learned from Blade. He probably didn't think anyone would use what he taught against him."

"Well, fuck a duck." I laugh. "I bet he didn't." The irony is just too damn good. "Still, you better get out of here. Blade might give you points for ingenuity. Raith won't. Not to mention, he'll force you to tell him why you're here. Did some of the other students put you up in this? They're not doing you any favors by tricking you into breaking into my room."

He shakes his head. "No one put me up to coming here. I —" He hesitates, and I realize he's embarrassed.

I groan inwardly. Don't tell me the kid has a crush on me. All I need is some lovesick tween following me around.

"I wanted to say thanks," he says.

"Thanks?" I frown. "Thanks for what?"

"For saving my life."

"What are you talking about?"

"You pushed me out of the way of that spear."

I had forgotten. He'd jumped in front of me. "That was brave, kid, but a little stupid."

His eyes drop. "It's my fault you got hurt."

"It's only your fault if you're the one who sicked the spear on me. Did you try to kill me?"

His head snaps up, eyes wide. "Oh, no. I would never do

that. It's my fault because I got in the way and you had to push me aside. That left you vulnerable."

I release a breath. "It's not your fault. The magic in the spear was very powerful. I wasn't getting out of that room"–I start to say 'alive,' but say—"unhurt," instead.

He shakes his head. "You're wrong. You used magic despite having Mr. Bordeau's sigil on your hand. If I hadn't gotten in the way, you would have beaten the spear."

I laugh. "What's your name?"

"Jonas."

"Well, Jonas. If nothing else, you're great for my ego." I study him. "You said you redirected Blade's magic. Does that mean I can get out of here?"

His face brightens. "Oh, yeah."

I cross to the door. He takes an uncertain step back when I clap a hand on his shoulder and step over the threshold. "Jonas, you may regret this, but you're my new best friend."

THIRTY

Leilah

I SEND JONAS BACK TO HIS ROOM WITH THE PROMISE that I won't rat him out to Blade, then quickly draw the curtains and arranged pillows beneath the blanket to look like a sleeping body.

An hour later, I get out of a cab in front of the White Plains police station. Pound Ridge doesn't list any homicide detectives, so I'm figuring the bigger city of White Plains handled Grams' case. They ruled the case suicide, but a detective had to investigate to come to that conclusion. I enter the station and go through security, then approach the front desk where a balding police officer sits.

He looks up from some paperwork and says, "Can I help you?"

"I would like to speak to the detective investigating my grandmother's death," I say.

Surprise flickers in his eyes, but he says in a neutral voice, "Who's your grandmother?"

"Miriam Crowe."

This time, the surprise in his eyes is almost palpable. "Hold on." He picks up the phone and says, "Lynn, do we have someone investigating the death of a Miriam Crowe?"

Someone speaks on the other end of the phone, but I can't discern the words.

"Uh huh," the cop says. "Yeah, that's what I thought." He nods as if the person on the other end of the phone can see him, then hangs up and looks at me. "Miriam Crowe's death was ruled a suicide. The case is closed."

"Does that mean the detective who investigated the case won't talk to me?"

"Detectives are too busy to spend time on cases that are already solved," he says.

"Who's the detective?"

"Doesn't matter," he grunts.

"I'm her granddaughter."

"I'm sorry for your loss," he says, but I don't detect any empathy in his voice.

"Who's the detective?" I ask again.

"Like I said, it doesn't matter. Now, get going."

I nod slowly. "I bet they'll know down at the paper."

He frowns. "Paper? What paper?"

"*The Journal News, New York Times.*"

He sneers. "We don't report to the newspapers."

"They'll look into the matter for me."

I turn and get half a dozen steps before he says, "Wait a minute."

I stop and face him.

"Maybe a detective can talk to you—for a couple minutes."

Five minutes later, a tall man about fifty years old is showing me to a desk in a room that contains about half a dozen desks.

He sits in a chair behind one of the desks and I take the chair opposite him as he says, "I'm Detective Moore. What can I do for you?"

"Are you the detective who investigated my grandmother's death?"

He nods. "You're her granddaughter, Leilah Crowe? You ran away from home seven years ago."

I blink. "Ran away? Who told you that?"

"Neighbors. How did you hear of her death?"

I smile. "Neighbors."

His gaze hardens. "If you're after the estate, you have to talk to an attorney. We don't handle that."

I go cold. "If I was after her estate, I would have it. I would like to see your report."

His brows shoot up. "The White Plains Police Department isn't in the habit of sharing internal investigation reports. You can request the autopsy report from the medical examiner. There's a form on the ME's website."

I nod. "As next of kin, I have the right to see the report you gave."

"I don't know who told you that."

"It's New York state law," I reply. That's a lie—well, maybe it's not a lie, but I found no laws governing the next of kin's right to see a homicide report when I searched the web on the cab ride over.

He shrugs. "You're mistaken."

I stand. "Can I quote you to the reporter at the *New York Times*?"

His mouth thins, but he gives a nonchalant shrug. "I don't make the law."

I turn and head for the door. I reach the front entryway a minute later and push through the exterior door. A woman calls, "Ms. Crowe."

I step back and turn. A fortyish woman wearing slacks and a long-sleeved, white, button-down shirt is standing at the same door I just exited.

"Do you have a moment?" she asks.

I nod and approach her. She allows me to precede her through the door, then I follow her back down the hallway and past the desk were Detective Moore sits. The office door she opens sports a plaque that reads Sgt. Decker. I enter and she closes the door after me.

"Have a seat," she says, and sits behind the desk.

I take the chair in front of her desk.

"I'm Detective Mills. Detective Moore tells me you've asked to see the report concerning your grandmother's death," she says. "As he told you, by law, we are not required to turn over the report to you."

"Then what am I doing here?" I ask.

She leans forward, elbows on the desk. "Ms. Crowe, I understand you need closure, but, please, take my word, this is not the way to achieve it."

"Take your word? Why should I?"

"Because the details in the detective's report would dredge up more emotions than answers." She leans back in her chair. "I understand you and your grandmother were estranged."

"If you think you can make me feel guilty, don't bother. It was my grandmother who kicked me out when I was fifteen."

Her brows raise, but her eyes betray knowledge. So, the sergeant knows more than she's letting on. That's nothing new for the police. I can't blame them. Just because I operate outside the law doesn't mean I don't appreciate the law's perspective—not to mention, it isn't their laws I'm breaking. From a human perspective, I'm a straight arrow. It's not like they would believe that I make magical disguises that hide wanted criminals from their direct sight. The fact I haven't broken any human laws is moot, though. Whoever's in the know will alert the Illumina of my actions. Let's see how the Illumina likes me talking to the cops.

"I know my grandmother," I say. "She's not the kind who would commit suicide."

"You were fifteen when you left," the sergeant says. "No offense, Ms. Crowe, but teenagers don't really know their guardians. Not to mention, you've been gone seven years. People change."

"What evidence is there for suicide?" I demand.

"She was found dead in her bed with an empty bottle of sleeping pills on the nightstand."

I wonder if Detective Mills knows there was no body, or if she's merely repeating what she read on the report. "You know my grandmother was a practicing witch?" Let's see if that gets anyone's attention.

She doesn't miss a beat. "My niece practices Wicca."

"My grandmother was a bit more than a practicing Wiccan. She was a powerful psychic." Psychic abilities usually go hand in hand with powerful magic, but we're taught from childhood to explain away our powers as simply being psychic. "She wouldn't take drugs," I say. "They…alter psychic abilities."

"Ms. Crowe, people who decide to commit suicide are no longer thinking clearly. They care only about the final results."

She has me there.

"I assume the medical examiner's report will detail the drugs in her body," I say.

The sergeant shakes her head. "We found no sign of foul play. Given her age and the pills, we found no reason to order an autopsy."

That shouldn't surprise me, but it does. I underestimated the Illumina.

I need to search the house, as well as check on Stony. Still, I can't leave here empty-handed. Is it possible for me to push through Ethan's sigil and cast a truth spell on the sergeant? The sigil didn't stop me from leaving The Academy, but I suspect that the instant I try to cast a spell, the dragon's magic will light me up like a firecracker and drag my ass back. I shudder to think how much stronger the spell on my next jail cell will be.

"I believe I'll have that talk with the *New York Times*," I say.

The sergeant angles her head in ascent. "That is your right, of course."

Damn, she called my bluff. Then again, it's a thin bluff.

I stand. "Tell your bosses that an interview with the *Times* will be the least of their worries."

She rises. "I will convey your message."

I hesitate, itching to cast a truth spell on her.

The sergeant escorts me from her office and, when we reach the front, she pulls a card from her jacket pocket and writes a number on the back. She hands me the card. "Call me if you feel the need to talk. That's my private number."

I glance at the number in surprise. Private number? Cops don't usually give out their private numbers.

I meet her gaze. "I'll keep that in mind."

THIRTY-ONE

Leilah

I arrive at Grams' house forty minutes later and hurry up the front porch steps. Anticipation hums through me at the thought of seeing Stony. I miss her so much. I reach the door and sense Grams' strong wards pushing back. I wonder again how the stranger got into her house—and worse, that damned green demon.

I push through the door and call out, "Stony, I'm hooome."

Silence follows.

"Stony?" I take half a dozen steps across the foyer and enter the living room.

Furniture still lies overturned and destroyed, the destruction untouched in the room after the demon attack. Only the green goo is gone. No sign of Stony. I search the kitchen. Empty Chinese food cartons litter the floor near the rear door. Blade has kept his word and fed her, and she's been eating. So, where is she?

I return to the foyer and head upstairs. I bet she shifted into a dog or cat and climbed the stairs to one of the bedrooms. I enter my old room first and stop cold. The room is a time capsule, frozen on the day I left. My old gym sneakers lie against the wall near the small desk where I did most of my homework. Even my old chemistry textbook lays open to—I cross to the desk—yes, the page on human genome. At fifteen, I wouldn't have admitted it to my friends, but I loved the sciences.

I trace a finger across the page, then snatch my hand back. Had Grams hated me so much that she couldn't bear to enter the room long enough to clear out my things? Tears sting the corners of my eyes. I swipe at one eye. No way am I going to cry. I'm done crying over a woman who didn't want me. I whirl to leave, but halt at the unexpected surge of magic emanating from the book.

I take a faltering step back. What the fuck? I stare for a long moment. Then, slowly, I reach out with my magic. The sigil on my hand flares with a fierce heat. I snap my eyes onto the sigil. My heart begins to pound. The sigil didn't heat that quickly even when I called forth those weird shadow balls to battle the green demon.

I look back at the chemistry book, take a careful step closer and ease two fingers back onto the open page. A tingle races up my arm. I tense, but nothing bad happens. Careful to keep the book open, I lift it from the desk and examine the covers. Nothing strange there, despite the pulse of magic still emanating from the book.

Damnit, I wish Stony were here. I lower myself onto the desk chair, set the book down, then turn the next page, then the next and the next before I realize the magic is waning. Waning, but still present. I flip back to the previous page and the one before that. Yes, there's no doubt, the magic is increasing as I turn toward the front of the book.

I slip a finger between half the pages and lay them on the right side of the book. Magic fairly leaps off the page. My stomach roils. Something is wrong, very, very wrong. With shaking hands, I flip the remainder of the pages to the right so that I'm looking at the title page. Magic dances across the page in thin, translucent ribbons of black energy.

What in God's name is this?

I lift a trembling hand and tap my fingertips to the page. A shock rips through me. A shriek rends the silence and I leap to my feet, knocking the chair over. The book spins and I cry out when the textbook morphs into a leather-bound journal much like—

I gasp. It can't be. Grams kept a journal like the one now lying on my desk in place of the chem textbook. This one appears worn, but not as worn as the one Grams kept.

I force my legs to move, right the chair and, once again, sit down at the desk. I no longer sense the enchantment that had cloaked my chemistry textbook. This has to be a spell book, right? But why would Grams hide a spell book in such an elaborate fashion? She guarded her potion recipes, as they were her largest source of income, but, at the same time, she often shared her recipes with people she felt would use them wisely. I'd never known her to go to such great lengths to hide, well, anything.

My heart takes a dive. I guess Detective Mills was right. People change.

I open the book and find the words written in an ancient language I don't recognize. Disappointment stabs. I flip through the book. A quarter of the book is filled, all written in that strange language. No doubt, not a real language, but a code created by a spell. Fuck. I glance over my shoulder at the window. Orange and grey clouds streak the sky. Dusk is falling. It'll be dark soon. I took a risk coming here after I left the police station, but I had wanted badly to see Stony.

Stony.

Where the hell is that pig? I snatch up the book and head for Grams' bedroom. If Stony were here, she would have sensed what happened in my room and come running.

As suspected, she's not in Grams' room or the guest bedroom. Fear tightens my stomach. *Easy,* I tell myself. Stony is anything but helpless. She can shift at will, and she's a ferocious warrior. My heart warms when I recall how she took on the Thol'guk. She really is my best friend.

I hurry back to the kitchen and pull open the drawer where Grams always kept paper and pencil. I ignore the surge of loneliness the familiar sight elicits and pull out one of the small pads and a pencil. I jot a quick note to Stony, telling her I had been by and promising to return as soon as possible, then attach the note to the fridge with a refrigerator magnet.

THIRTY-TWO

Leilah

———

Forty minutes later, I direct my Lyft driver to pull off the road a quarter mile from The Academy. The driver does as I ask, but gives me a doubtful look as I pay him and get out in what he clearly thinks is the middle of nowhere in the dark. He pulls away and I head toward The Academy, Grams' spell book safely tucked into my jeans' waistband at my back.

I reach The Academy wall in five minutes and drop noiselessly onto the other side. It's dinnertime, so most students are in the dining hall. That's not to my advantage. The Academy doesn't treat the kids quite like public high school students, but it's far easier to pass unnoticed in a crowd. It would be just my luck to get spotted by one of *The Three* or by a damned Watchman.

I scurry through the trees, then break out onto the walkway when no one is in sight. On the walkway, I slow to a stroll. Better to appear casual than like a person trying to hide something. If I'm stopped, the worst I'll be accused of is taking a walk—well, that and breaking out of a spell-bound room.

I reach the dorm and slip inside my darkened room. If I play my cards right, I can come and go as I please and no one will be the wiser. I turn, lean against the door, and release a breath. The aroma of food wafts to me. My jailer must've left dinner on my desk and then left, thinking I was sleeping beneath the covers where I'd stuffed the pillows. I'm a little surprised that he didn't notice the spell no longer surrounds my room. Maybe Raith sent a minion to deliver the food. This arrangement might work out.

My stomach growls. The food at The Academy is excellent and I'm hungry. I push away from the door and pull my t-shirt over my head as I head for the desk. I toss the shirt onto the chair to the right of the desk as I reach for the cover of the food, then freeze.

I'm not alone.

My heart pounds. Blade's magic is supposed to keep me from leaving and prevent others—my would-be killer, for instance—from entering.

I grit my teeth and throw out my senses in an effort to draw a bead on the intruder's whereabouts. The sigil heats with unexpected intensity, but not before I realize he's to my left. I whirl, throwing my leg high for a roundhouse kick. Strong fingers seize my ankle and yank. I topple backwards onto the bed, yank my legs up, and encircle my assailant's waist. When I tighten my legs with all my might, he gives an audible woof as air rushes from his lungs.

Gotcha! I think, and twist.

He grunts and goes down, but not as I expect. His heavy body falls on me the way a one-ton bull crashes to the ground. The breath rushes out of me and I wheeze while reaching for my magic. The sigil heats to singe level and I can't halt a cry.

"If you think distracting me with your body will keep you out of trouble..."

I recognize Blade's voice and freeze.

"Well, you *might* distract me," he continues. "But trouble will still follow."

I'm suddenly aware of every hard plane of his muscled chest against my nearly bare torso. Then there's the erection that's digging into my abdomen.

"What the fuck?" My protest comes out a hoarse whisper that sounds sexy.

"My sentiments exactly," he says, though his voice doesn't hold the sensual note it usually does.

"What are you doing creeping into my room?" I demand.

"You're the one who snuck out," he replies.

I try to draw a deep breath, but he's damned heavy and is making no effort to lift his body off mine.

"You locked me in my room like a child," I growl.

"Because you refuse to act like an adult. Bloody hell, Leilah, just two days ago someone tried to kill you. If you won't take the threat seriously, I will lock you in a cage that you—or Jonas —can't escape."

"It's not his fault," I blurt.

"I have already dealt with the boy."

"Dealt with him? How?" I demand.

"That is none of your concern."

"I tricked him," I say.

"That's not his story."

"He's a good kid. He doesn't want to see me get into trouble."

"Trouble?" Blade says in a dark voice that freezes the blood in my veins. "You have no comprehension of the trouble you're in. Have you any idea how I felt when I found your room empty?"

I roll my eyes. "Sorry I pissed you off. I imagine you told Raith."

"And Ethan," he says. "We aren't playing games, Leilah."

The heat of anger flashes. "You think I'm playing games?"

"You bloody well don't understand the stakes."

"The stakes are your, Ethan's and Raith's pride," I snap.

"Foolish girl," he mutters.

In the dark, I can't discern his expression, and I'm damn glad he can't see mine, which is hot with embarrassment, but his gaze burns into me. To my knowledge, the Fae, unlike vampires, don't have a particular ability to see in the dark. I don't need eyes to see the erection that grows harder by the minute. I wonder if I might distract him. I wiggle suggestively.

"Lie still, Leilah," he growls.

I wiggle again. He sucks in a harsh breath and I know I have him. I arch my hips and grind against his hard cock. My clit tightens almost painfully. God have mercy.

"Bloody wench," Blade mutters, and pushes off me.

I lever myself onto my elbows. "I thought you were more fun than this, Blade."

"This time, the spell around your room will be invincible," he says.

I jump to my feet. "I have the right to help search for the person who tried to kill me."

He gives a low laugh that makes my stomach do somersaults. "Sorry, love, but you don't."

"I didn't come here to be locked up in a fucking room." I grab his arm. "You can bet your ass I'll find a way out."

He grabs my shoulders and shakes me—hard. "We're not going to lose you, you understand?" He adds something under his breath that sounds like, "It's too soon."

Now, I'm going crazy.

He shoves me toward the bed and says, "The last thing you want to do is to piss off Raith. You think being confined to this room is harsh… You truly get Raith's ire up and you'll wish the only thing we had done was lock you in this room."

"You're crazy," I whisper.

He snorts. "In that, we are agreed. I must let Ethan know you're home."

"Home?" I scoff, and ignore the longing the word elicits. "You call being locked in a room *home*?"

"I call being surrounded by people who love you 'home.'" The words are spoken in a level tone, but naked fear drips from his voice.

Then I understand.

"Who was she?" I ask.

"She?" he repeats.

"The woman you lost."

A heavy silence follows. Yeah, I hit pay dirt. I remind Blade of someone he loved—and lost.

"Whatever happened, this isn't the same," I say. "I can take care of myself."

"The way you took care of yourself when you nearly bled to death on Raith's couch?"

I shrug. "Everyone has a bad day."

"We will not risk you being harmed," Blade says.

"You can't keep me here indefinitely."

"Don't be too sure of that."

I let a moment of silence pass, then say, "I'm hampered by this damn sigil, and you know it."

He releases a breath. "Without it, you won't return."

"I returned today."

"Don't insult my intelligence," he says in a weary voice. "We both know that the sigil would have forced you back."

So that's how it works.

"Exactly where were you?" he asks.

"What if I promise not to run away?" I say, instead of answering his question.

Silence stretches out.

"A promise won't stop you from pulling stunts like you did today," he finally says.

"We can work something out," I say. "One thing that will

help is Stony. She can take any shape I need her to." I don't mention that she won't like it.

"The howling night pig might be a good idea," he says. "She would have to remain small. A mouse, perhaps."

"And the sigil?" I wince at the hopeful note in my voice.

He starts for the door and my heart falls.

The doorknob jiggles and he says, "It would have to be a blood pact."

Blood pact? I shiver. Blood packs are virtually invincible, and they bind the partners together for…well, life.

"That's overkill, don't you think?" I say.

"Overkill? You nearly died right in front of us."

Fucking Fae. They're too damn smart.

"Draw up the agreement," I say. "Keep it simple. You three don't own me."

His low laugh drifts to me in the shadows. "There's never been the slightest confusion on who owns who, love."

Without another word, he leaves me wondering if he has a brain tumor or something. The guy is off his gourd.

THIRTY-THREE

Blade

____

IT IS STRANGE HOW ONE FORGETS PAIN. IT'S BEEN forty years since we lost Ciarah. Her near-death two days ago frightened me. Somehow, finding her room empty frightened me even more.

I draw in a deep breath of the cold winter night air and slow my walk across campus as I pull my cellphone from my back pocket. One tap unlocks the screen, a second strikes the number two. Ethan's name appears on the screen and I press the phone to my ear.

He answers before the second ring and demands, "Have you found her?"

"She returned to her room," I reply.

"It's time we tell her the truth."

"What?" I blurt, then smile at two passing male students. I wait until I'm out of earshot then say, "You've gone mad, Ethan."

"No," his reply is calm. "She's different this time."

"Did you expect her to stay the same?"

"You know what I mean."

I do, and it frightens me. "She always dies young." Pain

flashes through me as I voice that truth and it takes all my willpower not to return to her room and make love to her until she swears not to leave again. I halt. Might that work? I picture her dark hair fanned out around her face, dark eyes locked with mine as I drive into her so deep I touch her soul.

Several beats of silence pass as I walk. Then Ethan says, "I'm afraid, too."

I jar from the image, my cock so hard I have to grit my teeth. A moment passes before I can say, "We're always afraid."

"She barely knows us," I say. "There's not a chance in hell she'll believe that we've known her for centuries. She hates Raith, and you've managed to piss her off by marking her with your sigil. As her jailer, I'm now on her shit list. We're the last people she'll believe are centuries-long lovers."

"If we tell her, she might remember something that will help us understand why we need each other," he says.

"Or we might lose her."

He gives a low, joyless laugh. "It won't be the first time."

"We need to figure out who sent the Thol'guk to her grandmother's house to kill her. That means the attack on her in your class was the second attempt on her life. Maybe the attacker isn't a student. The magic that called forth the creature couldn't have been more than minutes old when she arrived."

"Someone followed her there?" he asks.

"Has to be."

"We didn't even know she'd left," he says. "Who's watching her? Someone was there with her. Any idea who?"

"Not a clue. Rebecca is back. I'm going to take the spear to her. Maybe she can glean something about the magic used on it. I couldn't find any connection between the magic at Miriam's house and the spear. The magic used to call forth the Thol'guk was less sophisticated. But then, I'm not the expert. Rebecca is."

"It's not terribly hard to call forth a lower demon," Ethan says. "Assign a permanent guard on Leilah's room."

The urgency in his voice is a sure indication that his armor is surfacing.

I halt. I told Leilah that my spell is invincible, but the girl has proven herself resourceful. I turn and head back toward her dorm.

"How soon can you get here?" I ask.

"Twenty minutes."

"I'll be waiting in the hall outside her door." I end the call and lock my gaze onto Leilah's dormitory.

Bloody hell, what I can do to her body in twenty minutes.

Two hours later, I catch up with Raith on his walk from his afternoon class to his office. He's looking far better than he's looked in years. Leilah's blood did him good. He gives me a sideways glance and keeps walking.

"I just came from Rebecca," I say. "She said the magic used in the spear is elemental."

He frowns. "That's advanced magic."

I nod. "Maybe a dozen people on campus are capable of casting such a spell. Off the top of my head, I can easily eliminate half of them."

"Who are the remaining six?" he asks.

I rattle off a list of names—four teachers and two students.

Raith gives a single shake of his head. "What reason could any of them have for wanting to hurt Leilah?"

"I would like to say I don't know, but it's clear the students associate Leilah with her grandmother."

"Not surprising," he says. I start to reply, and he adds, "I'm not saying anyone has a right to kill her. I'm not sure that's enough for any of these kids to commit murder. Is it possible someone breached The Academy wall?"

I want to reply with an emphatic *no*, but have to say, "I don't know. The search Ethan and I made along the wall turned up no evidence that anyone—or anything—breached the wards. The attack with the Thol'guk and the spear make two attempts on her life. I have no real leads. I'll take a look at our six obvious suspects."

He glances at his watch. "Get Hamish to fill in for Ethan's afternoon classes and have him help with the investigation."

"Ethan is guarding Leilah's room," I say.

He looks sharply at me. "You didn't reinforce the spell around her room?"

"I did. But she's too damn resourceful. Ethan and I agree that someone has to keep watch on her." I wonder if Ethan is making love to her. I was a fool not to take her into my bed before they discovered she was back.

Raith stares straight ahead and walks a little faster. "We can't stop her if she wants to leave."

"Actually, we can. She's agreed to a blood pact with us."

A corner of his mouth curls upward. "I have no intention of making a blood pact with her."

"It will force her to keep her word, and we can remove Ethan's sigil from her hand. That will give her back the use of her magic." I brace for an argument, but he goes quiet. I know enough to let him think.

"She shouldn't be practicing magic," he finally says.

"The devil, you say."

"She needs to grow up," he replies.

"She's twenty-two," I say, though I know that's not what he means. "You intend to make her pay for a perceived treachery."

"It isn't perceived," he snaps. "She openly betrayed me. That has nothing to do with this situation."

"Lie to yourself, Raith, but don't insult my intelligence by lying to me."

"You and Ethan are so afraid of losing her that she's got you both wrapped around her finger."

I laugh. "I happen to like being wrapped around her finger. Don't take part in the blood pact. But, at least, be honest with yourself. I don't know what all the fuss is about. You're nearly already there. You drank her blood."

"That isn't the same."

"Drinking her blood has done you good."

He casts me a narrow-eyed look.

"You can't blame me for speaking the truth," I say.

THIRTY-FOUR

Leilah

GRAMS TAUGHT ME THAT MAGIC IS EVERYWHERE JUST waiting to be unearthed, and once a person understands that, it's a simple matter to set it free. My first memory of her telling me that, I was three and a half years old. Her voice still rings clear in my head: *"Don't let anyone tell you magic has to be compli-cated. Some is—that's necessary—but most is peeking out from its hiding place begging for us to remove it's constraints."*

Big words for a little kid, but I eventually understood. Obvi-ously, not well enough.

I've spent the last three hours since my final class staring at Grams' spell book. The desk light is the only light on in my room and shines directly on the open pages. The magic contained in the book hasn't so much as sent up the wisp of a smoke signal. I shouldn't be surprised. Grams was a tangle of contradictions—something I think she reveled in—and she probably had a big laugh at the thought of someone trying to decipher her spells after she was gone.

I would laugh, if not for the dread heavy in my stomach. Magic isn't needed to tell me this book holds the spells she was using in the end. I should hand the book over to the Illumina. A single question stops me: why hide light magic?

I stare at the foreign marks on the open pages. How do I persuade the letters to rearrange into coherent words for me? I glance at the sigil on my hand. The damn thing hasn't yet acted up. But, then, I haven't tried *real* magic. I've repeated a few incantations, requesting aid from nature spirits, with no luck. Should I try pushing through the sigil? If the spells are...not quite right, will I set off warning bells? Without my magic, I might not be able to put a halt to anything that goes wrong.

Blade said they would remove the sigil if I agree to the blood pact. He caught up with me between classes and told me we were on for tonight. I said okay, but, truth is, I'm not sure I'll go through with the rite.

I made one blood pact in my life. I was twelve; he was sixteen. Seton, the big brother I never had. With a laugh I can still hear, he finally gave into my pestering. While any blood pact is powerful, we made several large mistakes that lessened the power of the pact. I suspect Seton knew that, but said nothing.

The confusion—and desire—I experienced when Blade caught me returning to my room yesterday has dissipated and, now that I've had time to think, I'm wary of making a pact with *The Three*. I feel pretty sure that instructors—especially Blade, Ethan and Raith—don't go around making blood pacts with students, which makes me suspicious.

Blood pacts are usually created between spouses, family members, or friends who knew one another in a past life. The last possibility sends a wave of chills from my feet all the way up my body and makes my scalp tighten like sun-dried leather.

This is bad. *Very bad.*

"Fudge," I mutter.

I rarely have such an extreme physical reaction, but, when I do, it means something big—something very big. Is it possible I knew these men in another life? I think back to the night I met Blade, two days after I'd arrived in New York. He sat down at my table, as casually as he had the night Ethan put the sigil on my arm, and flirted shamelessly. Blade always flirts shamelessly, but he never follows through with me—and Blade is capable of following through.

The night we met, we talked into the wee hours of the night. I found him incredibly attractive, but was oddly relieved when he didn't ask me to go home with him. He put me in a cab and paid the driver to take me home. I remember wondering if the world knew what a gentleman he is.

But he really isn't a gentleman. He's more the *'Tonight is all I have to give, baby'* sort of man rather than the *'send a woman home safely in a cab'* kind of guy. So, why was he so sweet with me?

Why does he lurk outside my dorm? He probably doesn't think I see him among the trees to the left of Penncarrow Hall. I might not have noticed him if I'd had anything to do other than watch the grass grow. Is it really possible we knew each other in another life? Maybe I knew him but not Ethan or Raith? I laugh. Raith dislikes me enough to have previously known me. Maybe I wronged him in another life. God, if that's so, then he really can hold a grudge. Vampires have a reputation for being unforgiving.

I release a breath. This last week has gotten me nothing but trouble. Raith said I could leave—if I'm willing to give up my magic. If I give up magic, I won't be in danger from The Shadows—only from criminals who have harnessed Shadow power. That's one helluva trade-off.

I look at the book. Without magic, I will never know what's in this book.

Who would I be without magic? What would I do? Get a nine to five job at some office. Party on weekends and, one day, settle down and have kids. My stomach sours. That's no life for me. I'm too old to become a James Bond agent and too young to settle for a dreary day job.

My choices are: one, wait powerless in this room, thanks to the damn sigil, until *The Three* find my would-be killer. Two, renounce magic. Three, enter into a blood pact with *The Three*. If I didn't know better, I would think they'd planned this. I sit up straight. Is that possible?

No. The stark fear on Blade and Ethan's faces couldn't be faked. So why suggest a blood pact? Why not just keep me locked in this room? A tremor ripples through my stomach. What might it be like to share a blood pact with Blade? I can see myself falling in love with the guy. Hell, I'm in lust with him, as it is. He's kind, and I've glimpsed the loyal man beneath the playboy exterior.

What had he said? *"I call being surrounded by people who love you 'home.'"*

Love? People you love? What the hell was he talking about? I might wish a man like him would want me, *really* want me, but I have no illusions. I'm not that special. But a man in love doesn't refer to himself as *people*.

This is crazy. When Blade talked about home, he clearly meant The Academy. Difficult as it is to believe, hardened playboy Blade Tyrion is a sentimental man.

I snort. Leave it to the Fae to be the biggest badass sentimentalists. That's the Fae paradox. An unexpected affection warms me. Shit, he actually cares about me.

I place the hand with the sigil on the book and give a slight push of my magic. The sigil heats. I release the magic. If I agree to the blood pact, they will remove the sigil and I can find out what's in this book.

This book is the closest I'm going to get to hearing the truth from Grams herself.

Dare I?
A chill replaces the dread.
I'm damned if I do and damned if I don't.

THIRTY-FIVE

Leilah

No surprise that the moon is full. The universe has a way of providing what's needed, and a full moon adds strength to any magic. Walking between Ethan and Blade feels more like an escort to the electric chair than safe passage to where we will enact the blood pact. From the corner of my eye, I look at Blade, who winks. I manage to halt an eye roll, but can't stop the embarrassment that warms my cheeks. How does he always seem to know when I'm watching him?

I covertly glance left at Ethan. He's scanning our surroundings, watching, I realize, for danger. They tell me they have no leads on my attacker. I suspect, they're not above lying. If Ethan is right and the spear magic was elemental, he assures me that discounts Jennifer, Ariel and Thomas. But that doesn't mean they don't know someone who is powerful enough to wield that kind of magic.

"Where are we performing the ritual?" I ask.

"In the woods." Blade tilts his head toward the front gate.

I give a slight nod. "Excellent choice."

He raises a brow. "Glad you approve."

I know the reason they chose the woods is because they

won't risk the magic bleeding into The Academy. "You're not afraid the elements will play tricks?"

"You know your magic," Blade says.

I snort. "Flattery will get you nowhere." *A total lie.* "Everyone knows that a spell performed in nature opens a door to tricksters."

"What's life without adventure?" Blade murmurs.

Butterflies skitter across the insides of my stomach. The man has no shame.

Ethan presses a hand to the small of my back. My heart—and body—wish that action indicated more than simple courtesy. Maybe it doesn't. Maybe he's just making sure I don't bolt.

We leave the sidewalk and start down the drive. Moments later, the gate comes into view.

"I want to read the contract," I say.

"As Blade told you, it's simple," Ethan says. You agree not to run away."

I lift a brow. "That's it?"

"You also agree to ask permission before leaving The Academy," Blade says.

There's the catch.

This is way worse than what I remember of high school.

"Why should I agree to the blood pact?" I say, and try not to think of the spell book.

Ethan looks sharply at me. "What do you mean?"

I shrug. "If I only have to contend with your sigil and Blade's spell around my dorm room, I have a chance of getting out every now and then. Your terms are way more constricting."

"You can have Stony," Blade says.

I narrow my eyes." That's dirty pool."

He shrugs. "So is you running away every time we turn our backs."

"Not every turn," I say, oddly offended.

"Twice in seven days—and you're talking about doing it again."

"I came back." I narrow my eyes. "How many other students have you made blood pacts with?"

"How many other students have assassins hunting them?" Ethan shoots back.

I shrug. "I would kill Jennifer, given the chance."

Blade lifts his brows.

I roll my eyes. "Okay, okay, maybe I would just maim her."

"I told you she needs to grow up," Raith says from the shadows.

I jump when he materializes on the lawn to my right, and I come to a halt.

"You scared the bejesus out of me," I exclaim, then realize what he said. "Hey, I'm plenty grownup."

"My offer to strip your magic still stands," he says.

"No chance," I growl.

"You can have a normal life," he continues. "Go to school, get a job, get married. Have kids, if you want them."

"I can do all that *and* keep my magic." Had the guy heard my earlier thoughts?

"You'll still have to stay here for at least four years," he says. "Then there's always the chance the Illumina will assign you a job."

"*Offer* me a job," I correct. "This is still a free country."

He gives a low laugh. "America is free. Margidda—High Potentials—not so much."

"Fuck you, Raith," I reply evenly.

He shrugs. "Then a blood pact, it is." He steps closer and I tilt my head back in order to maintain eye contact. "Be warned," he murmurs. "I will ensure you adhere to the terms of the agreement."

"You have some *special terms* you want to add to the pact?" I shouldn't goad him, but I can't help myself. His eyes darken and I manage not to step back. Shit, he's pissed.

"You aren't capable of handling any *special terms* I might add," he says.

"Coward," I whisper. Sure, that was stupid, but he's a bully and I hate bullies.

"Friday nights," he says.

I blink. "Huh?

"Raith," Blade and Ethan say in unison.

"She thinks she's grown up and she wants to play with the big boys," Raith answers them, but his eyes remain on me.

"So, what? I'm supposed to be your sex slave every Friday night?" is my sarcastic retort.

His lips lift in lazy arrogance. "We see where your mind is, Ms. Crowe."

"I—" Heat suffuses my cheeks.

"Friday night will be devoted to studies," he says.

"Studies?" What the fuck? "You want me to promise to study?"

"With me as your tutor," he says.

Despite my immediate repulsion, my stomach flip-flops. "We're talking the study of magic?" my voice is breathy and I want to kick myself.

"And whatever else I deem necessary," he replies.

"Raith," Ethan growls.

I tense when the tattoos visible below the cuffs of Evan's sleeves begin to glow.

"What do you say, Leilah?" Raith asks. I hesitate, and he adds, "Who's the coward now?"

Ethan's tattoos glow hotter.

"Relax, Ethan," Raith says, eyes still on me. "I'm not going to hurt her. Just teach her a lesson or two."

"Maybe it will be me who teaches you a lesson," I retort. God, I'm a complete idiot.

He shrugs and I want to slap him.

"I get Stony," I say.

Surprise flickers across his face. "The howling night pig?" His lips thin and he glances at Ethan. "I imagine I know who to thank for that stipulation."

"The howling night pig will protect her," Ethan says, and I know he's not just talking of protecting me from my would-be killer.

That makes me want to laugh, but I manage some restraint and settle for giving Raith a big smile.

"Let's get on with it, then," he says.

Without a word, I start walking toward the gate. Blade catches up with me and Raith and Ethan walk several paces behind, speaking in tones too low for me to hear despite straining my ears.

"Give it up," Blade says.

I snap my head up to meet his gaze, and say dumbly, "What?"

He gives a little shake of his head.

I say, "You know they're talking about me. I have a right to know what they're saying."

He emits the same laugh he gave when he caught me returning to my room. "You keep talking about your rights."

I grasp his arm and stop him. "I'm not your *or their* slave. I have the same rights as every other student in the school."

Raith and Ethan reach us as Blade says," You don't have the right to risk your life."

"I do," I snap.

"No one here at The Academy is allowed to risk their lives," Ethan says, but I have the odd feeling he's mentally adding, *especially you.*

"Then what the hell are you teaching us?" I demand.

Raith passes me. "How to stay alive."

THIRTY-SIX

Ethan

I FLANK LEILAH'S SIDE SO CLOSELY, I CAN FEEL THE warmth from her body. By the time we reach the small clearing Blade prepared for the ritual, the moon is nearing its zenith. Crickets and frogs play a magnificent symphony that calls to the fire straining to break free of my will. In the center of a circle of rocks lies a neatly stacked pile of leaves and twigs. A knife, one snow white cloth, and a sheath of paper half covered by the cloth lay beside the pyre.

We stop beside the circle and Raith and Blade look at me. I extend my hand, palm up. The command for fire barely forms in my head and the tattoos in my body heat as a baseball-sized ball of fire bursts to life on my open palm. For two heartbeats, I revel in the heat and beauty of the flame, then, with the merest of breaths, I blow the sphere into the pyre. The wood and leaves ignite with an audible whoosh.

The nighttime symphony falls silent, but my blood heats in anticipation of the blood pact. I haven't said anything to Blade or Raith, but I believe the pact might connect us to Ciarah in a way that could release her memories of our many lives together. I can't begin to understand what that might mean for us—except that we will no longer have to pretend. That possibility alone heats my fire.

How much hotter will my fire burn during lovemaking when Ciarah knows me, *really* knows me? How much more devastating will that knowledge be when we lose her again? Maybe, if she remembers us in this life, she will take those memories with her into the next life. Maybe, if she remembers, we will be able to hold onto her longer. Always, has her life come to a tragic end before its time.

She's strong, but wary. She doesn't fear the magic. She fears the bond the blood pact will create among us, the power we will have over her. Little does she know the pact will increase her power over us.

Blade shifts two of the stones that comprise the circle. We file through the opening and take up positions inside the circle. I stand to Leilah's left, the south corner, and Raith stands opposite her, on the west side of the fire. Blade repositions the stones then stands to her right, on the north corner.

"When we're done, we go get Stony," she says.

I nod. She lifts a brow and looks pointedly at Raith and he angles his head in ascent. I half wish Raith wasn't here. He said he wouldn't come. Raith rarely changes his mind once he's made a decision. While that often saddens and angers me, at least I know where he stands. His change of heart worries me. It's got to be that he's using the blood pact to punish Leilah for burying that knife in his heart forty years ago. There's nothing I can do to stop him—from trying. If he hadn't taken part in the ritual, Leilah probably wouldn't have thought much of it. If he persists in punishing her, he'll do something he regrets, something she won't forgive.

Blade picks up the cloth and tosses it onto his shoulder, then scoops up the paper and knife. He begins to murmur in the mysterious Fae tongue. After all these centuries, I still know only a handful of Fae words. The fire crackles and the small flame leaps into the air as if to break free of the pyre.

The Fae are amongst the most beautiful creatures on earth, aside from angels, but they're not of this world. Blade's eyes slowly shift from their earthly blue to the gold unique to the Fae when they are immersed in Fae magic. This is when Blade is at his most pure. He extends the sheath of paper toward Leilah. She takes it and he gives a slight nod, an indication that she should read the words.

She scans the document. Our Leilah is no fool. To read the words out loud while inside a closed circle with beings as powerful as us three gives power to the words even without the comingling of our blood.

She gives an almost imperceptible nod, then reads aloud, "I swear to ask permission before leaving The Academy—for the next six months."

"No," Raith growls.

She meets his eyes squarely. "I will not indenture myself to anyone for a lifetime."

"Two years," he shoots back.

She snorts.

"A year," I quickly put in.

She shifts her gaze to me. "Are you saying it will take more than six months to find who tried to kill me?"

I should have known she would find a way to thwart us.

I nod. "Six months."

Raith opens his mouth to reply, but I say to Blade, "If you are in agreement, nod."

He nods.

I ignore Raith's unintelligible mutter and instruct Leilah, "Repeat the promise."

She holds up a finger and pulls a pen from her back pocket. I stifle a laugh when she adds 'for the next six months,' to her written promise. She stuffs the pen into her back pocket, rereads the promise, then hands me the paper.

I read, "I agree that Leilah Crowe shall be allowed to have her familiar at The Academy," then hand the paper to Raith.

He takes the paper and extends a hand to Leilah.

She frowns.

He says, "The pen."

Her lips thin, but she pulls the pen from her pocket and hands it to him. He scribbles something on the paper, then hands paper and pen back to her.

She reads it, then looks at him, brows raised. "Really?"

He shrugs. "You insisted we specify your familiar be returned to you."

Leilah scribbles something on the paper that I can't make out, then she reads, "I swear to report to Raith every Friday after class for more *lessons*," and shoves the paper toward Raith.

Raith is acting as much a child as Leilah, but this form of punishment isn't all that bad. She could do with more discipline. Raith is nothing if not disciplined.

He takes the paper and scans it. The twitch at the corner of his mouth is slight, but I know him well. Ciarah—Leilah—has managed to amuse him.

He reads, "I agree that Leilah Crowe may keep her familiar Stony with her at The Academy. Her lessons on Friday night will not last longer than two hours."

I bite back another laugh. It's not easy to best Raith. Of course, Ciarah is one of the few people who can best any of us.

Raith hands the paper to Blade, who murmurs, "I agree that Leilah Crowe may keep her familiar Stony with her at The Academy, and the sigil shall be removed from her hand immediately."

Blade grasps Raith's hand, slices a tiny, neat cut on the tip of his second finger, then smears a droplet of blood on the paper. I'm next. Blade is a master and I feel not the slightest pain with the cut. He smears my blood on the paper. His blood is next. When he grasps Leilah's hand, I discern a small tremble in her fingers.

A corner of Blade's mouth lifts and I discern the small squeeze he gives her fingers. Leilah's eyes lift to his and he makes the cut so quickly that her surprise comes an instant after the cut.

She narrows her eyes on Blade. "You tricked me."

"Just a little," he says. "If you will." Blade holds the paper flat on his palm.

She hesitates and my heart beats fast. What if she decides at the last minute not to go through with the pact? No, she wants my sigil off her hand. She wants her magic back. She wants her familiar. Still, she fears the pact.

"There's still time to call this off," Raith says.

She smears her droplet of blood onto the spot where our blood blots the paper. The flames leap up as if reaching for the sheet. Blade snatches it up in the nick of time, but the sheath of paper rips from his grip as if yanked by an unseen hand and the wind spirits it up and outside our circle.

Raith curses under his breath. My tattoos heat and armor slides down my body like dominoes. I step closer to Leilah. Blade stretches his arms out at his sides and throws his head back. His eyes glow an even brighter gold as he chants in the Fae tongue. The fire leaps higher. Heat radiates off the flames like an inferno. I step in front of Leilah. Flames jump toward me. A feral growl splits the air. Raith leaps across the fire and up and over us to where the signed document whips on the current of air that grips it. My heart jumps into overdrive.

The circle is broken.

The flames call to me. I command my wings and they burst from my shoulders. I swing them around to cover Leilah. The flames surge toward Blade.

Leilah thrusts out her right hand and shouts, "Fire, extinguish!"

"No," I shout, but too late.

My wings are blown back by her magic. My sigil on her hand glows red hot. I command the flames back, but they are already retreating from her as if in fear. An unearthly shriek sounds in the instant before her magic meets the flames and the coals sizzle as if water has been poured onto them.

Blade's arms drop to his sides and he stumbles toward the smoking pyre. Raith reaches his side and catches him. Blade blinks. His eyes are again their natural blue.

Raith's gaze snaps onto mine. "What the fuck was that?"

Before I can reply, Leilah sinks to the ground.

THIRTY-SEVEN

Leilah

I am falling. A lone wolf howls through a whirlwind. Through the hair that whips around my face, I glimpse Raith and Ethan exchange glances. Blade's now blue eyes shift toward the howl. When the contract flits across my vision, I grab for the paper but it whips out of reach. A hand closes around my wrist. I scream and twist, fighting to escape the iron hold. Wind shrieks. The hand yanks and I slam against a hard body.

"No!" I shout.

The vicious wind halts and strong arms encircle me. I jerk my head up and meet Blade's concerned eyes. What— Beyond the circle where we stand, the contract floats through the air like a boat on water.

"The contract," I cry. "If anyone gets their hands on it…"

"You are lying to yourself," Blade says.

I look back at him. "What?"

"You've always had the power."

Power? The Fae has lost his mind. I look at Ethan for help, but he just stares at me. Raith is the only one who seems worried. His jaw is set and his stare is so intense, I practically feel him drilling a hole through my brain.

No, not my brain. My soul.

I hate vampires.

I look over my shoulder for the document, but it's nowhere in sight. I look back at the men. "Aren't you afraid of what will happen if someone gets their hands on the contract?"

Raith's lips pull back in a snarl. "Others are not who we need to fear."

I reel as if he's backhanded me. I'm not the one who should be feared!

"Why are you so cruel?" I demand.

Blade shakes his head.

"What?" I demand .

"Poor Leilah," he murmurs. "Doesn't know how to face the truth."

I yank free of his hold. "Fuck you."

"Don't tempt me," he murmurs, and desire streaks through me with such intensity my breath catches.

"I told you she hasn't changed," Raith says.

"Changed from what?" I demand, but he just shakes his head. "You guys may not care if someone tries to use our blood pact against us, but I do."

Raith gives a harsh laugh. "She's incapable of telling the truth."

Fury whips through me. I want to hit him more than I've ever wanted anything. Warm fingers close around my left hand. I start and snap my head up. Ethan's so close I can see his green eyes swirl.

"Do you think we can hurt you?" he asks.

I snap my gaze onto Raith, who stares through obsidian eyes. "*He* can," I say.

"No." Ethan says. "He doesn't have the power. None of us do. We never have."

My surroundings spin and dizziness assails me. "He has already hurt me." A phantom knife pierces my heart and I fall to my knees.

"We aren't the ones who can hurt you," Ethan's voice is far away, like the wolf's howl that sounds again.

I jam my eyes shut and shake my head violently—

The wolf howls.

My eyes snap open. Raith, Blade and Ethan are kneeling over me. I'm lying on the ground.

Blade smiles gently. "Glad to have you back, love."

I seize his arm. "Did you hear that?"

He frowns. "Hear what?"

"The wolf." I start to push upright. The world tilts.

Ethan slides an arm beneath me and eases me into a sitting position. The trees make a slow spin.

"Take a deep breath," Blade urges.

I do as he instructs and, thankfully, the spin slows and then stops. "What happened?"

"We were going to ask you the same thing," Ethan says.

"What did you expect?" Raith says. "She used her magic while wearing your sigil."

I stare stupidly.

"You should have let us extinguish the fire," he says with a trace of impatience.

"Fire?" I repeat. Then remember. "Where's the document?" I glance wildly around the small clearing.

"Easy," Blade soothes. "We've got it."

"Where?" I demand.

He looks at Raith, who pulls a folded paper from his back pocket. I snatch it from his grasp, open it and scan the contents. The words are the same, handwritten notes and all.

"What happened, Leilah?" Blade asks.

A dream, that's what happened. A goddamn dream. I look

up at Blade. "I guess Raith is right. I shouldn't have used magic while wearing the sigil."

Raith's brows shoot up and I know he's surprised that I agree with him. I don't care. I can't admit that I'm shook up over a dream. I hand the document back to Raith and start to stand. Blade gasps my hand and pulls me to my feet. I stumble a pace and he catches me. I look up and meet his eyes. He stares down, and his compassion causes my heart to lurch.

I push away from him and he sets me at arms' length, still grasping my shoulders. "Okay?" he asks.

Thankfully, I feel steady, and nod. He releases me, though I'm almost sure I glimpse regret in his eyes.

"I suppose it's time we fetch that familiar of yours," he says, and I want to throw myself back into his arms and cry.

THIRTY-EIGHT

Ethan

We pull up to Miriam Crowe's house in Raith's MacLaren. Thankfully, Raith drove. He barely shifts the car into drive when Leilah jumps out of the car and races toward the door. We three follow at a more sedate pace and enter the house to find her, kneeling on the floor of the kitchen, her arms around the pig. Her familiar is snorting loudly, clearly as pleased to see Leilah as she is to see the creature. I release a silent breath and hope the pig will help Leilah better settle into The Academy.

Leilah, at last, rises and faces us. When she extends the hand marked with my sigil, I sigh.

Her eyes narrow. "A deal's a deal."

I grasp her hand and revel for an instant over the warm silk of her slim fingers in mine. Then I press the back of my hand against the sigil and the mark disappears. Her eyes widen slightly and I know she's sensing the natural flow of her magic. I can't blame her for missing that strength. I couldn't live without my fire.

She pulls her hand free and regards me. "You're sure I can use *all* my magic now?"

"Give it a try," I say.

She lifts her hand, palm up, and a swirling ball of multi-colored energy appears just above her palm. She smiles in kid-like delight and bounces the ball off the floor twice before closing her hand around the energy. The ball disappears.

"We should get going," Raith says.

Leilah shakes her head. "Not just yet."

"Leilah," he growls.

"Don't get your knickers in a wad," she says. "I figure that while we're here, you all owe me a look around."

"Owe you—" Raith begins.

"I'm not an idiot, Raith," she cuts in. "Miriam was my grandmother, for fuck's sake. You all want me to believe that she consorted with Shadows. As her only living relative, am I not due the right to see the evidence for myself?" Raith hesitates and she adds, "You said she blew a hole in the basement. I want to see it."

His mouth thins and I start to say she's right, but Blade says, "She has a point, Raith. She needs to put this to rest. If she were anyone else, you know we would present them with the evidence."

Raith's eyes lock with Leilah's. "No funny business. Understand?"

She angles her head and starts to turn. He grasps her arm. Her head snaps up.

"We collected all the remains of Shadows—that we located." He hesitates. "The Shadows are…crafty."

Her dark eyes widen slightly.

"We can never be certain they are truly gone," Raith adds.

Leilah's expression softens.

"If anything happens—anything at all—you are to stand down and let us deal with it," he says. She opens her mouth to reply, but he shakes his head, and growls, "It's that or we leave this instant. Don't make the mistake of thinking I can't carry you out of here."

Stony half growls a squeal and Raith looks at the creature. "You know I am right." He ignores the familiar's snort and looks at Leilah.

She gives a single nod and he releases her, though I am certain his grip lasts a heartbeat longer than necessary.

"I will lead," he says. "Ethan will follow, then you, then Blade." He looks at us and we each nod.

Raith crosses the kitchen to the basement door and eases it open. To my surprise, the pig squeals loudly. We all look at the creature as it morphs into a sparrow.

"Stony," Leilah cries. "You don't have to."

The sparrow swoops toward Leilah, then shoots across the room, past Raith and through the open door. Raith reaches inside and flips on the basement light.

The sparrow chirps from the basement and a smidgen of tension eases from my shoulders. Reuniting Leilah with her familiar is probably the smartest thing we've done since she's come back into our lives.

Raith's eyes shift to me and I start toward him. Leilah follows with Blade taking up the rear. We descend the stairs. We reach the basement to find the familiar back in pig form and sniffing around the five-by-five-by-five foot hole in the concrete floor of the basement. As was the case when we first investigated, there is no debris. It's as if the blast sucked everything down into the earth.

Leilah draws a sharp breath but says nothing as she slowly circles the hole. She drops to a squat on the far side and extends a hand over the hole.

"Leilah," Raith growls.

She shoots him a thin-lipped look. "I'm just seeing if I can sense any magic."

She closes her eyes and her expression relaxes. We remain quiet until she finally pushes to her feet.

"Sense anything, Stony?" she asks. The pig gives a low snort and Leilah finishes her walk around the circumference of the hole. "Who found The Shadows?"

No one answers. She halts and looks at us.

"We did," Blade says.

"After someone else found this hole."

It isn't a question.

"If you're implying that someone planted The Shadows, then, no," Blade says.

Her head snaps up and her eyes lock with his. "You can't know that."

"I can," he says quietly.

"How?" she scoffs. "Because the great Illumina told you?"

Blade releases a sigh. "Because I'm the one who found The Shadows here."

Her mouth falls open in surprise. "No—"

He nods. "Yes. I'm the one who investigated Miriam."

THIRTY-NINE

Leilah

THE FOLLOWING MORNING, I QUICKEN MY PACE along the walkway and duck against the bitter wind that blows from whatever cold hell exists in the farthest reaches of the north. The air smells like snow, though I'm sure it's too cold to snow. The Watchman at my side matches my stride, and I'm getting the usual stares from other students, but don't care. Blade's words kept me up all night and still ring in memory.

"I'm the one who investigated Miriam."

The sense of betrayal, fear and downright fury have my insides tied into a knot even Grams wouldn't be able to unravel, like those impossible knots in my shoestrings she dissected when I was a kid. Blade's treachery is made worse because he waited until we were bound by a blood pact before admitting that he's Grams' accuser.

An accuser who might be right, that persistent voice in my head whispers.

An accuser who hid his identity from me and made me—

My thoughts come to a screeching halt. *Oh, no.* There is no fucking way I am going there. I do not have feelings for Blade. And if I did, he killed them by lying to me.

That big ass crater in Grams' house isn't Blade's doing. Then, again, maybe it is. Who says *The Three* didn't set up Grams? If they lied about finding Shadows in her house, they could easily lie about this.

But they're not lying, and I know it—at least not about Grams making that hole. There might not be a trace of Grams' physical body, but her energy lingers around that fucking hole.

What the hell were you up to, Grams?

A barely detectable movement in my jacket's front pocket snags my attention. I didn't have to coax Stony into taking the shape of a mouse. Well, this morning, that is. Last night, she was her usual piggy self when she took over my bed. I spent the night glad for her comforting snore.

For the thousandth time, my eyes burn with the need to cry. I can try to lie to myself that I'd be crying out of joy of having Stony back, but the flood of tears I'm working hard to dam are all on Blade's head. Had I known the truth, there is no way I would have made a blood pact with *The Three*. They *all* knew Blade was Grams' accuser yet kept quiet.

The blood pact.

God, what a mistake.

At least, the dragon's sigil is gone. The natural thrum of magic I've known my whole life flows through me. But the warmth of dragon magic hovers like a specter on the edge of consciousness. The dragon, no doubt, purposely left some magic behind. The first chance I get, I'm going to demand he remove the remnants of his magic. I don't need him. I don't need any of them.

I choke back a laugh. Hard as it is to believe, Raith has been the most honest of *The Three*. He doesn't like me and never pretended otherwise. Except last night. I'm sure I sensed fear and even a little tenderness when he demanded I comply with his safety measures.

I blow out a frustrated breath. The Watchman looks my way, but I ignore him as we reach Leeds Hall and hurry up the four steps to the main entrance. Warmth washes across my face as we enter the building. In the hallway, I receive the usual stares as students part like the Red Sea so the Watchman and I can pass. Fuck them. I've got Stony. I gently pat my pocket and am sure I feel her wiggle as I near the newly reopened Potions class.

I've been assigned to the advanced class. No surprise there. I'm a Crowe, after all, a detail not lost on anyone as I step through the door. Heads turn. Whispers float through the room. I catch sight of shelves lined with jars and I'm swept back to my first day at school when Ethan found me here. God, I can almost feel his cock pressed against my ass. He'd been so hard.

A girl doesn't needs dragons when she has a pig?

I mentally grimace. That might be going just a *little* too far.

I glimpse a narrow-eyed glance a girl shoots my way. What had made me think I would find any welcome at The Academy? Given that everyone believes Grams was practicing Shadow magic, can I blame them? Why would they think I'm any different?

Am I different? I have Grams' spell book, a spell book that might contain Shadow magic. I had intended to get the book to give up its secrets immediately after Stony and I returned to my room, but hadn't had the energy. I haven't even told Stony about the book.

My heart skips a beat. I'm withholding important information. Does that make me the same as Blade? Will Stony think I've betrayed her? Will *The Three* think I've betrayed them? What if the book does contain Shadow magic? I think about Eddy Hanks. Oh God, what if I am like Grams?

I reach the last row of desks and notice Thomas leaning

against a small wooden worktable. He says nothing...well, verbally, anyway. His eyes spit fire.

Eddy Hanks, my inner voice whispers. Shame warms my face. I break eye contact with Thomas and drop into the desk seat as the door opens and Headmaster Domini enters, quite suave in a white, button-down shirt and navy slacks. That's right. He's a Master of Potions, but I hadn't realized he actively taught. He leans against the table at the head of the class, crosses his arms, and begins a talking about basic herb potions.

Ten minutes later, I conclude that Grams could have magicked circles around Domini. As advanced as this class is, it's still beneath my level. I'd learned everything in this current lesson by age eleven, but I don't mind the refresher course. The headmaster is easy on the eyes and something about his voice is mesmerizing, like the roll of waves on a beach. I slump in my seat and relax, wishing I could sleep with my eyes open.

Near the end of class, there's a pop quiz. I pass with flying colors even though my thoughts wandered during the lecture. I shuffle out, ignoring the wide berth other students give me.

While I lived with Grams, I was a typical kid. I laugh at myself. Well, maybe not typical, but more average than I became on the streets. Oddly, the nearly fifteen years spent with Grams seems like a dream compared to my homeless years. I don't remember what it feels like to be a part of society. Margidda's underworld. Abaddon, is a dark place. Even there, I operated under the radar by steering clear of the big dogs and by staying small. Except for Eddy Hanks. I guess there's good reason for my being accustomed to being on the outside. Still, it hurts that the students so easily swallow Thomas and Ariel's lies about me. Are they lies?

I leave the classroom and the Watchman falls into step alongside me. I've got a two-hour break before martial arts class. A shiver ripples through me. At least, martial arts is outside—away from spears mounted on walls. A lighter shiver prickles across my arms, only this one isn't remembered fear. I look left and spot Blade striding toward me from the walkway leading to Penncarrow Hall. Before I can halt the reaction, my pulse quickens.

I'm ashamed to admit that I'm not sure if my reaction is because Blade is just so damned beautiful dressed in jeans and a leather bomber jacket or if it's the blood pact connection. A group of young female students wave to him and giggle when he smiles at them as he passes.

He reaches us and nods to the Watchman. "Thanks, Joseph. I'll walk Leilah to her dorm."

"No need to bother," I say, and keep walking.

The Watchman hesitates and Blade adds, "Why don't you wait for us at her dorm?"

Joseph—I'm ashamed to admit, I never asked his name—nods and strides on ahead of us.

I want to shout for Blade to go away. I want to punch his jaw so hard he feels pain clear down to his balls. I want to run away and never see him. But there's not a chance in hell I'm going to fuel the rumor mill. Not about this.

"That man is the size of a troll," I say in a conversational tone. I keep my gaze straight, but I'm aware of Blade's glance.

"That's common for the Watchmen," he says. "They're like the knights of old, large, skilled and fearless."

"I had a crush on one when I was thirteen." I lengthen my stride. "He wasn't as large as Joseph, but he was huge." I recall the man. Tall, dark and very handsome. He had kind eyes. "At least, my thirteen-year-old self thought he was huge. I was only five feet tall at the time. He had to be six five."

Blade angles his head in my direction and says, "You like tall men, do you?"

A tremor ripples through my stomach. I hate myself for still finding him attractive. That voice. God.

Something white lands on my eyelash. I blink. A snowflake.

Another, larger one, lands on my eyelash. Blade grasps my arm and pulls me to a stop. I freeze when he cups the side of my face and brushes a thumb across the eyelash that the snowflake clings to. Two male students approach, but my legs don't obey my command to start walking.

Blade's gaze lingers on my face, not on my eyes. "It's snowing."

I nod. The tenderness in his voice startles me. God, his eyes are so blue.

"Did you know who I was when you first met me?" I ask.

He blinks and his hand drops away from my cheek. He steps back. I sway slightly at the loss of warmth that had cocooned us.

"You did." Pain tightens like a vice around my heart. I'm a complete idiot.

Blade motions with his head in the direction we were headed. "I'd better get you to your dorm. The snow is starting to come down pretty hard."

I realize he's right. Snow is falling in big, thick flakes that promise a winter wonderland in the next couple hours. So much for practice outside. It looks like class will take place in that damn practice gym.

We reach Penncarrow Hall and I brush past Blade, hoping he won't follow me inside. Of course, he does. We climb the stairs to my floor, where the Watchman stands guard, and continue past him to my room. I open the door and turn to close it.

"If I could prove Miriam's innocence, I would defend to the death," he says.

I meet his gaze. "That wouldn't serve the Illumina, now, would it?"

"I've been accused of many things, but nothing quite so dastardly as to convict an innocent woman."

"How sweet," I say. "I'm your first."

Hurt appears in his eyes. I should feel bad. I should demand to know why he kept the truth from me. I should explain that deceit is the one thing I can't abide—that, and the willingness to sacrifice another person for one's own ends. But there's not the tiniest part of me that wants to do any of those things. So, I just close the door.

FORTY

Leilah

Stony has her doubts about me using magic to decipher Grams' spell book while on Academy grounds but, at my insistence that I will proceed with or without her help, she agrees to stand guard. She snorts from her position in front of the door.

I open the cover of the book on my desk. "I'll be careful."

I lift my wand and angle the point so that it's nearly touching the first page and chant:

Words on these pages
    Verses in this book
    Decipher me your riddles
    Your wisdom shall be mine

Wind gusts with a force that drives me backwards. Stony's squeal mingles with the howl of wind. My hair whips around my face.

I grip the wand with both hands and point it at the book.

"Wind, be gone!"

The wind cuts off and I stumble forward, but catch myself before crashing into the chair. Stony is at my side, snorting loudly.

I spit out a tiny strand of hair. "I know, I know," I say. "Too much magic."

I snatch up the book. Foreign words still fill the pages.

"Dammit," I mutter. "Maybe if I put a shield around the book and amp up the spell."

Stony squeals loudly. I look at her and frown. She's right. If I overdo the magic on Academy grounds, that is sure to set off alarms.

"There's no way *The Three* are going to grant me permission to leave school grounds until they figure out who tried to kill me," I tell her. "I can't wait. I have to see what's in the book."

"Decipher one or two pages," she snorts in piggy English.

I lift my brows. "Speaking English, now?"

She snorts, again, this time piggy snorts, but I know the look. *Don't be a smarty pants.*

I return my attention to the book. "A few pages... You think that's enough to get an idea of what's in here?"

She snorts.

"No, I don't want anyone to know I have the book." I release a breath. "I guess it'll have to be enough."

A knock sounds on the door. I lunge for the book and shove it inside the top drawer.

"Who is it?" I call.

"Open the door, please."

Shit, it's Ariel.

"What do you want?" I call.

"We heard noises. Open the door, please."

The word 'please' is emphasized in a way I interpret, open the door before *I huff and I puff and I blow your house down.* If I didn't have Grams' spell book, I would double dog dare little

Ariel to try. But not tonight. I cross to the room and open the door.

Ariel pushes past me into the room.

"Uh, most people ask permission before entering someone's room," I say.

She scans the room. "Someone reported noise from this room."

"Am I supposed to *not* make noise?" I ask.

Ariel whirls on me. "*Unusual* noise."

"Like a pig snorting?" I nod at Stony, who's sitting on her butt staring up at Ariel.

Ariel curls her lip and looks at Stony. "So, that's *the* pig."

Stony snorts.

Ariel's eyes narrow. "Careful, piggy. I happen to like bacon."

I take two quick steps, so that Ariel's nose is level with my chin. Her head snaps up and I stare down at her. "Don't you ever threaten my familiar."

Her pupils dilate but, to my surprise, she doesn't back down. "Make sure your familiar stays out of my way."

I give a low laugh. "I suggest you stay out of her way. And, for the record, right now, you're in *my* way."

Ariel stares for several heartbeats, then spins and walks to the door, Stony trotting along behind. Ariel steps into the hallway, then looks over her shoulder and says, "Anymore unusual noises and I'll—"

Stony pushes the door shut with her snout.

"That's gonna cost us," I say.

Stony tosses her head and says, "Too hot tonight."

I hesitate.

She snorts and I snap my gaze onto her.

"Truth is, we don't know I'm not like Grams," I say.

"I know," she says in as plain an English as I've ever heard her use.

I grimace. "Yeah, well, you're not always right."

FORTY-ONE

Leilah

Overhead, geese too stubborn to have flown south when winter set in a month ago, honk against a cold wind. Two days have passed since the blood pact and I'm headed to Raith's for my first Friday night lesson, the Watchman, Joseph, at my side.

The curiosity I'd felt at the prospect of seeing what Raith has in store for me is gone. I haven't seen the vampire since we picked up Stony that night, and I would be glad never to set eyes on him again. He has maintained that Grams killed herself while practicing Shadow magic. That, as they say, is that. How naive I'd been to think I could get information from him. Then again, a blood pact with one of the oldest vampires alive hadn't been part of my plans, either.

Gooseflesh skims atop my arms. *The Three* have been pointedly silent about the way the ritual ended. But we all know something unusual happened. No ordinary wind snatched the contract from Blade's hand and blew it outside the circle.

I didn't tell them about my dream—and don't plan to tell them anything in the future. I did tell Stony what happened, and she didn't like the weirdness any more than I do. That's why she insisted on sticking with me today. The weird dream had to be due to the blood pact. I straighten. Wait a minute. Might I be able to use lucid dreaming to capture elusive dreams?

A prickle of fear tingles my spine. Can I afford for the connection among the four of us to be brought into sharper view? My pulse quickens. Blade isn't one of the young wolf bikers I dated in Chicago. If I get too close to the Fae... I'm not sure just what will happen. Given the way Ethan touched me that first day in school, he—

He hasn't made another overture since that day, I realize. The other woman he mentioned to Miss Mack must be the reason why. I blow a strand of hair that's escaped its ponytail and fallen across my eyes. Ethan sure as hell didn't hold back that day. Why, if he had someone else, did he come on so strong? God, men love to talk about how deceitful women are, but men are so without honor. Unless... Maybe the someone came into his life after that day? I jam my hands into my hoodie pockets. Good, it's not like I care about the three of them.

The three of them?

When did I say I wanted Raith?

Just what the fuck are my plans? I made a blood pact that will keep me here for six months. Can I stand to see them every day, knowing they hid the truth from me? A thought occurs. The blood pact demands I ask permission to leave. I made no promise to stay if they refused that permission. Is that a loop-hole I can really use?

I spot Chelsea, the young girl I sparred with the day I met Raith. She's with two male students at least four or five years older than herself, all of them walking toward us. As the students approach, Watchman Joseph steps up to my side the students will pass. I shoot him a *you've got to be kidding* look, but he ignores me. I swear, the guy's a sphinx.

Chelsea watches me from the corner of her eye. The dumb kid probably doesn't realize I know she's watching me. They pass and I wonder if The Academy allows underage students to fraternize with older students. So far, I haven't noticed a great deal of *fraternizing*. Then again, I haven't been included in a damn thing. Not even by Fran. As if summoned, Fran emerges from a path to our left, waves, and hurries to catch up with us. The Watchman tenses.

"Relax," I say. "I know her."

He doesn't reply, but his hand casually rests on what looks like a small pepper spray can on his belt.

Fran reaches us, spares a glance for the Watchman, then says, "Some of us are going to Silwood Hall for a party. Want to come?"

I'm startled—and touched—that she's asking, but before I can reply, Joseph says, "She can't."

"She can, if you come with her," Fran says. "Plus, she's got her familiar."

I barely suppress a gasp. The little tattletale knows too much for her own good.

Joseph shakes his head. "She has an appointment with Raith."

Fran's eyebrows shoot up. "Have to see Raith, huh? Maybe you have a party of your own going on."

"Not hardly," I blurt. "His Majesty has decided I need tutoring."

She grins and I realize my mistake. "Tutoring?" Her grin widens. "You clearly don't need a party."

"It really is just tutoring," I insist.

She tosses her hair and laughs. "Promise to give me the juicy details later." Fran starts away, then faces us and walks backward. "It'll be our secret."

I groan inwardly, pretty sure that's code for *I'm going to tell everyone the moment I get to the party.*

I watch as she turns around and continues toward Silwood Hall and wonder what it would be like to be go with her to the party instead of to Raith's. Grams said that men were a nice thing, but to never underestimate a woman's need for the friendship of other women. I haven't had a lot of female friends. Women tend to avoid the company of pretty women. Too much competition. Fran said she wanted Blade, but that clearly doesn't stop her from being my friend. She disappears around the science building and I return my attention to the walkway.

Joseph and I reach the administrative building and I get glances from a group of students as the Watchman and I head up the half dozen steps to its oak door. I'm relieved to enter the building.

The Watchman halts inside the door and nods toward the sweeping staircase directly ahead. "Take the stairs to the top floor. If you're not up to the climb, there's an elevator there." He nods right.

I don't bother to look. I was here four days ago, covered in blood. My stomach does an unexpected somersault as I turn toward the stairs, and I consider the possibility of skipping this damn lesson. First, I would have to get around the Watchman, then I would have to avoid *The Three* for, well, for the next six months. I can't help a morbid laugh at the thought and start up the steps.

At the top of the stairs, double oak doors stand open. I cross the hall, knock lightly on a door, and step inside as Raith says, "Come in."

Of course, Raith looks better than a man has a right to. The sleeves of his white button-down shirt are rolled up and reveal muscled forearms. I note that the dark hairs on the nape of his neck are beginning to curl slightly as if he needs a haircut. I start when a woman rises from a squat in front of a fireplace at the far side of the room. She dusts off her hands then faces us. I know it's stupid, but embarrassment makes me want to turn and run.

"Rebecca, this is Ms. Crowe," Raith says without looking up from the papers on his desk.

She reaches me and extends a hand. "Very nice to meet you, Ms. Crowe."

I clasp her hand and say, "Nice to meet you."

She smiles politely, but I sense a secret beneath that polished veneer. Does she think I'm here for a quickie with Raith? No, even Raith wouldn't flaunt his one-nighters to his staff. One-nighters? Is that how I think of him. No, I realize. She's worried that's what this is. Fuck, she's in love with him. First, Miss Mack with Ethan. Now Raith's assistant and him.

"Will that be all Mr. Vanderkoff?" Rebecca asks.

"Yes. Thank you."

Rebecca hesitates for the barest second, then gives me another polite smile and heads for the door. This woman's feelings for Raith aren't like the desperate teenage infatuation Miss Mack has for Ethan. She genuinely cares for him. She reaches the doors and pulls them shut behind her with a soft click.

"Have a seat, Ms. Crowe."

I jump at Raith's command and blurt, "That was mean of you."

He looks up. "You and I will get along better if you stop seeing persecution in everything I do."

"I'm not talking about me, dammit. Your assistant."

He frowns in genuine confusion.

I roll my eyes. "Men are such idiots."

His brows lift.

"She's in love with you."

He blinks in shock. Deep shock, I realize with surprise.

"You didn't know," I say slowly.

He leans back in his chair. "What kind of adolescent game is this, Ms. Crowe?"

Stony stirs in my pocket. I start to ask if he doesn't think we're beyond the formality of addressing each other by our surnames, then realize it's better to preserve the distance.

I drop into the wing backed chair in front of his desk. "Think what you want. She's in love with you."

He opens his mouth to reply, then doesn't. A thought strikes and I concentrate on what he's thinking. I start at the sensation of hitting a brick wall. My head—or is it brain—feels like a pool ball bouncing off the inside of my skull.

"I have spoken with your instructors," he says. "I gather you feel no compunction about using magic anytime you like."

Wow, he's unaware I tried to connect with him through our blood pact. "I don't know how you came to that conclusion, considering I wore that damn sigil," I say, and mentally cheer that my voice remains steady.

"In fact, the sigil was deactivated in some of your classes. And, lest you forget, you have pushed through the sigil to use magic."

I shrug. "Isn't that why I'm here? I'm a High potential. That's a sign of how powerful I am."

"Headstrong," he replies, though I detect no rancor in his voice—damn his soul.

"You don't like me, why bother with me, at all?" A thought occurs, and I add, "You have to know that I was selling fake IDs. That's against the law. Why not just turn me in?"

"You think the Illumina doesn't know about your illegal activities?"

"So, the Grand Witch knows?" I hadn't considered this possibility. I am beyond stupid.

He shrugs. "I can't say that such inconsequential news has reached her ears."

"Why not tell her?"

"You're a High Potential. Who am I to question who the Stone names?"

A shadow flickers in his eyes and his words in my dream repeat, *"They are not who we need fear."*

"Why are you afraid of me?" I ask.

Surprise slips through his cool mask. "If you mean, why do I fear the trouble you make, the answer is, you act before thinking."

He isn't completely wrong. But he's lying. I realize that his secret is closer to the surface than usual. I want so badly to demand to know what he's hiding, but I can't pry the truth from him even with magic. Or can I... Just how hard would it be to use a truth spell on him?

"I would think twice about that," he murmurs.

I jump. What did he say? *I would think twice about that?*

He can't read my mind. Can he?

"Think twice about what?" I ask.

"Whatever it is you're contemplating."

"Who says I'm contemplating anything?"

He stares.

"What's tonight's lesson? How to win a staring contest?"

"The consequences of using magic for personal benefit," he says.

My mouth falls open. "You're kidding?"

"Do I look like I'm kidding?"

"You're telling me you never use magic to help yourself?"

"I have lived as long as I have by not being a fool."

"Just how long have you lived?" I ask.

His expression remains neutral. "Personal details of my life are not a part of this lesson."

"Personal details like why you didn't tell me that Blade was the person investigating my grandmother—which makes him the person who judged Grams guilty."

"You are misinformed, Ms. Crowe. Blade only reported the facts gleaned from his investigation. One of Blade's finer qualities is the ability to be objective. He had no personal stake in

Miriam's guilt or innocence. It was the evidence that damned her."

"Damned her?" I repeat.

I swear, something sizzles in the air.

Raith lifts a brow.

Yes, that sizzle was Stony. She doesn't like Raith.

"You have you familiar in your pocket." It's not a question.

Good. I'm asking the questions. "What evidence damned Grams?"

"You've seen the Shadow husks. You've seen the hole in her basement."

"If that's all you've got—"

"Remnants of Shadow magic are unmistakable," he cuts in. "We detected Shadow magic long before she killed herself."

"She didn't kill herself," I snap.

He angles his head. "Before she accidentally blew herself up."

"I'm supposed to take your word?"

"Ethan and I have no more personal stake in Miriam's guilt or innocence than does Blade."

"The Illumina does."

"We are not the Illumina."

I snort. "The fuck you aren't."

Stony squeaks.

"Your familiar is to remain in your pocket and not interfere," he says.

I flash a smile. "You have nothing to worry about—as long as you don't threaten me."

"I don't make threats, Ms. Crowe."

"You make promises."

"You wouldn't see me coming," he says with such nonchalance that I know he's not talking out his ass. But then, I never doubted his badassery.

He leans back in his chair. "You have never experienced the effects of using magic for personal gain?"

"Like casting a truth spell on someone to find out if they're framing an old woman for treason?" I flash another smile.

His eyes flash. Yep. I got him.

"You muzzled a student your first day in class," he says.

I shrug. "She—"

"—doesn't like you," he cuts in.

I wave a hand dismissively. "She didn't like me before I muzzled her. Are you really telling me this is the lesson?"

"Are you really telling me you have never experienced ill effects from using magic for personal gain?" he counters.

"Everyone has," I say. "For the record, I'm not an idiot. I don't go around arbitrarily casting spells on people."

He angles his head. "What do you use magic for?"

"Not that much."

"That doesn't answer my question."

I shrug. "I protect myself. Sure, I use magic to clean house, sometimes." *Though not that often.* "Who doesn't?" I add.

"No influencing employers to get a job?" he asks. Before I can answer, he adds, "No, you sell magic."

I don't flinch. "We already established my trade."

"You don't call that personal gain?" he asks.

"I'm not using magic," I reply, unruffled.

"Your grandmother taught you magic from childhood."

I nod. "Of course."

"What about your parents?"

"I never knew my parents. They left me with Grams when I was a baby."

I'm surprised by something that looks like compassion in his eyes. No. I have to be wrong. Raith Vanderkoff isn't capable of compassion.

"So, Miriam was your only teacher," he says.

He says her name as if he knows her. I lean forward. "You

knew Grams?"

"I know all coven leaders. She was the head of her coven—until two years ago."

Grams knew Raith? I shouldn't be surprised, but for some reason, I am. I pin him with a stare. "Is that how you discovered she was practicing Shadow magic?"

"If you're asking if I pretended to be her friend while spying on her, no. We weren't friends."

"That much I believe." Raith is no one's friend. "You have no concrete proof Grams was practicing Shadow magic. Everything I know—everything I've learned since I've been here—says The Shadows are insidious. How do you know they didn't infect Grams?" I hadn't actually considered this possibility until now, but what if it were true? She might do things she wouldn't have otherwise done. What fears and anxieties might The Shadows have latched onto in order to infect her so that she might practice Shadow magic? "Bottom line, you can't prove she did a damn thing wrong. You need concrete proof, something like—like a spell book written in her hand."

His gaze sharpens.

"The house is mine," I hurriedly add. "You can't stop me from living there."

"That's not my job," he says slowly, clearly surprised by my sudden change of topic—and clearly still cogitating on my statement about needing a spell book.

Shit, I fucked up. I stand. "This lesson is over." I start toward the door and get four paces before an unseen force drags me backward. I gather my will and shout, "Release me!"

I'm nearly thrown into my chair. I glare at Raith. "What the fuck did you do?"

He shakes his head. "Nothing."

Then I understand. "The blood pact." I promised a two-hour lesson with Raith every Friday night.

Fucking blood pact.

"Shall we begin again?" he asks.

Stony stirs in my front pocket. She's not happy, but there's not a damn thing she can do. There's not a damn thing I can do.

Fucking blood pact.

AN HOUR AND FORTY-FIVE MINUTES IS AN ETERNITY when you're confined to a small room with a stick-up-his-ass vampire—even a gorgeous one. I keep expecting his good looks to diminish as a result of his being a grade A jerk, but no go. I don't know if that makes being here easier or harder.

Vague images of a tall man flit across my brain. A warm mouth on my body. Impressions of memories, I suspect, of when he drank my blood and—I shiver—I drank his. Memories that have eluded my every effort at recall. Aside from the impressions—and dreams—I haven't noticed any negative effects of the blood sharing. Except maybe for the betrayal I feel as a result of his complacency in Blade's deception. The hurt has to be a side effect of the blood pact.

It's not like I'm friends with Blade. *The Three* are doing their jobs, despicable as those jobs may be. All I have to do is keep my distance for the next six months—that, and make sure the Illumina doesn't destroy *my* house—my first real chance for stability.

"Ms. Crowe."

My head spins for an instant, then Raith's face snaps into focus.

He's staring, brow lifted. "The ingredients for the spell?"

My cheeks heat and his gaze sharpens. I manage an even voice as I run down the list of ingredients used for the spell to cleanse a home of negative energy. He rattles off three other spells that I'm supposed to list ingredients for, then returns his attention to his paperwork.

I comply and, when I've finished, frustration has replaced embarrassment. I pin Raith with a stare. "Why are you wasting both our time with this drivel? You have to know I learned these spells by the time I was eight."

"Patience," he says without looking up.

"You're not paying attention." I wince at my wheedling tone.

He looks up and recites the ingredients I just told him, in the order I gave them.

I roll my eyes. "Everyone knows those are the ingredients for that spell."

"How about the spell to contact the dead?" he asks.

I hesitate. "That's one helluva jump from grade school spells."

"You do know how to call someone from the dead?"

"Every witch worth her salt knows—" I break off, understanding dawning. "You have got to be kidding. You actually think I've tried calling my grandmother from the dead?" The thought had occurred to me—numerous times.

"Have you?" he asks.

"Hell, no."

"Why not? That would give you your answers."

"You clearly didn't know my grandmother well. She won't answer my questions any quicker in death than she did in life."

"Was she in the habit of lying to you?" he asks.

That's a question I've asked myself a thousand times, but that's family business, and Raith isn't family. "No," I say. "If you want answers, why don't you call her from the dead yourself?" Then I realize, "You did try, with no luck."

Not just anyone can call spirits from the dead. That magic is generally the purview of witches and wizards—mostly witches—but not just any witch, witches who are recognized by the dead. I happen to be one of those witches.

I give a slow nod. "Like I said, if Grams doesn't want to talk, she won't."

"Maybe we didn't use the right spell," he says.

We both know that's bullshit. A witch who can call the dead practically only has to command them forth by name.

I glance at the clock. Ten more minutes and I can tell Raith to fuck himself, at least until next Friday night. Guilt niggles. Truth is, once we got past the initial bullshit, the lesson hasn't been terrible. Well, aside from being forced back into third grade. I almost laugh at his paltry attempt to get me to help him call Grams from the dead.

I shouldn't be angry. I've wasted my time in worse ways. Raith is exercising his authority. Why should that bother me so much? Because I'm powerless? Because the blood pact forces me to uphold my side of the bargain for the next six months?

Guilt digs deeper. The Illumina takes seriously the training of High Potentials. High Potentials are the ones taken in the Reaping, the ones most successful at fighting The Shadows. They are Margidda's first and last defense against annihilation. Was that what Blade meant when he said High Potentials aren't free to choose?

Shit.

I refocus on Raith. "How did you stop The Shadows? Don't give me that same bullshit about stopping all magic."

"You learned in Reaping Preparedness that we fought The Shadows within dreams," he says.

I frown. "That's it?"

A corner of his mouth lifts—a ghost of a rare smile. "You didn't learn the exact magic we used in the lucid dreams, but, yes—that's it."

"What *exact* magic?"

"You'll learn that in time."

"In time?" I shoot back. "By not teaching us how to fight The Shadows, you leave us vulnerable."

He sighs. "Would you have us place a grenade in a child's hand?"

I blink. "What?"

"Power is responsibility," he says.

"Knowing how to defend yourself is—"

"Power," he cuts in. "Would you hand a machine gun to just anyone—even to protect themselves?"

Fury whips through me. "Is that why so many died in the last Shadow attack—because you didn't teach them how to defend themselves?"

"You think lucid dreaming is easy?" he asks with a patience that makes me want to scream.

"That's why you teach people," I snap.

He studies me. "Isn't that what we're doing?"

"All people," I growl.

"People who would be infected or killed within minutes?" he asks.

"Not if you teach them."

His eyes lock with mine. "Send into battle people who aren't capable of fighting." I open my mouth to protest, but he cuts me off, "Do you honestly believe everyone can fight The Shadows?"

"They have a right to try."

He shakes his head. "Do you ever think before speaking?"

Fury pools in my belly. "If I didn't, you would be hearing what I'm thinking now."

Amusement sparks in his eyes then vanishes. "I suppose we have to start somewhere."

I jump to my feet. "Blood pact or no blood pact, this lesson is over." I whirl and head for the door. I draw magic into my fingers to combat the pact. I reach the door without resistance, then look over my shoulder. "You did use magic on me earlier."

"No." Raith indicates the clock on the mantle. "The lesson was over five minutes ago."

FORTY-TWO

Blade

By now, Leilah has finished her first lesson with Raith and is safely back in her dorm room. I slow my walk around the side of the Administration building. Snow falls in tiny flakes. On a winter's night in another life, such snow clung to Ciarah's golden hair as I kissed her beneath the ancient oak tree in the garden of the castle we five shared. I startle at the realization that her favorite soap had been rose scented, the same soap she had used that night I saw her in the cigar club.

As I knew she would be, Leilah is angry with me. She thinks I should have told her that I am the one investigating her grandmother. That would have given her one more excuse not to accept the truth about Miriam. Say what she likes, but Leilah is slowly being forced to see the truth.

In all the lifetimes we've known her, I don't recall committing such a grave sin against her. Then again, in all the lifetimes we've known her, she wasn't once the granddaughter of a powerful white witch who turned to Shadow magic.

Fury heats my belly. A bloody white witch. Miriam saw what The Shadows did to us. How dare she think she could ally with our greatest enemy and escape detection. She'd been lucky that she blew herself up. She saved herself the public humiliation of a trial and execution.

I release a breath. I hope the damn blood pact doesn't give Leilah an ability to see more deeply into my soul. I grimace. She would most definitely flay me alive if she could read my thoughts.

I round the rear of the Admin building and sense an angel's presence before I catch sight of Zadkeil, standing on the path up ahead. Speak of the devil. Angels pride themselves on maintaining a heavenly image: long, flowing hair, loose robes, armor and, of course, wings. All of which are absent in Zadkeil. In jeans, a tight t-shirt, a heavy leather jacket and black boots, the angel could be the leader of a rock band. Women would go mad for him.

I squint as I approach him, then stop. "Did you cut your hair?"

His expression doesn't alter. "You know that is forbidden."

I shrug. "Sure looks short to me."

With a sigh, he turns his head. His dark hair is held with a tie low on his nape.

"Ah. Your news must be important to have risked a public appearance dressed like"—I grin—"one of us."

"It is after midnight. We are alone," he replies. "But, yes, it is important. Your witch left quite a mess for us to deal with."

I raise a brow. "Indeed?"

His lips compress. "The Shadow remnants you recovered from Miriam Crowe's home represent only a fraction of The Shadows she used."

Only a fraction? I keep my expression neutral. "What exactly does that mean?"

His expression hardens. "It means you should thank my Lord that she didn't blow a hole large enough to take Westchester County with her on her way to Hell."

That would be one way to get around breaking the spell that

keeps the Hell Gates closed. What the bloody hell was Miriam doing with such powerful Shadow magic?

"I assume you found no trace of her?" he says.

"Not so much as a hair follicle. I had hoped you would."

"We must discover what spells she used."

I found no spell book in her home. That doesn't completely surprise me. Magic was first nature to Miriam. She had more magic memorized than a dozen talented Margiddians combined. She likely memorized any magic she used and didn't risk writing down spells. Still, I'm disturbed by the complete lack of remains. How does a witch blow herself to Kingdom Come and leave no trace?

"We cannot have her finding a way into Hell," Zadkeil says.

"What?" I blink. "You aren't serious in thinking she was trying to blow a hole big enough to enter Hell? That isn't possible."

"I never said it was possible," Zadkeil shoots back.

But he had. Then I realize what else he'd said. "What do you mean, *'We cannot have her finding a way into Hell?'*" I stare. "You don't believe she's dead." My mind races. We'd found the hole she'd blown in her basement and assumed... I narrow my eyes on Zedkeil. "What aren't you telling me?"

"We *must* have the spell she cast."

"The spell to enter Hell?" I say slowly.

He gives a curt nod.

The angel has gone mad.

"I've gone over that house with a microscope. There is no *evidence* she was trying to reach Hell." I shake my head. "In fact, the idea is ludicrous. Which means, you have information from another source. Has your god finally involved himself?"

The god of angels has good reason for not wanting the Hell Gates open. His once-favorite son is the ruler of Hell. The longer The Morning Star stays locked inside, the less trouble *Elyon* has to deal with. Even if it is possible to find another way into Hell, why would Miriam Crowe, a powerful white witch, want to enter?

And why is Zadkeil so worried about the possibility of someone entering Hell? If Miriam did get into Hell—something I don't believe for an instant—in no way does that— My thoughts freeze. If a powerful witch is *inside* Hell, might she be able to open the gates from that side?

The possibility is too bloody fantastical. Even if it were possible, why would a white witch want to open the Hell Gates? Another, even stranger question: if Miriam found a way into Hell, why would Zadkeil worry about *how* she'd done it? Why not worry about reinforcing the gate so that she can't get out? Maybe *Elyon* has someone else working on that issue and tasked Zadkeil with finding out how Miriam accomplished the feat.

"You will report any new findings to me," Zadkeil orders.

I blink snow off my eyelashes. "I thought we were partners in this investigation."

I start to ask what evidence he's found that leads him to believe Miriam was trying to reach Hell, but he says, "We cannot have Miriam Crowe's magic falling into the wrong hands."

I rein in my frustration. "Zadkeil, you're worried over nothing. She left no trace of her magic."

"Other than The Shadows she used," he hisses.

He's angry, but there's another note in his voice I can't quite identify. "What does your god have to say about Miriam supposedly entering Hell?" I demand.

Zedkeil's eyes narrow. "If *He* wants you to know what *He* is thinking, *He* will speak to you. For now, we need to find the spell Miriam Crowe used."

"The spell she was using when she blew a hole into Hell," I murmur. That small crater did almost look as if someone had drilled downward. I pin the angel with a stare. "Why doesn't

Elohim look into Hell and tell us if she's there?" I'm not the first person to ask this question. Interestingly enough, the god of the angels has remained oddly silent on that point. "That's right." I snap my fingers. "Even *He* can't get past the magic that sealed the Hell Gates all those centuries ago. Are you certain Senorn and Eledin weren't goddesses themselves to have used magic so powerful that even *Elohim* can't penetrate the spell?" Never mind that Senorn was a black witch. That'll get Zedkeil's blood pumping.

Sure enough, a righteous flame bright enough to blind a human ignites in the angel's eyes. "How dare you speak blasphemy. Our Lord would never enter the seat of evil."

"Even to ensure the safety of his own creation?" I counter with more heat than intended. "Maybe if he spent a little time there, he might think twice about sending to Hell anyone who doesn't agree with him."

Zedkeil sucks in a loud breath and his eyes go wide.

I stare. "Bloody...fucking...hell," I breathe.

This isn't a reconnaissance mission. This is a rescue mission.

I hold his gaze. "Elohim is locked in Hell."

FORTY-THREE

Leilah

I have to find out what's in Grams' spell book. Stony is behind me a hundred per cent this time, and sits with her butt against my dorm room door. I've also locked the door. Why I didn't think to do that the first time is beyond me.

"Stupid is as stupid does," said Forest Gump. He must have been thinking of me and my time at The Academy.

A dream-like quality clouds my brain. Not surprising. No one wants to acknowledge what might be the worse truth they ever have to face.

Once again, I stand over the spell book, positioned on my desk and open to the first two pages. I grip the wand in my left hand, my cell phone in the right.

I look at Stony. "Ready?"

She snorts affirmation.

"Here goes nothing." I tap the camera on the phone and hold it steady over the book, my thumb hovering over the button. I point the wand at the first page of the book and chant in a whisper:

. . .

WORDS ON THIS ONE PAGE ONLY
    For the barest of three heartbeats
    Decipher me your riddles

A BREEZE FLOWS ACROSS THE PAGE. THE WORDS shimmer, then slowly bleed into focus. I jam my thumb down on the camera button. The words fade and, once again, the foreign letters fill the page.

I set the wand and phone on the desk, then grab the book and stuff it beneath the blankets on the bed where Stony likes to sleeps. She won't let anyone get near her bed.

I lower myself onto the chair. Stony's hooves click across the floor. She reaches the bed, jumps up and drops onto the blanket and book. She watches me, her black eyes intense. We haven't talked about it, but we both know that just looking at the words of a powerful witch's spell has a power of its own.

I draw in a deep breath. Exhale. Then tap the image. The picture fills the screen.

I stare at the first line. This is no spell.

THE POWER IN THE SHADOWS IS UNMISTAKABLE.

MY HEART THUNDERS. I STEADY MY MIND, THEN continue.

THERE IS NO DOUBT THEY ARE THE KEY I HAVE BEEN SEARCHING FOR these last ten years.

. . .

"Sweet God," I mutter. My hand trembles so badly I nearly drop the phone.

I know God will forgive me—though everyone else will condemn me, and some would kill me if they knew the truth. I pray He is still able to help me.

The Shadows are not as difficult to control as I'd expected. That frightens me. In the end, though, does fear matter? Once I control them, nothing else will matter.

Once she controls them? Tears stream down my face. Stony jumps from the bed and nudges my leg with her snout as I read the next line.

Denique in occursum mihi Fatum meum

I stare at the Latin words. Why didn't the spell translate the Latin? Somewhere in the far reaches of my mind, I understand. My spell only removed the spell that hid the words written on the page. Grams wrote the last sentence in Latin.

"*Denique in occursum mihi Fatum meum,*" I murmur aloud. My Latin is decent, but my brain struggles to focus.

Stony says something. I look at her. She blurs.

"At last I meet my destiny," she says in piggy snorts.

I look back at the words. "Using Shadow magic is her destiny?"

Real, real, real!

The evidence against Grams is real. Blade—Ethan and Raith —are right.

I collapse into tears.

I'm vaguely aware that Stony stands over me in her natural form. The next thing I know, she lifts me in her arms and lays me on the bed. I curl into a ball as she pulls the covers over me. The bed dips and a warm body presses against my back. She rests her snout on my side and waits.

FORTY-FOUR

Leilah

I SLEPT THAT NIGHT, THOUGH I HADN'T EXPECTED TO. Emotions and the body are funny that way. They protect themselves. I dreamt, but remember only fleeting images. Thank the dream gods for small mercies. I stare at myself in the mirror that hangs on the back of my door as I tie off my one long braid and toss it over my shoulder. Had I known three days ago what I now know, I would have allowed Raith to strip me of my magic and would have left The Academy. Now, I'm bound here for six months and, every day, I must face the three men who have been telling me the truth about Grams all along.

I can never tell them about the spell book. Not that Grams deserves my loyalty. It's just that I can't bring myself to tell the truth. That truth leads straight back to me. If Grams can turn, then anyone can turn. Me included.

Eddy Hanks. The name bounces off the insides of my skull.

Without magic, I won't have the power to help a scum bag like him.

All I have to do is keep my distance from *The Three*, become a model student for the next six months, then I—

Wait. Do I have to stay here the full six months? What if I

allow Raith to strip me of my magic now? Maybe I can make a deal with the Illumina. Strip my powers, give me Grams' house, and I'll be out of their lives forever.

I shove aside the panic that rises. It's possible to live without magic. Millions of people do. This is the only way. I don't deserve to be a witch. Grams didn't deserve to be a witch, damn her soul.

She must be in Shadow Hell now, paying the price for her betrayal.

I will live a quiet life as an average mortal.

Can I live in Grams' house, so close to *The Three?*

I know right away that I can't. I'll have Raith strip my powers. That should please him to no end. I'll get the house, sell it, and move to some far away warm place with lots of sun, rum and hard bodies. Even if the Illumina destroys the house—which I won't let happen—they can't stop me from claiming the property. I'm Grams' only living relative. Stony and I—

Oh, God. Stony. Is Raith right? If I give up my powers, will I have to give up Stony, too? I glance in the mirror at her. She's sprawled on her side on the bed. She's looking at me way too intently. I tear my gaze from her and take two steps to the closet.

"The best thing about the War Games is that I get to use my swords," I tell her. Did my voice crack a little?

I pull the leather scabbard holding the short sword from the wall, then slide the blade halfway out. I love blades. That's probably something that should worry me, but I comfort myself with the fact that steel, instead of fire, is my vice. I've known a couple fire bugs and they're creepy. Martial arts is something I can pursue even without magic. I slide the blade back into the scabbard.

Ethan instructed us to choose two of the weapons assigned to us. I chose the short, Celtic Roman sword and a set of Japanese curved blades. Okay, so technically, that's three blades, but the Japanese knives are a set. If Ethan argues the point, I'll make him take one of the knives from me.

A tremor ripples through me. He would have to get damned close to *try* and take the blade. My insides gel when I recall the rush of security I felt when he caught me after the spear had pierced my body. I recall his face as clearly as if he were standing in front of me now. The pain in his green eyes still tears at my soul.

My mind freezes. Where the hell did that *memory* come from?

A loud squeal slices through my thoughts and I jar back to the present. Stony has pushed up to a sitting position on the bed and is snorting.

"Yeah, I'm okay," I say. But I'm not okay.

Is this new memory an effect of the blood pact? I don't care for that idea. What if *The Three* figure out that I have a secret? Is that possible?

I pause while slipping my belt through the leather knife sheaths. If I'm experiencing effects of the blood pact, does that mean *The Three* are also experiencing strange effects?

I have no choice. I have to let them strip me of my magic. I can't chance that I will one day rationalize the use of Shadow magic. I have to dispose of Grams' book before the temptation to read the spells grabs me. If not for the war games, I would go to Raith right now and demand he immediately strip me of my powers. But I can't make a fuss in the middle of these damn games. I can't be sure that Raith would strip my powers immediately, before rumor got to the Grand Witch. If she got involved, I could be in trouble. I can't let her know I found Grams' spell book.

I finish looping the belt through the sheaths, then add the sword scabbard and strap and buckle the belt. The weapons hang with comforting weight at my waist.

How I wish I could crawl back into bed and bury myself

beneath the covers. I'm in no mood to play at war. But I can't let on that anything is wrong. I can't even let Stony know what I'm planning. I face her. Can I really give her up?

I lift my hands from my sides and turn. "What do you think?"

She raises her snout in the air and snorts twice.

I shake my head. "The Excalibur sword is too aggressive. Better not to further piss off people."

She snorts again and shakes her head.

"I know they haven't caught my wannabe killer, but you'll be riding along in my pocket. Besides, I have my magic now. I'm not such an easy target." Will I be able to use my magic, even in self-defense?

Stony's little eyes narrow. Yes, a pig's eyes really can narrow —well, Stony's can, anyway—and I realize that she's not happy with the idea of being a mouse again.

I shrug. "If you really want to walk all over the woods, then, be my guest and stay in pig form. If you want me to carry you, then a mouse it is. You could stay here," I add. "With *The Three* around and all the other students, I'm not really in any danger." I have no idea if this is true, but I have the sudden need to put some distance between myself and my familiar. My heart lurches. That has never happened before. Am I already giving into my dark side?

"I'm going," Stony snorts.

"It's freezing out there—"

A knock sounds on my door. I turn and take three steps the door and open it. Fran stands in the hallway, decked out in tight leather that reminds me of the Avengers' Black Widow. She holds a chakram by its curved, center handler. It's a beautiful weapon, constructed in different shades of silver.

"You look fabulous," I say.

She turns like a runway model.

I lift a brow. "That outfit doesn't leave a single body cell to the imagination."

"That's what makes it so perfect," she says. "Love the braid, Rapunzel. Nice sword. I'm surprised you're not wearing leather." Her eyes slide past mine and she squeals, "Stony!" Fran races across the room and drops onto the bed beside Stony. "I remember you the day Leilah arrived. You are adorable."

Stony, the original ham, rolls onto her back and presents her stomach for a rub.

Fran giggles and happily obliges. "I love her." To my surprise, Fran hugs her. "Are you bringing her to the games?"

"I've been trying to talk her into staying in. It's so cold—"

Stony snorts loudly.

I roll my eyes. "I guess she's going."

Fran pulls back and smiles down at Stony. "I hope I end up on your team. We could have so much fun with her. I think she likes me."

I don't tell Fran that Stony likes anyone who showers her with attention. Truth is, Stony is an excellent judge of character and can sense evil a football field away.

Fran gives Stony another good stomach rub, then stands and faces me. "We have to do something about your outfit."

I look down at my t-shirt and jeans. "What's wrong with my clothes?"

Fran rolls her eyes. "Everyone dresses up for the War Games. It's like Comic Con."

"Fran, I'm really not—"

"Come on, Stony," she says. "Let's get Leilah in the right frame of mind for the games."

"I'm in the right frame of mind," I blurt.

Fran's gaze turns speculative. "You can't kid a kidder, kid."

.   .   .

TWENTY MINUTES LATER, I'M LOOKING AT MYSELF IN Fran's dorm room mirror and I have to admit, the girl has fashion sense. She's shorter than me, so her clothes are too short—and too small in the chest—but Fran isn't adverse to a little magical tweaking to make her clothes fit me. The dark brown, skin-tight pants show off my muscled legs. My breasts are pushed up over the top of a maroon leather bustier that would make Xena, Warrior Princess jealous. Yes, I'm a total Xena fangirl. The TV show is older than dirt, but that Xena looks fabulous in leather.

The ensemble is finished off with a calf length, quilted, dark brown waistcoat that matches the pants and will keep me warm. The sword strapped on my side gives me a badass look that, I think, would make Xena proud.

I still long for my bed, but can't afford for Fran to figure out that something is seriously wrong. I grimace as if embarrassed. "You sure about this?"

"You bet," she says.

Stony snorts agreement.

I give myself a final once over and find myself wondering what *The Three* will think when they see me. Shame rolls over me. What would they think if they knew I withheld evidence that my grandmother is a traitor?

I face Stony. "What's it going to be, walking or riding?"

Stony tilts her head and appears to consider. I shake my head and wait. It's always better to let Stony put on a show when she is so inclined. Fran drops to her knees beside Stony and I strain my ears to hear what Fran whispers, but no luck. Stony gives a squeal of delight and Fran rises as Stony shifts into a mouse. Stony scurries the few feet to me and climbs my pant leg, then up my arm and around to the inside front pocket of the waistcoat I open for her.

Once she disappears inside, I look at Fran and ask, "What did you say to her?"

Fran's eyes light with mischief. "I told her to think of all the fun we could have with no one knowing she's with us."

"That's a pretty good angle." I'm a little embarrassed I didn't think of it.

"You have your envelope?" Fran asks.

I nod. I'd stuffed it into the bodice of my bustier. The Academy gave each student an envelope and instructions not to open it until given permission. I was curious when I woke up to find the envelope slipped beneath my door, and even more curious with the order not to open it. Of course, my first inclination had been to try magic to peek inside.

Cheater, my mind whispers. Even in small things, I think nothing of cheating.

We head out. On the way downstairs, we distantly trail a group of six girls dressed in camo and heavy, hunting-style jackets. Two have swords strapped to their sides. One glances over her shoulder, turns back, and whispers to the group. They slow and look over their shoulders, then face forward and giggle. I send a questioning glance Fran's way but she just shrugs.

An inch of new snow covers the ground and a sheen of ice coats the trees. Most people like spring with its hint of bloom promising rebirth, but I love winter. The crisp air leaves no room for the grime that frequently reaches this far north of the City. That purity goes soul deep, cleansing the grunge that has seeped into my being. The thought has barely formed when I mentally laugh. I might like the idea of cleansing, but not the reality. If I did, I would suck it up and hand over Grams' spell book and take my rightful place as another witch fallen from grace.

The air isn't cold enough to freeze my lungs, but is cold enough to rouse me better than any cup of coffee. I breathe deeply, and my lungs feel as if they're frosting over.

Halfway across campus, the numbers of students headed for

the assembly field increase. I spot a building beyond the trees. "What's that?" I angle my chin.

Fran looks in the direction I indicated and says, "The shooting range. You like guns?"

"I'm better with swords."

Everyone wears or carries a weapon—knives, swords, throwing discs like Fran's—but I don't miss that no one else is dressed in the medieval leather Fran and I wear. The suspicion that I've been had is confirmed when we reach the field and not another student is dressed in medieval armor. The condescending look Chelsea Nightlow gives me cinches my suspicion. I know the kid doesn't like me, but she clearly thinks my outfit is stupid. She's probably right.

I give Fran a narrow-eyed look. "Why?"

Fran shrugs. "I didn't want to hog all the attention."

A tiny squeak emanates from my pocket. "Hush," I admonish Stony in a whisper. She squeaks louder and I roll my eyes. "It's just a form of speech. Fran isn't going to turn into a hog."

"Of course not," Fran quickly confirms as we emerge from the trees into the clearing where, apparently, the entire student body has assembled. "Sorry, Stony," Fran adds in a whisper.

Another squeak follows and a guy to my right looks my way and frowns.

Fran and I hurry past and I whisper to Stony, "Be quiet or I'll make you walk. It has snowed and it's pretty damn cold out here."

This time, no squeak.

I decide to use magic to change clothes into something less conspicuous, then realize this is kind of what Raith was talking about, using magic for personal gain. This really isn't that bad, though—

Is this kind of reasoning that started Grams down the path of darkness? How long does it take for a person to finally cross the line? How long before Grams kicked me out was she dabbling in black magic? This has to be why she kicked me out. My thoughts come to a halt when I catch sight of *The Three* near a group of students.

"Oh God," I breath. "Don't look over here."

Of course, Raith looks past Ethan and Blade straight at me.

Raith blinks, then I see—it can't be—amusement in his eyes. "The end of the world is at hand," I mutter. "Raith Vanderkoff almost smiled."

"Oh my God," Fran hisses. "Is Raith looking at us?"

The equivalent of a mouse growl emanates from my pocket.

A tiny smile curves one side of Raith's mouth.

I blink. No way is he a Xena fan.

Blade and Ethan turn toward me and the man standing to Raith's right becomes visible.

I freeze.

It can't be.

FORTY-FIVE

Blade

———————

It's a perfect day for our War Games. Even my lack of sleep over the strange meeting with Zadkeil last night—and Leilah's cold demeanor—doesn't quite squelch my joy in being outside. I breathe deeply of the crisp air as Ethan and I cut across the sparring field behind half a dozen students headed for the assembly field. I wear loose-fitting brown pants, matching leather armor that hangs to my thighs, and a short gambeson that protects my upper torso and arms. My favorite part of the outfit are the swede boots. They remind me of the clothes my kind wore eons ago, before the world became populated with too many people, and fashion became a way to impress others instead of a connection to the earth.

The games awaken my urge to run free in the woods and reconnect with my fae cousins, the nature spirits. Today, however, even with the bright January sun, I would have preferred to delay the games. Ethan has not spoken since he caught up with me outside my on-campus apartment, but I know something weighs on his mind beyond the worry that the War Games make Leilah an easy target.

Wait until he hears my news.

The students ahead leave the walkway and disappear into the trees thirty feet ahead. I open my mouth to speak, but Ethan says, "I discovered what Raith's problem is with Leilah."

That surprises me. I wait.

"He hasn't forgiven her for putting the knife through his heart forty years ago."

That should surprise me but doesn't. "Vampires rarely forgive."

Ethan looks sharply at me. "You don't believe she betrayed him?"

I slow as we near the trees and Ethan follows suit. "It was bound to happen," I say. "Raith incites a desire in others to put him in his place."

"She would never betray any of us."

"She isn't the same person every lifetime," I say. "Yet, she always loves us." My heart swells with anticipation of seeing her. Even angry, Ciarah is magnificent.

"Still, we —" Ethan begins.

"You're not naïve," I cut in. "She hasn't been a sweet lamb every incarnation." I snort. "She has never been a *sweet lamb*— and, in truth, she was more reckless in her last incarnation than she'd been in centuries." I smile. "But then, her parents were Greek and Spanish. A volatile combination."

"I had no idea you felt this way," Ethan says.

I look at him. "What way? That I see her for who she is? That doesn't stop me from loving her."

"Her volatility doesn't mean she betrayed Raith."

I shrug. "She stabbed him and left him for dead."

"Vampires are nearly impossible to kill," Ethan says.

We enter the trees and I veer right instead of staying on the pathway. Ethan shoots me a curious look.

"If Cordero had found Raith, he would have separated Raith from his head," I say

Ethan shakes his head. "There has to be something we don't know."

"Raith made his own bed," I reply. "Half the bloody time I want to kill him. We have never been able to control Ciarah. Raith goaded her by forbidding her to see Cordero."

"She doesn't deserve to be punished in this life," Ethan growls.

I laugh. "You think you can control Raith any easier than he can control her?"

"He's never been like this," Ethan says.

He's right. "Raith must work through his anger."

Ethan turns his intense green eyes on me. "You'll stand by and let him hurt her?"

I blurt a dark laugh. "Raith is powerful, but no vampire has ever controlled magic like the witches."

"Magic can't save a witch from everything," he says, and I know he's remembering the damn spear.

I shudder at a flash memory of Leilah lying on Raith's couch, the cushion and her shirt soaked with blood, and Raith drinking from the wound.

"She didn't have her magic when the spear wounded her," I murmur. "She does now—and that bloody familiar. The animal is worth an army of bodyguards. And she has us."

Already, I sense the magic of the pact invading my system—even my dreams. That is unexpected. Ethan makes no reply and I would wager he's feeling the connection, as well. grimace. The last thing I want is to be closer to the vampire. How is it possible for the blood pact to be drawing Ethan, Raith, and I closer? We made no blood promises to one another, only to Leilah.

"We should have insisted she stay in her room during the games," Ethan says.

I snort. "Because that's worked so well for us in the past?"

"We could have enforced her compliance with a spell."

"Even if you, Raith and I combine our magic, with that sigil off her hand, she can break any spell we cast. You know that." I clap his shoulder and squeeze. "I'm concerned, as well, Ethan."

He barely nods.

I wish Matthias were here. He always knows what to say on these rare occasions when Ethan overloads.

"I can't believe we haven't found a single clue as to her attacker," he says. Real heat radiates off his body. If we do find Leilah's attacker, Ethan will tear him limb from limb—if I don't find him first.

I nod. "They're damned smart."

"Which worries me," Ethan mutters.

"I'm hard pressed to believe anyone can get to her now with the wards Olympia set up to inhibit black magic," I say, but still, worry niggles.

Ethan casts me a sideways glance. "Is that why you've been camped outside Ciarah's dorm room these past few days?"

I grin. "One reason."

None of us has ever begrudged the other's place in Ciarah's heart—or bed. Well, after those first few incarnations, that is, when we began to understand that the five of us were somehow bound to her. Early on, we nearly killed one another. I smile at the memory.

"If we have trouble with the walkies, change to channel fifteen," Ethan says. "We shouldn't. They're military issue, but you never know."

I nod. Ethan, Raith, and I carry radios for the games, as do the officers. Today, however, Ethan, Raith, and I have an extra radio clipped to our belts for the private channel where we will communicate about Leilah, if necessary.

Ethan turns toward the meeting place. I grasp his arm and pull him to a stop.

He looks at me and frowns. "What is it?"

"There's been a development in the investigation." He

starts to reply, but I shake my head and say, "Not Leilah and not Miriam. It's Zedkeil. I believe I know why the angels are so hot to help out in the investigation." I pause, still not quite able to process the possibilities. "You are not going to believe this, but their god is locked in Hell."

Ethan blinks, then his eyes go wide.

I nod. "You heard correctly. *Elohim, Elyon*, The Most High, the god who lays claim to all creation, is locked in Hell."

"How is that possible?" Ethan breathes.

"I guess that spell Senorn and Eledin cast to close the Hell Gates is Grade A magic."

"How did you find out?" Ethan asks.

I shrug. "Zedkeil gave it away. He denied it, but you know what they say, 'Me thinks the angel doth protest too much.' It's true, all right."

"I can't believe it," he says.

"Neither could Olympia."

He looks sharply at me. "You didn't tell her?"

"Come now," I say. "You know I can't keep something like this from her."

He nods slowly. "I can't begin to imagine how she will use this to her advantage."

"She'll use the knowledge to leverage Heaven for a time when we need them."

"I suppose so," he says slowly. "Not in a thousand years would I have guessed this. How have the angels kept it quiet all these centuries?"

"They're a clannish lot who know how to keep a secret. Remember how long it was before anyone figured out the demon known as the devil was his son The Morning Star?"

Ethan snorts. "I can't blame him for that one. I don't think I would want to own up to having that bastard as a son, either. What does the Grand Witch think about all this?"

Two male students step from the trees to our left. They

must have veered off the path. They look in our direction and Ethan and I start walking. The students walk ahead of us. Five minutes later, clusters of students emerge through the trees up ahead. Anticipation hums in my belly like a live wire. Nothing tests our skills and endurance like the War Games.

Through the trees beyond, I see the field where we are to begin. Raith is standing with three of our generals. Seton Alexander is there. Adrenaline pumps through me. I am going to enjoy kicking his arse this year.

We reach Raith's group and Alexander angles his head toward me. "Blade."

"Seton," I reply.

Raith's eyes shift past me and his pupils dilate. I turn and my breath catches in unison with Ethan's audible intake of air. Leilah's dressed in brown leather with a brown quilted waist-coat. A short sword is strapped to her belt along with Japanese curved blades. She's even braided her hair...a hairstyle she wore in the late fourteenth century when Pope John XXII issued his *super illius specula* authorizing the use of inquisitorial procedure against witches.

I've never forgotten how magnificent she was, a sword in each hand, wisps of escaped hair whipping around her face in the gale-force wind, as if the gods themselves had joined the fight. Of course, Ciarah had called that wind. She and a dozen women accused of witchcraft stood against fifty soldiers sent by the church to arrest them for heresy. The soldiers were fortunate that Ciarah was the only true witch among the accused that day.

"Fuck," Raith says under his breath, and I know even he is remembering that day.

Leilah stares, eyes wide. Then she breaks into a run. She passes Ethan and I, and we spin as she throws herself into Alexander's arms.

FORTY-SIX

Ethan

MY DRAGON ROARS TO LIFE. I TAKE A STEP TOWARD Leilah.

A hand clamps down on my shoulder and I spin toward Blade. He gives a tiny shake of his head and slants his eyes toward the small stage at the far side of the field where Olympia sits on the stage overseeing the assembly.

"Not this time," I hiss with enough heat that fire flashes from my palms.

"Look at *her*," he whispers.

I hesitate. Can I bear to see Ciarah in the arms of another man, yet again?

"Look," the Fae says in a gentle voice, and I force myself to turn.

Leilah has buried her face in Alexander's chest. He's stroking her hair and making soft shushing noises. This isn't the embrace of lovers, but of sister and brother. I send a questioning look to Blade.

He shrugs. "I guess they know each other."

"Good guess," I say with asperity.

I look at Raith, but he just gives a tiny shake of his head.

"Anyone want to tell us what's going on?" Blade asks in a conversational tone.

"Not that it's any of your business," Leilah says, her face still buried in Alexander's chest, "but I grew up with Seton."

A sliver of relief eases the tension in my shoulders, but only a sliver. She's not the fifteen-year-old girl who ran away. She's a woman, and Alexander could easily fall in love with her.

She draws back and looks up at him. "What are you doing here?"

He winks. "You didn't think you were the only High Potential in our neighborhood, did you?"

"You attend The Academy? Why didn't you tell me? That would have made being here so much better."

He laughs. "I graduated four years ago. Still, I didn't know you were here until just now. I think I could bring *you* to task for going MIA for seven years," his tone is airy, but I detect deep curiosity.

She gives him another tight hug, then releases him and steps back. "You're one of the alumni here to take part in the War Games?"

He grins. "That's right, and you'd better hope you're on my team."

Leilah arches a brow. "I'm a lot tougher than I was when you last saw me."

His expression softens. "Not too tough, I hope."

"Tough enough to kick your ass."

Alexander looks at Raith. "I think that's a challenge."

"I'd say everyone is here," Raith replies. His eyes shift past me and I turn slightly as Gabriel Carter halts beside me. "I wasn't sure you were going to make it," Raith says.

"Traffic from Jersey was a bitch." His gaze shifts to Leilah. "Well, who do we have here?"

"A student who needs to assemble with the rest of the students," Raith says.

She scowls at him, then says to Alexander, "If you're placing bets, my team's a sure winner."

He laughs as she starts toward a cluster of students who are unabashedly watching.

"I think I should be assigned to *her* team," Carter says. "You know, in case anyone needs CPR."

Raith surprises me by saying, "No one is going to need CPR."

Carter's eyebrows shoot up. "Do I detect a note of ownership?"

"What you detect is the reminder that these War Games are a helluva lot more than games," Raith replies.

Carter's eyes light with his signature mischief. "Of course, my lord."

Raith openly ignores him and starts toward the eighty-plus students. I can't take my eyes off Leilah. She looks so much like Brin as she stood against the knights sent to arrest the witches. My fire ignites and I have to will my cock not to respond. We five had been there to protect the women. To protect *her*. But she'd protected the women, and the air had crackled with electricity as the warriors ran for the woods, followed by nightmares that, I'm sure, haunted them to their dying days.

Raith's voice projects over the wireless PA system as he instructs the students to open their envelopes. The tearing of paper fills the air for a long moment, then a murmur washes over the students.

"Team One, to the left," Raith orders. "Team Two, to the right. Team Three, opposite Team One, and Team Four, opposite Team Two."

The students shuffle until everyone is standing in the correct locations with their assigned teams. As planned, Leilah is on Team Three with Darryl Jones, a young mage with experience in our war games. It is hard knowing we're here as observers and can't accompany Leilah into the virtual Shadow world.

"Ethan, Blade and I will monitor your progress through the virtual Shadow world. Seton Alexander and Gabriel Carter are standing by in case of a medical emergency."

Whoops and shouts go up. Alexander bows to the crowd. As he passes Leilah on his way toward Carter and the waiting medical kits, he waggles his eyebrows. She shakes her head but laughs.

"Our battlefield is there." Raith points to the right of the field where a subtle shimmer is visible against the trees. "This year, we have created a virtual world that reflects a city like New York or Chicago during the Shadow War."

A loud murmur ripples through the students. Even Carter's brows rise in surprise. I don't blame them. I'm still uncertain about the safety of a virtual Shadow world.

"You have each been assigned to a team that we believe will best utilize your abilities and training," Raith says. "You are allowed to use magic when needed. But part of this training is to teach you to differentiate when you should and shouldn't use magic. Be prepared for a Shadow attack if you do use magic." He turns to face Team One. "Team One will guard the streets against roaming demons. Anyone in Team One know how to kill a demon?"

"You can't kill demons," a student, Jonathan Bennet, calls out. Jonathan lifts a silver talisman hanging from a cord around his neck. "You have to trap them in an enchanted object."

"Very good," Raith says.

I hear pride in his voice.

Raith shifts again. "Team Two will aid humans and Margiddians infected by The Shadows." He pauses. "Can anyone in Team Two describe the best way to deal with humans infected by Shadows?"

"Soft earth magic," Maggie, a young siren, calls. "Harmony, peace. Get them some place safe."

Raith nods slowly, then faces Teams Three and Four. "Teams Three and Four will infiltrate the home of the crime lord, whose house is protected by Shadow magic. You will capture him, then break the spell he cast on his human bodyguards. Remember, it is forbidden to kill humans who are under a spell. Your team leaders will identify the officers in your teams and will instruct you. As each team is ready, your team leader will lead you into the war zone."

Whoops and shouts go up—mostly from students who have been at The Academy for a year or longer. Some of the newer students turn their heads toward the shimmer, brows drawn in apprehension.

"Unlike the real world, no one can be killed in our virtual Shadow world," Raith goes on. "At least, not by virtual inhabitants, so don't aim at any of your fellow students."

Laughter ripples through the students and a few "Better watch your back" and "Ooohs" filter through the murmur.

"As instructed, newer students are to stick close to their team leaders and tell them if you start feeling overwhelmed. Watchmen are stationed inside the virtual world to help keep everyone safe. We will also be watching."

I force my attention away from Leilah and remind myself she is in no real danger.

FORTY-SEVEN

Leilah

MY HEART POUNDS AS I WAIT IN THE REAR OF TEAM Three, as Team Four enters the virtual war zone ahead of us.

Seton is here. He was a student at The Academy. If ever the fates decided to bless and curse me, it's now. I want to cry and scream at the same time. Seton, of all people, has the ability to know something is wrong in my life. If he figures out that I intend to give up magic, he will fight me tooth and nail. I must speak with Raith immediately, once the games are finished, and get my magic stripped.

The guy ahead of me disappears through the opening into the virtual world. I take a deep breath and step inside after him. The late morning sunshine cuts off behind me and I enter misty darkness. I guess the hour to be approximately two o'clock in the morning. In the distance, skyscrapers, slim and sleek, rise into a thick fog that the full moon barely penetrates. Even insects and night creatures are silent.

Ahead of us, members of Team Four melt into the darkness that surrounds the estate we're to infiltrate. Five feet to my left, I discern the small form of Chelsea Nightlow alongside a tall boy who's part of our team.

Darkness, the kind not seen with the eyes, presses close around me. I shiver and resist the urge to hug myself. I hadn't thought I would see a single Shadow in my lifetime. The wisps of fear that probe my consciousness tell me this world is filled with damn good imitations of the real thing. My pulse jumps. The feeling reminds me of what I experienced when I read the words in Grams' spell book.

I suddenly wish I was buried under my bedcovers, Stony and I watching reruns of The Big Bang Theory. I lift a hand to pat the pocket where Stony remains suspiciously quiet but stop myself. I can't risk her being taken away. Not yet.

Darryl, our team leader, motions us forward. I wish Fran was on our team, but she'd been assigned to the demon hunting team. Our trek through the trees is almost noiseless. The rustle of leaves underfoot comes from Chelsea's vicinity.

We reach the estate's eight-foot-high wall, and the wards intended to keep out intruders pushes against my senses. I concentrate on light and murmur the spell created during the Shadow War to penetrate wards: "Light and love, surround me in your peace."

Embarrassment ripples through me, but I will my pulse to remain slow and steady. Much as I want to believe this is all BS, there's no doubt that our warriors managed to stop The Shadows from annihilating us, and I must admit to a little curiosity at trying out these easy spells even on virtual Shadows.

I twirl the index finger of my right hand in a circle and am rewarded with a subtle but strong sense of peace. I breathe deeply and ask the nature fae to lift me with their wind. I crouch and leap, landing with the barest snick of my boots on the top of the wall.

Thank you, I telepath to the unseen nature spirits, then drop to the ground on the other side.

Darryl and two other students land soundlessly to my right.

To my surprise, Chelsea follows next. Darryl crouches and motions us to follow, then starts forward. I fall in behind Chelsea, who glances over her shoulder at me before she hurries ahead.

We reach a large elm and halt as two other students catch up with us. An image flashes of us walking through the door and getting mowed down by machine gun fire. My heart leaps and I realize fear is pressing against my chest like an unseen hand. Fuck. Is this Shadow fear? I shiver. Does Stony feel the darkness? I touch the pocket where she's hiding and am comforted when my fingers discern the slight bulge.

I release a breath. Team Four will do their job and all will be well. They have to enter the mansion through a skylight on the east side of the house, then disable the security system located in the security office on the ground floor.

Half a dozen students catch up with us and Darryl leads us across a darkened expanse of lawn to a large oak close to the circle of light cast by night lamps that illuminate the house.

A minute later, the last two of our team arrive. We drop flat to the grass and I hold my breath as two guards approach along a walkway that skirts the house. They wear body armor and carry AR-15 assault rifles in addition to sidearms. Fuck, did Elijah Walker's guards carry AR-15 assault rifles? My mouth goes dry. What if the instructors are wrong and we can be killed?

No one twitches so much as a muscle as the guards near. My heart pounds so loudly I'm sure everyone can hear. The guards are almost past us when one abruptly stops. The other swings around as the first one turns in our direction. He reaches for the small flashlight on his belt.

Movement snaps my attention right. Chelsea pushes up onto her knees and hurls two curved throwing knives so fast that the blades blur before they hit their marks. The two guards fall to the ground with so little noise it's eerie. My heartrate jumps to a gallop.

Darryl surges to his feet and whispers, "Everyone up."

We stand.

Darryl faces Chelsea. "Give me your remaining weapons."

She hesitates.

"*Now*," he orders.

"But the men were evil," she whispers. "They liked being under the influence of The Shadows."

"What?"

"I felt their love of The Shadows."

Darryl extends a hand. Chelsea's lips thin in rebellion, but she pulls two more throwing knives from her belt and lays them in his hand. He slides them into his knife sheathe, then motions us to follow as he hurries toward the house. The others crouch and follow Darryl. Chelsea falls in line behind me. I can't tear my gaze from the two men and their weapons as I hurry past them. How could the authorities have allowed anyone to walk around with assault rifles? Had Elijah Walker's men murdered Margiddians?

We reach the house and press against its stone wall. Darryl glances at his radio watch and gives a tiny nod that I hope means that Team Four has disabled the alarm system. He edges toward the side yard, peers around the corner of the house, then motions for everyone to follow and darts around the corner.

I edge around the house behind a tall guy and catch sight of Darryl at a side door, picking the lock. A wolf howls in the distance. I slow and scan the darkened lawn, searching for the source. The Academy really went all out to make this experience spooky.

I reach the other students as Darryl eases the door open. He peeks inside, then twists and motions us to follow. I enter behind the tall guy. Chelsea takes up the rear. We creep through a pantry, cross a kitchen, and enter dimly lit servants' stairs. As I sidle past a sharp corner in the stairs, darkness, hatred and fear thicken. I recall a beautiful glade drenched in sunshine, with blue skies that go on forever. That is the place I will visit when we leave here.

Until then...

The tall guy ahead of me reaches the second floor and disappears to the right. I step from the stairs into a hallway softly lit by crystal wall sconces. I tense, startled by an unexpected intrusion of magic.

Lightning shoots up the stairwell behind me. I jerk aside as students drop to the carpet. The blinding white bolt shoots past me and ignites the wall opposite the stairwell. I grunt and blink my gaze into focus on my left arm. A singed black line mars my armor.

Footsteps clattering down the stairs cause me to whirl in time to see Chelsea disappear around the turn in the stairway. Shit, the kid must have gotten scared when the lightning bolt—

My thoughts shift with a horrifying realization. That lighting was conjured by magic, not the dark magic that protects this place. Chelsea's magic.

Darryl jumps to his feet and is saying something, but the deafening hum in my ears drowns him out. I draw a sharp breath and throw out my senses, searching for The Shadows we were warned would attack if we used magic.

I lunge down the stairs, taking them two at a time. Seconds later, I leap the remaining two steps and burst into the kitchen in time to see Chelsea halfway to the pantry. In the corner of my eye, movement causes me to snap my head in that direction. A long, black ribbon of energy tangling with itself is streaming after Chelsea.

Time seems to stop. The Shadow is so damned beautiful.

The wisp shifts as if looking in my direction. I reach out a hand—

And crash into something hard—the middle island, I vaguely realize as I hit the floor shoulder first. Pain shoots down my arm. I roll and leap to my feet, panting. Chelsea has reached the pantry. I don't see The Shadow. Oh God, has it reached her?

"You want magic, mother fucker?" I growl. "Come get me. Dragon!" I shout, and throw out a spell strong enough to choke the fucking Shadow.

A dragon half the size of a refrigerator appears. Chelsea whirls, wide eyes on the beast. Her head swings in my direction. Our eyes lock.

A blur snaps my attention left. Raith appears just as the dragon howls and exhales fire.

A wolf howls.

A flash of light blinds me.

FORTY-EIGHT

Raith

I'M ASSIGNED TO THE SOUTHEAST CORNER OF THE virtual world and to Team Four, but am watching Team Three on the tablet the surveillance cameras feed into. Leilah flanks Mason up the stairs of the crime lord's mansion, with Chelsea Nightlow in the rear. Thus far, Leilah has followed orders.

The first students reach the second floor of the mansion and Blade's voice announces over the radio Velcroed to my belt, "They're doing great."

Except Chelsea, I think, but grab the radio, depress the talk button, and say, "You're supposed to be watching Team Two."

"I assigned Carter to Team Two," he replies.

I start to reply.

A lightning bolt illuminates the stairs.

Students drop to the hallway floor—except Leilah, who is hit by the bolt in a blast of light that fills the screen like the detonation of an atomic bomb.

"What the fuck?" Blade shouts over the radio.

"Chelsea," Ethan growls over the channel. "She—"

"Was aiming for Leilah," I cut in.

I'm running before I shout, "Get in there!" and slap the radio onto the Velcro.

The VR world is a fraction of the size it seems, and I reach the kitchen in seconds. An emerald green dragon hovers between Leilah and Chelsea. Fire billows from its mouth.

I can't stop the games. Even I don't have that much power. But I can stop Chelsea.

I lunge toward her. My fingers close around a slim arm, then around thin air. I stumble forward.

"Raith!" someone shouts.

I whirl, dragging in huge breaths. Chelsea is gone. Leilah—

I look wildly about the room. The dragon bellows. I seize the creature's neck and tear the left wing from its body. The dragon screams. I sink my fangs into its thick neck. Bones crunch in unison with my snarl. Blood fills my mouth. I throw the lifeless dragon onto the tiled floor. A large hand seizes my shoulder. I spin to face Ethan. He stumbles back two steps into Blade.

"Where the fuck is she?" I demand, but the stark fear on his and Blade's faces answers my question. "No," I whisper.

My heart thunders.

A Reaping. Impossible.

And Leilah was taken.

Along with her would-be killer.

Sneak Peek

Rogue Witch

AN ILLUMINA ACADEMY REVERSE HAREM NOVEL
BOOK TWO

She sold her soul and now she wants it back…

Condemned by her peers for her grandmother's crime of treason, street witch Leilah Crowe's very identity is brought into question, as well as exactly who holds the pink slip to her soul.

Her world further spirals when wolf Caleb Dakota and gargoyle Matthias James enter her life. Her love-hate attraction to vampire Raith Vanderkoff, dragon Ethan Bordeau and Fae Blade Tyrion were confusing enough. How is it possible to love five men—men who are willing to share her…men who would go to Hell and back for her?

But it may be Leilah who must find a way into Hell to reclaim her own soul and save them, along with the Academy that has branded her a murderer and a traitor.

ONE

Leilah

Sunlight blinds me. I throw up a hand against the glare. Where the hell am I? Seconds ago, I had crashed to the floor while chasing Shadows in a dimly lit kitchen. I slap a hand over the shoulder I fell on, but there's no pain. I turn in a circle, heart pounding. Gone is the mob boss's kitchen in the virtual War Games. Gone is the dragon I conjured to battle the Shadow chasing Chelsea. Gone are Chelsea and Raith. Now, sunlight, silence and cold surround me.

"Leilah."

I whirl at the sound of my name, but I'm alone. My imagination? Or an echo from the world from which I was just ripped? I'm standing on an icy road in a rural countryside that looks like…God, this could be upper Westchester County, New York where Grams used to live before Shadows consumed her mind and spirit.

"Damn you!" I shout to the wind. "Send me back."

I close my eyes then snap them open again, but nothing changes. Is this a part of the War Games we weren't told about? Would The Academy do that to us? Would the Grand Witch do that to us? Raith sure as hell would. That fucking vampire threatened to expel me from Illumina Academy. He would love to see me fail and get kicked out. If he's playing some trick to get me expelled—

My thoughts screech to a halt. If he's playing some trick to get me expelled, why should I fight him? I would love nothing better than to be allowed to leave The Academy. Then I could return home—my new home, Grams' house.

So, how do I oblige?

I look down at my clothes. I'm still wearing the skin-tight, dark brown pants, leather bustier, and calf length, quilted, dark brown waistcoat I wore in the War Games. Even the burn mark from Chelsea's lightning bolt still mars my right sleeve. I clap a hand over the Celtic short sword strapped to my belt on the left and the other hand over two Japanese curved blades on the right. Still there.

I scan my surroundings. Across the street, a large stone house stands twenty feet off the road. To my left, beyond the open field, sits a two-story stone home that's at least forty-five hundred square feet. The road winds around a curve and disappears into trees. All as perfectly normal as any rural street in upper Westchester County. Wherever *here* is, appears just as real as the virtual Shadow world where the war games were taking place. Only that world took place at night, near a large city on the grounds of a crime lord's estate.

Are any of the other students here? Is Chelsea here? When last I saw the teenager, she was fleeing from the house of the crime lord we were sent to capture, a Shadow hard on her tail. I'd conjured a dragon in an effort to get the Shadow to chase me instead. But the Shadow was hungry for fear and Chelsea had plenty of that. Then Raith arrived an instant before all went white. Now, I'm here in—whatever this is.

Instructors aren't supposed to interfere with the games. But then, Commander Raith Vanderkoff, Mr. Vampire Asshole, does exactly as he pleases. *Wait*. Are the teachers still observing us? God, that's perverse and—

Fear whips through me when I remember.

Stony.

I stuff a hand into the inside pocket of my jacket where Stony, in mouse form, had been hiding a moment ago. My fingers encounter the lining. I search left, then right. Nothing.

No. No. No.

I choke back a sob. I just got my familiar back two days ago. To have her ripped from me again so soon is…cruel. I slap my thigh and force back the tears that threaten to spill from my eyes. Stony knows to meet me at Grams' if we get separated.

"Figure out what's going on and we'll be reunited," I tell myself.

Think. I release a slow breath. If the War Games' virtual world has gone wonky, maybe we were transported to somewhere near The Academy in Westchester? But it was just night, now it's day. I look up at the sky at the sun, which is—

No way. *No-fucking-way.*

I stare at a light blue sun.

I shake my head almost violently. This isn't my reality. Where am I? What—

Did the Shadow I was chasing infect me? The Shadows feed on our fears. Some people simply can't find their way out of the darkness The Shadows create, and psychosis consumes them. If we're lucky—if being driven insane with fear can be called luck —the infected only take themselves down. If we're unlucky, we start killing each other like we did in the recent Shadow War where millions died.

If the Shadow did infect me, it would have occurred seconds ago in the War Games. Was the magic I'd used to stop the Shadow enough to open the door to infection? I'd always believed the Illumina was overreacting when they preached that even the slightest use of magic in the presence of a Shadow can allow them entrance into your psyche.

I've practiced magic my whole life and never seen a Shadow until the War Games. The game hadn't been real, though. The Shadows were part of the virtual world—virtualverse, the students called it—created by the Grand Witch of the North— key word being *virtual*.

Fear twists through me. "Stony!" I cry. "Where are you?"

Where am I?

My thoughts abruptly jumble with a horrifying thought. On God, is it possible…is this a…Reaping? I resist the urge to look around for the floating obsidian ribbons that are Shadows. Are they close? Will they attack if I use magic in an effort to figure out where I am? Is Illumina telling the truth? Does our magic feed The Shadows? Damn the Illumina. They make us fear our natural state.

The possibility this is a Reaping is too fantastical. What are the chances that Illumina Academy students could be swept into a Reaping—a magical reality that tests our skills against our mortal enemies, The Shadows—while in a magical virtual reality designed to test our skills against The Shadows? The last Reaping took place five years ago. They never reappear for at least twenty-five years. This has got to be the virtualverse gone wrong.

A bitter wind whips my hair. I shiver. Clouds scuttle across the weird blue sun and the wind turns colder. I smell oncoming snow in the too-crisp air. I glance left then right down the road. Does this reality come complete with cars whizzing by too fast on these narrow roads? In the real upper Westchester County, it's dangerous to walk on the roads, which doesn't stop fools from doing so. There are no sidewalks, and the densely wooded terrain leaves no place to walk except on the shoulder of the road. I take a deep breath and, like just another fool, start walking.

Minutes later, I round a curve in the road. A large red barn borders the road up ahead to my left. The purr of a car engine draws my attention to the road behind me. I step off the road and face the oncoming car, as a blue sedan appears around the curve. I stick out my thumb as the vehicle approaches. An elderly woman is driving. She keeps going. I turn and watch the car disappear down the road, and belatedly remember the sword and knives strapped to my belt. Hell, I wouldn't have stopped for me, either. I'm dressed like a medieval warrior. I have my fellow Illumina Academy student, Fran Shelton, to thank for the funky outfit. I hope she's safe at The Academy.

I start walking, again. Through the trees, I glimpse a massive house about eighty feet behind the barn. Up ahead on the right is a two-story home painted mustard yellow with a stone wall in front.

I shiver with cold and stuff my hands in my jacket pockets. In memory, I smell the cinnamon rolls Grams baked on similar cold winter days. My mouth salivates in longing for the hot chocolate she served with the rolls. No one makes hot chocolate like Grams. I release a fog-filled breath and the sense of well-being increases. I haven't felt this good since…since the last time Grams made cinnamon rolls and hot chocolate.

I'm startled to realize that the last time Grams served cinnamon rolls and hot chocolate was the day before she kicked me out of the house. I was fifteen. An unexpected sob escapes me. My God, I had forgotten that. All these years, I'd focused on the day she kicked me out. Why am I remembering this now? My breath comes out as steam in the cold air. The sense of well-being vanishes and the sweet memory of Grams' cinnamon rolls and hot chocolate collides with the memory of her shoving me out the door.

My attention snaps to rapid movement in the trees ahead. I halt. A figure is racing deeper into the trees. I break into a run across the road, past the stone house to my left, and enter the trees beyond the house. Underbrush and low-hanging limbs force me to slow.

"Hey," I shout. I've lost sight of the person, but they can't be far ahead. "Hey!"

I advance at a fast walk and scan my surroundings but spot no sign of human life. I turn and catch sight of a fist hurtling toward my face an instant before pain splinters through my cheek. All goes black.

www.ingramcontent.com/pod-product-compliance
Lightning Source LLC
Chambersburg PA
CBHW061309190726
48288CB00002B/424